DANGEROUS LIBERTY

"Do you really believe I would put you in the way of any but the most honorable employment, child?" de Lisle asked wryly.

"Well, my lord, I do not think respectability is among your chief concerns," Melissa retorted with some audacity. "You cannot expect to be considered a worthy patron of a chaste young woman, now can you?"

"You are wise to be wary of me and all men, infant. We are exceedingly selfish and prone to consider no wishes but our own."

Melissa eyed him suspiciously. "I do not see why I cannot know now what position you have secured for me. I might not like it, my lord, and then you will have been put to all this trouble to no avail," she protested.

"Oh, I think I have the means of persuading you, my dear." He smiled mockingly. "You are rather at my mercy, you know."

A frisson of some undefined emotion shook Melissa at his words.

Before she could argue further he had taken hold of her arms. "Am I to believe you would rather warm my bed than pursue gainful employment?" he asked, challenging her to defy him so that he could subdue her in a manner he would enjoy.

He drew her closer . . .

VIOLET HAMILTON

THE HIDDEN HEART

ZEBRA BOOKS
KENSINGTON PUBLISHING CORP.

ZEBRA BOOKS

are published by

Kensington Publishing Corp.
475 Park Avenue South
New York, NY 10016

First printing: April 1987

Printed in the United States of America

Chapter One

At first glance the gentleman lounging against the squabs of the richly furnished carriage did not appear to be awake. His tall beaver hat tipped over his brow, his eyelids drooped deceptively as he swayed easily with the motion of the swiftly travelling coach. Dressed in the latest stare, he wore a capped greatcoat covering fine, cream kersey breeches tucked into glossy Hessian boots, the epitome of restrained elegance. In one negligent hand he held a gold-headed cane which he suddenly raised and prodded gently at the pile of rugs folded in a heap at the end of the opposite seat.

"I think you may safely emerge now and let me see what kind of an uninvited passenger I am entertaining on this tedious journey," he drawled, pushing aside the wrappings with a flick of his cane.

A startled gasp came from the figure who struggled from the concealing rugs and eyed the questioner in surprise. Wearing shabby breeches and a rough cotton shirt covered by a leather jerkin, the stowaway seemed to be a lad of tender years, with flushed downy cheeks and a head of golden-brown curls framing a pointed chin set defiantly against any tendency to betray anxiety.

"Oh, sir, there must be some mistake. Yours was not the carriage I intended to enter," the young voice quivered despite the best efforts to hold it steady in the face of the gentleman's quelling glance.

"I quite agree you have made a mistake. Just whose carriage did you mean to burden with your presence?" the gentleman asked cynically. Despite his indolent pose, which had not altered, a suspicion of menace lurked in his soft, sneering tone which promised retribution to any miscreant who defied him.

"Well, you see, sir, I have not the fare for the mail coach to London, and I rather hoped the elderly couple whose carriage I had chosen might take pity on my dilemma and let me journey with them. They seemed kind, and I cannot think how I came to enter the wrong coach." The response came tentatively, revealing the realization that the gentleman whose privacy had been invaded would not be such an easy target, nor so easily gulled by a pathetic story.

"Running away from school or a cruel guardian, I suspect," the gentleman mused, running a dark eye over the tousled form, seeming intent on probing beneath the rumpled garb of his victim.

"How clever of you to guess, sir, and you are quite right. My guardian is an absolute monster," the young person responded eagerly, smiling winsomely in the hope of averting the wrath which was fully anticipated. The gentleman looked a formidable adversary, not at all in the mode of the kindly couple who had been the original chosen refuge. He had pushed his hat back now to reveal dark wavy hair above piercing black eyes masked by heavy lids, a disdainful, weary expression marking deep lines on either side of a sensuous mouth, drawn now into a sneering expression. His sprawling posture did not disguise the long, well-muscled length of him, a promise of strength leashed into fashionable indolence but still apparent under that casual demeanor.

"How boringly obvious. Surely you can embroider a better story than that, my dear," he replied.

The young passenger tugged at the tattered jacket that hung loosely over trembling shoulders. Had the sharp appraising eyes penetrated the imperfect disguise, adopted out of desperation, in the hope that the clothes would protect the wearer from unwanted attentions?

"Boring to you, sir, perhaps, but only too true. My guardian's inordinate and cruel demands made it impossible for me to live any longer under his roof," came the pert answer, a jaunty effort to hide the trepidation which the situation engendered.

"So borrowing some serving lad's togs you rushed heedlessly from your cruel guardian's house, not realizing that you might be embroiling yourself in an even more desperate situation," the gentleman continued, his knowing eyes roaming insolently over his passenger. "You might have done better to retain your skirts and throw yourself on my mercy. I have a reputation for being kind to damsels in distress," he mocked.

"You saw through my disguise. You know I am a girl," was the anguished reply.

"I am too practiced a hand to be taken in by musty breeches and badly cropped hair, you know. It's quite obvious no lad ever enjoyed that creamy complexion or your more obvious attributes," he said gazing meaningfully at the bosom she had tried to hide beneath the too tight jerkin.

Blushing she hurried nervously into the explanation, "Well, you see, it seemed safer to disguise myself if I meant to loiter about the Hawk & Dove searching for a possible conveyance," she answered, her light, refined voice more evidence that her deception would not have fooled any but the most credulous.

The Marquis Theron de Lisle raised a sceptical eyebrow at the innocent disclosure, and settled back to hear the story, prepared to be amused, if nothing else, by a contrived tale. "I am waiting with bated breath to hear this harrowing account," he said, but with a suave air his passenger found far from sympathetic.

Melissa, her violet eyes edged with luxuriant lashes

widening in apprehension, took a deep breath as she appraised the gentleman whose unwelcome guest she was. How much should she reveal of her flight to the inn at Exeter? Somehow she had the impression he would not be easily gulled by some Banbury tale. It might be best to tell him as much of the truth as she could, hoping he might believe her and enable her to continue the journey in his company. If not, he might just abandon her on the roadside, an unhappy prospect as she had little more than a few meager coins in her pocket and no idea how she could find another rescuer.

"My name is Melissa . . . Mason," she stumbled over the words and then went on with more confidence. "My parents died when I was quite young and I was taken in by a friend of my father, who had spent most of his life in India. That was where they had met, I am told. My guardian was also in business there. I have been in his care since I was nine. I am sixteen now," she added, showing pride in her advanced years.

"A great age indeed, but obviously not one which has led you to years of discretion, I vow," the Marquis interposed in that hateful tone she was beginning to dread.

"I know, but really, I had to leave. Mr. H. . . . ," again she hesitated, unwilling to divulge her guardian's name, ". . . wanted me to marry his nephew, Algy—Algernon, a most odious young man. He has wet lips and damp hands, and is altogether unattractive," Melissa insisted, her speaking eyes clouding with the thought of her narrowly escaped fate.

"And if you refused to accede to the disagreeable request of your guardian he threatened to lock you in your chamber, starve and beat you into submission, I suppose," the Marquis replied in a bored tone, obviously far from appalled at the melodramatic prospect.

"Exactly," Melissa agreed, ignoring the sceptical inflexion which greeted her disclosure. "There really was no one to whom I could turn until I remembered our former housekeeper who was always kind to me, and who now resides in London. I believed if I could reach her she might give me sanctuary, put me in the way of some respectable position."

"I doubt very much if your housekeeper could find you a respectable position, but perhaps another kind of situation would fit your talents more agreeably," the Marquis replied, his eyes roaming over her body in a manner Melissa found insulting.

She glared at her antagonist, crossing her arms protectively across her bosom as she returned his bold stare. "I don't care for your tone, sir, and although I seem to be at your mercy in this equivocal position, you are no gentleman if you are suggesting that I might entertain some disreputable offer."

"You are quite correct in your assumption. I am not a gentleman, and you are in a most equivocal position," he agreed, not one whit disturbed by her reproof. "It seems to me that you have very few choices. If you reach this mythical housekeeper, I cannot see that she can place you in a household where you would be comfortable. I do not see you as a domestic, and there are few matrons who would employ you as a governess or companion, too much temptation to the young men of the household. In the end you would find yourself on your back in some bed, and if that is your fate, much better to sell yourself to a protector who will appreciate your charms with the proper remuneration."

"You are disgusting, sir." Melissa gasped, amazed at the bold speech of this odious man. "I have no intention of becoming a light skirt, whatever you may think."

The gentleman ignored her outrage, seeming to be amused at her predicament, which only confirmed Melissa's assessment of his character. "You may not have any choice. Of course, you could return to the eager arms of the obnoxious Algy. But no, I believe you would be wasted on him, a no doubt bucolic youth from the provinces, whose crude embraces would be a sad disappointment I fear."

"Since I have forced my presence upon you, willy-nilly, I suppose you have the right to insult me, but I find your suggestions and alternatives repulsive in the extreme,"

Melissa said indignantly, although she suspected it would be to her benefit to behave a bit more ingratiatingly. Her intention to throw herself on the mercy of the elderly couple in whose coach she had chosen to hide was completely overset at facing instead this sardonic man, probably a rake of the first water, with an inflated idea of his own consequence and a cynical attitude toward life and young women in desperate straits. Certainly he was no knight-errant, eager to protect the innocent and virtuous. He was much more likely to take advantage of her vulnerable position, she concluded shrewdly. No doubt he was unaccustomed to rebuffs by women of any sort.

"This righteous wrath of yours is quite tedious," said the Marquis de Lisle, for that was his title. "If we are to travel together to London I hope you will try to behave with some gratitude for my forbearance and not enact these Cheltenham tragedies. I might possibly be persuaded to solve your rather mundane problems, but only if you cease fulminating and allow me to reflect. I suggest you settle back and take a nap. I promise not to ravish you before we reach the next posting stop. Be quiet, that's a good girl." His patience at an end, he tipped his hat over his eyes again and settled down comfortably, signalling that further discussion was unwelcome.

Melissa, realizing for the moment he would not eject her from the coach, breathed a sigh of relief and obeyed. She felt she had brushed through those explanations rather well, not revealing what she intended to keep hidden. She suddenly felt exhausted from her recent adventures and the searching catechism and found her head nodding. Within minutes she was fast asleep, unaware that her companion was studying her beneath lowered lids, planning to use her artless disclosures to his own advantage.

Darkness was drawing in as the Marquis de Lisle's coach, skirting the Salisbury Plain, reached the Wiltshire town of

Amersbury on the great North Road to London, his lordship having decided to put up for the night at the George & Dragon.

Postboys and minions from the inn hurried across the cobbled courtyard as the Marquis' footmen let down the carriage steps, recognizing the crested conveyance promised good tips for service rendered. De Lisle descended leisurely, shuddering at the cold wind which blew in from the Plain, and turned to assist his passenger. Melissa, still muddled from her sleep, stumbled down the steps. She refused the proffered hand of the Marquis and, in confusion, turned to look about her at the bustling courtyard.

"We are halfway to London, at Amersbury, infant, and will stop here for the night. Now do not get on your high ropes. I have bespoke accommodations and you will be properly housed." The Marquis smiled suddenly at his unwanted guest. He found her embarrassment amusing, suspecting she feared what faced her in this commodious lodging.

Within moments a bowing landlord had arrived to welcome the distinguished guest and to escort him to the bedroom and private parlour prepared for his arrival. A contrite Melissa followed in his wake, already grateful that she was not forced to settle in the public taproom where her disguise might not protect her from the speculation of the regular customers. She wondered how the Marquis, whose name and title she had yet to discover, would explain her presence. She should have known. Arrogantly ignoring any speculative glances from the landlord, the Marquis demanded hot water, several bottles of Madeira, and a meal to appear shortly. When the door had closed behind the subservient landlord, the Marquis turned to face her.

"You will feel all the better for a wash and some refreshment. We will be having an early night as I want to reach London before evening tomorrow, and must make an early start. Now cease shying like a fawn when I come near you. You will sleep in this parlour on a trundle bed, the sleep of the pure and virtuous, I promise. I have not decided yet what to do with you, but for the moment you have my assurances I have no designs on your person. Incidentally, I have not introduced myself, Theron de Lisle, at your service." He bowed mockingly, amused at his reception from the tousled urchin who barely acknowledged the introduction in her relief that, at least for the moment, she was safe from his unwanted attentions.

Gathering her wits about her and determined not to be cowed by his haughtiness, Melissa nodded. "De Lisle, I suspect is your title. You are a nobleman, are you not, my lord?" she asked.

"Yes, fledgling, a marquis, no less, which no doubt will do nothing to allay your suspicions, and quite rightly, too. I have a fearsome reputation." He flashed a blinding smile, wiping the cynical lines from his face and thus making him appear much younger than his thirty odd years.

"Well, I confess I am relieved. With so exalted a rank, I need not worry for my virtue, then. No doubt, your lordship has a spate of mistresses, far more experienced and amenable than I," Melissa responded outrageously, determined to hide her trepidation behind a bold front.

"Absolutely, but perhaps not a spate. That sounds too exhausting even for me. Now settle down while I remove to the bedroom to rid myself of this travelling dirt. You will feel much more the thing after a good supper." The Marquis ran an admonishing eye over her then turned and entered the inner chamber.

Relieved to relax her guard for the moment, Melissa turned to the fire, rubbing her hands before its comforting warmth. Still not completely reassured by the Marquis' unexpected kindness, she felt he had not wholly accepted her story and might still enact some price for escorting her to London. However, she had no choice but to go along with whatever plans he had made, at least until they reached the city. There she should be able to outwit him and vanish into the streets of that crowded metropolis. Amused and intrigued as he might be now at her predicament, she doubted he would summon the energy to follow her, or care what happened to her once she had disappeared. A very puzzling and provoking man, Melissa decided, but formidable for all that, and one she would challenge at her peril. But she had come this far without harm and must trust to luck and her own contrivance to come safely into harbor. Nothing would impel her to return to Horace Hawksley's gloomy house and the hateful fate her guardian had planned for her. Unaccustomed to gentlemen of the first rank, or any gentlemen at all for that matter, she found herself puzzled by the Marquis' attitude. Perhaps he found her dilemma amusing, an antidote to a boring journey. Still she would be wise to keep her wits about her. She suspected that beneath the facade of sophisticated ennui lurked a ruthless opponent, a man who would brook no opposition to his desires.

She was interrupted in her thoughts by the appearance of the chambermaid with water and she proceeded to tidy herself as best she might. The maid gave her a searching glance, obviously burning to know what a fine nobleman was about travelling with such a ragamuffin, even sharing his chambers with such a one. Melissa ignored her. Soon the girl left her to her ablutions, and her thoughts which were far from easy.

If the Marquis entertained any but the most casual interest in her he hid it most successfully, Melissa concluded when they met over the evening meal. Her exhausting day had not dulled her appetite. She ate heartily of every dish put in front of her—some tender pigeons, sirloin of beef and various enticing comfits. The Marquis, she noticed, ate sparingly, but drank a full bottle of wine, and broached a second one. Melissa eyed him warily, accustomed to seeing her guardian well foxed after much less, but obviously the Marquis, whatever his other faults, had a much harder head.

"Now, my intrepid child, we must come to some resolution of your affairs," the Marquis remarked.

"I am grateful to your lordship for your forbearance in allowing me to ride to London with you, but I fail to see how my affairs are any concern of yours," Melissa protested in her most haughty tone, the affect somewhat diminished by the sweetmeat she was chewing.

De Lisle leaned over, removed the tempting dish from her hands, and continued as if she had not spoken. "I assume you have some female garb in that tattered carpet bag you clutched so determinedly when we arrived here. But I think perhaps you had better keep your disguise, pathetic as it is, until we reach our destination."

"I have every intention of doing so. When we reach London, I will be off to my housekeeper and you can forget all about me." Melissa hesitated before grudgingly continuing. "And I suppose I must offer my gratitude for your escort."

The Marquis grinned mockingly, knowing how much her gratitude went against the grain. "Spare me your thanks, my child, I have a feeling before we are much further along in our acquaintance you might have every reason to damn me. Now pay attention. I have no intention of dropping you off in some slum to make your way into goodness knows what coil. I am taking you to my cousin, the Comtesse de Frontons, who will show you how to go on, and tog you out in some suitable garments," he said decisively. Before she could protest he continued in terms that brooked no argument: "If you have any idea of eluding me to follow your own pursuits let me tell you I will have no compunction in turning you over to your guardian, and letting him marry you off to the odious Algy. Despite your valiant attempts to gull me as to his name and your own, I vow I would have little trouble finding the gentlemen in the depths of Devon."

"You wouldn't do that," Melissa railed. "Oh, you are worse than Algy, far worse to pretend to help me and then behave so despicably." She had no idea how appealing she looked in her distress, her violet eyes swimming with tears, and her cheeks flushed with anger.

"I would be far more despicable if I left you to your fate in London. I would wish to take you to a more suitable home than

Aimee's but the one couple who might shelter you and with whom you would be happy is now in America, although I expect them home shortly. Sarah Valentine would find you most appealing and sympathize with your predicament, since she herself is equally heedless of trouble in following her heart. But Aimee will have to do until I can make other arrangements." The Marquis' brow furrowed as he thought of his cousin, a sophisticated lady of the town who would only welcome her unwanted visitor under some duress. "And do not think that if you find your situation with her uncomfortable you can run away to that ubiquitous housekeeper. Incidentally, what is the address of that noble lady?"

"I won't tell you," Melissa defied him, determined to thwart his intrusion into her life.

"Oh, I think you will," he replied suavely, rising to his feet, and pulling her out of her chair and into his arms. Before she could challenge him again he had taken her chin in his hand, lowered his head, and kissed her fiercely, surprising her with the force of the strange emotion this punishing embrace engendered. Melissa tore her mouth from his and struggled against the iron hands which held her.

"You are an unprincipled cad, sir, to force yourself on an unprotected female," she stammered, but defiant all the same.

"I quite agree. I am unprincipled, but let me assure you, I will go to some lengths to get my way in this matter and you would be wise to submit now before my passions get out of hand," he insisted mockingly, well aware that she was more frightened than she would admit, admiring her courage, but determined to discover that address.

"That would be rape, sir." When he pulled her close once again, she quickly capitulated. "Bessie lives on Bread Street, Cheapside, at least she did the last I heard some months ago." She faced her adversary bravely but her breath was coming in short gasps, and the color flooded her cheeks, to her humiliation.

"It would not be rape, my dear. Surely you give me credit for more expertise in the bedroom than that. But it's as well you told me, for when my devil is roused I am capable of anything, even ravishing childish virgins. Now what is the rest of this admirable Bessie's name," he insisted, still holding her in a tight grasp.

"Blount, Bessie Blount. And I wish I had never left my guardian's home. Even Algy would be preferable to your disgusting attentions," Melissa retorted, ashamed that she had not dealt more firmly with her tormentor.

"If you find my attentions disgusting, my dear, I shudder to think what your reaction would be to what you would endure in Cheapside, where, no doubt, you would end up in some kip house or worse." The Marquis, feeling a bit ashamed of his actions, spoke in irritation. For a moment, feeling her slight form in his arms, he had half hoped she would defy him, forcing him to carry those punishing kisses further. Disgusted, he reminded himself that seducing virgins was not his style, no matter how enticing the challenge. Angry at losing his control, he said harshly, "Just be grateful I am not abandoning you to Bessie and Cheapside for you have no idea what horrors might await you there. Now for heaven's sake stop behaving like a pea goose. You are safe from me for the night, which no doubt will be a long one for me." Reaching for the bottle on the table, he took it and his glass, crossed the room, and entered the bedroom, slamming the door behind him.

Melissa stood trembling with shock, exhaustion and another strange emotion, engendered by those few moments in the Marquis' arms. She wondered what would have happened if she had continued to resist him. All she did know was that the Marquis de Lisle was a dangerous man, whom she would defy at her own risk.

Chapter Two

Having had long experience with her guardian when he had partaken deeply of spirits, Melissa did not find the Marquis' black silence the morning following their tempestuous encounter in the parlor of the George & Dragon too surprising. She prudently suspended conversation after her cheerful "good morning" elicited a growlish response. She was tempted to point out that over-indulgence in wine brought a heavy head and a lowering humor, but decided this was hardly the time or the place for that opinion. Following meekly in his lordship's wake she entered the travelling coach, prepared for a long and uncomfortable ride. After a few dozen miles, however, the Marquis' mood lightened and he condescended to speak a few words.

"I am pleased to see you are not a chattering female in the morning. Nothing is more abhorrent than the twitterings of your sex after a night spent unwisely with a bottle," he admitted ruefully.

"Many gentlemen seem to indulge in that direction," Melissa agreed smugly, implying that the Marquis was subject to the normal failings.

He laughed a bit grimly. "I hope you have no intention of delivering a temperance lecture. I would not receive it kindly."

"Not at all. I am sure you would pay no heed." Melissa eyed

him tolerantly, all sweet smiles for his discomfort.

"You are a minx, and will no doubt lead some poor fellow a terrible dance, if you manage to snare an unexceptional husband. Even in that ridiculous garb, you have a certain out-of-the ordinary charm," the Marquis teased, his mood considerably improved.

"I am not at present hanging out for a husband; but, when I do secure an eligible beau, I will not send him to you for a recommendation. Somehow I do not believe any respectable young man would be reassured by your endorsement," she answered pertly, unwilling to let the Marquis believe that his careless words of approval pleased her.

"Perhaps you are right, fledgling," the Marquis agreed good humouredly. "An endorsement from me would not be the thing, more apt to result in the poor fool calling me out."

Deciding that to pursue that train of thought would lead to difficulties, and realizing that the noble lord had no intention of apologizing for using her so roughly on the previous evening, Melissa decided that it behooved her to question him about their destination.

"Could you tell me, sir, where we are bound, and just what you have in mind for me?" Melissa asked gently hoping to soothe any suspicions he might entertain that she might not fall meekly into his plans. The Marquis obviously went his own arrogant way, unaccustomed to considering any desires but his own. For the moment it suited her to abide by his decision to house her with his French relative, but this was only a temporary expedient. The sooner she reached Bessie and removed herself from the Marquis' custody the happier she would be, for she did not trust him. He found her plight amusing now, but he might just as easily become bored and turn her over to her guardian as he had threatened. She did not seriously believe he had other designs upon her, for she felt if her innocence and naivete were not protection enough her lack of the more obvious charms necessary to engage the interest of a top-of-the-trees man of the town did.

"I have told you I am taking you to my cousin's house in London, but as to what I have in mind for you, I am not prepared to tell you just now. You will have to compose yourself with patience, and remember that you still have a choice. You can leave your fate in my hands or return to your guardian's house. Do not think any other options are open to you, because they are not," the Marquis concluded grimly.

Melissa decided that further argument would avail her little at this juncture, but she seethed with anger at the thought that this high-handed nobleman believed he could order her future in whatever fashion suited him. Obviously he was unaccustomed to having his dictates challenged, and much as she wanted to refuse his offer of lodging she realized that he did indeed have the power to force her to accede to his plans. Refusing to thank him or agree with his demands, Melissa sat stubbornly silent, which did not seem to cause her companion any disquiet. She would have been even more annoyed if she knew he thought her defiance amusing, as she perched on the seat of the carriage, in her tattered boy's dress, her slim body stiff with anger and frustration.

As the coach entered London in the early afternoon Melissa abandoned her pose of outrage in her excitement at seeing the great city for the first time. Until this moment Exeter had represented the epitome of sophistication for her, raised as she had been in the wilds of Devon and rarely allowed beyond her guardian's house and fields. Her first reaction was stunned surprise at the crowded motley thoroughfares, teeming with hawkers, vendors of all kinds, beggars and merchants, clerks and urchins, all of them rushing helter-skelter on the day's business. Secretly she admitted she was fortunate to be arriving under the Marquis' care, for she would have found herself at quite a pass trying to negotiate this maze of streets to Bessie's address in Cheapside. The coach rattled along the cobbled streets into a quieter more elegant section of the city, finally rolling to a stop before a tall narrow house just beyond a tidy square.

"Come infant. We have at last reached our destination. I sent a post boy ahead with the announcement of our arrival so your hostess should be on hand to welcome you," said the Marquis. He took Melissa's arm in a firm grasp, leaving her no recourse but to precede him up the high scrubbed stone steps to the entrance. Rapping his cane on the door, he waited but a moment before the door was opened by a dark clad personage, rather sour of face and mien, who greeted the Marquis with a stiff smile.

"Good afternoon, your lordship. The Comtesse is expecting you, and your . . . companion." The butler looked disgustedly at Melissa as if to say he thought she would be better received below stairs than in milady's drawing room.

"Quite so, Evans. Please see to Miss Mason's luggage," the Marquis ordered, wresting the carpet bag from Melissa and handing it with his great coat, hat, cane, and gloves to the much-tried butler. Not relinquishing his grasp on her arm he dragged her over to the left of the tiled hall toward the salon which ran the length of the house. Before Melissa could take in the sight of the resplendent brocaded furnishings, and the high moulded ceilings, her attention was caught by the black haired beauty who rose from a chair by the window to greet them.

"*Bon jour, mon ami,* I see you have brought the promised guest. Not quite what I expected, but then, knowing you, I should not have expected anything in the ordinary way," Aimee, Comtesse de Frontons, greeted them, her soft languid voice with its noticeable accent in tune with her garnet silk gown and her intricate coiffure. She was a study in elegance, her matte-white skin showing not a blemish, her luxuriant raven tresses pulled into a smooth chignon, and her luscious figure accented by the rich lace of her gown which was designed to make the most of her white shoulders and full bosom. She put Melissa in mind of an over-ripe peach, but perhaps that was unfair, occasioned by her own jealousy and knowledge that she herself would never achieve such bounteous beauty.

The Marquis crossed to the lady, bowed low and kissed her hand. "Your servant, my dear Comtesse, and how charming you look as always, a delightful sight to brighten these weary eyes. But allow me to present the infant, a Miss Melissa, ah, Mason, I believe she calls herself, my uninvited guest but now, alas, a charge upon us both." The Marquis explained in his maddening manner, causing Melissa to blush with mortification, which was, no doubt, exactly what he intended.

"Ah yes, well, I must hear all about your adventures my dear, but for the present I think perhaps you might enjoy a bath and a change into a more seemly costume," the Comtesse suggested. Melissa considered she had received her no-doubt unwelcomed guest with more tact and charm than could be expected, and it was small-minded of her to take the Comtesse in dislike because she looked so voluptuous and was on such intimate terms with the Marquis.

Evans, the butler, appeared in answer to the Comtesse's summons, and escorted Melissa from the room. She deliberately did not look toward the Marquis, although she was determined that she would not be seeing him again. Politeness demanded that she thank him for his escort but she felt that any attempt on her part to express her gratitude would raise his suspicions. With a muttered "Thank you, milord," and the sketchiest of nods, Melissa slipped from the room. Theron de Lisle watched her leave, his eyes narrowing thoughtfully. The child was up to some rig. He did not trust that meek and mild demeanour, but he would deal with her later. He turned to the Comtesse who was inviting him to take a chair.

"Well, Aimee, I suppose you are due some explanation of this rather odd occurrence?"

"Yes, it is not quite your style, Theron, rescuing urchins from folly along the road," the Comtesse replied languidly. She had little interest in the Marquis' protégé, but it behooved her to express some if she wished to keep in his good graces. Theron might appear blasé and indifferent to amusements which excited more conventional men, but the Comtesse knew he could be exceedingly stubborn and unyielding in pursuit of whatever caprice currently engaged his interest. And obviously he had plans for this urchin *manqué*. Although Aimee de Frontons did not contemplate an extended visit from Melissa with equanimity she had too much sense to express her displeasure to Theron. He could turn quite haughty and even nasty if brooked. She knew what the removal of his sponsorship could mean to her own future. No, she must keep him sweet at all costs.

"She spun quite a heart-rendering tale, but whether or not it is true I have yet to ascertain. I want you to shelter her for a time until my plans for her are fully developed. She needs a complete new wardrobe, and of course, I will stand the reckoning for that. Take her to Mme. Charles. And find a hairdresser to tame that ugly crop into some kind of order. She looks a fright right now, but I believe she can be fashioned into some kind of looks under your fashionable hand, *ma chère*." He smiled at her, quite shamelessly using the charm of which he was overburdened when he wished to use it, which was less often than might be supposed from such an experienced rake.

"You know, Theron, you never cease to astound me. Here you are a practiced libertine, up to every dubious start, and yet you evidence signs of charity and warm-heartedness which do not suit the image you have so carefully cultivated." Aimee considered the Marquis thoughtfully.

"Do not be deceived by my kindness in this instance, Aimee," he replied carelessly. "If I have a motive in befriending this child, I am not willing to discuss it now, or perhaps ever. But do not be gulled into thinking I have lost my suspicion of people in general. Unfortunately, the world does not consist of chivalrous, virtuous, unselfish, kindly people, but rather of worldly, self-seeking, greedy and devious characters who will seize every advantage to their own ends."

"Surely you are much too cynical, Theron. I don't believe that, in your heart, you really have such a jaundiced view of people," the Comtesse protested with a charming smile.

"I am surprised you think I have a heart, my dear," he replied. "But do not mistake my very natural interest in the lusts of the body for romantic impulses."

"Really, Theron, how unusually uncouth of you. I prefer to think you have a heart, and I believe a much finer character than you describe," Aimee de Frontons insisted.

The Marquis, not deceived by her gentle hints that they shared a special intimacy based on more than physical desire, ignored her efforts to win some type of declaration from him, and returned to the matter in hand. "I thank you for taking in my stray, Aimee, but do not suppose for one moment that this gives you special rights in respect to my affairs. I don't believe I owe you any favours," he spoke sharply, his tone warning her to go no further.

"How cruel of you, Theron, to remind me how much I owe you for my deliverance from that ogre, Napoleon. I would not presume to question your decisions. I will, of course, be happy to help you in whatever way I can with your . . . ward."

The Comtesse's momentary hesitation over the last word signified that she still had doubts about the Marquis' intentions toward the young woman foisted into their lives in such a singular fashion. But she knew enough of her cousin not to press her enquiries further. A difficult man, Theron, who could only be handled with a very light touch. Angry as she might be at his refusal to give her any promise for the future, she was too experienced to press him.

Aimee de Frontons had decided from the beginning of their relationship that she wanted the Marquis as her next husband. Married young by her exigent parents to an older aristocrat who had not treated her indulgently, she had been relieved when Madame Guillotine had claimed him. Because he had left her on their Burgandy estate, she had avoided a like fate. Theron had rescued her on one of his mysterious visits to France. She had expressed proper gratitude by welcoming him into her bed where he proved to be an exciting and skilled lover, but showed no indication of regularizing their intimacy.

She wondered if she had been unwise to submit to him before the vows were sealed, although she had every confidence she could bring him around eventually. She believed he had suffered a rebuff at the hands of the American granddaughter of Lady Ravensham, who had preferred to marry an earl's son with a rather better reputation. Lately, however, she had been forced to revise her thinking. Theron appeared to care little for the joys of domesticity, little interest in confining his lovemaking to one partner, or even for the succession to his distinguished title. She still considered herself first in the field, however, for he scorned the respectable misses on the catch for a husband, and had no difficulty enjoying the fleeting pleasures of the bed for which he paid generously. Certainly the Comtesse was too vain, too worldly, and too confident to feel she had anything to fear from a grubby little girl who had thrown herself on the Marquis' mercy. Whatever his intentions toward Melissa, Aimee did not for an instant believe they were romantic.

Chapter Three

"Well, poppet, you do pay for dressing," Theron conceded at his first view of Melissa in her new wardrobe. She did indeed look a treat in an azure blue silk redincote over a cream shift, her short golden brown curls tamed into a fashionable crop which accented her pointed face and huge violet eyes. He raised his quizzing glass and raked her with that world-weary glance she found so annoying. "Yes, quite an improvement. You make a charming ragamuffian lad, but an even more enticing girl."

His amusement angered Melissa who considered herself togged out in the latest stare and did not appreciate being treated with careless condescension. She thought she looked exceedingly modish even if she remained obviously in the shade next to the Comtesse's elegance.

"I am most grateful to you and the Comtesse for generously outfitting me, although I am not quite sure how I will repay you. But you must keep an account, for I intend to recompense you for this unnecessary expense," Melissa said grudgingly.

"Oh, I am sure I will be recompensed, infant, never fear," the Marquis replied mockingly, and then as if the whole subject bored him turned to Aimee who had been watching the pair with narrowed eyes. "My congratulation, *ma chère.* You have achieved wonders," he approved.

"I am glad you are satisfied, Theron. Although her figure is a bit too slight to show off the latest fashions to the best advantage, I believe she will do," the Comtesse preened, soothing her own emerald silk over more generous curves.

The Marquis, eyeing Melissa's slight bosom under the blue redincote, raised an eyebrow at the obvious comparison, noticing that his protégé blushed with anger under his scrutiny but then turning away as if bored with the spectacle of such naivete.

"Now that I am properly gowned, what is your plan for me, my lord?" Melissa asked.

"Later, later, infant. I am not ready to reveal my nefarious schemes yet. Now run along and stitch a sampler or read an improving tract while I have a small coze with my cousin." The Marquis dismissed Melissa in that manner she found so maddening.

Snorting with disgust, Melissa flounced from the room, not at all pleased with being directed in such a cavalier manner, and feeling very much like a member of the nursery set relegated to childish pursuits while her elders discussed matters of more importance.

The Comtesse, smug in the knowledge that the young woman could not hold a candle to her own more obvious and mature attractions, signified that Theron could take a seat, and settled herself to hear what he had to say.

"I am in your debt, Aimee, for following my instructions so well. You have definitely improved the chit. I am grateful," Theron said, ignoring her gesture to sit beside her on the cream settee and choosing instead a chair some distance removed.

"And what do you have in mind for the young woman, Theron?" Aimee asked. "It is not your usual style to take so many pains with a schoolgirl."

"Are you concerned that I intend to set her up as my latest mistress? Never fear, such innocence is quite beyond my touch. Chaste flowers have never appealed to me, as you must know," the Marquis replied cynically, entertained by the

Comtesse's probing. "The chit's chastity is quite safe from my lecherous demands." He suspected his cousin's fears for Melissa's future were not founded on any emotions of protection but were based on more selfish motives.

"Well, you are being very mysterious. What do you mean to do with her?" the Comtesse asked languidly, now satisfied that the Marquis' intentions did not endanger her own status.

"As you know, I am involved in some very tricky business with our pestential enemies. You have benefited by my contacts with our friends across the Channel, but there is still much more to be done, and Melissa will fit in very well with my plans to sow dissension in that quarter. That is all I am prepared to tell you, right now, but let me assure you that your guest will not be with you much longer." The Marquis was well aware of the Comtesse's lack of enthusiasm for the young woman foisted on her.

Aimee did not hide her relief, but her problem with Theron still remained. He was a slippery customer, not easily manipulated, and she owed him a great deal. Despite her confidence in her charms she did not seem any closer to achieving her aim of becoming his marchioness, and she must play her cards carefully. Giving a light laugh she turned the conversation to less controversial affairs, and he followed her lead with graceful acquiescence.

Melissa, banished from the drawing room by her elders, took refuge in the book room, where she pondered over her next move. She shared her hostess' speculation about his lordship's arrogant motives for championing her, but for the moment decided not to challenge him. She quite enjoyed her taste of London life although the Comtesse's chaperonage had not exposed her to much of it. She had not abandoned her idea of locating Bessie Blount and enlisting her help in finding a situation. She could not continue in the Comtesse's house indefinitely. Her hostess' practiced manner, her surface amiability and generosity did not make Melissa comfortable. Obviously the Comtesse's relationship with the Marquis was a close one, and certainly the two were well suited. Both sophisticated, experienced, and well versed in the flirtatious badinage which seemed to be the coin of the haut monde. Although the Marquis' cynicism and haughty disregard for any desires but his own infuriated Melissa, she had to concede that he had been surprisingly kind to her with what purpose she could not define. But she did not trust him. A price for his patronage would be exacted, and she did not intend to linger in his vicinity in the event she would be called upon to pay it.

Perplexed, Melissa examined her choices. Even if she did succeed in reaching Bessie, the Marquis knew of the Cheapside address. Remembering how he had pried that information from her, Melissa blushed. A practiced seducer, he might easily have carried that brutal embrace much further, and then how would she have responded. She was not impervious to his sensual enticement, she knew, ashamed as it made her to remember her reactions to that kiss. His determination to install her with the Comtesse, to check on her progress daily had at first led her to think he might want to set her up as his mistress, but lately she had been forced to conclude he had little romantic interest in her. Obviously not a gentleman inspired by love of humanity nor chivalrous instincts, he had some devious design for her, one she was convinced she would not find to her liking. Despite her independent and resourceful spirit, she doubted that she could defy him effectively or even dissemble long enough to lull his suspicions. He was perfectly capable of using her for whatever purpose he had in mind and then abandoning her, indifferent to her welfare. He was not a man influenced by the gentler emotions, and innocent as she was, Melissa feared his ruthless and arrogant attitude. She had little hope of appealing to his better nature. She did not think he had one. Meanwhile, her only recourse was to be on her guard, act the grateful guest, and not be beguiled by his charm which he assumed whenever it suited him, and was based on little more than his own convenience.

Theron de Lisle left the Comtesse's home shortly after their conversation, promising to escort her to a fashionable rout that evening, not including Melissa in the invitation. He did not intend to expose the child to society, for that would endanger his scheme. Certain that he could impose his will on her, he had not forgotten her intention to find Bessie and escape from him. Although he doubted much of the story she had told him, he did think she had some compelling reason to flee her former home. About the only information he could rely on from her reluctant lips was the address of that fabled housekeeper, for she had been forced to reveal that under a great deal of provocation, and without time to think up a better tale. Theron de Lisle had tasted just about every vice in life of incredible dissipation and was not a stranger to the wiles of women, but he had very little experience with innocents, and that very innocence could prove disarming.

He had always steered clear of eligible young women, for he had few illusions about the fairer sex. The respectable ones, paraded during the season in search of wealthy titled husbands, learned at their parents' knees to prefer a fat purse and lavish rent rolls to love. Disillusioned early by a promiscuous, self-indulgent mother who had died eloping with her lover, he had never dallied with chaste young girls even in his salad days. A rake, a womanizer, and a libertine, feared by respectable belles, he spent his time with demimondaines, impures, ballet dancers and worse. His romantic escapades were a scandal. Few respectable families would allow him near their daughters, no matter that his ancient title and wealth, as well as his undeniable physical attractions, made him an appealing figure to the young ladies. Recently he had abandoned his libertine ways, more from a surfeit of such pleasures than a desire to reenter the society to which his ancient and noble lineage entitled him. He had exchanged the ennui of indulgence for the adventure of serving his country, rather surprised at the patriotism which had led him to such a path. Danger and excitement were proving to be more stimulating to his jaded appetite than the round of gambling and whoring which had occupied his leisure until now. His thirty-odd years had been glaringly misspent, and if he did not entirely regret them, he decided that his present course provided far more satisfaction. Ruefully, he conceded that if he had not completely abandoned his licentious ways, or his scornful rejection of society's shibboleths, at least he had found a purpose to life instead of a determination to go to the devil as quickly as possible. His sponsorship of Melissa had begun on a whim, but upon consideration he had discovered she might fit very well into his design to unmask the traitors who had proved so damaging and elusive.

Shrugging off his distaste at the role he had chosen for her, he proceeded to the Foreign Office where he intended to reveal his plot to Castlereagh, who had until very recently been too concerned with the Irish reform bill to give much attention to the war with France. But now Castlereagh had steered the Irish Bill through the Commons and had been replaced by Cornwallis in Ireland so his priorities had shifted to the damaging French intrigues against His Majesty's government. Many of his contemporaries found Castlereagh cool and aloof, but under that facade his passions ran deep, and his sincere patriotism could not be denied. Beneath his suave, social manner and that handsome mien was a mind of amazing astuteness, and de Lisle admired his indifference to specious popularity, an attitude he himself found useful. Currently president of the Board of Control, Castlereagh was soon to be appointed Secretary of State for War, and in a better position to implement his policies. His cooperation was vital.

De Lisle made his way to No. 18 St. James Square, Castlereagh's London home, confident that the minister would endorse his plan, based as it was on the information the Marquis had inadvertently discovered on his latest trip to Plymouth.

The Viscount received him graciously, but spent little time in small talk.

"I believe you have some valuable leads as to the latest

incursion of French spies into our midst, de Lisle," Castlereagh began. "This influx of emigrés is an ongoing problem. We cannot, in all justice, deny them sanctuary, but among the honest victims of persecution there are too many rogues and opportunists who owe little loyalty to either the ancien régime or to the new republic. They infiltrate everywhere, and there is so much loose talk in London. What have you discovered for us?"

"For a time, the network we uncovered through the traitor General Apsley-Gower put a crimp in French intelligence, but I have reason to believe that affairs have been reorganized, and the spies are even more prevalent," de Lisle reported. "One of our couriers was found murdered on an isolated beach at Devon, but in his pocket was a torn fragment of a playbill from the Majestic Theatre in Drury Lane. I do not think this was mere coincidence, or that the fellow had been merely idling his time at a recent performance. I intend to put an agent into the theatre to discover if we can unmask the chain which is leading to all this treason in our midst."

"Can you rely on this person? It seems a strange venue for spying," Castlereagh queried. He had some reluctance to trust de Lisle, who had very suspect ties to France himself, but he was eager to take advantage of the Marquis' rather surprising efforts to serve his country. The libertine lord had showed little evidence of concern for aught besides a wearying round of dissipation, a pose Castlereagh found despicable, but he would use whatever tools came to hand if that would assist the government, now besieged on all sides by the French war.

De Lisle, not unaware of the minister's opinion, did not intend to reveal the details of his design, but gave him a brief outline of his scheme. Castlereagh objected to his agent, but finally gave his grudging approval, still doubtful that any worthwhile results would insue. For his part de Lisle was reluctant to show all his cards. Sufficient to the moment was official agreement. He did not want or expect gratitude, and he received none, only the knowledge that the government understood his aim and methods. Spying was a dirty and ungrateful business and His Majesty's government, although seeing the necessity for it, preferred to turn a blind eye until the traitors were unmasked. De Lisle acknowledged cynically that Castlereagh was willing to use him even if he did not like or trust him. That neither disappointed him, nor disturbed him. He bid a restrained farewell to Castlereagh satisfied that he had achieved his purpose.

Chapter Four

"You see, Thomas, Mistress Blount, is an old friend who has fallen on bad times, and I wish to meet with her to see if I can assist her in any way." Melissa smiled engagingly at the young footman. In her hand was the letter she had written to Bessie, hoping he might take it to Cheapside. Smiling wistfully at the young servant she confided, "I am sure the Comtesse would not approve of me trying to contact one who has come down so disastrously in the world, so might this remain a secret between us? No need to worry the Comtesse, or to make trouble," she pleaded, widening her speaking violet eyes in appeal.

"Well, Miss, it would mean my place if Evans discovered what I was up to, but I would like to help you," the footman replied, anxious to acquiesce but well aware of the penalties. He did not particularly admire the Comtesse, and thought she made an odd chaperone for this young woman whose surprising appearance had the servants all gossiping. Still, he was not too eager to risk a good position.

"Oh, I am sure you are too clever to be discovered, Thomas. You seem well awake on all suits," Melissa coaxed outrageously. "Please do this very small errand for me. I will see no harm comes to you." How she could guarantee this, she hoped he would not ask.

"Very well, miss. But just this once, you understand," he obliged, taking the letter from her and making all haste from the hall before either Evans or anyone else should see him, or before Melissa could demand other services.

In her impatience to escape the Comtesse's surveillance, Melissa had decided she must urge Bessie to come to her, either here when her hostess was occupied elsewhere with the Marquis, or in some innocuous rendezvous where they could meet undetected. She had suggested that Bessie give the footman an immediate answer and could barely restrain her eagerness to set the appointment.

On de Lisle's arrival that morning she greeted him nervously. Melissa had no doubts that he would disapprove of her actions and would take suitable measures to thwart whatever ruses she might take to escape his orbit. She had quite enough of the noble lord's patronage and had no intention of continuing in this anomalous position in which he had placed her. Innocent she might be, but she knew full well that the Comtesse and the Marquis were involved in a liaison and she did not enjoy acting the gooseberry to their dalliance.

"Well, my pet, what maggot have you in your head on this bright morning? You cannot beguile me with that wistful expression and those fluttering downcast eyes, you know." He frowned at her, suspecting she was up to some rig, and he had every intention of discovering it.

Melissa barely repressed a gasp of astonishment. Could he read her mind? Or was it just his nasty, suspicious nature? Well, he could not cozen her into confessing anything to him.

"I have no idea what you mean, my lord. But I must protest your treatment of me. I cannot stay here indefinitely, and I must say it's a bit boring not to be allowed any freedom to explore London or to meet any one," she replied, determined to let him see she would not assent tamely to his dominance.

De Lisle inspected her closely. Of course, the minx was not happy in this situation, but he had come to tell her what he had decided and would brook no rebellion. She had, after all, little recourse but to obey him, without funds or friends in London. And he had not discounted Bessie Blount.

Summoning all the charm which had always served him with her sex, he soothed, "Now Melissa, I have only your best interests at heart, and knowing how you hate to be under obligation to me, I have a proposal which will discharge any debt you feel and remove you from this unhappy situation. Although I cannot see that you are in any distress here compared to living under the hateful condition which your guardian imposed."

Oh, he was a clever devil, Melissa conceded. He knew full well she would endure much rather than return to her guardian. And he had been kind enough to find her shelter and provide her with an extravagant wardrobe which somehow she must repay. She had kept her boy's clothes, now brushed and cleaned, ready for any contingency. She might yet have recourse to the disguise which had served her badly.

"Just what do you have in mind, my lord?" she asked warily.

"Now listen to me carefully and do not raise your hackles until I have finished," he warned, warming to the delightful picture of innocence she made in her cherry red cambric gown, the light from the tall bowed window glancing golden in her short curls. If only she did not look so young, so vulnerable. Who would believe she could play the part he had destined for her? Still it must answer.

"I have taken suitable lodgings for you and a position which I am not able to reveal just now, for all the arrangements are not quite completed. Unfortunately, I have been called out of town for a few days, and your removal will perforce have to be delayed until I return. But you will not be unhappy to leave Aimee's menage, I vow, will you, infant?" he spoke kindly, unwilling to reveal what he had in mind until he had her under the roof he would provide.

"The Comtesse has been all kindness, but it is a difficult position, being an object of charity. I hope this position you have secured for me will enable me to repay the considerable outlay you have made on my behalf," Melissa answered, her spirits rising at the thought that she would no longer be beholden to the Comtesse, but not completely certain of what the Marquis had decided for her. "I assume this position is a respectable one," she countered, her doubts rising again.

"Oh, yes, and I think you will find it most agreeable. Do you believe I would put you in the way of any but the most honourable employment, child?" he asked, aware that she did not trust him even yet, and surprised at his disappointment in her lack of confidence in his good intentions. He had never had cause to reassure any woman yet of his credibility and most of them cared little for honour when money was involved.

"Well, my lord, I do not think respectability is among your chief concerns," Melissa retorted with some audacity. "No doubt you have never to worry about appearances, nor care, I suspect. You cannot expect to be considered a worthy patron of a chaste young woman, now can you?"

Really, she was most ungrateful, but the Marquis showed little evidence that he considered her aught but a troublesome burden. She need not fear for her virtue at his hands. She would more likely encounter indifference and boredom, and who could blame him, burdened with a troublesome girl who had not even been honest with him. Her wide violet eyes clouded. She wished she could confide in him, place all her problems on his wide shoulders, but that would never do. She had learned, to her cost, to be wary of trusting anyone.

The Marquis, understanding more than she realized, wanted to calm her fears, and ask for her trust, but, he conceded cynically, he had done little to deserve it, and would be doing even less in the future, placing her in an anomalous, even dangerous position, and, one which might ruin her reputation irretrievably. What was wrong with him? He normally entertained no conscience about his arrangements with the fair sex. Of course, he rarely dealt with innocents. That might explain it, but he could not dispel the sudden chagrin he felt at using her thus.

"I will be away but a few days, and when I return we will ttle your future. Try to contain your questions until then." ould he tell her now? No, he did not think she was in the best mour to receive his intrigues, and he did not want her nfiding in Aimee. The less the Comtesse knew about his ans for Melissa the better. All Theron's instincts told him to lay as long as possible acquainting any woman with a secret. e looked her over in a considering fashion.

"You are wise to be wary of me, and all men, infant. We are ceedingly selfish and prone to consider no wishes but our vn," he warned. Looking at the ingenuous picture she made, r fresh complexion glowing with youth and expectation, he ain wondered if she could play the role he had destined for r. If he had a spark of decency he would leave her out of his achinations. She should be enjoying the usual pursuits of a ung woman just out of the schoolroom, flirting with dewy-ced young men, gossiping, stitching, shopping, all the safe d mildly pleasurable antics common to her state. But then, r very naivete made her perfect for his scheme, and her own irit of adventure would be piqued by the challenge. Why was e making excuses to himself? He must use the tools at hand d she was tailor-made for his purposes. After all, he would be n hand to protect her—though, he scoffed, he was hardly a roper protector of the morals of a school girl.

Melissa eyed him suspiciously. She was no milk and water iss to obey his dictates without demure. Whatever he had in ind for her she suspected it was far less respectable than he laimed. Well, if she did not like what he had arranged, there as always Bessie and her own plot to elude him and the omtesse. Shrewdly, Melissa divined that the worldly renchwoman would be happy to see the back of her and make o push to protect her from whatever future the Marquis had ecided.

"I do not see why I cannot know now what position you have ecured for me. I might not like it, my lord, and then you will ave been put to all this trouble to no avail," she protested.

"Oh, I think I have the means of persuading you, my dear. He smiled mockingly, implying all sorts of punishment. "Yc are rather at my mercy, you know."

A frisson of some unnamed emotion shook Melissa when sh realized to what he was referring. She was certainly no matc for the noble lord, if he planned a repeat performance of th confrontation in the inn which had led to her revelations abo Bessie. Before she could argue further, he had taken hold o her arms, eyeing her narrowly. "Am I to believe you woul rather warm my bed than pursue gainful employment?" h asked, half hoping she would defy him, and he could subdu her in a way he might enjoy.

Melissa gasped, "You are a devil. And I don't believe yo mean to carry out these threats. I am not up to your touch, m lord," she cried, wondering at her own temerity. He drew he closer and seemed about to put her fears to the test when th door opened abruptly and the Comtesse appeared.

Aimee de Frontons raised her eyes at the intimate pictur before her. Could she have been deceived? Was Theron' interest in the chit deeper than he had allowed? No trace of he anger at seeing the pair so intimately involved showed in he smooth address.

"Here you are, Theron. Evans told me you had called. I ar sorry not to have been ready to receive you. Have you finishe your catechism of Melissa? She looks quite aghast at whateve budget of news you have given her," Aimee said suavely implying that she should be given an explanation of thei compromising attitude.

"On the contrary, ma'am. We were just discussing m future. I cannot stay here indefinitely, you know, and my lord has a suggestion as to a position for me. But no doubt he wil tell you all about it," she assured the Comtesse, not liking th speculative glance that lady had given them. Stepping bacl from the Marquis, she gave a little nod of farewell and whiske herself from the room, only too eager to leave their presence

"Well, Theron, what are you doing, dallying with th

nursery? I believed your tastes lay elsewhere," the Comtesse reproved him, her tone sharper than she intended.

"You really have a vulgar mind, *ma chère*. My plans for Melissa do not include what you obviously think. But I am removing her from your milieu, which should please you. She has not been a comfortable guest, I believe," he sneered, furious that she had caught them in a pose which could be misconstrued.

Realizing she had gone too far, exposed too much, the Comtesse hurried to soothe his sensibilities. She would deal with Melissa later. She had put up with quite enough of that young woman's company, and she did not intend to allow the Marquis any further opportunities to practice his charms on this intruder who threatened her own plans.

Chapter Five

Disturbed and distracted by her interview with the Marquis, Melissa wandered into the garden room, where she might be private to ponder over her next move, and wait impatiently for Thomas' return. She had not liked the Comtesse's inferences about her status, and his lordship's cavalier disposition of her future did not promise well either. No time could be more provident for her to leave the dubious shelter of the Comtesse's house. Despite the Marquis' assurances that he had found her a respectable position, she had not relished the suggestive glances he had bestowed on her, nor his assumption that he had the means to compel her to obey him. A dangerous and unprincipled man, the Marquis, and one she would be wise to avoid if she did not want to store up trouble for herself. He had entirely too much charm and experience and too little regard for women to make him a safe champion.

She had fallen from one desperate situation into another. Neither her guardian nor the Marquis cared a fig for her own wishes, only intent on using her to implement their selfish purposes. Marriage to Algy would have been horrible, but did the Marquis offer her a more pleasant choice? His threats to take her virtue did not frighten her, for she could not really appeal to him, but the situation could be humiliating. She could not put her faith in a man who boasted of his libertine ways and was incapable of any deeper emotion toward a woman than satisfaction of his physical desires. She must escape now while he was absent. Much longer in this invidious position and she would be meekly submitting to whatever he asked of her. For if he put her to the test, she doubted her ability to resist him. This weakness in her character, she despised. He would scorn her appeals and mock her deepest affections.

Not for the first time, Melissa wished she were a woman grown with all the worldly experience of the Comtesse. Still she would not be defeated. She would find Bessie and prevail upon her good nature. Surely her old housekeeper could find some means of protecting her from the perils her orphaned condition had engendered. How lovely to grow to womanhood protected by loving parents who would see to it that she married a man of her choice, kindly, respectable and eager to secure her happiness. Well, no use repining like some ninny, she must just cope as best she could with events. Her natural spirits and independence of mind came to her rescue. No one, neither Horace Hawksley nor the Marquis de Lisle, would use her as a pawn in their schemes. Setting her pointed chin, Melissa, not naturally fainthearted, resolutely set herself to win out over them both.

Her resolution was to be tested earlier than she knew. Peeking out of the garden room, she saw Thomas crossing the hall and hesitating by the library door. He must not interrupt the pair in there, asking for her. Hissing at him, she beckoned him to her side, and pulled him into the garden room.

"Quickly, Thomas. Did you find Mistress Blount?" Melissa asked, all excitement.

"No, miss, I didn't," he answered, his open freckled face drawing into a frown. "I made some enquiries in her former lodgings and all I learned for my pains was that she had left some days ago. An old biddy there who claimed to be privy to her plans, says she thinks Mistress Blount was bound for Bath where she had some relatives. Not a nice neighborhood, that. Bath is sure to be a happier destination. 'Tis a good thing you did not venture there, miss."

"No doubt, Thomas, and I do thank you for attempting my fruitless errand," Melissa smiled coaxingly. She had no coins to give him, and only hoped his inherent kindness was reward enough.

"Well, I hope this news puts your mind at rest. Your friend has probably landed on her feet, finding refuge with relations and at least out of that stew in Cheapside," he tried to reassure Melissa, seeing her downcast face and troubled expression.

"Yes, I know. No doubt she has done the wise thing. I feel happier about her," Melissa said, although this was far from the case, but Thomas must not be drawn further into this conspiracy. His open countenance and willingness to oblige made him a poor protector of secrets. Evans or the Marquis would have the whole story out of him in a trice.

She thanked him prettily, and again requested that he not mention her errand to anyone. Not for one moment did she think the Comtesse would care if she sent clandestine messages to her former housekeeper, but she did not want that lady privy to her secrets, and she had little faith in Aimee de Frontons' promises to keep any confidences Melissa reposed in her from the Marquis. Now that Thomas had revealed Bessie's location, Melissa realized that her choices were limited even further. Her only recourse was to follow Bessie to Bath, and how she was to accomplish that was beyond her imagination for the present.

Whatever the Marquis' plans for his return, Melissa knew she must lose no time in absenting herself. Retiring to her bedroom, she rooted out her boy's costume, which she had hidden in the back of the wardrobe. If she journeyed to Bath aboard the mail coach she must go as a lad. To travel unaccompanied in her present guise would be foolish in the extreme. But a place aboard the coach would cost money and her funds were dangerously low. Even if she were to ride atop, as the more improvident passengers were prone to do, she doubted if she had enough for the fare. Puzzling over her dilemma, Melissa did not at first hear the knock upon her chamber door, but before she could gather her wits about her, the Comtesse entered, raising her eyebrows at the breeches and jerkin, Melissa had laid across the bed. But the Comtesse made no mention of the boy's garb.

Seating herself languidly in a slipper chair by the window, she smiled tightly at her guest, but Melissa noticed that the Comtesse did not enjoy her usual composure.

"I don't know quite how to put this to you, Melissa," Aimee said in her mannered voice. "No doubt the Marquis told you he has been called out of town on government business and will be gone for several days, if not longer. I would hope, between us, we could dispose of your future before he returns."

Melissa remained silent, content to let the Comtesse offer her views. She would not give her the advantage of either arguing or agreeing with her, but her hostess' suggestion did not come as a total surprise to her. She had realized from the first that the Comtesse had not welcomed her unexpected arrival with enthusiasm.

Aimee de Frontons, in the face of her guest's silence, was not entirely certain how best to put her ruthless dismissal. However, that intimate pose in which she had so recently surprised Theron and his protégé, plus his refusal to confide in her, strengthened her determination to be rid of the girl before his return. Rarely did Theron put himself to the trouble of chasing any woman who might have caught his fancy. Out of sight, out of mind, was a philosophy he embraced, knowing that there were other equally attractive lights of love available at his nod. Why should he prove more stubborn over this one? If she hesitated at all, it was because she must choose her words carefully.

"I was most happy to oblige the Marquis by providing shelter for you temporarily," she said, "but obviously your position here is subject to misinterpretation as well as being awkward for you. As the Marquis' protégé you will not be received in society, for his unfortunate reputation implies that you are far from respectable. We both know that he rescued you from the kindest of motives, but, I fear, the Marquis' philanthropy is limited. Your presence in my household makes it awkward for us both. When he has completed his current assignment, we plan to announce our marriage. Surely you can see that your peculiar residence in my home will cause raised eyebrows. Theron, of course, is oblivious to society's opinion, but I am not. I would prefer not to be put in the embarrassing position of explaining your relationship with him. I must prevail upon your generous nature to help me out of this equivocal position. I understand that you have no friends in London, but surely there is some refuge available to you?"

"Well, it is difficult, Comtesse," Melissa replied, ingenuously. "I am an orphan, you know, with a horrid guardian, who is trying to compel me into an unfortunate marriage. I cannot return to his care, as the Marquis agrees." It would do no harm to let the Comtesse know of de Lisle's intent in that direction. From the beginning she had sensed that the Marquis had foisted her on his fiancée without that lady's cooperation, and she could quite understand the Comtesse not wanting her underfoot. But now she must use the Comtesse's eagerness to remove a rival to her own ends. The Comtesse's jealousy, no matter how unfounded, could answer her own dilemma. "You see, I am not only an orphan, but completely indigent. Much as I agree it would be best to leave the shelter of your roof, I have no money to effect my departure," she added sweetly.

"I assumed that Theron had proved generous to you in your unfortunate dependency," the Comtesse said coldly. Avaricious herself, she expected others to use every situation to an advantage. "I cannot spare you much, as I am in straitened circumstances myself, being an emigré with my estate in Burgundy sequestered, but certainly I will give you a few guineas to see you on your way," she concluded grudgingly.

"I would be most grateful, Comtesse. I, too, find my position embarrassing here, and I can only hope to relieve you of my presence as soon as possible. I do have a friend who might take me in, but this involves a journey of some length." Melissa could barely surpress her pleasure at the turn of events. She had no compunction in taking money from the Comtesse, who was quite willing to go behind the Marquis' back for her own reasons. Melissa wondered at Theron, such a skilled evader of the matrimonial yoke, beguiled into a parson's noose by the Comtesse who appeared little better than an adventuress herself. Still, he would have difficulty, with his reputation, in securing a more eligible bride, perhaps. Melissa, who did not want to contemplate what the Comtesse's news meant to her own feelings concerning Theron de Lisle, hurried to seal their bargain.

"Can you be off this afternoon?" the Comtesse asked. "I do not want to press you, but the sooner you leave, the sooner you will find safety. I doubt that Theron will push to discover your whereabouts, for once out of his sight, I am sure he will be relieved at losing the responsibility for your welfare. He is easily bored with these sudden gestures toward humanity, and he might abandon you or cause you to be placed in a situation you might find even more unhappy than the marriage your guardian planned. We women are victims of men's passing desires, and we must do our poor best to settle our futures with some attempt to secure our own comfort." Now that she had achieved her aim, and with less trouble than anticipated, the Comtesse was all amiability. "I am sure you will settle happily in your new life, and you can rely on me to explain your departure to Theron," she concluded.

I am sure of that, Melissa agreed to herself. But since the Comtesse was aiding her to achieve her own heartfelt desire to escape the Marquis' protection, she could not cavil. Promising to bring the needed guineas immediately, the Comtesse made her farewells, obviously with few qualms as to Melissa's fate once she left the protection of her home, and delighted to have brushed through the interview so easily. For her part, Melissa wondered at the Comtesse's assurance that she and the Marquis were to make a match of it. With her hardly gained knowledge of that enigmatic gentleman, she was surprised that he would bestow his title on his cousin. She quite understood that sophisticated lady's eagerness to rid herself of a guest who distracted the Marquis' attention from her own obvious charms.

As she packed her valise, with only a few necessities, and one or two of the plainer frocks now in her wardrobe, Melissa refused to dwell on her own emotions concerning Theron de Lisle. He was far from the kind of man whom she would allow to touch her heart. He had little heart himself and made no apologies for using women to satisfy his desires without permitting them any closer intimacy of mind or emotions. It was a cause for rejoicing, in fact, that she was not the kind of woman who would interest him. And yet, she felt unaccountably bereft, chagrined that her innocence and youth made her so unacceptable. He only wanted to manipulate her, use her for some nefarious purpose. His kindness meant little, a facade to gull her into obeying his every wish, a position she would not allow herself to occupy. Far better that he continued his liaison with his alluring French cousin. Aimee de Frontons was sensuous, ambitious, experienced, and clever, all qualities Melissa lacked herself, and obviously ones which the Marquis found attractive. She would be far better to put him from her mind and concentrate on what awaited her in Bath. Somehow, this determination to banish the Marquis to his rightful sphere proved to be more difficult than she anticipated.

Chapter Six

Melissa had to agree with Samuel Pepy's that Bath was "the prettiest city in the Kingdom" with its classical John Nash facades and the spires of the twelfth century abbey rising majestically above the town. It was much larger than Melissa had expected, its noble avenues and crescents radiating for blocks from that impressive edifice.

On arriving at the George aboard the mail coach, disguised in her boy's garb, she was appalled at the task she had set herself, to find Bessie in this grand expanse. Finding lodgings was another problem, but she was fortunate there, securing an attic room off Guinea Lane, near the market.

Her landlady, a buxom, cheerful widow, took immediately to the likely lad who had spun her a tale of hardships which had brought tears to her eyes. Melissa warmed to the widow Blakely who had lost her husband in the American war for independence, and felt safe beneath her roof. She explained her peculiar circumstances, her boy's clothes, on her fear of travelling unescorted on the public stage. She confided to the widow that her parents had died, leaving her orphaned and with few resources. She was searching for her cousin, known to be in Bath, and who would shelter her when she learned of her piteous state. Her cousin could find her gainful, respectable employment, and this was greatly to be desired as she did not have unlimited funds. The widow Blakely offered her a temporary job helping her care for the apartments of her lodgers in return for a reduced rent on the room, but agreed that discovering Bessie's whereabouts in Bath might prove more difficult than Melissa expected.

A shrewd and kindly woman, Mistress Blakely did not completely accept Melissa's story, for it was obvious the girl was quality, and not the offspring of tradesmen, but she could not resist her beseeching violet eyes and vulnerability. She did not fear for Melissa's virtue in her house, for she kept a severe eye on her lodgers, most of whom were out all day at their various employment and none of them young men who might cast out lures to the girl. Mistress Blakely did not take in many single men, not approving of their habits, strong drink, tobacco, loose women, and gambling, all leading to ruination. Her lodgers were mostly prudent sober folk who worked at respectable establishments. There was a middle-aged milliner, a superintendent at the Roman Baths, a waitress at the Pump Room, and a foreman for the new buildings going up near Crescent Lane. Only the foreman was suspect, a burley, rollicking man inclined to pinch Melissa's chin and ogle her suggestively, but with little real malice in him.

Melissa felt she had indeed fallen on her feet, for she had no illusions as to what her fate might be in a less salubrious place. She enlisted Mistress Blakely's help in how she might go about locating Bessie and found her landlady's advice sensible. She doubted that Bessie would spend any time at the Baths or the Pump Room as these were amenities more suited to the gentlefolk who came to the spa on repairing leases or for their health. But Bessie had to eat and the Walcot Street stalls, offering meat, poultry, and fresh produce, seemed a likely place to find her. Melissa took to haunting the area in her free time, wondering with some trepidation if she would recognize Bessie on sight. After ten days in Bath her vigilance was rewarded. Hovering about the bins of carrots, potatoes, and other vegetables one Wednesday afternoon, she saw a thin, idy woman, dressed in a sober, brown merino dress and shawl approach the stall with a basket on her arm from which protruded a chicken. Her severe mousy hair, tucked tightly into a bun, her weathered cheeks, and button bright brown eyes were unmistakable. It had been five years since Melissa had last seen Bessie, but she had changed little in the interval.

Approaching her tentatively as she haggled with the stall keeper, Melissa said, "It is Bessie Blount, is it not?"

The woman looked up startled and then her tight lips parted in a welcoming smile. "Good gracious me. It's Miss Melissa. What are you doing here?" She sat down her basket and enveloped Melissa in a warm hug. "What a lovely young girl you have grown to be. Last time I saw you it was all legs and scrawny arms, and now you have become a real beauty!" Bessie's eyes misted a bit, recalling the child she had known in Devon in the past.

"Oh, Bessie, it is so wonderful that I have found you. I have been searching for days. All I had was your London direction and I thought perhaps you had disappeared, and Bath is much larger than I expected." Melissa herself was close to tears.

"What is Mr. Hawksley thinking of allowing you to wander about Bath without a chaperone, child? And why are you here at all? I thought he insisted you stay close to home in Devon." Bessie remembered very well her former master's obdurate attitude about Melissa and his unwillingness to allow her much liberty.

"I have run away from Hawksmoor, Bessie. Can we not go have some refreshment nearby and I will tell you what has happened?" Melissa pleaded, anxious to put her tale before the former housekeeper who had always tried to comfort her in the past when her guardian had treated her harshly.

"Certainly, Miss Melissa. There is a little cafe around the corner here where we can have some chocolate and cakes, good Bath buns which you always liked, as I remember," Bessie answered.

Over the chocolate and Bath buns Melissa told Bessie most

of her story. She did not mention the interlude with the Marquis, implying that she had come to Bath searching for Bessie straight from a short stay in London where she had learned from her companion's former neighbor about her changed address.

"So you see, Bessie," she concluded, "I must have some employment. I cannot return to Hawksmoor and the hateful marriage Mr. Hawksley has arranged for me. If he ever finds me, I greatly fear, he has the means to compel me to it, as he threatened. I will not marry Algy, nothing can force me to that pass." She shuddered in remembrance of the loose-lipped, groping nephew of her guardian. "If only father had not died. I cannot think what he was about, entrusting me to such a one as Horace Hawksley."

"I often wondered that myself, dearie, and I must admit it gave me great discomfort to leave you to his mercies, but I had no choice. I can tell you now, he turned me from the manor when I protested at his treatment of you, keeping you away from everyone, refusing to send you to school, and only employing that nasty Miss Mercer to teach you, a right mean madam she was, too," Bessie remembered, anger in her eyes. "But you did quite right to seek me out, although what I can offer you is not the life which should be yours by right."

Melissa pressed her hand gratefully, comforted by Bessie's championship, and feeling the cares of the past few troubling weeks fall from her shoulders. She looked at the woman who had come to her rescue, seeing beneath the rather grim features and the drab gown to the warm and kindly nature of the real Bessie, whose sternness was a mere facade.

Banishing the emotions which threatened to overset them both, Bessie spoke briskly, unwilling to let Melissa see how much her story had moved her to compassion.

"I am now working as a wardrobe mistress at the Theatre Royal, replacing my cousin who had to return to Devon to care for her ailing father. I was quite fortunate to find this position because I had been doing rather rough work in London—partime cleaning. Your uncle did not give me a reference, you now. But enough of that mangy man and his deeds. All has urned up trumps now. And I believe we can get you taken on t the Theatre as an assistant. As I remember you were always a lever little needlewoman," Bessie recalled, practical and eassuring.

"Oh, Bessie, that would be capital. No one would look to ind me there, amidst play actors, surely," Melissa's natural lithe spirits rose at the thought of such a refuge. Then she esitated for a moment, as if in doubt. "Still, I had better keep ny lodgings. If by some chance my guardian traced you to Bath, I might be able to escape his vigilance by living apart rom you. And the widow Blakely is most kind to me, and runs a most respectable establishment, quite near here in Guinea Lane."

"Yes, I have heard of her. Of course, it is not what you are accustomed to, but she is a reputable body and will allow no goings on in her establishment. I believe your guardian might try to discover your whereabouts, if he is determined to marry you off to his nephew. We must just hope he has lost all interest now that you have disappeared." Bessie tried to speak with conviction, but, in truth, she was worried about Melissa's future. For her part Melissa was not so concerned about Horace Hawksley's tracking her down, as that the Marquis might decide to ferret out her location, a prospect she viewed with mixed emotions.

So it was settled. Melissa took up her duties at the Theatre Royal within the week, finding the play actors a motley but not unkind group, and the manager, a brusque, harried type, uninterested in her once he was assured by Bessie that her assistance was vital to the costumes in her care. Fascinated by the behind stage activity of the company, Melissa watched breathlessly as they rehearsed, quarreled, pranced and pirouetted through the life of pretence which had its sordid, as well as appealing, aspects.

The leading lady, Angela Ankers, in particular caught

Melissa's attention. She was an aging star, petulant, and constantly fearful that her position as the reigning actress of the troupe might be endangered by the younger women in the company. Mistress Ankers clung valiantly to roles which were unsuitable for her ripe attractions, and flirted roguishly with her leading man, Cecil Stone, her junior by ten years and a man eager to tell all and sundry that his talents were wasted in this backwater, and that soon he would be trodding the boards at Drury Lane or the Mermaid where sophisticated London audiences would appreciate his abilities. The two bickered and postured, their acting as blatant offstage as it was on as they both had powerful egos and gave little quarter in their constant battle to steal the limelight from one another.

The bit players and character actors proved to be an unexceptional lot, cheerful and business-like, amused by their stars but willing to follow their lead in whatever drama the two enacted before the curtain or behind it. Of middling ability, the troupe, in general, amazed Melissa by the vast range of their repertoire, assuming the roles of so many characters in farce, melodrama, comedy, or tragedy. Melissa, forced by her isolated circumstance into omnivorous reading, was well versed in Shakespeare, but the plays of Sheridan, Congreve, Goldsmith, Farquahar, and Vanbrugh were new to her. Added to this impressive list of performances were the occasional harlequinade and pantomime to be mastered, striking Melissa with awe at the many lines to be learned, the complicated business to be mastered. The actors, whatever their faults and foibles, their mercurial tempers, and passionate moods, inspired her admiration. She often lingered in the wings after her day's duties were concluded watching the transformation of rather ordinary people into these magical figures who captured the audiences rapt attention with their skills.

The company accepted Melissa with little curiosity, content that she mended flounces, supplied missing props, polished scabbards, and generally made herself useful under Bessie's competent aegis. For these duties she was paid a few shillings a week, but it seemed to her, with never a sou to call her own efore, a vast sum. Two or three weeks went by in this omfortable fashion and gradually the days with the Marquis nd Aimee de Frontons faded into the distance, only occurring o her at odd times when she was alone in her attic chamber.

Then, just as she was settling into her behind-the-scenes outine, protected by Bessie from any approaches from entlemen in the company or from the military officers who aunted the Green Room and stage door, a dramatic change ame in her circumstances.

Mistress Ankers may have fancied herself, as the leading ctress, the cynosure of all eyes, but in truth both the company nd the audience preferred the ingenue—one Perdita Fane, a ovely blond creature, of charming manners, but neglible alent. As Rosalind, Juliet, or Dorinda in "The Beaux Stratagem," she looked so appealing that few cavilled at her nability to play other than herself. Besieged by offers from the officers who nightly greeted her appearances with fervour, Perdita had every reason to fancy herself the reigning belle of Bath. Vain, vapid, and greedy, the discipline of the theatre often wearied her. Learning lines became a chore to be scorned when she could be riding in some ensign's phaeton or strolling hrough the Assembly Rooms with a coterie of eager admirers hanging on her every word. Consistently late to rehearsals, bored with the business of acting, she at last decided to accept one of the many offers which came her way. Without a word to any of the company she decamped suddenly one afternoon with a rakehell lieutenant who promised to set her up in luxury with jewels and a carriage and pair. This left Samuel Thornton with more than a dilemma. He had to have an ingenue, prepared to play Ophelia to Cecil Stone's Hamlet the next evening or cancel the performance—at which prospect his frugal soul protested.

Unknown to Melissa, Thornton, who looked at every woman from sixteen to sixty assessing her suitability as an actress, had been watching her for some time. Although not an accredited beauty in the fashionable mode of lush curves, blue eyes, and golden curls, she had a certain quality compounded of breeding, vivacity, and vulnerability which drew the eye. And most important of all, her speaking voice had a clear bell-like resonance which would project across the footlights. The rest could be taught, Thornton concluded, if he could get her to consent to appear on the stage. He sensed she might not approve of such a career and would prefer to stay behind scenes in the humble capacity of assistant wardrobe mistress. There was a mystery about Melissa, which hinted at origins not usual to theatre folk. He approached her warily. Melissa on her part was equally ill at ease, for she could not imagine what the august director wanted with her and only hoped she would not be dismissed from her post.

The interview took place in his office. He came around his burdened desk and insisted she seat herself. He noticed her upright carriage, straight shoulders and the direct gaze from those amazing violet eyes. Yes, she should do, he noted with a restrained smile.

"Miss Mason, undoubtedly you have heard that our ingenue Perdita Fane, has decided that the theatre no longer appeals to her and she has decamped rather hurriedly, leaving us with quite a problem." He chose his words carefully, watching her reaction.

"Yes, sir, so I understand," Melissa said, wondering what this had to do with her.

"Mistress Blount tells me you have quite a command of Shakespeare, and would need little study to learn the part of Ophelia. I hope you will help us by playing the part in tomorrow's performance of "Hamlet." There are not too many lines to learn, and as you know, Ophelia appears only briefly in the tragedy. If you would consent to take on the part, the whole company will be exceedingly grateful," he urged.

"But sir—Mr. Thornton," Melissa protested, aghast at what he was asking. "I am not an actress. I know nothing about the theatre except what little I have learned in the few days I have been here assisting Mistress Blount."

"You have a lovely voice, and a certain presence. Ingenues often have not as much. Certainly Perdita was no artiste. I think, with a little coaching, you could do it, and the salary is better than that of a wardrobe mistress, I can guarantee that. Four pounds a week, far better than the few shillings you get now," he coaxed, seeing her hesitation. "And it is so important to the company. If you do not consent we must cancel the performance and refund the ticket money, not a good practice, as I am sure you will agree. We would all be much in your debt. And if you found it too disagreeable, you can return to the wardrobe duties after this evening. But I think you might enjoy it."

Stunned, Melissa sat back, hardly knowing what to answer. The courage and audacity of the actors facing the turbulent audiences had impressed her, for Bath's theatre patrons were not a subdued and appreciative lot, venting their criticism with hearty catcalls and equally violent approval. The thought of facing such a group was daunting, but she was moved by Mr. Thornton's appeal for her help. She had always believed him to be an austere aloof man; yet, now he seemed quite human, almost humble in his efforts to persuade her. In the end, she reluctantly consented to try the part, with the understanding that if she failed she could return to her previous anonymity behind stage. Her only stipulation was that her real name not be used on the program. She would appear as Melissa Langford, which had a professional ring to it. Melissa only hoped she could fulfill the promise of the name.

To the surprise of the company, Bessie, the audience, and even Melissa herself, in fact to all but the prescient Samuel Thornton, Melissa's debut as Ophelia in the following evening's rather pedestrian "Hamlet" was startling. Rarely had an actress so tellingly embodied the innocent, touching and stricken Ophelia, driven to madness by the rejection of her lover and the death of her father. Her clear, flutelike voice singing wistfully, "hey, nonny, nonny" in the final throes of madness brought tears to many an eye and her ethereal figure, floating gracefully around the stage in her diaphanous white draperies caught the throat, so tender were the emotions she inspired in the jaded audience. In short, she was a huge success, quite putting Cecil Stone's Hamlet in the shade, and causing that young man to eye her with a certain jealousy during the curtain calls.

Melissa, surprised to find herself the cynosure of all eyes, exhilarated by the applause, and most of all by the thrill of losing herself in the character and forgetting all else, was charmed by this novel experience. Thornton told her later she was a born actress, although, he added, she had a great deal to learn. She agreed and set immediately to conquer her ignorance. For the moment her unhappiness over her guardian, her interlude with de Lisle and the Comtesse, even her poverty and loneliness was forgotten. The future held the excitement of this new challenge and she met it resolutely.

The *Bath Gazette*, in reporting the performance, hailed the birth of "a delightful, believable Ophelia," and "a charming addition to the company now appearing at the Theatre Royal." Even Angela Ankers graciously deigned to praise Melissa's performance, not finding in the eager and respectful ingenue a rival to her own more worldly attractions. Only Bessie seemed a bit hesitant to add her bouquets to the many congratulations the new sensation evoked.

"It's not the way for a lady to behave, Missy, traipsing around the stage for all to gape at. Your Pa would not have wanted such a life for you. Actresses are regarded as little better than light skirts by the ton, you know." She frowned, fearing the pitfalls ahead for her charge.

"Bessie, dear, Papa is not here to advise and protect me so I must just make my way the best I can," she reproved. "And believe me, the Theatre Royal is a far happier venue for me than Horace Hawksley's house or marriage to his odious nephew. And I have you to stand guard over my virtue," she added gaily.

Bessie, not convinced, sniffed her disapproval, but did not relax her vigilance.

Chapter Seven

Following her triumph as Ophelia, Melissa had neither the leisure nor the inclination to enjoy her new popularity. Samuel Thornton proved to be a hard taskmaster, setting her immediately to learning Juliet's lines, for he felt she would score yet another success in that role. Although the words came easily to her, the action did not, and she found it difficult to react convincingly to Cecil Stone's Romeo. She had not fully realized, watching the company from behind scenes just how much hard work went into each production, not only lines to be learned, but also positions and business to be plotted and absorbed. The touring troupe might pretend to be careless, improvident and self-indulgent, but once on stage most of them took their craft seriously, and did their utmost to create the fantasy their audiences demanded. She could do no less than emulate them in this new career that had been thrust upon her willy-nilly.

Two of the bonuses of the discipline Thornton imposed were that she had little time to worry over private concerns, and even less time for the bucks and officers who haunted the Green Room. Bessie would allow no dallying with the young men who threw out lures to the new reigning belle of the Theatre Royal. Sniffing scornfully at Melissa's decision to abandon all the precepts of a well-born and respectable lady for the ramshackle life of the theatre, she let it be known that no matter how misguided Melissa might be, Bessie had constituted herself as her champion, and woe betide any man who challenged her right to protect her charge.

While Melissa studied her lines for "Romeo and Juliet," and Bessie warded off the most persistent of the actress' importuning suitors, neither could know that their most effective adversary was plotting his campaign as he drove at a furious pace from London. Theron de Lisle's cool mastery of his horses belied his inner rage, well camouflaged, but increasing with every mile he traveled. He was furious at Aimee, Melissa, and, most of all, at himself for trusting any woman; but once he caught up with the ungrateful chit, she would feel the full power of his anger. He did not wonder why his gorge was raised by Melissa's flight. Never before had any woman challenged him in such a manner and retired triumphant, and he did not intend for Melissa to be an exception. He would not admit to himself the dismay, disappointment, and fear for her safety he had felt when he returned to London to find his bird flown.

If Melissa had escaped his wrath, Aimee de Frontons was available to experience the biting scorn he heaped upon her when he discovered that not only was she unconcerned at her guest's departure, but also apparently had made no push to discern her direction. The blithe dismissal of Melissa, which Aimee had congratulated herself had been handled so adroitly, suddenly appeared not quite so clever. Theron raked her over the coals in a frightening fashion, with that cold sneering tone all the more effective because he did not raise his voice. A shouting, blustering man she could deal with, but this quiet, deadly sarcasm completely undid her.

"But Theron, *cher*, I had no idea you would be so alarmed. I thought you might even be relieved to have the matter settled without further annoyance to you. This girl had no claim upon you, and she certainly was not the type of light skirt to engage your interest, even if that were not already occupied." Aimee used her eyes with what she hoped was suggestive effect. Surely Theron would admit her own mature charms were much more appealing than the raw, unfledged attractions of this stray he had picked up. But when the dark scowl did not lighten on his face, she continued in a cajoling tone. "I know you inferred you had made some arrangements for her future, but I thought that was only a boring expedient to get her out of the way. I cannot see that her decision to take her fate into her own hands is an occasion for all this anger. After all, even if she owed you some gratitude, she had a perfect right to leave. I just did not urge her to remain when I saw how unhappy that would make her." Aimee was doing her best to soothe Theron, but was forced to realize from his manner, that he had no intention of letting the matter drop. Just as well the girl was gone. She had never seen him so interested before.

"I am happy to see you so sanguine about Melissa's fate, thrown out into a city with no money, resources, or friends, prey to every ruffian, blackguard and low type who crosses her path. 'Tis my own fault for bringing her to you in the first place. You are not exactly renowned for charity to your own sex are you, ma'belle?" he asked mockingly, the white line around his tightly held mouth indicating that his anger, barely controlled, might yet explode over her carefully coiffed head.

Not for the world would Aimee let him know of her chagrin and embarrassment at his scathing criticism. She could not afford an irreparable breach, so she must do her best to bring him about to a more equitable state of mind. He was perfectly capable of walking out of her drawing room and never seeing her again. Damn that girl. Who would have expected him to react thus, like a guardian uncle with one precious chick.

"Believe me, Theron, I did nothing to force her to leave. She knew she was welcome to stay as long as you or she wanted. I can only suspect that upon learning what you had in mind for her, she took fright and rushed away. You scared her, threatened her virtue, perhaps, so you see, *mon cher*, you are really the culprit," she taunted audaciously, determined to carry the battle into his camp before he could question her more closely and expose her lies.

Startled out of his brooding, considering the truth of Aimee's suggestion, Theron's eyes narrowed, and then he sneered, "Oh, no, Comtesse, you will not assuage your own guilt by placing the fault at my door. I am convinced you invited her to leave, hoping it would not matter to me, or that you could explain her absence away somehow. But I do not look kindly on interference in my affairs, especially by a woman of your stamp." He ignored the flush of mortification reddening the Comtesse's cheeks, and the clenched hands which signified she was within an ace of losing her own temper. Before she could demur and try to offer further excuses, he gave a curt bow and left her, prey to much disquiet about her future, and the knowledge that she had played her hand badly.

The Marquis de Lisle tooled his curricle into the courtyard of Bath's most elegant hostelry, York House, on the late afternoon of the day preceding Melissa's scheduled debut as Juliet. Arranging to have his horses stabled, and appraising the innkeeper that his carriage with valet and luggage would be following him, he commandeered the best private parlour and bedchamber and ordered a bath and a meal in short order. The landlord, recognizing a Corinthian of the first stare, hurried to do his bidding, leaving de Lisle to brood over the wine, his booted feet stretched in front of him as he contemplated his next move.

In the first heat of his anger he had rushed off to Bath, ascertaining Mistress Blount's direction from that same obliging Cheapside neighbor. No more than Melissa before him did he have any idea where to locate that elusive madam in the town, but he had resources unavailable to Melissa, and he was confident of tracking his prey. What was causing him to brood, was not the whereabouts of Mistress Blount, but his totally inconsistent attitude in rushing pell-mell after a young woman who had already caused him more trouble with less reward than any female he had ever encountered. True, he had need of her services in this master plan he had devised to apprehend the French spy ring, ostensibly operating from a London headquarters he determined to penetrate. But Melissa was not the only young woman available for the masquerade he had in mind; so why had he been so disappointed to find her fled and why had he reacted so violently to Aimee's accusations? He had had many more gorgeous and amenable lovelies in keeping than the elusive and independent Miss Mason. Obviously she feared for her virtue at his hands, and perhaps she had reason to, no matter his assurances to the contrary. Despite his best intention to treat her as an elder brother or guardian uncle he had been taken by her elegant figure, that appealing pointed face from which those unusual violet eyes stared so fetchingly. Under other circumstances he might have made a push to seduce her, but his loose moral code did not include the ravishment of virgins, innocent school girls.

He laughed sardonically as he threw down his third glass of wine. Remembering his last meeting with that independent young woman, she probably would have boxed his ears if he had taken any further liberties. His famous address and reputation carried no impact with her. She considered a life with the ubiquitous Bessie, no matter how humble, preferable to enduring his protection. A deserved setdown, but he refused to accept it. He would find Miss Mason and they would have a reckoning, on that he was quite decided.

"I cannot tell you, Miss Langford, how much I am looking forward to your performance tomorrow evening as Juliet. And I could not believe my good fortune when you agreed to have supper with me this evening, when so many better fellows were besieging you," Ensign Percival Ashburton stammered, his fair face flushed with excitement and eagerness as he carefully ushered Melissa from his phaeton before the York House.

"You are too kind, Ensign Ashburton. I am quite looking forward to supper." Melissa smiled at the young man, barely out of his teens who looked so concerned and guileless.

Bessie had acceded to his fervent and frequent requests to escort Melissa to an innocuous supper because she recognized in the young officer a suitable companion for her charge, who entertained nothing but the purest and most honourable of intentions. Indeed, he was the very pattern card of the type of young man whom Melissa should be meeting if her guardian had done his duty toward her. Bessie sent the young couple off to supper with never a qualm, and in this belief she was entirely correct.

Ens. Ashburton, lately of the 14th Foot, gazed upon Melissa with the utmost respect and admiration, unbelieving of his good luck in winning her presence at supper when so many of his fellow officers had failed. He was an unconceited young man, heir to a modest competence and the only child of doting parents who had consented reluctantly to his desire for a martial career. Not above middling height, with a shock of blond hair, imperfectly kept in order, honest clear-blue eyes, and a complexion from which the down of youth had barely receded. His temperament was as uncomplicated and disarming as his appearance. He had a deprecating manner and treated Melissa with all the politeness which she might have expected in the most circumspect society. Having been exposed to the lascivious and suggestive manners of so many stage door habitués who believed actresses fair game for any insult or proposition. Ens. Ashburton was a welcome relief. Melissa treated him with the open camaraderie of a brother, to which he responded like a grateful puppy. They found much to talk about over supper, sharing a love of the country and rural pastimes.

Unknown to the young couple, they were watched from a corner table in the large dining room by a group of senior officers who had dined well and were now dipping deep into the brandy. The ring leader appeared to be a major, rather a dashing type with hard, dark eyes and a swagger to his walk and whose full lips broke into a sneer at the sight of the two supping across the room.

"Would you believe that that haughty little madam, who is probably no better than she should be, turned down countless offers to have supper with the Ashburton cub?" he asked his companions, his voice slurred from anger and drink.

"Yours among them, eh Gratton?" a corpulent captain joshed as he reached for the bottle again.

"Oh, I am not so charmed by our latest thespian as many. She has a certain innocent appeal, but I imagine on closer acquaintance I would find her a common bore. These actresses, no matter how handsome, often are, you know," he answered carelessly, implying a wealth of experience.

"Oh, I say, old man, aren't you being a bit harsh? Not all actresses are women of easy virtue. Some of them are quite respectable. Mrs. Siddons for example," argued the portly officer, more from a desire to taunt the major than any real conviction.

"The Divine Sarah is the exception to every rule, but these little soubrettes and ingenues of touring companies are on the boards for only one reason, to display their wares, hoping to attract a wealthy protector, and I doubt Miss Langford is any different for all her winsome, innocent appearing ways," sneered the major, now staring at Melissa and her companion with some disgust.

"Well, she certainly is saving her charms until that protector appears, for it's impossible to get beyond that gorgon she has guarding her. I should say she is still unplucked," another officer stated coarsely. The quartet, now dipping deeply into the brandy, were becoming quite bawdy in their comments and suppositions about Melissa.

Ens. Ashburton, hearing a raucous burst of laughter from the group, turned to look at the revelers, and recognized his superior officers with some chagrin. He suspected he and Melissa were the object of comment and he did not want her exposed to such ribaldry. Chivalrously he suggested they leave, as the hour was latening and the company such that she might find embarrassing. Grateful for his solicitude, she consented and the pair made their way from the dining room to the ensign's phaeton, thereby missing by minutes an encounter with the Marquis de Lisle.

Chapter Eight

Standing in the wings of the Theatre Royal, Melissa tried to subdue the terror she felt, the first night nerves members of the company had warned her to expect. With Ophelia she had rushed into the performance hardly aware of what it meant to face, as a novice, an audience of critical boisterous theatre goers. But in "Hamlet," the burden of the play had not rested upon her. Tonight she felt every eye would follow her amateur efforts, her lack of confidence, her insecurity, her embarrassment at being the center of attention. When Samuel Thornton had first proposed the role to her she had assented blithely, her success in "Hamlet" having tempted her, but this play was a far different thing and the new notoriety given to her by the theatre appalled her more than it thrilled her. Behind her fear of the footlights was a deeper fear that somehow Horace Hawksley might discover her whereabouts from this appearance on stage and drag her back to the isolation of dour Hawksmoor where he would force her to marry his nephew. But she must not think of that now. Scene II of the first act was drawing to a close. Then she heard Lady Capulet's words, "Nurse, where's my daughter? Call her forth to me."

Taking a deep breath, Melissa walked onto the stage, dressed in her white draperies, her golden hair shining under the lights, looking as vulnerable and innocent as a fourteen-year-old should—in truth, a rare Juliet.

The audience warmed to her heart-breaking portrayal of young love, and from the moment of her entrance it was obvious that Samuel Thornton had scored a major success with his unknown ingenue now reborn as a full-fledged star. Her clear resonant voice, her fragile appearance, the elegance of her slight figure, the proud set of her head all heightened the image. Rarely did an actress so perfectly represent the delicate and emotional Juliet. Not just her looks but her ability to portray tragedy won every heart in the audience. Cecil Stone's Romeo suffered greatly by comparison—too hard, too experienced, too crude to do justice to the part opposite such a Juliet. The evening was indubitably Melissa's and once into the part she lost all nervousness, all fear and became in truth the doomed young Capulet. For once not a sound could be heard in the normally noisy house as the final act drew to its tragic close and Juliet cried, "Oh happy dagger! This is thy sheath; there rest and let me die."

The audience rose as one to applaud the new star, who seemed dazed by her triumph. Melissa would play Juliet to equal praise again, but those fortunate enough to see her in her debut would never forget that initial performance. Back in her dressing room after the many curtain calls, she removed her makeup, exhausted and a bit depressed now that the ordeal and the success was behind her. For the past twenty-four hours her every thought and all her heart had been involved with learning her lines, hoping to portray Juliet with conviction and appeal. Now she had triumphed; yet, she felt depressed, still wrapped in Juliet's tragic end, disappointed that the curtain had fallen, and the challenge had been met. She hardly heard the congratulations of the company, who rushed around her, eager to add their own plaudits to the new star's crown.

Samuel Thornton, making his way through the crowd who clustered about her, dispersed her fellow actors with a gruff. "Away with you now, and let the poor girl alone. She has done us proud and we have seen a star born, but she must be tired and longing for her supper. Shoo, now, let her be," he ruthlessly ordered the actors out of the dressing room, and then turned to Melissa.

"Thank you, my dear. You were incredible. I have seen a score of Juliets in my time, but not one, even the glorious Sarah Siddons, to rival you. I knew you could do it. I applaud myself, too, for seeing in you the makings of a great actress," he preened, willing to allow Melissa her due, but taking onto himself most of the credit for recognizing her talent.

Melissa laughed, coming down to earth, and seeing in Samuel Thornton, a human and fallible man, who had yet taken a chance with her through necessity rather than choice, for which she did not fault him. Rather did she thank him for introducing her to this fascinating life of play-acting.

"I had planned a little supper in your honor at York House, my dear. So hurry and dress and we will repair to that fine hostelry and toast your success," he beamed, eager to capitalize on the evening and show off his star.

"All right, Mr. Thornton. But it is not necessary, you know. I would be just as happy to go home to bed. I am quite tired." Melissa rather dreaded facing her public beyond the footlights, but realized the debt she owed to Thornton. If he believed her appearance at supper important to the success of his company, then she would do as he wished.

"Nonsense, you deserve a treat. Hurry up, now." He surprised her by bending over and giving her a chaste kiss on the forehead, before leaving the dressing room. Melissa smiled. She had not guessed the gruff and reserved Mr. Thornton, so often harried and cross over company concerns, could behave in such a fashion.

Her next visitor was Bessie. Still disapproving, she reluctantly admitted that Melissa had acquitted herself well, and reminded her that even if she had descended to the iniquity of acting, she must behave like a lady and not subject herself to the kind of treatment actresses usually received from the bucks and officers who besieged the Green Room. That very moment there were a score of the young fools clustered about the stage door waiting to importune her when she appeared. Bessie snorted as she helped Melissa into her simple muslin gown, and tidied her curls, now grown to a respectable length and framing her gamine face in becoming disarray.

"Not to worry, dear Bessie. I am so tired from the recent ordeal I can barely face anyone. I will never treat actors with condescension again. Learning all those lines, that action, and then portraying a character with sincerity and force, is a monumental task. I have a great deal to learn, and it will take all my leisure to master this craft I have chosen," Melissa said firmly, her chin set.

"I hope not all your leisure, my dear. I have other plans for you," a familiar suave voice came from the doorway.

Melissa, who had turned her back, swiveled around, scarcely believing what she had heard. Standing in the entrance to her dressing room was Theron de Lisle, dressed in impeccable evening clothes, eyeing her through his quizzing glass, disdain and boredom warring with that sensual magnetism which was uniquely his own.

Melissa, taken completely by surprise, did not know what to say, and could only gasp, "What are you doing here?"

"Looking for you, my elusive child, and finding you it seems in this most unlikely venue. I must say, for all your naivete and lack of experience, or perhaps because you embody those qualities, you make a very delightful and believable Juliet. I congratulate you, Melissa." He bowed mockingly, and came into the room. "However, I think you owe me an explanation for your precipitate flight from London, don't you?" He continued to look at her with that raking glance which reduced her hard-won poise. She would have preferred to face a hundred hostile audiences than the Marquis de Lisle. How maddening that he had found her, spoiled her debut, her evening of triumph.

"I am waiting, my child," he drawled, but his eyes menaced her, promising retribution. He turned to Bessie. "You must be the famous Mistress Blount. I have a few things to say to your charge. You can safely leave her in my company, I assure you."

But Bessie was having none of that. "I don't know who you think you are, forcing your way in here, and threatening Miss Melissa, but you can just take yourself out again," she bridled, conscious of her young companion's dismay at finding this fancy lord accosting her in her own dressing room. "She needs no fine London nob trying to scrape up an acquaintanceship. You may have known her before she came to Bath, but I doubt you were ever introduced by her guardian or met Miss Melissa in any approved fashion. You can't cozen me with your fancy manners, nor Miss Melissa either, I warrant."

Bessie glared at the Marquis, who did not appear to be very impressed, raising a slightly questioning eyebrow at Melissa and saying softly, "I am happy to see you are so closely guarded from harm, my dear, and by such a dragon, too."

Not waiting for Melissa's reply, for in truth she was too bemused to answer, cast all in a pother over his sudden appearance as if conjured up by a spell, he turned his attention to Bessie.

"Mistress Blount, let me assure you, I have no fell designs on your nursling here. I met Miss . . . er, Mason, was the name she gave me, although I vow it is not her true one, under very peculiar circumstances, and was able to do her a trifling favour. Before we could discuss her future, she fled London as if the devils were after her. Not very flattering or grateful of her, I am sure you will agree." He ignored Melissa and turned his full attention to Bessie, charming away her bad humour with his rare smile, and treating her as if she were a duchess, rather than a mere wardrobe mistress. She was no proof against that magnetism, that worldly charm which had seduced far more sophisticated women than poor Bessie Blount. She blustered for a moment, then her defenses fell.

"Well, I don't understand all this, sir, but it's obvious that you know Miss Melissa, and whatever your business with her, I am sure it is respectable. She is not the kind, sweet, clever gir that she is, to attract a top of the trees buck like you. For all he triumph tonight as an actress, she is naught but a schoolgir still, you know." Bessie stared at de Lisle as if daring him t contradict her claims. De Lisle made no answer but raised a wry eyebrow as if to imply that Bessie's championship was a bi ridiculous in the circumstances. He waited patiently, and a neither Bessie nor Melissa made any push to answer him o even to continue dressing, he opened the door, and gestured t Bessie.

"I have a few words to say in private to Miss Melissa. I will not be long, and then you may return to continue your ministrations." He held the door and waited for Bessie to leave Reluctant to abandon her charge to this mysterious lord, and consumed with curiosity as to his business with Melissa, Bessie stood her ground.

"It's all right, Bessie. I will be quite safe. You go along. I think Mr. Thornton wants you to attend the supper at the York House. I can manage. I will see you later." Melissa smiled at her friend, unwilling to cope with the Marquis, but equally averse to having Bessie a witness to their discussion. Bessie, impressed despite herself with the arrogant lord, decided on a dignified retreat.

"All right, I will leave, but I will be within call. You'll be needing assistance with your gown. Just give a holler when you are finished with this fine gentleman," she huffed.

"Thank you, dear Bessie," Melissa smiled although she shared the wardrobe mistress' anxiety as to the Marquis' intent.

"Thank you, Mistress Blount," de Lisle bowed her out the door, and then turned to face Melissa, raking her up and down with a critical gaze.

"You never cease to surprise me, Melissa, and I thought I was up to every rig and start of females. This play acting talent of yours is quite fortuitous. It fits in very well with what I have in mind for you," he said, seating himself in the one rickety chair available and regarding Melissa with an indulgent smile, which she did not for one minute trust.

"I have no idea what you mean, my lord. And I cannot see the necessity for your visit here. You no longer have any responsibility for me. As you can see I have managed quite well without your sponsorship. Actresses may not be considered the thing by the society in which you move, but I am determined to continue with this fascinating career, and stay respectable, too," she spoke determinedly.

He was not going to cow her with his worldly manner, and cynical beliefs. True she owed him a great deal for escorting her to London and finding her a temporary refuge, but her days with Aimee de Frontons had not been especially happy ones. Now she was master of her own fate, and if she was wise, she would put a great deal of distance between herself and this rakish lord who threatened her new life in some strange way. Whatever he wanted from her, she sensed she would be wise to refuse it.

"I am sure you are the soul of probity, my child. How long you will remain virginal and chaste in your chosen career, is a matter of some dispute. I care little for that," he replied sardonically if not with entire sincerity. "I do not allow my protégés to escape my milieu until I am bored with them, and you are no exception. You had no business to leave the Comtesse's chaperonage, unless there is some aspect of that decision of which I have been kept in ignorance. Aimee tells me you decided on the spur of the moment to leave, and she did not feel compelled to stop you, for which she will pay a heavy price," he added ominously.

"The Comtesse was very willing to let me go, and it is no affair of hers, or of yours either, if I choose to begin a new life in Bath," Melissa said mutinously. She did not care for his tone, nor his calm assurance that she would do his bidding and he certainly did not sound as enamoured of the Comtesse as her fiancé should. "Now that you have seen I am capable of managing by myself, you can take yourself back to London, to the Comtesse, and whatever other, no doubt, libertine activity you enjoy there," she added scornfully, eager to let him know that she was well aware of his disreputable past, and that she wanted no part of it.

"It's not quite that simple, my erstwhile Juliet. I think you owe me a little more than a casual farewell, and at any rate I refuse to take my congé. In the absence of the disagreeable guardian, I feel I have a duty to protect you, and in return, I crave a small service from you, which will fit very well into your new disguise. I am sure you would not want Thornton to dismiss you, or to find yourself barred from gainful employment in the theatre anywhere, and I promise that is what will happen if you do not obey me in this," he spoke harshly, impatient with her valiant efforts to remain independent. Obviously he was not about to waste his much vaunted charm on a mere thespian, Melissa decided. He talked to her as if he were, indeed, her guardian, and was quite as capable as Horace Hawksley of settling her future.

Then changing his tactics most unfairly, he rose, and drew her up into his arms, holding her eyes with a compelling stare. "Come, come, Melissa, there is no reason to be at daggers drawn with me. You will enjoy what I have in mind, and I promise your virtue is not endangered. I have no time for innocents, as I once told you, but since I have helped you, you now have the opportunity to repay the favour. But enough of this. Obviously you are too distracted by your triumph to hear me out now. I will escort you to this cast party tonight and tomorrow we will discuss my plan in some detail. I promise that you will find it intriguing, just the thing for one of your spirited and independent ways. Trust me, my dear. I have your best interests at heart," he smiled at her, all seriousness now, and Melissa could not withstand him. She forced herself to shrug off his embrace before she succumbed to further advances. What was it about this man that overset her senses? Domineering, ruthless, selfish, with no concern for any will but his own, he still had a power over her she found at once exciting and frightening. She would be well to be on her guard.

Chapter Nine

Melissa's surprising triumph as Juliet brought her little satisfaction, she discovered the next day. On awaking her first thought had been for the meeting with the Marquis. The evening before, when he escorted her to the celebratory dinner at York House had not provided any opportunity for intimate discussion. De Lisle had not seemed discomfitted by the postponement of the promised interview, but she had no reason to believe he would forget the inevitable confrontation.

Samuel Thornton had hosted a gay supper for the company who had been too flushed with the success of the performance, to question Melissa about her cavalier. De Lisle had watched the gathering with that air of mocking amusement which so infuriated her. His proprietal manner toward her had not gone unnoticed, but in the midst of the revelry Melissa had not been forced to parry questions from her fellow actors. Even Thornton had been unusually jovial and relaxed, but he cast a wary eye on the Marquis whose appearance rather worried him. He had some experience with practiced rakes seducing his actresses, distracting them from their careers, and casting out lures which they found difficult to refuse. This bang up Corinthian with his blasé, world weary assurance and obvious wealth could only mean trouble, he was convinced, but that evening was not the time to challenge Melissa about her

London beau. Enough time for that when she showed signs of restive dissatisfaction with her new role.

The York House thronged with customers, many of them eyeing the rollicking company as they toasted the success of the evening. Among them was a group of officers including Percival Ashburton who tendered his shy congratulations to the new star, and was forced to introduce his companions, who all vied for her attention. Ens. Ashburton, noticing the suave Marquis in attendance on Melissa, wondered where she had met such a London swell, but was too gauche and diffident to put himself forward or contest the Marquis' apparent claims. Not so his commanding officer, Maj. Henry Gratton, who insisted that his junior present him.

Bowing low over her hand and ogling her suggestively, he praised her performance effusively. "My dear Miss Langford, you have brightened the dull environs of Bath beyond all belief. Can we hope that this evening's performance will be just one of many triumphs? We fear your talents have not the proper showcase in our stuffy watering place. Perhaps you will soon be off to London, where your charms will titillate the jaded metropolis," he said, his hot glance roaming over her in a manner she found embarrassing and unwelcome.

"Not at all, Major. I find Bath quite to my taste," she answered cooly, not wanting to continue the conversation. Where Ens. Ashburton treated her much like he would any female met in his mother's drawing room, there was no mistaking the Major's hungry, lascivious stare. She tried to turn away but he continued to hold her hand and then confused her further by inviting her to ride with him the following day.

"Miss Langford's leisure is spoken for, I am afraid Major, and you must restrain your ardour for her company," the Marquis intervened smoothly, making the major feel uncomfortable. Somehow he found himself shunted to one side, unable to complete what he had assumed would be an easy conquest of the new actress.

"Stuck up pop-in-jay," Gratton muttered as he retired to his table, followed by Ashburton and his fellow officers. His bold oily good looks and uniform usually brought him all the female attention he desired, and he did not appreciate being set down by a London nob. "Like to get him in a good fight with the Frenchies, and then see how his high-and-mightiness behaves," he complained to his companions. "And that filly had better watch her step with his lordship. He looks a nasty customer to me."

Ashburton, in an effort to soothe his irate commanding officer, who could be an ugly opponent when aroused, proffered an excuse. "Perhaps he is a relation. Miss Langford is not in the usual way of actresses, I believe. She is obviously a lady."

"Don't you believe it my boy. That is all just a veneer acquired for her roles. She looks a hot little number to me, and has her sights set on a wealthy well-born protector, but he will soon be bored. His kind never keeps a light skirt for long," the Major sneered.

"Oh, I am quite sure you are mistaken, sir. Miss Langford is not of the muslin company," Ashburton demurred, fearful of angering the major but stalwart in his defense of his goddess.

"Well, we shall see. It's early days yet, and the girl may be sorry to have turned away her more humble admirers. She must capitalize on her charms while she has the chance," argued the Major, and called for another bottle in a querulous voice.

The Marquis, impervious to all the excitement and furor aroused by Melissa's success, suggested that he escort her home as the evening had proved a tiring one and would accept no refusal. Before she knew quite how it happened Melissa found herself bundled into de Lisle's curricle and driven away from the merry crew intent on making a night of it.

Annoyed at de Lisle's bland assumption of ownership, Melissa hastened to take issue with him once they were alone.

"I am perfectly capable of deciding when to retire, my lord.

As you can see I no longer need your sponsorship, and I quite dislike the implication of your commandeering me in such a way. I am sure Mr. Thornton and the company have put the wrong construction on our relationship," she spoke severely, furious at the position in which he had placed her.

"And would they be far wrong, my dear? I fear you need a protector or you will find yourself in a far more invidious position than any I could offer. Actresses are fair game for the meretricious bucks and military types that haunt these watering places," he said, tooling his rig swiftly through the streets.

"I can protect myself, and I do not enjoy being considered a light skirt, my lord," Melissa argued, her chin firm and the light of battle in her eye. Although loathe to admit it, the thought of occupying the position of de Lisle's mistress brought an anticipatory thrill which she forced herself to deny. She would not succumb to this libertine lord's lures. That way lay madness, and she was not so innocent that she did not suspect he had deliberately encouraged the false assumption of their relationship. She was shocked at herself, that she should even consider complying with any suggestion that she fulfill such a role in his life for even a brief time. Peeping at him from under her eyelashes, she had to admit his appeal was a formidable one. When he was not smouldering with anger, or sarcastically taking her to task he could be incredibly attractive, as no doubt many a credulous female beside herself had discovered.

"I might remind you, Melissa, that you have by your own actions placed yourself in this invidious limelight. You have exposed yourself to every insult you might be offered, while if you had remained tamely in London you might have enjoyed all the pleasures of a properly reared maiden," he answered mockingly. "Ah, here we are, at your rather seedy lodgings. Surely you could have found a more salubrious abode, my dear," he complained as he drew his horses to a halt before Mistress Blakely's boarding house.

"I like it here," Melissa sniffed. "It's no business of yours where I choose to live. I have been offered nothing but kindness by my landlady and her guests." She ignored his proffered assistance and scrambled down from the curricle in an undignified way, her anger almost oversetting her. Arrogant devil, trying to intimidate her.

"I cannot keep my horses standing, but let me assure you Melissa, we have a great deal of unfinished business to settle. I will be around to drive you out tomorrow morning, so do not accept other invitations, or scurry around to the theatre, hoping to avoid me. Thornton tells me you have no performance tomorrow, so expect me early. You have a few explanations to make and I intend to have them," he promised severely, not one whit discomposed by her anger.

"Good night, my lord." Melissa refused to meet his eyes, or signify that she accepted his strictures and flounced into the house with the echo of his laughter in her ears.

And now it was the morning of the interview and she could not lie abed, cowering under the linen, hoping to defer the promised interview. On the one hand she dreaded confronting de Lisle, on the other, her curiosity was aroused. What could he want with her? Did he really intend to make her his mistress willy-nilly, or did he have some other ploy in mind? His bland manner gave nothing away and she had no recourse but to rise and ready herself for the meeting. Sighing deeply Melissa prepared to make her toilet, wondering, not for the first time, if she could really trust the enigmatic Marquis. Surely he could not have a deep romantic interest in her. She was not his style at all, and she suspected that what really annoyed him was that she had evaded him once, and he was stubborn enough to follow her just to prove that she could not thwart him.

Mistress Blakely, bringing her breakfast, was all agog at her roomer's new fame, and plied her with questions about the performance. Melissa, reluctant to hurt her feelings, tried to parry her inquisition, but the garrulous kindly soul was not easily put off. Finally the landlady departed, complimenting herself on her astuteness in garnering such a famous guest, and quite sure she had seen Melissa's possibilities from the first meeting. Melissa, taking herself to task for her meekness in awaiting his lordship's pleasure, fumed in impatience as the morning lengthened, and by the time de Lisle arrived for the promised interview had worked herself into a state of righteous indignation.

It was close to noon when that gentleman finally made his appearance, impressing Mistress Blakely with his consequence, and infuriating Melissa by his casual acceptance that she would await his pleasure. He did nothing to soothe her ire by gazing at her critically through his quizzing glance when she descended the stairs to greet him coldly.

"I quite realize that in your flight from London, you could not take your new wardrobe with you, but surely you could have chosen a more stylish gown," he drawled, raising his eyebrows at her plain blue cambric dress and matching cashmere shawl.

"No doubt your lordship is accustomed to ladies of the first stare, but fashion was not my first concern in fleeing from the Comtesse's rather indifferent hospitality," Melissa replied nettled that he found her appearance lacking.

"No matter. Your new clothes have been bundled up and await your arrival. And my child if you continue to call me "your lordship" in that off-putting tone, I will not be responsible for my actions. My name is Theron and you have my permission to use it," he granted amiably.

Vowing to do no such thing, Melissa answered wickedly "Oh, no my lord, I could not presume."

"What you need, my girl, is a good spanking, but come along. I thought we would ride out to a nearby inn for a luncheon and discuss your future," the Marquis replied, not at all upset by her attempts to put him in his place.

Tossing her head haughtily, and ignoring his smile of amusement Melissa allowed herself to be handed into the Marquis' curricle.

Despite her intention to keep her distance, she found herself thawing as they rode out of Bath, the fine April day matching her surprising mood of bubbling spirits, which she admitted to herself had a great deal to do with her companion. He made no effort to engage her in disputatious conversation but chatted lightly of her performance, the elegant buildings of Bath, and the efficacious tonic of the waters.

"I had thought of taking you to the Pump Room to sample the waters in hopes they would ameliorate your temper but decided we could be more private in the country," he teased. "Have you tasted the famous palliative yet?"

"No, I have been much too busy pursuing my livelihood," she retorted smartly. It was just as well to let him know she was committed to her life in the theatre, and did not need his assistance in making her way.

Theron ignored her pitiful attempt at rebellion but continued smoothly to chat of negligible matters until they arrived at the White Hart, nestled by a small pond, resting place of a collection of ducks, and bordered by a meadow of budding daffodils, truly an idyllic spot for a rendezvous. Melissa could not restrain her pleasure at the sight. Ushering her into the inn's private parlour where he bespoke a light meal, Theron continued to charm her in the manner which had always stood him in good stead with females, and she had to admit he was a master at beguiling away any suspicion.

"Now, my infant, to business," he said, his mood sobering, as the servant cleared away the remnants of their meal. "I have not chased you from London merely to chastise you for your ingratitude. I concede you may have had some reason to take the Comtesse in dislike and also that I may have been a bit high-handed in my treatment of you. You are such an independent little madam, I fear I should have used more cajolery. My methods lacked finesse, perhaps," he admitted, smiling in that devastating way which overset Melissa's determination to remain aloof and disinterested.

"I admit, when I discovered you in my coach, I had every

intention of handing you back to your guardian at the first opportunity. I am no gallant knight, eager to rescue distressed maidens. I seek my pleasures elsewhere," he continued.

"Quite the opposite, I vow," Melissa interrupted pertly. "You are more apt to ruin them, I suspect."

"You wound me, child. You must not believe quite all the tales of my wicked reputation. But enough of this foolery. What I have to ask of you is a real boon, and perhaps I should not involve you in what may turn out to be a dangerous undertaking, but your recent success in the theatre is too good an opportunity. I hope to take advantage of your triumph. In fact, that was why I was so tardy in arriving for our meeting. I spent the morning in a productive encounter with Samuel Thornton, who has proved quite cooperative. He is willing, for a consideration, to release you, for I understand you have no contract, to accompany me to London where I will secure for you a much more attractive showcase for your talents at the Majestic Theatre."

"But I am perfectly happy with my job at the Theatre Royal. I am not sure I am ready to face London audiences after just a few appearances on the boards here," Melissa protested.

"You are too modest, my dear. You will charm London as you have Bath, I am convinced. But that is not the reason for my desire to remove you to London. I must confide my real motive which I assume you will keep secret. I have been engaged on some investigation for the government into the recent spate of French infiltration into our most private correspondence and negotiations. We have reason to believe that the traitors are using the Majestic as the headquarters of a notorious spy ring. You are in the perfect position to discover and unmask these conspirators who would look askance at an ingenuous young actress from the provinces. And I will be on hand to protect you from any harm," he spoke with assurance, but hesitated then, loathe to tell her how he would be in a position to do this, for it placed her in a light she would find repugnant.

Melissa's huge violet eyes sparkled with excitement. And she had to admit some relief. So this was what he wanted of her, her assistance in a matter of national security, the safety of the nation besieged in war. She warmed toward him. He was not the heedless pleasure seeking rake he pretended, but indeed was inspired to serve his country in the most difficult and unrewarding way.

Theron eyed her narrowly. He had expected that the adventurous aspects of the mission would prove vastly appealing to her romantic soul but he knew not how she would take his next suggestion.

"In order that I may be constantly on hand, both to learn what you might discover and to be accepted by the company and the hangers-on in the Theatre, I must appear to be your protector. In short, my dear, you must agree to behave as my mistress, not an enviable role for one as aggressively virtuous as you appear to be. You will be acting both on stage and off," he concluded, bracing himself for her recriminations.

Melissa gazed at him appalled. He could not be serious. It was one thing to act as a spy for her country. All her patriotism rose to the challenge, but to chance her virtue in defense of her country was another. "Is that really necessary, my lord? Surely we need not go quite so far in our masquerade."

"Believe me, my child, this is no game we are playing. These people are determined and dangerous. They would have no compunction in making an end to you if they thought you were aught but the ingenue you must pretend to be. I cannot expose you to the possible danger without my constant protection. As it is, I feel reluctant to ask you to take the risk," he spoke gravely, for once dropping his social sneering manner which so irritated her. She saw that he was in earnest.

"I am not so craven I fear the machinations of some paltry traitors. But I trust, my lord, that you mean to give only the appearance of having me in keeping. I do not intend to allow you any license in that respect, you must know," she answered severely.

"Ah, you disappoint me, Melissa, but you have my word I will not presume, however tempted I am to sample your favours," he replied lightly, hoping to brush through the matter quickly before she could realize the difficulties ahead. Indeed, the more he saw of the fascinating Miss Langford, the more tempted he was to try his chances with her, but then she might cry off, and he really needed her cooperation if he were to achieve his mission of unmasking the French spy ring. He must convince her of his bona fides, his intention not to harm her or let anyone else place her in jeopardy.

"So we are to be partners in this desperate undertaking, Melissa. Agreed?" he asked winningly.

"I cannot refuse this appeal to my patriotism, Theron, and yes, I will do it, if you think I can. I will hold you to your promise not to allow the pretence to become a reality. Even so, my reputation will be ruined I fear," she agreed, not too overset by the thought of losing her good name in aid of the adventure which faced her.

Theron sighed with relief. He had brushed through that quite well, but he knew, as she could not, just how much her cooperation would indeed put her beyond the respectable society which was her right. Somehow he must see to it that she did not suffer for her acceptance, and he vowed that he would accomplish that as well as his mission.

"You are a brave girl, and I applaud your courage. You will not regret helping us, I promise. I and the boffins in the Foreign Office will be in your debt. But, come, back to Bath, we have much to do in readying you for your task." He stood up, prepared to usher her from the inn, denying the uneasy feeling that he had committed her to an action they might both have cause to deplore before the business was finished.

Chapter Ten

Between them, Melissa and Theron decided that she must remain in Bath for a brief time while he returned to London to set in motion their plans. Since she would be deserting the Theatre Royal shortly, Thornton agreed to continue with "Romeo and Juliet" for several more performances and Melissa was not put to the trouble of learning another part. Her new fame, as the reigning star of the Bath stage, caused her some little disquiet, as she was accosted whenever she appeared in public, and even a short stroll to the Circulating Library brought ogling from the passers-by and attempts to scrape an acquaintance. Bessie was so disturbed by the motley trying to encroach on her charge that she insisted on accompanying her wherever she went in public, reminding her of the unsuitability of respectable females wandering unescorted in public.

Melissa had not quite decided what to do about Bessie. She wanted her to travel with her to London, but she knew Bessie would be appalled by the Marquis' role in her new life, and there was no question of confiding the real reason for his protection. Finally she decided that she must ask Bessie to come with her, and hope that she would accept Melissa's shocking pose as the Marquis' light-o-love. Melissa steeled herself to endure Bessie's strictures, but on no account could she confide in her as to the real situation. Having Bessie at hand would protect her, too, in case Theron decided to alter the terms of their arrangement.

Bessie, unfortunately, was not at hand on the day that Melissa had her distressing encounter with Major Gratton.

She had decided late in the afternoon that she must run to a nearby drapers to replenish her chemises and other unmentionables. Throwing a shawl over her dress she rushed from her lodgings to the shop a few blocks distant. Her purchases completed she emerged from the shop to be confronted by Major Gratton, who had been hovering about her lodgings hoping for just such an opportunity. He hastened to confront her.

"Ah, my dear Miss Langford," he greeted her with appreciation and a wide smile, "what a fortuitous meeting. May I drive you back to your rooms? You seem a bit burdened with parcels."

Melissa, who had not warmed to the officer upon their prior meeting, hesitated. But as if he had conjured up the weather to assist him, the first drops of rain began to fall. She decided his presence was preferable to a wetting and allowed him to help her into his barouche, which offered some shelter from the rain.

Smirking to himself at her acquiesence, Gratton mounted and took the reins. Turning to Melissa and smiling ingratiatingly he said, "I have been awaiting another meeting with you with much eagerness. I feel perhaps that our introduction at York House the other evening did not allow us time to really become acquainted." There was more than a tinge of familiarity in his manner to which Melissa took exception. He was sitting much too close to her and she edged warily away.

"This is most kind of you, Major Gratton, to rescue me from a soaking. If you will turn left here my rooms are just a few streets away," she answered, ignoring his reference to further friendship. Her limited experience warned her that he was a sensual man with an earthy taste in women, one to beware of.

Strangely she condemned him out of hand for his obvious intentions, although Theron had admitted to the very same inclinations and she had not found them disagreeable. But she trusted the Marquis in a way she could never extend to this encroaching coarse-fibered man. Why that should be so, she refused to admit to herself. Later she would excuse the comparison by rationalizing that the Marquis was, despite his many faults, a man of breeding and refinement, qualities the major lacked.

"I hope I may prevail upon you to give me just a few more moments of your time," Gratton said, paying no heed to her directions and whipping up his horses, ignoring the turning she indicated. "On further acquaintance I feel we might come to an understanding which would give us both pleasure," he said, running a leering glance over her form which caused Melissa to blush hotly.

"I must insist you drive me to my lodgings immediately, Major. I have a performance this evening, and much to do beforehand," Melissa answered bravely, chiding herself for allowing such a coil to develop. She should have risked a short wetting and refused his offer of a ride.

"Just a few minutes of your time, my girl, I know you actresses are always on the lookout for the best offer, and I suppose you think you have secured it from that London nob who was escorting you the other night, but I notice he has hared back to London. Your provincial charms paled quickly, I see," he sneered. "Do not be so hasty to turn down my suggestion. I am quite warm in the pockets and can do you well, if I am pleased, as I am sure you can see that I will be."

Melissa, by this time in no doubt of his insinuations, was tempted to plant him a facer—not the reaction of a lady, but then he had not treated her as one.

"I hope I have not understood your disgusting implication correctly, Major. But in any case, I want nothing to do with you. Now take me home immediately," she cried.

"Or you will do what, my beauty?" he taunted. "You might

jump from the carriage, but I hardly think you will attempt that. Play your virtuous game if you will, but I can wait. You will not be so high and mighty for long. I know your kind well."

"I'm afraid you have miscalculated, Major. You do not know me at all. I would not want to complain to your commanding officer that you made improper proposals to me, and constrained me against my will," Melissa answered cooly, now thoroughly in command of herself, not at all impressed with this bounder's ugly words.

"Well, you are a bold little madam to threaten me thus. Come, come let us not brangle. I apologize if I have offended. I will take you home and we will continue this conversation at another, more convenient time," he backed down. The threat had not really impressed him, but he saw that he must use other tactics. Damned if she was worth it, but she had his fighting spirit up. He was not used to being dismissed so cavalierly. She would regret it, he vowed.

Melissa did not deign to answer, and shortly he deposited her at Mistress Blakely's making no effort to assist her from his carriage. She clambered down, somewhat impeded by her packages, but had the last word after all.

"I will not thank you for the ride, Major, as I found it far from agreeable. I suggest you look elsewhere for romantic entertainment. You will not find it with me." She hastened up the steps before he could respond.

Odious man. If that was the treatment she could expect because she had chosen to follow a career on the stage, the sooner she left it the better. Why were actresses considered fair game by such libertines, she wondered. Possibly because so many were, she had to concede. Just as well that the Marquis was returning to shield her from such unwanted advances. Well, she had jumped into this predicament with hardly a thought for the consequences, and she must not depend on that sardonic gentleman to guard her from all dangers. He might protect her life from dangerous adversaries, but he could do little to save her reputation. She would have to manage that herself. And if depressing the pretensions of such as Major

Gratton was necessary she felt well up to the task.

Before the evening's performance Melissa approached Bessie about accompanying her to London. The dresser did not seem surprised that Melissa would be leaving Bath, but she warned her yet again of involving herself with the Marquis.

"That man, for all his toplofty airs, is no better than he should be. And I have a good idea what he has in mind for you, missy, so don't be gulled by his fine ways and lard. He's not on the lookout for a wife, but a far different companion and that is a role you would find very unhappy. Mark my words," she warned.

"I am quite sure you know best, Bessie, but the Marquis has always been kind and generous to me. I owe him a great debt. And now he has secured me this wonderful opportunity at the Majestic. And if you are with me, you will have every chance to guard my interests," Melissa responded. "I don't say you are wrong about him, mind. But you do not know the whole story," she continued, hoping to mollify her companion whose warm concern touched her.

"And I suppose you will not tell me until it suits you, missy. Well, I am coming with you, for it is not right for you to be alone in that den of evilness without some friend to guide you. The Marquis will answer to me if he causes you any harm or sorrow," Bessie stated grimly.

Melissa rewarded her with an affectionate hug, and smiled to herself. She had every faith that the Marquis could handle Bessie, and indeed just about anyone. That was the difficulty. He was a disarming devil, able to cajole females with seemingly effortless ease. And he knew just what he was about. If she felt as confident of her own powers it might be as well. She had a notion that her life would soon be far more complicated than it was now, and not just because she had agreed to his dangerous proposition. But Melissa was far from faint-hearted and approached the coming adventure in a blithe spirit. For the moment she would concentrate on learning her craft.

* * *

Theron arrived back in Bath two days later, in time to view Melissa's last performance at the Theatre Royal. He took a box, in which he sat alone, and ignored the many eyes directed on his elegant person, as he watched the stage. Melissa had expected him, since he had the forethought to send her a missive apprising her of his attendance, but the knowledge that he was among the audience rather unnerved her. With his note had come a huge bouquet of roses, a signal of his position in her life, given for appearances only, she was sure. Still the gift had pleased her.

Samuel Thornton had decided to announce her departure only after the final curtain had descended and she had received the rapturous acclaim of her fans. The reception of the news was tumultuous with catcalls and raucous displeasure echoing throughout the theatre. Somehow Melissa had expected Bath to produce genteel theatre-goers, but they were rarely quiet. Neither Melissa nor Thornton paid much heed, both knowing that the fickle theatre goers would soon hail another idol. Despite her sudden fame Melissa had no conceit about her abilities or her popularity. Although she enjoyed portraying Shakespeare's heroines, and quite looked forward to testing her skills in London, she acknowledged in her heart that she had little of the passionate dedication to the theatre that was necessary for a permanent career on the stage. She still clung to her idealistic dreams of a life in the country with a loving husband and family. More than ever, it seemed beyond her reach. Her brief sadness at leaving Bath, the company, and the bracing comfort of Mistress Blakely did not depress her spirits for long.

The Marquis' attendance in her dressing room banished all thoughts of the past and reminded her that she must keep her wits about her if she was to perform credibly in her new role.

"Well, my pet, you have closed the door on your Bath adventure and are now about to launch yourself on London. Does this give you pause?" the Marquis asked, watching idly as Melissa removed her makeup, his long figure stretched indolently in the one spindly chair the room provided.

"Of course I am a bit nervous about what lies ahead, but I must just do my best and hope that London audiences will be kind." Melissa eyed him thoughtfully, remembering that it was not just the London audiences she had to fear, but a host of new experiences, not least of which was her relationship with the Marquis. She had a spate of questions to ask him, but could not do so with Bessie hovering about her, sending baleful glances at Theron, as she bustled about the room.

"That will do for now, Bessie. I can finish. You may await me outside," Melissa said finally, smiling kindly on that austere woman. "And thank you for all you have done, dear Bessie," she concluded softly.

"I will be going back to my rooms to finish packing up for London now, dearie, and you had better do the same shortly. You need your rest, not gadding about to champagne suppers and the like," she warned darkly, casting a speaking look at the Marquis. However much she admitted his attraction, Bessie was still suspicious of his actions toward her ewe lamb. He remained impervious to her hints, his dark eyes hooded, not revealing his thoughts.

Melissa sighed with relief as Bessie left, and ducked behind the screen to remove her costume and don her gown.

"Bessie mistrusts me, I fear. I must win her round, as I cannot endure her constant dark looks and ominous conjectures for your future under my aegis," Theron said mockingly.

"Oh, I am sure you will charm Bessie, as you do most females," Melissa replied a bit tartly as she struggled into her frock, emerging from behind the screen, still wrestling with the buttons.

"Here, turn around and let me do that for you. I am quite adept at ladies' toilettes," Theron said, standing up. The feel of his fingers on her bare back gave her quite a shudder which she had difficulty in controlling, but he paid no heed, finishing the business in a matter of fact way, as if dressing young women was all in a day's work. And probably was to him, Melissa muttered to herself ill-humouredly.

"There you go, infant." He released her, patting her gently

on her backside, rather as if she were still in the nursery, she thought angrily.

"I can see you are bubbling with questions, but I believe we must defer them until we are more private," Theron said as he held out her shawl. "I have bespoken a supper at York House in a special parlour where we can talk unobserved, and then I will bundle you off to the estimable Mistress Blakely's because we must make an early start tomorrow. Thank goodness, once we get to London you will be able to dress in a more seemly fashion."

"I am sorry if I appear a dowd to your lordship," Melissa answered hurt by his aspersions, but forced to admit that her present wardrobe did little to enhance her charms.

"I refuse to wrangle with you, Melissa. Come let us face your adoring fans," the Marquis teased, offering his arm and escorting her from the room.

Melissa gave one last wistful look around the shabby dressing room with its dingy walls and rickety furniture. She had been happy here, and who knew what lay ahead—more commodious and lavish surroundings perhaps, but also danger and suspicion. She would not forget Bath and the Theatre Royal.

They emerged from the dressing room to encounter a small group of military men and hangers-on who had grown impatient in the Green Room when the star had not made the expected appearance. Among the officers clustering in the hallway was Ens. Ashburton, who stepped forward shyly proffering a bunch of rather wilted spring flowers.

"Oh, Miss Langford, your performance tonight was wonderful. I am only sorry it is your last and we will not see you grace the Theatre Royal again. But perhaps, I will see you in London, if we are posted there soon." A blush rose to his eager open face, as he beheld his ideal.

"Thank you, Percival. You are too kind. I have enjoyed our friendship and I, too, hope we will meet again," Melissa replied kindly, for she could not ignore his devotion which was so respectful, so artless.

Behind him she encountered the sullen stare of Major Gratton, whose eyebrows rose as he noticed her escort. Beyond a frigid nod she ignored him and allowed Theron to sweep her to the entrance, relieved that she had him to protect her from the suggestive ogling of the officer. There was something about the man which made her skin crawl.

In the curricle, Theron turned to her before taking up the reins and jibbed, "I see you have enthralled the military, my dear. How sad that you must bid farewell to that tame puppy and the rest of the uniforms, so enticing to a young woman, I believe," Theron spoke in that sneering manner which always raised her hackles.

She hastened to defend Percival Ashburton. "Some of the officers are insolent and suggestive, but Ens. Ashburton has been all that is respectful and honourable to me," Melissa argued vehemently. "I like him."

"A pathetic lad whom you have ensnared, no doubt, but you will have to forget him now. There will be many of his stamp to pay you homage in London, but do not forget you owe me your loyalty and allegiance, and must appear to be enamoured with me. Too difficult for your acting talents, do you think?" he teased, not impressed with her rebuke.

"You are a hateful, cynical man that no sensible girl would entertain as a cavalier for a moment. But since I am committed to this course you have outlined, I must put up with you, but do not think that I enjoy being the cynosure of all eyes as your light skirt, my lord," Melissa reprimanded him sharply.

"So it's back to 'my lord' again. I have offended. Well, perhaps I will talk you into a better humour over supper," Theron mocked, delighted to have raised her hackles. He intended to keep this relationship firmly light hearted, or their problems would only be increased by any closer relationship. But as he eyed her wistful face and huge eyes he wondered, not for the first time, if he could keep to his good intentions.

Chapter Eleven

The narrow white-pillared house which Theron had chosen for Melissa in Stanhope Gate held none of the grandeur of the Comtesse de Frontons' mansion. A short carriage ride from the Majestic Theatre in Drury Lane, Melissa's new home appealed to her, its neat small garden and tall shining windows overlooking a quiet backwater. She suspected the Marquis had owned the house as a suitable lodging for his former mistresses, but if so, no sign of their occupancy was evident in the newly furnished house. The staff was made up of a housekeeper and several maids; there was no austere butler to impress Melissa with his consequence. The small drawing room could accommodate only a few visitors. Bessie, impressed against her will, made a thorough tour and reported her qualified approval, but she let Melissa know that such abodes were more properly the residences of light skirts, Covent Garden dancers, and members of the demimondaine, not at all suitable for a respectable country miss. Melissa laughed and reminded her dresser that she must be considered to be among that company now that she had embarked on a theatrical career.

Theron had explained to her on their journey from Bath just what her role entailed. The Majestic, a popular theatre, nevertheless had none of the cachet of the Drury Lane or the 'heatre Royal in London. One reason he had been able, with he passing of much largesse, to secure Melissa a role in the ompany, was that the manager, George Whitebread, had etermined to challenge the reigning stars with a fresh new alent. Mrs. Siddons had been queen of the city's stage long nough. His company had youth, ambition, and enough ability o achieve his aim. What was needed was a magnetic new ersonality who could win audiences with a fresh appeal, a aiety and charm which would offer a welcome change from he mannered and grandiose posturings of the traditional casts. Vhitebread had not been overly receptive to the Marquis' laims that he had discovered just such a star in the provinces. In astute and cynical impresario, Whitebread suspected that he elegant nobleman only wanted a showcase for his mistress, ut hard pressed as he was financially he agreed to take on Aelissa.

She did not at first warm to the manager, a corpulent, alding man whose jollity hid an overweening ambition and a ar from generous nature. He had none of the gruff kindness of amuel Thornton, but he seemed willing to be persuaded that Aelissa had possibilities. With Theron standing by ready to ntercede to remind Whitebread just what was owing to the ctress, he had to tread warily. What he did insist upon was hat she would be introduced in a lighter role, not the Ophelia r Juliet Melissa had already mastered. The Majestic patrons vanted livelier fare and he had chosen Farquahar's *Beaux itratagem,* an enraging romp which would feature Melissa as Dorinda, a young heroine well suited to her immature charms.

With Theron watching inscrutably from the sidelines, Whitebread introduced Melissa to the company. Robert Rathbone, a veritable Adonis with sculptured profile, blond wavy hair, and agate blue eyes, was the leading man, quite conscious of his position, and unwilling to cede his position of dol to any upstart actress from the provinces. He bowed over ner hand charmingly, but his stare was cool. Far less easy to nandle, she surmised, than the preening Cecil Stone, who for all his posturing, was naught but a foolish, vain man without an ounce of malice in him.

"I look forward to appearing with you, Miss Langford. Here's to a fruitful and enjoyable alliance," he murmured softly, his glance passing over her and on to the quiet but vigilant figure of the Marquis, standing negligently against the proscenium arch. Theron said not a word as the introductions went forward but there was not a member of the company who could mistake his presence, nor his interest in this new young member of their troupe.

Molly O'Hara, the character actress, seemed welcoming, her buxom figure and merry eyes, beaming warmly on Melissa. Then there was Alison Andrews, who might have reason to object to Melissa, since she had often played many of the roles which would now be the new ingenue's. Guy Gordon, a mature well-set-up gentleman of some forty years, who obviously enacted the villain's roles. He would make a splendid Iago, Melissa considered, with his lean, fine features, height, and sardonic look. He gave little emotion away, and she wondered at his choice of career. He seemed more of a gentleman but perhaps had fallen on bad times and must perforce support himself where he could.

The minor members of the company were a motley lot, neither over ingratiating nor aloof, just accepting her as yet another addition to their troupe.

All of them might speculate about the Marquis' presence but they ignored him, in no doubt as to Melissa's relationship to the aristocrat. Melissa, who should have felt some shame at the knowledge that the company considered her Theron's mistress, felt surprised that she had so little embarrassment. What troubled her more was that she could not believe that this company of unexceptional actors could hide a traitor, a mastermind of a spy ring. None of them seemed capable of such deception, although she knew that imposture was part of their stock in trade. And how was she to ferret out their knavery? Well, she must await on events. Promising to attend rehearsals on the morrow and thanking them prettily for their welcome, she allowed the Marquis to escort her from the theatre, a bit weary from the morning's experiences.

Whitebread ran the cast through a rough rehearsal of that evening's performance, a turgid melodrama that demanded little refining. On dismissal Alison Andrews approached Molly O'Hara to ask the veteran actress what she thought of the new addition.

"She seems a likely lass, but I warrant not brought up to the casual ways of theatre folk. Still, she will probably not have much to do with us. Her fine protector will see to that. I wonder he allows her to continue on the boards, with no need for it. She must take to the life. But she does not seem the kind to be a light skirt, more likely a distressed gentlewoman fallen on evil times and making her way the best she can," Molly concluded charitably.

"She's a fool to parade around the stage when she could lead a life of luxury with her protector. He's a real nob. For all his fine ways, I wouldn't want to cross him. He looks a difficult customer," Alison answered shrewdly. "I am not sure I would want him to have me in keeping."

"Nonsense, my dear," interrupted Guy Gordon, who had heard their discussion of the new import. "You would be very fortunate to attract his lordship, but I believe he would not be content with the obvious. She is not quite in the common mode. I wonder what attracts him, as she seems little more than an innocent," he pondered the thought. "One thing is certain; our leading man will get short shift in that department."

While the company discussed Melissa in a manner which would have given her pause, Theron drove her back to Stanhope Gardens and reminded her of the conspiracy on which she had embarked so lightheartedly. He seemed distrait, and concerned, not his usual style at all, Melissa thought.

"Are you wondering if we have made a mistake, that the Majestic is not a hot bed of spies?" she prodded Theron. "I must say it seems most unlikely. Of course, Guy Gordon is a perfect villain, but somehow I do not think he is a traitor."

"They are actors, my dear and well up to dissembling. No, I am only regretting that I have forced you into this situation. They appear to be a decent sort, but who knows. I only hope I can protect you from any harm," he said, wondering at his concern. He had rarely felt the possessive and protective urges that Melissa inspired when dealing with the myriad women who had crossed his path in the past. But then none of them had her qualities of well-bred innocence. He reminded himself that he did not know her true background, an omission he must rectify before too long. That neither Mason nor Langford was her true name he was convinced. He would have to investigate this mysterious ogre of a guardian in Devon. For it was certain she would reveal little and he hesitated to compel her. She was in enough deep water as it was, and seemed heedless of it. Her next words convinced him that she did not really see the danger of her position.

"You worry too much. I think the whole affair a tempest in a teapot, but I intend to take what the gods, or should I say, you, offer. No doubt I would never have managed to become an actress at the Majestic if you had not bribed Mr. Whitebread. I just hope he did not rob you blind," she said blithely.

"That would be impossible, my girl. I am well up to protecting my interests. Let us just hope that I can protect yours as well. And what did you think of the matinee idol, the blond Adonis? You must not let your mercurial affections stray in his directions. I would not take that in good part. Quite a blow to my reputation if I lost you to a strutting player," he teased, trying to put the uneasiness he felt behind him.

"I am sure, my lord, you have no occasion to doubt your superior attractions. I thought him too good to be true, quite the most handsome man I have ever seen, but I promise to resist temptation, although I quite anticipate our love scenes," Melissa countered mischievously, eager to test his reaction.

"Concentrate on rooting out our spy, my pigeon, and avoid

any trysts with the gorgeous Rathbone. You are not up to his touch," he answered in a quelling tone, annoyed that the thought of Melissa in the actor's embrace could cause him such disquiet. Perhaps this pretence had not been such a clever idea after all. He should have come up with a different ploy to discover the Majestic's traitor, for despite Melissa's disclaimers, he still believed the miscreant was there.

Chapter Twelve

Although the Majestic could not compete with the Theatre Royal or the Drury Lane, its decor was elaborate—glittering chandeliers holding a host of candles, the warm red walls setting off the gold-trimmed boxes, and impressive arcades inviting patrons to enter. George Whitebread and his backers had spared no expense in providing a showcase for the company, which might not have earned the éclat of some London theatres but had nevertheless a stylish aura about it. Even in the shrouded dimness of rehearsals, the Majestic remained impressive, inspiring the actors toward creations of fantasy. Melissa found it contrasted nobly with the Bath play house, and that the actors had attained a professional polish which impressed and daunted her. She wondered if she, still so much an amateur, could achieve the standard they had reached through tested experience. She expected some resentment and was prepared to act accordingly, for she did not have an inflated view of her own talents, and had no trouble reminding herself that whatever her slight abilities she owed this opportunity not to her gifts but to the Marquis' patronage. She had no doubt that George Whitebread would have showed her to the stage door if she had arrived pleading for a job on the basis of her slim Bath appearances.

She suspected that the cast looked upon her elevation with

some cynicism, and as a result she behaved with a charming humility and saw to it that she learned her lines promptly. She had little leisure to brood over her other purpose, the unmasking of the spy in the company. Looking over her fellow thespians she yet found it hard to believe that one of them might be a traitor, and continued to confide her scepticism to Theron.

He had been assiduous in his attentions, driving her to and from rehearsals, displaying all the attention which could be expected, although Melissa was forced to concede that he in no way acted besotted by her charms. He behaved more like an elder brother protecting her from unwelcome advances, and she wondered if the troupe, or even Whitebread himself, believed he had any romantic interest in her. She thought she might take it upon herself to chide him a bit about his rather off-putting attitude.

A few evenings before her debut he surprised her by escorting her to supper at the Clarendon, a tonnish hostelry much frequented by the nobility who sometimes conducted their various liaisons within its discreet portals. He had bespoken a private room, which she suspected was less from any desire to make advances toward her than to discuss their serious business in seclusion, while giving the appearance of sampling her charms in secret. He talked amusingly during the lobster and champagne supper, common to such occasions, but a real treat to Melissa whose culinary habits were simple. When the last dishes had been removed, they settled to a discussion of their problem.

"I realize that your time has been heavily devoted to learning your lines and preparing for tomorrow night's debut, but have you made any new assessments of your fellow thespians, having spent so much time with them these last days?" he asked, toying with his brandy and watching her with an expression which she found difficult to define. What an enigma the man was, obviously a sophisticated libertine, well versed in all the pleasures of the haut monde, and even of a more dissolute society, but still sincere in his efforts to thwart his country's enemies. What a strange combination of self-indulgence and disciplined strength he was, impervious to the gentler emotions, unconcerned with aught but his own desires, which happened now to coincide with the government's.

"I have found no reason to think that the company is hiding your miscreant. They all seem most involved with their careers, the women with fashions and romance off-stage, and the men of an egotistical nature, for the most part, jealous of their positions. It's hard to believe they have either the time or the inclination to delve into politics," Melissa reported.

"I could not be wrong. That play bill must have some meaning. Our agent was not a man who frequented light entertainment, indeed was as sober and dedicated as one could find. He would be at a performance for another reason, and that reason could only have been that he was on the track of the traitor who somehow discovered his danger," Theron answered firmly, unwilling to concede he might be mistaken.

"Are you certain, Theron, that I am the person to discover this spy for you. I have been little in the world, and my judgment of people is far from extensive. Surely you might have enlisted one of the many women you know who would be far more experienced in this matter," she offered tentatively, her doubts surfacing.

"My dear child, one of your chief assets is your guileless manner, and believe me that cannot be assumed. You are quite right, my extensive experience in the petticoat line has enabled me to taste a wide range of females, from duchesses to the muslin brigade, but in neither set would I find an innocent with the daring spirit or the temerity you possess to take on this dangerous chore. Most females care little for much beyond gossip and wealth, damn their avaricious little souls," he concluded bitterly.

"Really, Theron, your jaded tastes have given you an unjustified disgust of my sex," Melissa chided, seeing nothing dicrous in reprimanding him so. "We are all not greedy nobbish fly-by-nights. Some of us care for the poor and the ersecuted, worry deeply about the safety of our country and e men who defend her. I do not know what has given you ich a distrust of humanity, but I think it is most quelling, and hope I never have cause to feel thus."

He smiled at her indignation, but remained unmoved by her assionate disclaimers.

"As I was saying, you are a true innocent. You will not long emain so, I fear, but I cannnot make that my chief concern. Ve must, and will, discover this spy. Sir John is about to aunch yet another offensive against Napoleon and we cannot isk our plans being disrupted. In looking over that acting crew e other day, I am inclined to put my money on the Adonis, athbone, a slippery character with an inordinate conceit," he aid.

Melissa, rather angry by his complete indifference to her irtue, took issue with him immediately. "I don't agree. Robert s obviously only concerned with making his way in the heatre. The popularity is the chief interest. No, Guy Gordon is possibility, but perhaps that is only because he looks so much he part," Melissa brooded, not convinced that either of the ctors had traitorous activities behind their more obvious haracteristics.

"I fear you have been bamboozled by the gorgeous Rathbone. Be careful there, infant, for his ego would swamp ou. Gordon . . . perhaps. But you must not ignore the vomen. Some of the most devious characters in this business re among your sex."

"Oh, you are impossible, Theron. You suspect everyone. I m surprised that you trust me," Melissa complained, horoughly aroused now by his attitude.

"I seem to have no choice, Melissa. But come, it's early days et, and although I am anxious to clear up this mess, I realize ou have only been at the Majestic a week, and I cannot expect niracles."

"But you do. You are a very demanding man, who brooks n opposition to your wishes. Really, you need to be taken down peg or two." As usual Melissa found herself considerin Theron with a confusion of emotions. But uppermost now wa a determination to solve his problem. She owed him that, and their relationship must be one of conspirators and naught els she would have to live with that. Oh, why was he so attractiv she sighed, peeping beneath her eyelashes to consider hi stylish form and strong features which revealed so little c what he really felt.

She admitted that few young women would not be influ enced by Theron's magnetism. Dressed as usual with im peccable austerity, in black evening clothes with a gold fo his only adornment, he put other men in the shade. He had a indefinable quality compounded of arrogance and ruthles indifference to any desires but his own which could b infuriating, but compelling at the same time. She suspected sh would come to regret their alliance brought about b coincidence and necessity, but she could not deny him. H exercised a strange dominance over her which she fough valiantly, but could not dismiss.

She could feel a warmth stealing over her, a lassitude, and a eagerness to acquiesce with whatever he demanded of her How foolish. He considered her a naive little girl, who jus happened to suit his purposes of the moment, and thos purposes did not include romantic dalliance. But then wha would she do if he seemed ready for her to fulfill the positio the world believed she actually held. Would she consent to b his mistress, waiting always for the moment when he tired knowing that he felt nothing but a slight affection for her Nonsense. She must not even entertain such shockin thoughts. Obviously he did not.

"I hesitate to ask this of you, but it seems you must try t invade their dressing rooms and search their effects. Ther might be a clue among them. I cannot hope for incriminatin letters or the like, but perhaps a trace of a French connectio r some similar indication. It could be very dangerous, and ou must not engender suspicion. You must be wary. I could vish I need not employ you in such a way, Melissa, but we have no other recourse. Just this morning I heard that another of ur agents had been intercepted on the coast. This damnable ituation cannot continue," he said, more to himself than to ıer.

"Never fear. I will take every precaution. I agree we must nove carefully but decisively. Standing around the wings eyeing my fellow actors will avail nothing. I find the thought of aking action positively exciting. I believe I will make a better agent than actress," she concluded merrily.

"I would do it myself, but if I was discovered it would be all ıp with us. You will be able to wiggle out of any embarrassing liscovery in your usual adroit manner. You have an uncanny ability to land on your feet, my dear," he smiled, disguising his worry under the urbane cloak he habitually wore. "I am convinced the company thinks you an ingenuous little madam, whose endearing and beguiling ways, have attracted a rake like nyself, to everyone's wonder. You are a born actress, my dear, never fear."

"So Mr. Thornton told me. I must now prove it, to myself, to you, the company, and the London audience tomorrow. Wish me luck, Theron," she asked, pushing any disquiet to the back of her mind.

"Oh, I do, my child. And I will be in my box to applaud you. And as it is growing late, I must return you to your virginal couch," he said brusquely. Melissa could see that he was troubled, but could not guess that he was damning himself yet again for exposing her to such peril, when he wanted to cosset and cherish her, emotions foreign to his nature, and causing him to curse yet again the coincidence which had led her across his path.

Chapter Thirteen

Fortunately, Dorinda, the ingenue in Farquahar's *Beaux Stratagem* was a silly creature, a product of the broad Restoration comedy that audiences of a century before had found irresistible, but whom Melissa thought privately of not much substance. And surely no girl with her wits about her would have been attracted to the melodramatic Aimwell played so broadly by Robert Rathbone. She found her acting talents tested far more by her off-stage role than that before the curtain. Chiding herself for being so blithe about the coming debut, she was reminded that even as mindless a role as Dorinda required study and interpretation. But her thoughts kept sliding away from the comedy to the real life characters of the company of which she had become a member.

Robert Rathbone's breathtaking good looks could possibly hide a more complex personality, but Melissa did not believe that gorgeous gentleman had either the brains or the energy to become a conspirator. His whole attention was centered upon himself and the impression he made upon his gullible fans, the star-struck ladies who watched him breathlessly and sought his favours. Melissa tended to dismiss him, wondering in passing if all leading men were so conceited and aware of themselves.

Guy Gordon posed a different problem, looking for all the world like a villain, but proving on closer acquaintance, quite well mannered and humourous, with a jaundiced opinion of his fellow man but kindly withal. She had come to like him, and thought him a finer actor than Rathbone.

Molly O'Hara was as Irish as her name, irrepressible, feckless and a bit fond of the bottle, but not a woman to whom secrets could be confided.

As for Alison Andrews, she was a bit of an enigma, apparently not resentful of Melissa's elevation, but a bit aloof and very reticent as to her past, although from the little she had allowed to fall, Melissa suspected she came from a country background and perhaps a shop. Hers was a bland and unexceptional manner which defied analysis at this point.

Of the lesser members of the company Melissa had not yet learned enough to make a judgment, and further research would have to wait upon tonight's performance.

In truth, the ease in which she had been accepted as an actress by this veteran troupe caused her some disquiet. Would Whitebread have agreed to give her a trial without the Marquis' patronage? She viewed this probability very sceptically. Well, she must do her best to prove worthy of Whitebread's faith, whatever the reason for it.

On this evening of her debut before London's critical theatre-goers she sat before her dressing table, grateful that she shared the room with no other member of the cast. It was a far more commodious and luxurious chamber than her former hidey-hole in Bath. Even the disputatious Bessie had raised no demur, and now was enjoying herself bustling about readying Melissa's costumes, and generally making herself useful while Melissa dreamed before the looking glass.

"I must say his lordship has done you proud. Two bouquets of yellow and white roses," Bessie clucked in approval eyeing the floral display with some complacence, but then spoiling her appreciation by adding, "I only hope the flowers are a sign of respect and do not signify some other intent."

"Bessie, you worry too much. The Marquis has been all that is most respectful. Besides you are always on hand to lend me credibility," Melissa reproved the dresser.

"You may know so, and I may know so, and even his high and mightiness may know so, but the world thinks far differently. It's not right, you being placed in such a position," Bessie argued stubbornly, unwilling to relinquish her fears for Melissa's virtue. "This play acting will lead to no good, mark my words."

"Dear Bessie. You are such a dragon. No one could doubt my purity with you in constant attendance. Now do leave off, I must concentrate on my role. I cannot seem to remember a word," Melissa replied, first-night nerves beginning to overset her as she glanced wildly around the dressing room wondering how she had come to such a pass. A knock on the door disturbed her anxious reverie, and Bessie admitted George Whitebread, looking somber despite his cheering words.

"I just looked in to wish you well, my dear," he said. "I am sure you will send the audience into transports. We have a full house. Obviously the advertisements did their work, and we have attracted all the ton as well as the pit regulars. Only the royal box is empty, but after tonight I expect that will change." He rubbed his hands together in satisfaction.

"I hope to justify your faith in me, Mr. Whitebread, and thank you for your floral tribute," Melissa acknowledged the splendid display of spring blooms which the manager had proffered.

"Not at all, my dear. I expect this evening to usher in a new era in the Majestic's life. You will be a triumph, I am convinced," he answered, then bowed to her and took his leave.

Melissa, left to her nervous anticipation, rather wondered why Theron had not come backstage to offer his good wishes for her debut. She knew he was out front, in his customary box, but he had told her he had invited guests to join him so perhaps he felt he could not leave them. She would have been grateful for his assurances. At least the first night tremors prevented her from worrying about the job she was really here to do. After this evening she must pursue her investigations, but for now she had to concentrate on Dorinda.

"Five minutes, please," came the call-boy's warning and a tap on her door.

Melissa gave a last, rather apprehensive, look to her appearance in the looking glass and rose to take her place in the wings, although her entrance was not among the first. Bessie looking at her with pride, gave her a hug and praised her handiwork.

"You do look a treat Miss Melissa. Much too good for that rabble out there. But I wish you good luck, nonetheless," Bessie offered, realizing that her charge was in a high state of tension.

"Thank you, Bessie. Well, I'm off," Melissa gave a final tug to the white muslin gown, with its chaste bodice and swept from the dressing room.

Dorinda was not a role which demanded great talent or expression from an actress, but Melissa brought to it an engaging ingenuousness, a fresh insouciance which had a charm of its own. And her clear resonant well-bred voice reached the furthest recesses of the house. Her spirited portrayal, as well as her piquant air as she pirouetted through the scenes, roused the house to enthusiastic applause. Always eager to see a new talent, the bucks and beaux, habitués of the London theatres, wildly hailed this new star to brighten their blasé horizons. The company took seven curtain calls, and Melissa and her co-star, Robert Rathbone, several more.

Now that her debut had been received with such success, Melissa had a moment to spare for the Marquis, sending a searching glance to his box, on the right of the stage, where he stood to join his own congratulations to those of the cheering throng. She turned to give him a special smile which suddenly wavered as she saw one of his companions, the soignée Comtesse de Frontons. So the lovely Aimee was back in favour. Melissa had no time to do more for the curtain fell for the final time and she was surrounded by her fellow actors proffering effusive approval, hailing her as a new luminary, extravagantly praising her performance.

Robert Rathbone was the first to buss her on the cheek, suggesting that this was but the first of many triumphs they would share. She could not but be thrilled by such an accolade and by the company's unstinted praise, but now that the first flush of excitement was over, her thoughts returned to the meaning of the Comtesse's presence in Theron's box. However, she did not forget to thank her supporters with that modesty and sincerity which was a rarity in that egotistical world of play acting. Finally, she escaped to the privacy of her dressing room where she had to endure Bessie's congratulations and ministrations but felt protected from the motley.

"That Mr. Whitebread says you must make an appearance in the Green Room. All the bucks will have gathered there to pay their respects, and he says it's good business to let them fawn and ogle," Bessie reported, sniffing at the thought of such a vulgar display.

"Oh, dear, and I hoped to have a moment to myself. But I suppose I must honour Mr. Whitebread's request. Just let me get out of this costume and put on my gown and I will repair to the Green Room," Melissa agreed, too kind to refuse though all she wanted to do was get Theron apart and discover what Aimee de Frontons presence in his box meant. Though why she should be so concerned about the Comtesse's reinstatement she refused to think about.

Bessie helped her into the gown she had chosen for this auspicious evening, a jonquil-yellow silk of deceptive simplicity, tamboured at the hem and bodice and edged with a small row of seed pearls, a perfect foil for her elfin figure and wide-eyed, pointed face. With trepidation she approached the Green Room from where a hectic babble of noise emerged. Facing an audience from the stage was one thing, but being the cynosure of all eyes in this throng was another. She wished Theron was on hand to support her, and just as she prepared to enter the room, he appeared.

"Well, infant, about to receive the plaudits of your public, and looking in fine fig. I am impressed, Melissa, and you must allow me to add my humble homage to the many you will receive in a few moments." Theron raised her hand and placed a warm kiss on the inside of her wrist causing her a shiver of delight.

"Oh, thank goodness you are here. I need support to face that braying crowd. Not one of them would pay me heed if they had seen me a few months ago in my shabby gown in Devon, or rescued me from my dilemma. Thank you, Theron," she turned starry eyes upon him. She had forgotten in her relief and gratitude her uneasiness over the Comtesse, but suddenly it came back to her. She withdrew a bit. "And where is the Comtesse?" she asked stiffly. "I saw her in your box."

"My guests are of no matter to you, Melissa," he answered coldly, assuming his more usual disdainful air, for he did not entertain questions about his behaviour with equanimity.

"Are they not, my lord? Pray excuse my temerity. Shall we enter?" Melissa responded, with an equally haughty tone, not liking the arrogant manner in which he evaded her query.

"Come now, my child, let us not spoil the brilliance of your triumph by wrangles. All will be explained in good time." He offered his arm, smiling quizzically at her high colour and speaking eyes.

He might enjoy getting a rise from her, but she would not forget the Comtesse, nevertheless, no matter how he cozened her. She owed that lady a reckoning.

They swept into the Green Room, where every eye turned upon them, and Melissa was grateful for the solid form of the Marquis who shielded her possessively from the crowd of suppliants who immediately pressed about her, offering their tributes and praising her inordinately. Most of the beaux, tulips of the ton, noted Corinthians, and some less distinguished men about town, tendered their obeisances politely, only too aware of the protective presence hovering over her. Theron de Lisle did not entertain competition and there were few who would subject themselves to his scathing sarcasm when aroused. His reputation precluded taking untoward intimacy with any female, even an actress, whom he had taken under his wing. One exception was a tall, sandy haired man, with bright blue eyes and a whimsical kindly expression, who came up to them and insisted on Theron presenting him to the star of the evening. Surprisingly, Theron greeted him with some cordiality.

"Well, Harry, I see you cannot restrain your impatience to make the acquaintance of Miss Langford. Melissa, this graceless rogue is Sir Harry Acton, of His Majesty's Hussars. He is panting to be presented to you but beware he has a fearful reputation with the ladies."

"Charmed, Miss Langford. May I say how thrilled I was with your Dorinda this evening, and that although I am invited to join you for supper, I could not wait to meet you," the officer smiled engagingly at Melissa, not one whit discomforted by Theron's sardonic introduction.

"How kind of you, Sir Harry. And I am so happy you will be among the guests at supper. I feel sure we will be friends," Melissa twinkled at him, liking his easy manner and his lack of any suggestive leer, so obvious among the other patrons of the Green Room. She knew that most of them would have been eager to make improper advances toward her, as was their wont, if they had not been inhibited by the Marquis. She chatted gaily with Sir Harry, not noticing the rather overdressed young man across the room who was looking at her with a speculative stare, as if unbelieving of her presence. His shirt points were too long, and his evening clothes, not of the finest tailoring, were accented with rather ostentatious gilt buttons, his waistcoat over-embroidered. After a moment's hesitation he crossed the room to her, elbowing his way through the crowd around her, impervious to the mutters of disgust at his rudeness.

"I say, it can't be, but you look uncommonly like my uncle's ward. It's Melissa, isn't it?" he confronted her with a malign expression.

Melissa, seeing the last man in the world she wanted to encounter, the despicable Algy, paled but quickly recovered, "I think sir, you have made a mistake. We are not acquainted." She turned away seeking comfort from Theron, who looked askance at the young man whose description matched to a farthing that of his protégé's erstwhile suitor.

"Now don't come missish with me, Melissa. I don't know what you are doing cavorting on the stage in this scandalous way, but be assured Uncle Horace will have a great deal to say when I tell him where you disappeared to. Fine behaviour, I must say," Algernon Hawksley smirked, realizing that he had thrown a rub in the way of this hoity-toity miss who had escaped his clutches, taking with her the fortune he so eagerly craved. But he would have his revenge. Now that he had found the miserable chit she would pay for her rejection of his honourable offer. Before he could continue however, he felt an iron hand on his arm.

"I believe you heard the lady. You have made a grievous mistake. Obviously, you will want to make your apologies for causing such distress." Theron's silky voice set ominously with the haughty stare and unrelenting grip he kept on Algernon Hawksley's arm.

Recognizing an aristocrat of the first stare, and an opponent to be reckoned with, Algy tried unsuccessfully to remove his arm and began to have second thoughts upon encountering Theron's quelling gaze. Could he be mistaken? Granted that Melissa had never looked so fetching back in Devon, with her frightened eyes, her shabby dresses, and her scrawny figure. Algy preferred females with voluptuous curves and bold charms, but he had been willing to make the chit his wife so that he could command the funds she would bring him. This girl looked enough like Melissa to be her twin, although more fetchingly togged out, and far more assured in her manner.

Surely he could not be deceived. But Melissa would never have attracted this haughty lord, who seemed to take such umbrage to his remarks. Not a man to tangle with, Algy felt, not liking the look of the Marquis, who increased the pressure on his arm.

"I apologize, Miss Langford, if I have offended you. I must have made a mistake, but you look so like someone I knew in the country. But then, she was a poor drab of a thing, now I recall, and could not hold a candle to you. Please forgive me," he concluded, eyeing her closely as he gave that spiteful dig.

Speechless, Melissa nodded, and turned away, summoning all her composure. "Shall we go, my lord. I am longing for my supper."

"Of course, my dear. I await your pleasure," Theron agreed suavely and ushered her from the Green Room ignoring the lamentations of the crowd left behind to toast the newest goddess of the theatre.

Chapter Fourteen

The celebratory supper proved not to be the joyous occasion Melissa had anticipated. She had been overcome by the confusion of meeting Algernon Hawksley and her efforts to fend off questions about that young man from Theron had been pitiable. She knew she had only postponed a reckoning. When she timidly tried to explain that indeed she had never seen that intruder before, he turned to her in his most off-putting manner, raking her up and down with one of those disdainful stares.

"Confine your acting to the stage, Melissa," Theron said harshly, and Melissa could see he was riding his temper on a tight leash. "I'm not impressed with your pretence. However, this is not the time for questions, but do not think you can evade them. I intend to get to the bottom of this business of your real identity. You have not convinced me that the tale you spun the day we met is a true one, and I do not like being gulled by a chit of a girl no better than she should be. If you endeavour to lie to me again, I will know it, and you will rue the day, I promise you."

She felt her own ire rising on his assumption that she owed him an explanation, but she also wanted to assure his continued protection. If Horace Hawksley came to London he had the power to compel her to return to Devon. That would not suit her, nor Theron if he wanted her cooperation in unmasking his traitor. Only Theron could deal with Algy and prevent him from creating mischief. Despite her anger with his peremptory challenge she knew she would have to tell him the truth eventually. But there was still the matter of the Comtesse, and she had no idea how she would handle that lady when they met at supper. Really, her wisest course was to keep her own counsel till Theron's wrath had cooled a bit. What a shame to have her anticipated supper spoiled by all these vexatious problems. Setting her chin, she kept silent, refusing to even look at her escort for fear that her resolution would waver.

After his outburst, Theron did not press her further. He, too, felt reluctant to spoil her triumphant evening by provoking a quarrel. He was convinced that Algy was indeed the rejected suitor and he had every intention of dealing with him, but it would not hurt this little minx to be kept on tenterhooks for a while. She was far too apt to go her own way, independent and willful, part of her charm but maddening all the same. She needed to learn he did not brook interference in his plans, nor rebellion against his wishes.

The two arrived at the Clarendon without exchanging any more words, neither prepared to enter the lists against the other, but both seething with a sense of injustice, not a climate for a celebration. That the evening passed off as well as it did was entirely due to the jovial efforts of Sir Harry Acton, whose irrepressible spirits lightened the atmosphere. Melissa was even able to greet the Comtesse with a certain amount of aplomb, taking an unholy delight in that lady's annoyance which perforce she had to conceal. The other guests were two Corinthian friends of Theron's and Sir Harry's, their rather supercilious affectations grating on Melissa, but who mellowed somewhat as the evening wore on.

"Allow me to congratulate you on a spirited performance, Melissa," the Comtesse remarked sweetly, her tone barbed. "Although I would never have thought the stage would be your choice of profession. You seem ill-suited to such a career."

"On the contrary, Aimee, our young star is an actress of tested skills. I believe she has spent most of her life preparing for just such a moment," Theron intervened suavely, his good humour restored watching Melissa's struggles to cope with the Comtesse's innuendoes.

He had invited Aimee in a whimsical moment, eager to see her confrontation with Melissa and how that young lady would handle the meeting. He had neither forgiven nor forgotten Aimee's role in Melissa's sudden departure from London, but it suited him to allow her to abase herself and seek his forgiveness. Whether he would grant it was another question and he had not allowed the Comtesse back into his good graces. He considered her attempts to reinstate herself as his *chère amie* rather amusing, reacting in the cruel manner he could adopt at times. He found the thought of welcoming her into his bed once again distasteful, although he was not prepared to examine his feelings for that uncharacteristic reluctance.

All in all the evening passed with a certain surface congeniality, only Sir Harry seeming to truly enjoy himself, and indeed he appeared impervious to the undercurrents. On both arriving and leaving the Clarendon, Theron and Melissa had been approached by several young bucks who had seen the performance and were eager to hail Melissa and try to wrest her attention from the Marquis. More to annoy him than because she had any desire to further their acquaintance she smiled sweetly on them all, inferring that she found their platitudes acceptable and even encouraging their efforts to press for further meetings.

Theron, not unaware of her ploys, managed to remain aloof, his usual mask of hauteur depressing any attentions of the men who crowded around her, but he found his humour severely tried by the experience. Not that the company realized his irritation. After a few insolent stares the admiring fans melted away, accepting ruefully that none of them had a chance with the new toast of London while the Marquis was in possession.

Sir Harry, who knew Theron better than most, raised a sceptical eyebrow at the notion that his impervious friend had been caught in the toils of such an innocent. He was convinced it was but a temporary aberration on the part of the blasé lord. De Lisle's taste usually ran to far different ladybirds, and he could not understand his preference for Melissa, delightful though she was.

By the time Melissa had been escorted back to Stanhope Gate she had an outsize headache and was in no mood to put up with any strictures from her protector. And he seemed perfectly willing to bid her an austere good evening and repair to dissipations more in his normal mode. Melissa suspected he would seek out the Comtesse who seemed more than eager to soothe his ego, and she refused to admit her dismay at the contemplation of their rapturous embraces. If that was what Theron preferred it was of no concern to her, she assured herself. Her manner was equally chilly, which amused the Marquis.

"Since you have no performance tomorrow," he added, "I will be by in mid-morning to hear your explanations, infant, and I hope the contemplation of that does not spoil your rest. You have had a tumultuous evening, and children oft find so much stimulation unhealthy. I forget how young you are, and I suppose I should make allowances. Sleep well, my dear," he concluded, his mood suddenly softening, and to Melissa's surprise he leaned over and kissed her gently, with none of the passion she had come to expect from him.

Not knowing how to respond, Melissa contented herself with a quiet good night and a thank you for the entertainment and slipped into the house to be soothed by Bessie's comforting ministrations, for in truth she was exhausted by the tension of the performance and its many aftermaths.

Since she had expected to toss and turn all night, reliving those fraught moments in the Green Room when Algy had made his insinuations, Melissa was surprised on awaking in the bright sunny morning to discover she had slept long and dreamlessly. By nature an optimist, she decided that she would face up to the Marquis and not allow him to intimidate her with his questions and threats. After all, she thought mischievously, he needed her as much as she needed him. More perhaps, since her cooperation was necessary in discovering the spy. Now that her debut had proved so successful, she could make her own way in the theatre without his patronage.

Still, she conceded, Algy was a problem she was not so confident in solving. If he wrote to his uncle that Melissa had become the leading light of the London stage, she had little doubt that her guardian would post up to London and drag her back to Devon. Why he was so determined that she wed Algy, she could not fathom. Could it be that he merely wanted to discharge his obligation without the trouble of securing her a more attractive husband by putting himself to the expense of tricking her out in expensive gowns and introducing her to the local society. Somehow she did not believe this was the reason. He must have a deeper intent, one he was unwilling to divulge, which meant it did not bear examination.

Melissa, although innocent about life and men in general, had few illusions about her guardian. He had never professed any affection for her, not that she would have welcomed it, for he was a far from prepossessing man, even more abominable than Algy, if possible. From her arrival at Hawksmoor, his dark manor house in Devon, he had treated her brusquely, offered no consolation to the lonely unhappy little orphan bereft so tragically of her parents, and had provided only the barest of necessities to the comfort of a growing girl. Her governess had been a mean, cold woman with few attainments and a propensity to harsh punishment for the least infraction. If it had not been for Bessie, Melissa would have suffered even more than she had. And finally even Bessie had been taken from her. She pleaded to go away to school, but was refused, as this was an unnecessary expense, her guardian insisted. The wonder was that she had survived so well under his grim treatment, her ebullient spirits so little quenched. But in the end, his insistence on her marrying Algy had been more than she could stomach. No matter what happened to her in this new life which had been thrust upon her she had a greater chance of finding some measure of security and happiness than if she had remained meekly in Devon to be coerced into a hateful marriage.

And she would never have met the Marquis. Melissa could not help but wonder what her reaction would have been if Mr. Hawksley had produced an eligible husband, kind, considerate, attractive, generous, and eager to win her love. Well, certainly the Marquis had neither of the first two qualities although she could not deny his generosity nor attractiveness. Measured against the Corinthians and gallants who had thronged about her in the Green Room last evening, against sweet Percy Ashburton, and even the congenial Sir Harry, he stood above them all. But he was not for her, even if she had a chance to win his affections. His cynical, distrustful attitude toward women had so pervaded his character that she wondered if he would ever marry. Woe to the misguided miss who gave him her heart and her hand. He would treat her casually, sequestering her in the country, no doubt, while he pursued his libertine ways, unaffected by the bonds of matrimony. Well, she would not allow him any license with her, or allow him to cozen her into his bed. Only heartbreak lay in that direction. She had enough sense to know that, and she must be sure that her head ruled her heart in this instance.

Having settled the Marquis to her satisfaction, Melissa ate her breakfast with a healthy appetite and dressed in a beguiling violet muslin gown which matched her eyes. This time he did not keep her waiting but arrived at Stanhope Gate soon after she had completed her toilette and demanded her presence in the drawing room. He raised his eyebrows at the floral displays which were already crowding the room, their scent pervading the air, but made only a passing comment as to their meaning.

"I see you are being overwhelmed by tributes to your charms already," he said after greeting her perfunctorily.

Melissa nodded her agreement, and seated herself on the small brocaded settee before the fireplace. "Yes, everyone is most kind."

"Everyone but me. Will you try to enmesh me in your toils, now that you have become the toast of the town? I warn you that others have attempted it, and failed although I am not averse to having a romantic fling with such a popular belle," Theron mocked, half serious but intent mainly on testing her mercurial temper.

"You are quite beyond my touch, my lord. I leave the field to the Comtesse, who seems much more suited to your talents," Melissa sparred, not forgetting that lady's possessive manner.

"Aimee is not your concern," Theron said dampeningly. "But we are not here to discuss your acting triumph or my romantic adventures. I intend to discover the truth about that disgusting puppy who approached you last night in the Green Room. And don't think you can put me off with some Banbury tale about mistaken identity. I am convinced he was in truth, the odious Algy, and if you want my help in dismissing him, you had better reveal the whole story, with none of your usual inventive embellishments."

Melissa sighed, stalling for time. How much should she tell him. Once she had been able to avoid his probing into her background, but she doubted she would find it so simple a second time. He knew her too well now and she had some experience of his stubbornness.

As she hesitated, Theron took a few strides around the room, barely concealing his impatience. Then drew her up from the settee, raising her chin with a firm grasp.

"I have thought from the beginning that your story about the wicked guardian was, if not a lie, far from the whole. And I want your real name, not this Mason or Langford you have adopted. If you want my help you must be honest with me, which is expecting a great deal from a female, I admit, but we have too much at stake now in our partnership for you to be putting the scheme at jeopardy with your falsehoods and embroideries." Theron looked firmly into her eyes, holding her gaze with the mesmerizing power he could exert when he wished.

"Oh, Theron, I do not know what to say. It's all so complicated," Melissa said, hoping to avert his ill humour but not expecting much success.

"I imagine it is not beyond my limited comprehension. Just start at the beginning. You will feel the better for it," he urged.

"I suppose I will have to tell you. What I said about Horace Hawksley, for that is his name, was the truth. For some reason he wants to palm me off on his nephew as a wife. I suppose he is tired of having me under his wing, and wishes to spend no more of his blunt on me. He has never been overly-generous. And it is true that my father left me under his guardianship, why I cannot fathom. When I was nine, after my parents death from the fever in India, I was deposited on his doorstep. I suppose he could not refuse to take me in, and I suspect some money came with me, although he has always complained about the expense of keeping me," she remembered woefully.

"And your real name?" Theron asked, brooking no evasion.

"Melissa Mansfield. I know my father was in the East India Company, and that he and my mother had fled her parents' wrath at their marriage, but I do not know who my maternal grandparents are. If they had not repudiated my mother, I suppose I could have been taken in their care, but obviously they never forgave her for marrying outside their wishes. I had a happy childhood in India and remember my parents as devoted to one another. When they died, an official of the company took me to England—I remember the voyage well. He left me with Horace Hawksley," she concluded, surprised to feel so relieved at having confided in Theron at last.

"Mansfield. . . . I wonder if I can discover anything from the East India offices. I will put my man on it. But that does not remove the threat of Algy," Theron meditated. "And he must be removed. We cannot have that complication added to the other, your mission to discover the French agent at the Majestic."

"I am sure it is within your power to deal with Algy and I must say I will be most grateful," Melissa said.

"And I wonder what form that gratitude will take, my child?" Theron replied derisively, giving Melissa a glance which caused a blush to rise to her cheeks. Oh, he was impossible, teasing her when so much was at stake, unable to refrain from flirting even now.

He laughed, enjoying her discomfort. "Well, I think I can cope with Algy. We do not want him writing about his discovery of you to his uncle. Then the demanding Mr. Hawksley will rush up to London and try to either marry you off or force you back to Devon. And we have no legal recourse, for he is your designated guardian."

"Oh, Theron, you would not let him do that, would you?" Melissa exclaimed, all dismay, her distrust of his sardonic lordship buried in her fear of coming once more under her guardian's dominance.

"I might, if you do not heed my wishes," he answered. Then seeing her real distress he relented. "No, chicken, I would not allow either Algy or Hawksley to have their way with you. You have become vital to my designs and I brook no opposition from some country cit or his bumbling relative. Besides, I do not think you would do well with Algy. I have another idea for you," he teased, hoping to distract her from the misery such a fate engendered.

Ignoring his hint, Melissa, in her relief, rose and threw her arms around him, pressing a grateful kiss on his cheek, "Thank you, Theron, I knew I could depend on you to solve my difficulties."

Startled, he grasped her more firmly, holding her in a tight embrace, and returning her kiss with a passion which surprised them both, his lips moving in a drugging insistence over her lips, cheeks and hair.

"You are a tempting handful, my dear. I cannot resist sampling what you offer so sweetly," he murmured, forgetting the reason for her enthusiasm, and allowing his better instincts to be overcome.

Before the weakness which his touch evoked swamped her entirely, Melissa was rescued by the entrance of her parlour maid. Neither had heard her tentative knock.

"Pardon me, madam, but a gentleman has called." The maid, properly trained, gave not a glance to her dishevelled mistress, but kept her eyes on the draperies, her face schooled into impassivity.

"Oh, yes, Rose, who is it?" Melissa tried to regain her composure, as Theron released her and moved away, arrogant and disdainful as usual, apparently not upset by the unexpected encounter.

"Sir Harry Acton, ma'am," the maid replied. And on this announcement the stalwart figure of Theron's friend made his entrance, hailing them both with enthusiasm. Perforce Melissa had to welcome him, and the three chatted for a moment, Melissa promising to drive out with Sir Harry later that day, before he and the Marquis took their leave.

"We will meet this evening, Miss Langford, when I hope you will take supper with me," the Marquis suggested, but implying she had no choice but to assent. Bowing over her hand, he escorted his companion from the room, leaving behind a much confused young woman.

Chapter Fifteen

Theron curtly refused Sir Harry's invitation to join him for a round at Gentleman Jackson's Boxing Saloon, and sawed on his horses with an unusual disregard for their tender mouths and skittish spirits. Sir Harry, raising his eyebrows at Theron's rare abuse of his cattle, went his own more sedate way, wondering if at last his friend had been caught in the romantic toils he had always scorned so bitterly. Theron was a man of mercurial moods, cold and ruthless in danger, sneering of society's rules, and impervious to the tender emotions, but he was acting very out of character. There was more to the relationship between the Marquis and his charming actress than met the eye, of that Sir Harry shrewdly warranted.

An hour later, brooding over a bottle at White's, Theron was inclined to agree with his friend. Why was it that this one female, no more than a schoolgirl really, with none of the sophisticated experience he normally demanded in his lights of love, aroused in him this curious desire to protect combined with a jealous anger at her stubborn ways? Females were for dalliance, and quickly abandoned when their charms palled. They had little to do with the main business of men's lives. His mistake was involving Melissa in this attempt to root out the French agent at the Majestic. If it were not for that he would turn her over to her guardian and forget the provocative little miss.

But he knew that duty was not all that prevented him from acting thus. Only once had he been in danger of surrendering his heart to a respectable female, and Sarah Valentine, in love with her stalwart colonel, had nipped any pretensions he might have entertained in the bud. Just as well, for Theron was convinced he would have made her, or any woman, an exasperating husband. He had always avoided matrimony with all the skill and adroitness at his command, for the thought of facing one woman over a dinner table for the rest of his life was too boring to contemplate. True, so far, Melissa had never bored him—maddened him, defied him, charmed him—but never caused that yawning ennui which in the past had signaled the end of every affair he had ever embarked upon. Even Aimee, for all her lush attractions and her cousinly claims, had evoked only a faint interest and response to her skills in bed. But now even his liaison with her had lost its appeal. He must be growing old, sated, or so involved with this spy search he needed no other antidote to the tedium of his life. Not being able to settle the problem of Melissa to his satisfaction, he deliberately banished her from his mind and turned again to the mystery of the French conspiracy.

While Theron wrestled with the problem of their relationship, Melissa, who would have been more than incredulous if she had known the tenor of his thoughts, determined to put that gentleman out of her mind, and get on with the business he had asked of her. She had persuaded herself, even with the evidence of that tender yet tormenting embrace, that he was using her for one purpose. The sooner she accomplished that the better, for then she would cry quits with the arrogant lord, and get on with her life, a lowering idea which she did not contemplate with enthusiasm. Banishing her tendency to wander off into romantic dreams, she ordered a hackney and repaired to the theatre. Work was what was needed, and perhaps the opportunity to make a search of the company dressing rooms would dispel the disorder of her thoughts.

Whitebread had surrendered to Melissa's tentative suggestions that a play with more meat might still appeal to the Majestic's lighthearted audience and he was tentatively considering a production of "Taming of the Shrew," Katherine's role challenging to his new star. She found the manager a difficult man to assess. He gave little away beneath the ingratiating manner of the professional he had donned in pursuit of his overriding ambition, to make the Majestic the equal of any theatre in London. He must be convinced that his company could perform "The Shrew," that the cast would not lose the momentum engendered by Melissa's recent overwhelming success.

Melissa approached him gingerly, unsure of just what attitude she should adopt to persuade him. She knocked on his office door with a great deal more assurance than she felt. Responding to his gruff invitation to enter, she sailed through the door and greeted him cheerfully.

"Good morning, Mr. Whitebread. I hope I am not disturbing you," she said noticing that he hurriedly covered some papers on his desk. Did he think she was trying to ferret out the secrets of the box office returns, or was he just naturally cautious. Shuffling his papers together, Whitebread hailed her with a smile.

"Ah, our reigning star. Sit down, sit down, Miss Langford. What can I do for you? You are not appearing on our boards this evening, and I admit our advance ticket sales reflect your regrettable absence. We must find a new role for you without delay."

"Yes, I do not want to rely on Dorinda indefinitely. Have you given more thought to "The Shrew"? I am quite enamoured of Katherine, and I think we could make a good thing of it," Melissa urged.

"Well, normally, I find my audiences not always as receptive to the Bard as I would like, but I believe the audience would turn out in great numbers to see you in anything," he replied. "You have quite captured the blasé attention of

London, my dear. And since I am grateful, I think you can begin to study the role. I will make the announcement to the company immediately. I only hope they are up to it," Whitebread finished, with some doubt as to his troupe's abilities. He was wary of offering any production beyond the bland and broad fare which was the usual Majestic stock in trade.

"I am sure you will not regret it, Mr. Whitebread, but for the moment I will continue with Dorinda, which you have announced again for tomorrow, I understand." Melissa thanked him with a pretty smile.

"Yes, and right now we will go over the last act again. There are some rough edges there, and Rathbone needs a little schooling, I fear," Whitebread rose and escorted her to the door, following her out. They walked down the empty aisles toward the stage where various members of the company had gathered in anticipation of the called rehearsal.

Rathbone did not take kindly to any criticism of his performance, and Melissa feared he held her responsible for Whitebread's remarks about his depiction of Thomas Aimwell, the ne'er do-well hero of *Beaux Stratagem*. Finally, his reading, and that of the rest of the cast, met Whitebread's approval and the company was dismissed. Melissa smiled sunnily on one and all and retired to her dressing room. She hoped to linger behind the dismissed players and make her forays into the various dressing rooms after they had all left the theatre.

She sat restlessly on the couch thumbing through a copy of "Taming of the Shrew" as she listened to the voices of the actors and actresses preparing for their departure. Molly O'Hara interrupted her reverie, popping her engaging face in the door.

"A few of us are repairing to the Crown and Garter for a snack before going home. Would you join us, dearie?" Molly offered tentatively. She did not like to presume, and from the first moment of their meeting, had accepted that Melissa was not quite one of them, of a quality a touch above the normal run of actresses who graced the Majestic. She looked at the girl's piquant face below the mop of brown-gold curls and had no difficulty in understanding the arrogant Marquis' attraction. She worried a bit about the obvious liaison between the two, for Melissa had little of the avaricious, hard-headedness of many actresses who used their charms to such economic advantage. Somehow she doubted that Melissa encouraged the Marquis from such base motives, and she hoped the girl had not lost her heart to the hardened libertine.

"I would love to, Molly, but I must spend some time with Katherine." She waved the script. "If we are going to put on 'The Shrew,' it means much study. But somehow I feel quite akin to that spirited heroine," she added, for she did indeed like Katherine and looked forward to portraying her.

"Just remember, that in the end, Shakespeare had her completely under the thumb of Petruchio. Is that a fate you contemplate?" Molly asked daringly, hoping for a confidence from Melissa. Despite her warm friendly manner with the company, Molly noticed that the new star kept her own secrets. She never boasted of her relationship with the Marquis, although both Molly, and more obviously Alison Andrews, had tried their best to discover how the land lay.

"Fortunately I have no Petruchio in my life," Melissa parried pleasantly. "Still I think of Kate as a real challenge. I can promise you I will give her my best. You run along and join the others. Perhaps I will look in later."

"All right, dearie. Don't wear out your pretty eyes studying the script," Molly said, cheerfully taking her leave. Impervious to snubs, she rarely took offence, and her presence in a company of tender egos was soothing and refreshing.

Once more alone, Melissa wondered if this was the time to further her investigations and visit the various dressing rooms in search for clues. Reluctant as she was to pry into the cast's private affairs, she realized that she must put aside her scruples and make the effort. Sighing, she admitted that as a spy she was not a great success, but fair heartedness would not win the day.

Since she had been elevated to stardom and had the luxury of a dressing room to herself, Molly and Alison were now sharing one. Melissa, looking carefully around the corridor, ducked into their joint dressing room, two doors down from her own. It held the usual welter of costumes, two chairs, two mirrored tables littered with makeup and toiletries. Quickly rummaging among the belongings, Melissa found little of interest, unless the possession of French powder was an indication of conspiracy. She doubted that either Molly or Alison were the conspirators, but she must cover any contingency. In one of the drawers of what must be Alison's dressing table she found only one item of interest, a cryptic note with no signature.

"My dear,

I fear I cannot grant your request at this time. I know you feel slighted by the current situation, and believe me I would do all in my power to relieve it. If you will have supper with me this evening perhaps we can discuss it further. I must prevail on your good nature to be patient."

There was no signature, so that Melissa could not discover who was pleading with Alison to be patient. Since the actress was such an enigma to Melissa, and not of a confiding nature, it would be difficult to find out the name of her cavalier. The script was scrawling and difficult to decipher, but had a vague familiarity. Melissa carefully replaced the missive where she had found it, and continued her search but found nothing suspicious.

A cursory examination of the other rooms was equally disappointing. She left Robert Rathbone's room to the last, somehow averse to examining his effects. Then, too, at any moment she might be discovered and how would she explain her presence? In the women's rooms she might say she was looking for some cosmetic, but she had no business in

Rathbone's room, and he would know it. But at last, she slipped into Rathbone's sanctum unobserved. The theatre's silence oppressed her, and she admitted she was frightened. Rathbone's dressing table was littered with the usual paraphernalia of costumes and makeup, his mirror lined with notes from admirers, but none of any significance. Hurrying in frustration and fear, Melissa delved through the drawers, finding nothing. As she prepared to leave she heard voices in the corridor. Panicking, she looked around the room for a hiding place. The only possible refuge was behind the large screen, over which a colourful dressing gown had been tossed. She scurried behind it, as the door opened.

"Really, Alison, I cannot think why you wanted to see me in private. Our relationship is finished, and I might remind you it was at your request that we end our romance," Robert Rathbone's fruity, full voice complained in a querulous tone.

"I have no romantic interest in you anymore, Robert, 'tis true, and that is not why I requested this interview," came the light voice of Alison Andrews. "I want to talk to you about our new star."

Melissa started. What was this? How embarrassing. She would now be privy to a conversation she felt could only be painful, but perhaps informative, as well. She conceded that if she were to act the spy she must not cavil at overhearing private conversations.

"Well, what about the charming Miss Langford? Surely you do not suspect that I have any intentions toward her? Even if I had, I venture the haughty Marquis might object. And I would not want to tangle with his lordship. He would not look favourably on any poaching in that direction, I am sure," Rathbone replied.

"Well, there's something very odd about Miss Langford, I vow," Alison said fretfully. "And I cannot believe that she is completely indifferent to your charms."

"Could you be jealous, my dear? How flattering," he said silkily.

"Don't be ridiculous. But I must admit there is more to her than meets the eye. She may be an adequate actress, but she is not what she seems, I am certain. And how did she achieve her sudden success? Overnight she has become the rage of London. She's not so very beautiful, and her talent is not so immense. No doubt the Marquis has sweetened Whitebread's pockets to give her this chance. He had no right to relegate me to supporting roles!" she complained.

"I rather thought your cheerful acceptance of second place to our new star lacked plausibility. You dislike her, don't you?" Rathbone queried her rather amused at her jealousy, and feeling complacent that she thought him attracted to Melissa.

"Well, it would not have been very clever of me to kick up a fuss," Alison replied angrily. "She might get me dismissed. But I am furious to be treated in this fashion, and I intend to have my revenge."

Melissa was shocked at the malevolence in Alison's tone. She had never given much thought to Alison's possible enmity over being displaced as the Majestic's star. The actress had cleverly hid her animosity.

"What do you want me to do? I will not endanger my own position by championing you, my dear. I do not owe you that," Rathbone answered, obviously annoyed that Alison would ask this of him.

"As her leading man, you have plenty of opportunity to make her look ridiculous on stage. You are an old hand at stealing the limelight," Alison suggested nastily.

"But why should I? Are you implying that if I go along with your idea, you might take me back in favour?" Rathbone suggested. "Come, Alison, it's true I enjoyed our liaison, but I am not going to earn a dismissal from the Majestic in order to get you back into my bed. Anyway, I thought you had a new paramour. You threw me out with little compunction, if I remember," he added carefully.

"Robert, you are a cool bastard. You never cared for me. I

was just a convenience to you," Alison said, her voice now coarse and shrill.

"In this game, my pet, we must protect our own interests, and mine do not include putting myself at risk for you. You must put up with the status quo. I do not think Miss Langford will be the reigning star of the Majestic indefinitely. I suspect his lordship has different plans for her. Meanwhile coming to fisticuffs with me is not your answer. Just wait it out. You will again be the leading lady, I am sure," he soothed.

"I hope you are right, Robert, but I do not like the idea of miss hoity-toity queening it in my place. I will just have to seek other methods of ridding the Majestic of her presence," Alison answered angrily.

"Come, come, my angel. Do not be so cast down in the boughs. You will come right. And such animosity does not become you. Let us cry pax," he placated her with what Melissa thought must be a kiss of consolation.

"Don't, Robert. I am not to be put off by your platitudes. I intend to get rid of that little miss, either with your help or without it," Alison concluded, and Melissa heard the door slam noisily as she departed in a huff. Holding her breath she waited. If Rathbone decided to settle down at his dressing table she was in trouble, for she could not crouch here forever. But evidently he had had enough of the confining room, and after a muttered curse, followed his former leading lady.

Chapter Sixteen

"Do I dare hope, infant, that your insistence on dining here at home with me, is an indication that you might favour me with closer intimacies?" Theron mocked, toying with his wine glass. The two were just concluding an elegant supper in the Stanhope Gate house. Melissa had insisted on dining there rather than in a restaurant, since he had demanded she spend the evening with him.

"Don't be ridiculous. I thought it might be more private and I want to discuss the results of my prying into the cast's dressing rooms this morning," she reprimanded him curtly, furiously blushing. Oh, he was a devil, implying that she was eager to allow him into her bed, on the strength of a supper invitation. He enjoyed teasing her, she knew, and found her innocence provocative, no matter how she tried to discourage him.

"Alas, I feared it was that. No matter how I try, I do not seem to make much progress in turning our equivocal relationship into something more satisfying," he sighed theatrically, knowing that he was raising her hackles, but unable to resist.

"You know perfectly well that I am not available for your lecherous interest," Melissa retorted. "I did as you suggested and investigated the cast's effects today. The only thing I discovered was a very puzzling note in Alison Andrew's dressing table unsigned by what I think must be an admirer. As I recall it she had evidently asked him for some help in solving a dilemma which he refused to grant. After what I heard later I think it might have been from Robert Rathbone. She hates me and wants to turn me out of the Majestic."

"Are you sure that's what it referred to?" the Marquis asked, all lightness gone from his tone.

"I fear so, because of what I heard later." Melissa went on to tell him of the overheard conversation.

"Yes, you seem to have made an enemy there," the Marquis mused, thinking over Melissa's disclosures, "and a clever one, for she gave no evidence of resenting you. But she is powerless to harm you, I think. And I am convinced the note had nothing to do with this French business. How annoying."

"Well, really!" Melissa protested. "Here I tell you of this jealous female and all you are concerned with is how it bears on your conspiracy. Can't you see how awkward it is? How am I to face them tomorrow?"

The Marquis raised a wry eyebrow. "You can't mean that you are overset by one jealous female. Since I have known you you have coped with a demanding guardian, the odious Algy, the indomitable Bessie, Ophelia, Juliet, Dorinda, and the Comtesse, not to speak of my own lecherous proposals. I do not think even Napoleon is beyond your scope and here you are worried over a second-rate thespian. No, my dear, you will not persuade me you fear the vengeful Miss Andrews," he concluded as if bored with the whole situation. "And I do not believe she is involved in our spy ring." He frowned. "But perhaps Rathbone is a possibility. He was not inclined to grant Miss Andrews' request and take you on. That may mean he is wary of any further complications."

Melissa, thoroughly annoyed that Theron's chivalry was not aroused by her apparent danger, protested. "All you think about is that damned spy ring. I wish I had never become involved in such a coil."

"Tut, tut, infant, such language from a gently bred female! And I understood you wanted naught from me but cooperation in our venture of exposing the traitors. Can it be that I was wrong, and that you entertain softer feelings for me?" he chaffed, obviously enjoying Melissa's discomfort and the blush that rose to her cheeks.

"You are impossible, my lord. I pity any poor female who becomes enamoured of you. You have not a compassionate bone in your body," Melissa responded, determined to take the war into the enemy's camp.

"Ah, I gather we are speaking of love, a much misunderstood emotion, I fear," Theron said cynically. "And any woman who is fool enough to think she might draw me into her coils is in for a deep disappointment. I am adept at avoiding their silken traps. Your sex, my dear, is much more attracted to my wealth and title than toward my person. Because I am a skilled lover does not mean that the emotion aroused is anything but a fleeting physical attraction."

Melissa, aware that they had ventured into dangerous waters, hurried to turn the conversation. "Well, I am in no danger from your practiced gallantries. Let us discuss our next move. What do you suggest I do next?"

"Still a scared little rabbit, I see. Don't you believe I could initiate you adroitly into the pleasures of the bed? Virginity is a much overrated commodity, I fear, but one to which you cling so resolutely I can see I have little hope of changing your mind, and force is not my style," he sneered, obviously bored with the tenor of the conversation. Melissa did not like the ugly light which flared in his eyes, and was too innocent to recognize desire when she saw it, although she had the uneasy feeling that Theron would not be held at bay for very long if he were indeed intent on seducing her.

"May I remind you, Theron, that the reason for our relationship has nothing to do with passion, but is based on patriotism, or is that too obvious a sentiment for you to endorse," she said coolly, nettled at his attitude. In this mood she found him far from attractive and much preferred his usual brotherly teasing to this provocative stance.

"Of course, my dear, as you say, our alliance is against Napoleon, not any other foe, even Cupid's much vaunted darts," he agreed, in the sneering manner she found so hateful. Then, as if tired of baiting her, he turned serious. "I do not know what our next move should be, but I have a feeling affairs are coming to a head. Rumour has it that the French want a truce, and there is some reason to believe His Majesty's ministers are amenable. It would be a mistake, but alas, my advice does not appear effective. And our military command is in disarray. We desperately need a strong commander in the field and an effective resistance at home. If I could expose this spy ring, Addington and his faint-hearted friends might listen to me," he concluded, angry at the thought of the government's conciliatory stance toward the country's enemies. "Napoleon will never be satisfied until he has subdued us, and we cannot allow that."

"I quite agree. Well, I will continue as before, hoping that I will stumble upon some clue," Melissa said, depressed at events and her helplessness.

Theron took his leave soon afterwards. No doubt to seek out a more attractive and complacent female, Melissa thought dismally. She certainly wanted to keep him at bay, and if he was involved with one of his many Cyprians, he would leave her alone. So why did that thought fail to lighten her spirits? she asked herself and repaired to study a copy of "The Taming of the Shrew."

During the next few days Melissa had little leisure to worry about either Theron's attitude or the discovery of traitors as *Beaux Stratagem* came off the boards and the company rehearsed "The Taming of the Shrew." Alison Andrews, who was playing Bianca in the production, showed none of the animosity toward Melissa that she had revealed to Robert

Rathbone. If it had not been for that overheard conversation, Melissa would have found it hard to believe.

George Whitebread appeared pleased with the rehearsals although his manner was strangely distrait. His professionalism came to the fore while he directed the cast, but as soon as rehearsals were concluded he rushed off on some private business which seemed to be causing him worry.

Melissa was spared Theron's attentions for the moment. He turned up occasionally to escort her home from rehearsals and the final performances of *The Beaux Stratagem* but refrained from the teasing provocative manner which had caused her such heart burnings. His manner was oddly aloof, almost bored. Could he be regretting their involvement she wondered or was he just disappointed that his schemes did not appear fruitful?

Melissa did enjoy the soothing and jolly company of Sir Harry Acton, who showered her with flowers and invitations. She found the engaging Sir Harry a distinct relief since she did not have to parry his advances. He seemed content to act as an adoring escort without making any outrageous demands.

Of Algernon Hawksley she heard nothing, and only hoped he had retired from the scene permanently, balked of intent to return her to Hawksmoor. She should be satisfied but felt oddly uneasy, as if waiting for some unnameable disaster which hovered over the Majestic.

On the final night of *The Beaux Stratagem*, at Whitebread's insistence, she agreed to appear in the Green Room to greet her many admirers. Wearing a sprigged apricot silk gown, her curls tamed into a fetching Grecian style, she created a small sensation among the bucks who thronged behind stage.

"My dear Miss Langford, you were, as always, a triumph," Sir Harry hailed her, hurrying to her side and staking a protective stance, blithely asserting his prior claims before the eager young men who sought a favour from the star.

"Sir Harry, you are too kind, and so good for my consequence," Melissa smiled.

"Is Theron going to honour us with his presence this evening? He was not in his box for the performance, I noticed."

"I doubt it," she answered, a bit piqued that the Marquis had not seen fit to attend this last performance of her success. "He has been quite elusive lately. Perhaps he has found a more engrossing matter to engage him. After all, he has seen the play countless times."

"How could he find anything more engrossing than the toast of London," Sir Harry replied gallantly.

"How indeed. Miss Langford has won London's hearts as she had Bath's," came a familiar voice, interrupting their tête à tête.

Melissa turned to see that the newcomer was Major Henry Gratton, the officer whose attentions she had found so repellent in the fashionable watering place.

"Good evening, Miss Langford. Dare I hope that you remember me from Bath?" Major Gratton said suavely, ignoring her frown of displeasure.

"I remember you only too well, Major," Melissa replied curtly. "May I present Sir Harry Acton, a good friend."

"Your servant, sir." Sir Harry bowed stiffly, sensing that Melissa did not welcome the Major's attentions.

"How fortunate you are to have gained Miss Langford's good approval," the Major said. "I fear I made the wrong impression on our first meeting and must now strive to put things right."

"Did Percy arrive in London with you, Major?" Melissa asked.

"Yes, indeed, the whole regiment has been posted to London before going to Devon where we will be keeping an eye on the Frenchies," Gratton replied. "I take it the cub Ashburton is still in your good books," he sneered, obviously annoyed at her preference for his junior officer.

"Percy is a delightful young man who was very kind to me in Bath. I do not forget my friends—or my enemies," Melissa replied in a warning tone. "Is he not here this evening?"

"I believe not, but no doubt you will be able to renew your acquaintance before too long. I understand he was supplanted," Major Gratton said suggestively.

"Not at all. I will be delighted to see him again. Perhaps you would convey my wishes to him?" Melissa said sweetly. "And now, I must bid you all farewell. Sir Harry is taking me to supper," she explained, much to that gentleman's surprise. He did not demur and they left the Green Room together. Gratton, so summarily dismissed, ground his teeth in irritation. Well, that chit would have her comeuppance before too long. He did not like being rebuffed, and she would regret her top-lofty air, he vowed. He owed her a lesson for her treatment of him and he planned to see that she learned he would not be sent to Coventry by a jumped-up actress.

Chapter Seventeen

If Melissa found Theron's attitude puzzling, that gentleman also found himself equally at a loss. To his dismay he spent much more time wondering about Melissa's real feelings for him than was comfortable. The annoying little minx inspired emotions he did not want to contemplate, a combination of irritation, desire and a need to protect, all quite foreign to his nature.

Rare was the female who could interest him for such a time. It must be because he had not been able to lure her into bed. Of course, his mocking suggestions had been no more than a ploy at first, but now he felt something much more compelling, and he did not want to admit how constantly she was in his thoughts, and those thoughts of a romantic nature. Romance had little to do with most of his conquests, satisfactions of his physical desires the paramount reason for pursuing any woman. And Melissa was scarcely a woman, no more than a child really. Of course he felt a responsibility for placing her in the equivocal situation in which she found herself, exposed to danger as well as the undesirable cynosure of sophisticated eyes who believed her his mistress. Did he want her to occupy such a role?

While he mused over the problem he determined to keep his distance, but he was discovering that he missed her inordinately. He would not allow himself to be put in thrall b any female, no matter how enticing. Already his situation wa causing raised eyebrows and wary treatment from his staff a the Grosvenor Street mansion which was the London home o the de Lisles.

Added to his uneasiness was the knowledge that he wa making no progress in unmasking the spy ring. Castlereagh ha invited him to a meeting to discuss the matter and had bee displeased at the lack of progress, suggesting that perhap Theron would be better off pursuing leads in Devon rathe than squiring an actress about town. The minister had not bee impressed with Theron's evidence about the Majestic and onl his own strong persuasions had finally convinced Castlereag that he was on the right track. Still, he must come up with mor proof that, indeed, the theatre was the headquarters of th ring, and that prospect seemed as distant now as it had from th onset of the affair.

Theron spent time at White's drinking and indulging i deep play, neither attempt to banish his problems being ver successful. On the evening of the final performance of th *Beaux Stratagem* he had forced himself not to attend th theatre, repairing to White's yet again, and broaching a thir bottle to banish his cares. The club's aristocratic members many of them long-time acquaintances, kept their distance unwilling to subject themselves to the Marquis' black mood Only one gentleman had no such qualms.

"What's this, Theron, drinking the night away in lonel splendour. I am surprised. I thought you had forsworn suc ramshackle ways," came the voice from a handsome, well-set up man, who crossed the room and extended his hand.

"Valentine, by all that's holy. I did not expect you back fron America so soon. Is all well with you and Sarah?" Theron ros and shook the gentleman's hand. Of an equal height to hi own, he shared the Marquis' dark good looks, but had a mor open smile and a calmer mien.

"Yes, Sarah's in fine fettle, although a little sad at leavin her grandfather. But the Army has need of me, and ordered me home, in expectation of an invasion, I fear," Col. Valentine explained.

"I don't believe Napoleon has that in mind. Instead there is talk of a truce, a ploy to give him time to regroup—and that timid crowd at the War Office will go along with it, I expect," de Lisle said ruefully. "But right now I am involved in another spy chase. I thought when Apsley-Gower was unmasked that that might be the end of this treachery for a while; but, yet a new group is burrowing away at our secrets, and I am having little success at discovering the ringleader," he admitted, loathe to discuss his failure, but needing advice and support from his friend. "Let me fill you in on the scheme I have in hand."

Theron proceeded to tell Valentine all about the Majestic and Melissa's role. The young colonel frowned as he listened but did not interrupt until de Lisle had finished.

"That playbill in your agent's pocket may have been a red herring. It seems slender evidence on which to base an investigation," he offered at the conclusion, ignoring the references to Melissa, for the colonel, who knew only too well Theron's proclivities, hesitated to take him to task for involving the girl.

"Castlereagh agrees with you, but in the face of the lamentable lack of any other pointers we must continue our investigations and hope that more clues will be forthcoming," Theron said, then went on with some reluctance. "I know what a chivalrous chap you are, Lucien, and although you have not said so, I sense your disapproval of my employing Melissa in such a fashion."

Valentine concealed his surprise that Theron could be so concerned about the actress' fate, which was very unlike his usual cynical regard for the ladies. He wondered what his wife would think of the affair, if that was what it was. If Theron had installed the young woman as his mistress in fact as well as a cover for his investigations, he could better understand it.

However, de Lisle would not happily entertain any criticism of his private life even from a good friend. Despite de Lisle's eagerness to unmask the traitors, his undoubted courage and ability, Valentine was in no way reassured that the practiced libertine had altered his attitude toward the fair sex. Sarah Valentine believed that Theron's cynicism was but a cloak for disillusionment which could be banished by the right woman, but Valentine was not so sanguine. The young woman in question might be in danger of not only losing her reputation and her life, but also her heart if she came under the spell of the fascinating rake. At one time Lucien had thought Theron a formidable rival for his own heart's desire, and still sometimes wondered how Sarah could have preferred a rather dull soldier to this skilled seducer. Theron could be trusted in affairs of state but not in affairs of the heart. Valentine did not quite know how to broach his concern without offending the haughty peer.

Theron, understanding Valentine's apprehensions, smiled grimly, then turned the conversation to queries about the Valentines' American visit, and sought information about the political climate there.

"With Thomas Jefferson's election, the colonies might be dragged into an alliance with France," Valentine informed him, "although Hamilton will do his best to thwart his arch enemy's plan in that respect, I have no doubt. I have a rather gloomy report to deliver, I fear."

"I am anxious to hear Sarah's views on the matter," Theron said. "She will have some forthright remarks, I am sure. And how did she feel about leaving her homeland? She is such a fierce little patriot and would not like to hear your reference to her native land as the 'colonies.' Put her up in the boughs in a minute, unless marriage has considerably altered her mercurial temperament."

Lucien grinned. "Not a bit. She's still a little rebel at heart, but we have declared a truce, even though, occasionally, the domestic scene becomes a bit heated. But come and see for yourself and dine with us tomorrow evening."

"Delighted. But only if you will join my theatre party. Melissa is opening in "The Taming of the Shrew" later this week. That will give you an opportunity to see the young woman for yourself and after the performance talk to her at supper. I have asked several other friends to be a member of the party. Sarah will enjoy it as I am sure she feels a kinship to Katherine," he added, laughing at Valentine's rueful agreement. The two men, in good charity with each other, continued to discuss the unhappy political climate and for the moment Theron, pleased at the reunion, was able to banish his black mood in the company of the estimable colonel.

Later that evening, in the Park Street mansion of his wife's grandmother, Lady Ravensham, where the Valentines were staying, Lucien gave Sarah an edited version of Theron's remarks. Marriage had in no way subdued Sarah Valentine's ebullient spirits nor dimmed her looks. The daughter of an American mother and a British father whose tragic romance had ended suddenly in the aftermath of General Howe's occupation of Philadelphia during the late rebellion of George III's colonies, she felt strong ties to her homeland which her alliance with a British officer had not altered.

Her sprightly topaz eyes glimmered with excitement as she heard of de Lisle's latest escapade.

"How enterprising of Theron. Despite his rakish reputation he might yet make a good husband to some fortunate female. He's devilishly attractive. I found him quite hard to resist myself," she teased, hoping to raise her usually calm husband's hackles.

"That will do, my girl. You are a respectable married woman now, and I will have none of this skittish behaviour. You had your chances with Theron. For a time there, I thought he might have offered for you," Lucien smiled, delighted at the picture Sarah made, her burnished chestnut curls and creamy complexion giving no sign of her new matronly status. He and Sarah had endured misunderstanding, danger, and the pull of opposite cultures before they had agreed to settle their differences in a lasting union.

"I doubt that Theron had any but the most dishonourable intentions toward me, which you successfully routed. No, Lucien, I fear that he is a lost cause. I only pray he will not ruin this girl, and claim her heart as well as her virtue. I suspect she is far from an ordinary light skirt, but of rare quality."

Sarah tugged at her curls, musing over Theron's latest excursions into Cupid's toils. Her husband watched her with some amusement. She could not resist a mystery.

"Can it be that you feel some reluctance to meet an actress? Are you insulted that Theron would make such a suggestion?" he asked teasingly.

"Don't be foolish," Sarah retorted. "I care nothing for the ton's rigid rules. But perhaps you wish to protect me from exposure to such a one? She might corrupt me, you know."

"Nonsense, my girl. Don't try my patience with such an idea. I can see you are dying of curiosity, and society's proprieties will not prevent you from getting to the bottom of Theron's actions," he replied, tugging off his cravat.

"I am quite fond of Theron but am under no illusions about him. He is a dangerous threat to any female under eighty. Even Grandma is quite taken by his charms. But I will see for myself when we attend the theatre party, and I will quiz him when he comes to dinner tomorrow. You can rely on that," she concluded with determination.

"Poor Theron, to be chastised by you. He has my sympathy. You are quite ruthless when aroused, as I know to my cost. But enough of the dashing Marquis. Let us to bed," he dismissed de Lisle impatiently, for Sarah's provocative appearance was an invitation to lovemaking and a year of marriage had not stilled his appetite. Sarah smiled mistily, tossed off her peignoir and blew out the bedside candles, only too willing to cooperate with her husband's suggestion.

Chapter Eighteen

Playbills advertising the exciting new actress in "The Taming of the Shrew" had attracted a full house for Melissa's debut. The pit thronged with noisy customers who waited impatiently for the curtain's rising, and even the boxes were crammed with their aristocratic owners who normally considered early attendance quite beyond the pale. Melissa had captured the fleeting notice of the ton, as well as the lower rungs of society. It was considered the fashion to patronize the Majestic and see this rather mysterious new star who had ascended to the dramatic pinnacle hitherto reserved for such luminaries as Mrs. Siddons and Jessica O'Neill. Rumour had it that the sensational Miss Langford, who was the notorious Marquis de Lisle's mistress, was of genteel background and was boldly denying her respectability for love of the Marquis. Certainly she was above the touch of the usual ladybirds who graced the Majestic's stage, and was not only attractive but talented, a rare combination.

Backstage Melissa had no thoughts to spare for her soiled reputation, the French spy ring, or Theron's aloof attitude. She was suffering from the onset of first-night nerves, not soothed by Bessie's stout cheerfulness, nor even Samuel Whitebread's assurances that the evening would prove another laurel in her crown. Her apprehension was fueled by the knowledge that not only Sarah Siddons, but Charles and John Kemble, fresh from their triumphs at the Haymarket would be among the audience, their theatre dark for the evening so that the famed actors could assess this new rival. What could she be thinking, exposing her slender ability to the eyes of such formidable and popular members of the profession?

Since her entrance did not occur until Act II she had more than enough time to fret and distrust the wisdom of attempting such a demanding role. Her hand shook as she applied the makeup and she paid no heed to Bessie's nostrums.

"You are a foolish one, Miss Melissa. There is no reason for you to be nervous, for you are well prepared and the house is full of anticipation. You look such a treat it will not matter if your skills falter," Bessie comforted. Then in an attempt to turn Melissa's attention away from the ordeal ahead, "You would be better served if you worried about the Marquis. He has brought your reputation in bad odour. I know everyone expects actresses to be loose in their behaviour, but many are of the utmost respectability. Still, if you consort with such as that one, no matter how innocent, you will be suspected of being his latest mistress in keeping." Bessie had in no way abated her disapproval of the Marquis, although she was certain her charge had not given way to his lecherous advances.

"Oh, do not chivy me about his lordship now. It's of no matter. I am shaking with fright and you wish to discuss my morals. Believe me I have more to fear from this blasé audience than I do from the Marquis," Melissa scoffed, refusing to allow thoughts of that enigmatic gentleman to distract her from the serious matter at hand.

"I see he has quite showered you with flowers, although at least he had not the effrontery to include more expensive gifts in his offerings," Bessie muttered, convinced that jewelry would signal the evilness of his designs. "Not yet, at any rate. But there now, my lamb, I didn't mean to upset you any more. Forgive Bessie."

"It's all right, Bessie. I know you are only concerned for me, but I promise you, this acting career is only temporary. I do not intend to make it my life," Melissa sighed. Right now even gloomy Hawksmoor and Horace Hawksley seemed an envied refuge from her present anguish.

"Ten minutes, Miss Langford," came the call boy's cry. Melissa wiped her wet hands and looked critically at her costume of green silk, styled appropriately in the mode of the Renaissance Padua. "Well, I cannot cower here any longer. Now what is my first line. I have forgotten completely. Oh, yes, 'Of all thy suitors here I charge thee tell'," she muttered and rose to take her place in the wings.

"Good luck, Miss Melissa—not that you need it," Bessie offered bracingly, and gave her a big hug, careful not to disarrange either her makeup or costume.

"Thank you, Bessie. Let us hope we both still have jobs at the end of this fiasco." Melissa smiled tentatively, appreciating her dresser's attempts to raise her spirits, but aghast at what faced her. This was no blithe, silly, Dorinda, a Fraquahar farce, but Shakespeare, and neither Juliet nor Ophelia had put her in such a taking.

Her entrance was greeted with loud approval. For a minute, startled, she lost the character. But heartened by the appreciation she spoke her first vituperative lines to her sister, Bianca. From then on she held the audience in the palm of her hand, for in truth she was a perfect Katherine, at first violent and unbiddable, but then falling deeply in love with her tormenting husband, until in the last act she could say with heart-stirring sincerity,

> "I am ashamed that women are so simple
> To offer war, when they should kneel for peace;

Or seek for rule, supremacy, and sway,
When they are bound to serve, love and obey."

The audience greeted the end of the performance with gratifying enthusiasm, cheering wildly as Melissa and Rathbone, then the full cast took their bows. Emerging from Padua and the cloak of the tempestuous Kate, Melissa felt a triumphant relief. Not only had "The Shrew" proved a resounding personal success, but the cast in general had excelled itself. As she swept low to receive the accolades bestowed upon her, her eyes for the first time went to Theron's box, which seemed crowded with strangers. She smiled in the general direction of the Marquis, but did not allow her glance to linger, for she noticed that the Comtesse was among his guests and this raised her ire. She was becoming as contrary as Kate, she decided, The curtain dropped for the final time, and she released Rathbone's hand.

Turning to her leading man, she congratulated him. "You made a splendid Petruchio, Robert. I think the whole thing went off magnificently, don't you?" she asked, admiring his efforts. He had certainly surprised her with the sincerity of his characterization. His handsome clear-cut profile, golden hair and manly stature had usually been enough to win the audience, but tonight he had extended himself, really acted his role without the usual posturings she had found so annoying.

"I have you to thank, dear lady. Your Kate demanded my best," Rathbone preened. "I think we make a fine team. Here's to many other successful efforts," he continued, raising her hand to his lips and kissing it in homage.

"If only he would confine his talents to the stage." Melissa found his posturings faintly repellent, but she had to concede he had portrayed Petruchio with fire and realism. Congratulating him again, she walked off to her dressing room. Now that the ordeal was behind her, Melissa realized how exhausted she was, and still ahead was the celebratory supper. All she wanted was to creep off to Stanhope Gate and her bed, but that was impossible. She must somehow summon the energy to cope with Theron and his guests.

Bessie, waiting eagerly to congratulate her, clucked when she saw Melissa's pale, drawn face and drooping shoulders. Hurrying to her side, she gave her an affectionate hug, and then prepared to remove her costume.

"I will try to keep them all out until you have time to rest a bit. You look tired to death, but let's get you out of this pesky dress and into your dressing gown." As she spoke Bessie was busily accompanying her words with action.

Melissa sighed. Where was the exhilaration which actors found so thrilling, the reason for their work and talent? The plaudits of the crowds and the applause should make up for all the nervous anticipation and the hours of rehearsal. Obviously, she lacked the egotism which inspired Rathbone or other members of the company. Her real métier was not the stage but some comfortable country house where she could lead a life of domestic tranquility. But such a future seemed more distant than ever. When she had run from her guardian and Algy, she had never dreamed she would end up on a stage, exposed to the world in such a fashion. Her disturbing thoughts were interrupted ruthlessly by a knock on the door.

"I'll soon get rid of your admirers, Miss Melissa. Don't you fret now but finish removing that makeup. It will spoil your lovely complexion if you leave it on too long," Bessie advised, hurrying to intercept the caller. It was the Marquis looking his splendid self in his evening clothes.

"Good evening, Bessie. May I come in and congratulate our star? I promise I will be brief," he smiled engagingly at the dresser, intent on overcoming her protective instincts.

"Well, for a moment, my lord. But Miss Melissa is exhausted, not fit for anything but her bed." Bessie admitted him grudgingly.

"Oh, I think she must honour us with her presence. All of London is waiting to applaud her." He crossed the room to where Melissa stood awaiting him.

"I don't need to tell you how marvelous you were, infant. You carried all before you. I had no idea you had become so accomplished, although Kate is a sympathetic character, much in your own mode," he teased, raising her chin with his strong fingers and gazing at her with admiration and some other undefined light in his eyes.

"Thank you, Theron. I must admit I was frightened half out of my mind, but thank goodness we brought it off," Melissa answered. Her eyes riveted to his, a warm glow stealing over her as she realized how much his approval mattered to her, and how relieved she was to see his black humour had disappeared. "And I must thank you for your flowers." She waved toward the numerous bouquets of yellow roses filling the room with their fragrance.

"Not at all. You deserve an even more extravagant tribute, but I doubted if you would receive it before. Please wear this trifling present this evening, and I do not want to hear a lot of rubbishy objections," he said, drawing a velvet box from his pocket, and presenting it to her. She gasped as she saw the magnificent amythest and diamond necklace within. He took it from her and fastened it about her neck, his hands lingering and sending a frisson of delight through her.

"Now I don't want to hear objections about my evil intentions with this gift. It is only a small token of my esteem and my gratitude for all your help. Now into your gown. Our guests are waiting, and we must be off to the celebratory supper." He smiled down at her, for once neither mocking nor cynical. "A glass of champagne is what you need to restore your spirits and then you can resort to your usual quarrelsome humour toward me. I have quite missed our wrangles," he teased, enjoying the flush that rose on her creamy cheeks.

"You are impossible, Theron, but thank you. I will accept the necklace since you offer it so unexceptionally, but you know, of course, it will only confirm the gossips as to our relationship. Perhaps that was what you intended?" she asked a bit shyly, reluctant to disturb this new mood of amity.

"There you go again. But I am in too good charity with you this evening to accept your challenge. Now I will be off. Hurry with your primpings because I do not like to keep my horses standing." He bowed, grinning at her irritation at his high-handedness.

Fingering the necklace with a wistful hope that it signaled a change in their partnership, Melissa changed into a violet silk gown that accented her eyes, and that set off the necklace to perfection. Looking in the mirror at her sparkling eyes and trim figure she felt well armoured for the evening ahead.

Chapter Nineteen

Sweeping into the Clarendon on Theron's arm some time later, Melissa was almost overwhelmed by the enthusiastic reception she received from the distinguished company who had also chosen the hotel for supper. Sarah Siddons and Charles Kemble, secure in their own reputations, were among the first to toast her. The divine Sarah, now no longer in her first youth but captivating for all that, embraced Melissa extravagantly and welcomed her into the band of thespians of which she had long been queen. The courtly Charles tendered his own approval in acceptable fashion, and was succeeded by a host of gallants who wished to meet the actress. Theron shielded her adroitly from the crowd descending upon them, and there were few, noting his protective attitude, willing to argue with his proprietory claim.

He had reserved a private room for the supper, and on entering the parlour, Melissa saw that not only the Comtesse but Sir Harry Acton were awaiting her. Also rising to greet her was a handsome dark-haired man of soldierly bearing whose arm was held by a lovely young woman with chestnut hair and warm topaz eyes, dressed elegantly in a gown of *eau de nile* silk.

"Melissa, may I present two friends of mine, Col. and Mrs. Lucien Valentine, who have just returned from an extended stay in America. You and Sarah should have much in common, both being of an argumentative and independent nature," Theron mocked as he introduced her to the couple.

"Pay no attention to Theron, my dear Miss Langford. He cannot brook the idea of any female not falling before him in humble submission," Sarah said, smiling kindly at Melissa. "And may we offer our admiration for your sprightly portrayal of Kate, always one of my favorite heroines, although her craven surrender to her husband at the end quite disappoints me."

"I quite agree, Mrs. Valentine," Melissa responded, quite liking this addition to their party, "but then Shakespeare being naught but a beset man, had to assuage his audiences by bringing her under Petruchio's thumb, I fear."

"I am afraid Theron, you have met your match, and I sympathize, having so much trouble with my own termagant," Lucien Valentine contributed, amused by the exchange between his wife and the young actress.

"You were jolly good tonight, Miss Langford. You even convinced me of Kate's reversal." Sir Harry joined the group.

Perforce the Comtesse had to add her own congratulations, although she could not resist a sting in her remarks. "I have always thought Kate was too foolish to fight against her best interests, but we poor females are often reluctant to submit to our natural masters. Don't you agree, Miss Langford?"

"Natural masters? Natural adversaries, I would say. But enough of Kate. I am ravenous and Theron has promised me champagne. Do I see lobster patties?" Melissa ignored the Comtesse's suggestive remarks and inimical appraisal, turning to the supper table.

The party continued on a light note, only the Comtesse behaving with a certain aloofness. She had immediately noticed Melissa's magnificent necklace and conceded that the young actress had scored there, her own reactions based on avarice rather than affection toward any gentleman with whom she consented to dally. But the Valentines and Sir Harry more than made up for Aimee's reserve. The Comtesse was too clever to show her jealousy outwardly, which she knew would only annoy Theron; but she determined before too long a time, to gain her revenge on the chit who had replaced her in his affections. Although he had left her bed, he still generously provided her with funds to supplement her meager resources and she had to tread warily. Soon, however, she would not be dependent upon him, and could deal with both Theron and this upstart little country girl, as they deserved. Adept at hiding her emotions, the Comtesse now turned her charms upon Sir Harry, who responded with practiced gallantry, disguising his distaste for the Comtesse's company.

"Will you now remain in England, Colonel?" Melissa asked Col. Valentine, as they availed themselves of a sumptuous array of delicacies, including the much prized lobster patties.

"I obey the whims of the War Department, Miss Langford, but we hope to settle in for a long stay. Sarah's grandmother misses her sorely when she is absent, and I must say a spell of London's delights would be most welcome. I fear Sarah often yearns for her homeland, but she is quite stouthearted about her exile and has lost much of her aversion to redcoats. But it took some persuasion on my part as she is a devoted little rebel," he smiled fondly upon his wife. Melissa, wistfully envious of the pair's devotion, so different from most London ton marriages, wondered if she would ever attract such affection.

Questioning the colonel, Melissa learned of his wife's background, and realized that indeed Sarah must love her colonel inordinately to abandon grandfather, friends, and country to accompany him wherever his duty called. She found them, in their old fashioned conjugality, rather odd friends for the cynical and arrogant Marquis who scorned such virtues, but she warmed to them both. Sir Harry, too, was such a sincere and forthright gentleman, quite a contrast to the Marquis, that he, too, seemed an odd choice for a trusted companion, but he obviously admired the Marquis and the regard was reciprocated. Only the Comtesse's presence marred the congenial evening, and Melissa decided to ignore the lady, much as she wondered about Theron's continuing interest in Aimee de Frontons.

Later that evening, as he was escorting her back to Stanhope Gate, Theron explained the inclusion of the Comtesse in the intimate party. For once he did not mock or sneer, and Melissa decided that although he could not be trusted in matters of the heart, his determination to expose the spy ring engaged his most passionate interest. For that she could almost forgive him his other transgressions.

"I have suspected for some time that Aimee is meddling in matters which are highly suspect," he said. "While she is far from being as clever as she thinks, she is greedy, vengeful and conceited, all qualities prone to lead her into trouble. She desperately desires the return of the de Fronton estates and would cooperate with the devil himself if she thought she could secure them for herself. She thought to lull me with her bed-worthy charms into marriage but I am not so easily trapped."

Melissa feared Theron might have taken a toss over the luscious Aimee, although she could hardly believe the Frenchwoman had succeeded where others, equally seductive had failed. And in this assessment she was correct.

"Do you think she is selling secrets? Where would she discover them? I am sure you are too experienced to give her any information." Melissa watched his grim face, but failed to read any expression but cool indifference in his hooded eyes.

"Quite right, infant, I am too canny to be cozened into indiscretions, no matter how appealing the enticement. I may be wrong, but she is hiding something. And I will discover it," he promised grimly, boding ill for the lovely Comtesse.

"Well, while you are plumbing her secrets, I have no doubt you are still enjoying her charms," Melissa replied tartly, not liking the pictures which rose unbidden of Theron practicing his expertise in the Comtesse's boudoir.

"Ah, a spy's work often takes him into strange environs. I will not deny the pleasures of pursuing the ladies adds a certain spice to the game," he mocked outrageously, noting Melissa' fiery cheeks and delighted at how easily she rose to his bait. Bu then turning to more pressing matters. "Incidentally, thought I recognized that bounder of an officer who wa pursuing you in Bath riding away from her door the other day Is the Major in town?"

"He appeared in the Green Room the other evening, but rebuffed him with Sir Harry's help. His regiment has bee moved to London, so you might have glimpsed him, but I doub he is up to the Comtesse's touch. Although he seems to hav plenty of blunt, certainly more than an officer's pay," sh mused. "What a dreadful man he is."

"Yes, beware of him, my poppet. I fear he is yet another wh has designs on your virtue. Does this mean that your mor respectable suitor is also in town, the estimable Perciva Ashburton?"

"I suppose so, although I have not been honoured with hi company. Percy is a dear boy, and I am quite fond of him," Melissa offered, hoping to see some reaction.

"Doing it too brown, my dear. I am hardly in a taking ove your preference for that downy cheeked lad. Much too callo for you. He would be under your thumb in a trice an completely cowed. Not a good prospect for wedded bliss," h scoffed contemptuously.

"What would you know about wedded bliss, my lord?" Melissa retorted. "You are the last person whose advice would take."

"Touché, Melissa. A hit!" he said, not one whit disturbed b her indignation. "And what example of the much overrate state of matrimony can you offer?"

"Well, there are your friends the Valentines. They seen very happy, still in love, and certainly she is far from under hi thumb. He respects her," she concluded.

"True, the Valentines are an exception. But Sarah is not i the usual mode of society's misses. She is a lively little rebel and led Lucien a merry chase. Almost did herself in, toc sticking her pretty little nose into matters far better left to her lord and master."

But before Melissa could give a hot retort to his condescension, they arrived at Stanhope Gate. He assisted her from the barouche and escorted her to the door, bowing low over her hand.

"You were a triumph this evening, Melissa. Perhaps it would be best if you concentrated on your acting and left the spying to me. I was reminded by your mention of Sarah Valentine that you might be in real danger with this scheme we are running. I would not want anything to happen to you. My conscience is uneasy at the thought."

"Pooh, my lord. Don't pretend to have a conscience. You are a ruthless, selfish libertine, concerned only with your own interests. Don't play the role of a concerned kindly protector. It's not your style. I am the actress in this partnership. I intend to pursue our investigations. But thank you for the lovely supper, and the introductions to the Valentines. I liked them, and am happy to think I am not so sunk in infamy that they would snub me. Normally the ton does not receive lightskirts, I know." She spoke lightly, but beneath her cheerful banter Theron sensed a concern over her disreputable position, exposed to the world as his mistress.

"The Valentines are a sensible pair," he said, frowning. "They are not bound by the silly strictures of the ton. They will be good friends to you, and Lord knows, you need them. Now off to your chaste couch. I will be around tomorrow to take you driving, and bring some healthy glow to those wan cheeks. Children need lots of fresh air and exercise," he joked, trying to lighten the atmosphere, but then, almost with reluctance, he took her in his arms, and gave her a gentle kiss, rousing all kinds of undefined feelings in them both.

Melissa entered the house, willing herself not to look after him. He had certainly disturbed her tranquillity, and endangered any plans she had to drop off easily to sleep.

Chapter Twenty

Both Melissa and Theron's frustration over the lack of progress in uncovering the French spy ring intensified as the King's troops massed on the Sussex shore, in expectation of a momentary invasion by France's bellicose First Consul. While His Majesty's ministers worried over the Nation's preparedness, George III retreated into one of his manic cycles and his son again became Regent, adding to both the military and civil administrators' problems. The turmoil in the country only inspired renewed pleasure seeking among the members of London society and Melissa's popularity reached dizzying heights.

Many a beau or gallant wrote poems to her violet eyes and sun streaked curls. They besieged her carriage when she rode to and from the theatre, and even camped relentlessly outside Stanhope Gate hoping for a glimpse of their goddess. Melissa took the whole rigamarole in good part, knowing that within the month a new fashion would engage most of the bucks' attention. She wondered how they could behave so frivolously when their country was in danger, but from the rumour about London, one would never know the country was at war. Melissa was spared the more annoying attentions of the rakes who thronged the theatre nightly, because few of them wished to tangle with the Marquis de Lisle, who continued his interest in the actress. He appeared, in truth, to be completely besotted by the new star, although his few intimates found that hard to believe, knowing from his lurid past that de Lisle never became permanently enthralled with any female. But whatever his interest in Melissa, he did not entertain rivals complaisantly, and London's beaux had to admire the actress from a respectable distance.

So intense was Theron's involvement with Melissa that members of White's began to lay down bets in that club's famed wager book as to the ultimate outcome of the affair. Traditionally, actresses were regarded as little better than the ballet dancers at Covent Garden or the pretty horsebreakers who flaunted their attractions in Hyde Park, and were available to the highest bidder. The Prince Regent's brother had settled down at Bushey Park with the Irish actress, Dorothea Jordon, who produced a bevy of illegitimate FitzClarences in between appearances on the stage. But the Duke of Clarence's domestic fidelity had not really brought actresses into respectability. True, Sarah Siddons was accepted as a lady, and the playwriter Richard Sheridan had married a woman who sang on stage, much to his family's dismay. Occasionally an aristocrat stooped to wed an actress as had Lord Derby whose preference for Eliza Farren had shocked society when he made her his Comtesse. But rare was the actress who married into the ton, and few believed Melissa would bring it off, especially with such a practiced seducer as de Lisle, who had cleverly avoided the pitfalls of matrimony, and shunned the company of debutantes. Several of the more curious members of the ton approached Lucien Valentine hoping to discover if de Lisle was, indeed, about to enter the parson's trap, but they received little change from that astute gentleman.

In the privacy of the Ravensham house on Park Street, Lucien was more forthcoming. Toying with his wine glass over the remains of dinner one evening, some days after their arrival in London and the Clarendon supper, Lucien was questioning his wife.

"Do you think de Lisle is fairly caught this time, Sarah? Very ungallant of him not to wear the willow for you, my pet," he chaffed.

"Nonsense, Lucien," she retorted, "there was never any possibility of that. Gossips would have it that Theron is a rake of the first water, but I don't believe it. He always treated me with the utmost propriety, at least, almost always." She laughed at her husband's raised eyebrow.

Lady Ravensham, Sarah's grandmother, entered the conversation, eager to hear the latest about the Marquis, having known the young peer from childhood.

"Could he really be serious about this actress? He is completely impervious to society's good opinion and will follow his own bent no matter how the scandal stirs. Is she as respectable as you have given me to believe? If so, she has ruined herself irretrievably by this alliance. And I fear Theron will not be beguiled to the altar no matter how much he holds her in affection."

"Grandma!" Sarah exclaimed. "You ought to be shocked. I fear you have appalling tendency to forgive that rapscallion any vice."

Lady Ravensham smiled benignly. "I would wish for Theron to marry a woman who cares for him, actress or not. He desperately needs an unselfish love to steady him. If he were ever truly in love I feel he could be tamed by the power of his feelings. He is not basically evil, you know, only disillusioned and unfortunate in his family background." A gentle white haired dowager of some seventy years, she was inclined to view affairs of the heart with a romantic sensibility, not borne out by her own experience.

"Well, Theron can take care of himself," Lucien said. "I fear Melissa Langford is much too vulnerable. She is not quite what I expected. Certainly she comes of genteel birth, no matter what her profession. There is a mystery about the girl and about her relationship with Theron. She does not behave like a lightskirt, and his attitude toward her is not that of a man toward his mistress."

"Yes, I wonder how they met and what induced her to play such a role," Sarah mused. "What could her family be thinking, allowing her to be so used? I vow her birth is quite creditable. She has all the appearance of a lady."

"I can see your brain is busy, Sarah. Do you feel this a cause worthy of your interference? What have you in mind?" Lucien smiled at his wife, knowing her susceptible heart was stirred by Melissa Langford's situation.

"There must be some way to discover who she really is and why she has come to such a pass. I believe the affair is worthy of my investigation," Sarah decided.

"Oh, my dear," Lady Ravensham chided, "it is really none of your business. Leave well enough alone. You have such a tendency to embroil yourself in dangerous situations. Lucien, you must restrain her," she pleaded helplessly, seeing the stubbornness on her granddaughter's resolute face.

Lucien snorted ungallantly. "Quite beyond me, Lady Ravensham. You should know from past experience there is no holding Sarah when she gets the bit in her mouth. A very aggressive lady, my dear wife."

"Well, I make no promises, but I will keep a close eye on the pair, and let you know the results of my inquiries," Sarah promised. She was most intrigued by the possibility of some judicious meddling, and her kind heart was touched by Melissa's position.

Lucien looked at Lady Ravensham and smiled a bit grimly. They both knew that Sarah could not resist a challenge, and this particular one was too promising to ignore. Lucien consoled himself with the thought that the most determined matchmakers had failed to capture Theron in the past, and even his enterprising Sarah might find the task beyond her.

"The Taming of the Shrew" continued to attract crowded

houses, much to George Whitebread's delight. Melissa began to feel more comfortable in the role, her first night nerves reduced to mere flutterings before her initial entrance. She now felt more at ease with the company, too, beginning to know them as individuals rather than just a supporting cast. Most of them responded to Melissa's overtures enthusiastically, but Alison Andrews avoided her. When forced into each others company, Alison treated her with a cool deference which Melissa found impossible to breach. Melissa at last shrugged and acquiesced, deciding that the actress would never find her acceptable. Everyone cannot like me, Melissa chided herself, and Alison has more reason than most to take me in dislike. I am becoming too puffed up, she thought, spoiled by the adulation of the Majestic's patrons, no doubt.

There was little hope that Theron's interest in her would engender any conceit, Melissa ruefully conceded. For all the gossip and the role of entranced protector he played in public, he treated her more like an older brother or indulgent uncle in private. Even the occasional careless embraces he had bestowed on her before had now come to an abrupt end. Bored probably with my naive charms, Melissa decided, and now trapped into this masquerade because of the spy ring. There, too, I have proved most unaccommodating, not discovering what I was placed in the Majestic to find. No wonder he is disgruntled, Melissa chuckled, then sobered. However she might want to put Theron in a taking, this was a serious business, and soon she must admit she had come to a standstill, unable to discover the culprit, and bring an end to this game they were playing.

If Theron's treatment lacked a certain warmth, Melissa could not complain about another of her cavaliers. Young Percy Ashburton had called, smiling with humble gratitude when she accepted his tentative invitations, and not resenting her more frequent refusals. He was in considerable awe of the Marquis, and although he never quizzed Melissa about the peer's presence in her life, even as naive as he was, he could have been in little doubt as to what role de Lisle played.

Theron, for his part, barely noticed the young man, Melissa thought. He certainly did not view him as a rival, and how could he, she conceded, for upon every suit Theron outshone the young officer. Theron had even ceased to tease her about Percy as a possible husband, much to her chagrin, and seemed relieved the young man was on hand to play escort when his responsibilities prevented him from occupying that post. Rather like a nanny relinquishing her charge to a nursery governess on her day off, Melissa decided in some annoyance. She was quite weary of being treated like a twelve-year-old by Theron.

Percy might have been inexperienced, but he had enough wit to realize that his commanding officer, the egregious Major Gratton, had unsavoury plans for Melissa. The Major chaffed Percy in the most vulgar way in the mess about his pursuit of the actress, and the two almost came to blows one evening when the Major had drunk more than his usual two bottles. So disgusted was Percy by the officer's constant badgering and disgusting illusions, he had put in for a transfer from the 14th Foot, but with the invasion scare so prevalent it did not appear on the cards.

Melissa, who had dismissed the Major from her thoughts, would have been surprised to learn he had neither forgotten nor forgiven her rebuffs. He had not appreciated the chivying he had received from his fellow officers in the mess, and Percy Ashburton's success only exacerbated his anger. He brooded over his plans for revenge, and set about plotting a scheme to bring the chit to her knees. Inadvertently, Percy had let drop some pertinent information about the Marquis' former mistress, the Comtesse de Frontons, and Gratton, received in some of the ton's drawing rooms, was able to pursue the matter. By contrivance he managed to meet the luscious Aimee, and within days the two had formed an alliance. It was indeed Major Gratton's curricle Theron had seen leaving Aimee's house one afternoon. Both the Comtesse and the

Major felt they had a score to settle with Melissa, and wished to devise a scheme to bring about her ruin. That their bargain led to a compact of a different sort was a bonus in which the unscrupulous pair took a great satisfaction.

"I fear, Major, that it is unwise for us to be seen together. It might give rise to suspicion," Aimee protested one afternoon when Gratton had called upon her.

"I suppose you are right, my dear Comtesse. But we need to meet to lay our schemes," Gratton smirked, a bit annoyed for he had hopes of cementing their relationship in her boudoir. She was a seductive lady and he had never turned away from any female who promised amourous delights.

"We will contrive another place. But it is most important that Theron does not discover we are friends," Aimee said with determination. The Major, although well-born and seemingly deep in the pockets, did not attract her in that way, although she was nothing loathe to encourage him to ensure his cooperation with her plans.

"I know of a smart little inn, not too far from town which might serve," Gratton smirked.

Aimee frowned. She had no doubts about her ability to handle the officer should he become pressing, but his suggestion did not please her.

"I think, perhaps, it would be as well if we confined our meetings to a public place," she said sharply. "Vauxhall is ideal, for we can both visit the gardens without suspicion. However, what we must put in train now is our chief objective, to discredit Melissa, both in her profession and in Theron's eyes. The Marquis is a downey bird and not easily gulled."

"You know best, dear lady."

Aimee smiled smugly. When she had finished with the minx neither the Majestic's impresario nor Theron would have anything more to do with her.

Gratton and the Comtesse parted well pleased with themselves.

Chapter Twenty-One

"Really, Bessie, you must not come to the theatre this evening. Your cold is worse and you have a fever. I am not so helpless that I cannot dress without you. What you need is to take a soothing posset and repair to your bed," Melissa urged her dresser.

Indeed Bessie looked miserable, her nose red, her eyes watering, caught in the grip of a furious cold.

"I hate to desert you, Miss Melissa, but, 'tis true, I do not feel quite the thing," Bessie replied, giving evidence of the truth of her words with a ferocious sneeze.

The two were in Melissa's chamber in Stanhope Gate, Melissa preparing to set out for the theatre. Rain was falling in a determined drizzle, only emphasizing the wisdom of Melissa's advice to her dresser.

"The Marquis is escorting me this evening, and I will come to no harm," Melissa said soothingly. "I am not some timid little miss who needs protecting every minute, you know."

"You always need protecting from his lordship. I grant that he has acted properly up to now, but he might just be biding his time. He is a rascally sort, mark my words. And who knows what he has in mind for you," Bessie sniffed, her suspicions of the Marquis not abated in the weeks she had been installed at Stanhope Gate. "His presence has endangered your reputation, no matter how unwarranted," she concluded.

"Oh, Bessie, you refine to much on his lorship's intentions. He treats me very well, and I have reason to believe he does not think of me in that way," Melissa argued, somewhat wistfully.

"He's a clever devil, and you are but a babe in the woods. All of London thinks you are in his keeping."

"Yes, well, as long as we know the truth, it matters not what all of London believes," Melissa responded, annoyed. "Not another word, now. And I promise to come home directly from the theatre, so you will have no need to worry. Come now, admit you will be better off in your bed."

Finally she prevailed and Bessie retired, still muttering to her bed. Melissa, wrapped in a warm pelisse, for the September evening was wet and chilly, went down to receive Theron, wondering if his mood would be a bit more approachable this evening. Lately he had been brooding and uncommunicative whenever they met, which was not often. Perhaps he was worried about this spy business and had little time for other concerns. If so, he was not confiding in her, and this caused Melissa disquiet. They could not continue the way they were, and must soon have a confrontation as to their next move in this dangerous game. Feeling uncertain and indignant over Theron's recent humour, Melissa greeted him with reserve.

"Good evening, Theron. Bessie is not coming with us this evening. She is not feeling well, and I have sent her to bed. Shall we be off? I will need some additional time this evening since she will not be on hand to assist me."

"So the indomitable Bessie is deserting us," Theron said lightly, running an appreciative gaze over Melissa, who looked enchanting as usual, the sapphire blue of her cloak matching her gown of the latest mode. "That must worry her to death. She does not approve of me, I fear, despite all my attempts to cozen her."

Shaking her head, Melissa smiled but did not rise to his mocking tones.

They had little conversation on the way to the Majestic,

Theron sitting moodily beside her in the landau. Usually he drove his curricle himself, but tonight because of the inclement weather he had perforce to join her in the covered carriage.

At the Majestic he accompanied her to her dressing room, surprising Melissa, because lately he had deposited her at the stage door and then gone about his affairs. He had not been attending the performances, having seen the play numerous times. In the snug room, Melissa removed her cloak and settled down to prepare for her role, while he stretched his long length in a chair and watched her with a brooding expression.

"I wonder how much longer you will be satisfied with this acting role, Melissa. Bessie is quite right, you know. It is not a proper occupation for you, and she's right, too, that you should distrust me. I dragged you into this play acting because it suited my selfish purposes." Theron frowned, his glance roaming over Melissa as her hands fluttered nervously over the toiletries on the dressing table. She kept her head averted so that it was difficult for him to gauge her expression.

"Surely you are not concerned about my reputation at this late date, Theron, or is it that you are put out to have earned the credit for seducing me in your usual adroit fashion without enjoying the pleasures of my bed," she said saucily, not willing to let him see how his words dismayed her. The thought of abandoning her theatrical career did not disturb her as much as the thought that when she did her contact with Theron would disappear, too. Could she be falling in love with this cynical womanizer who was incapable of offering her the kind of love she craved? Rallying her spirits, she suppressed the fear that she had already allowed herself to feel an emotion for Theron which he would never welcome except on a very temporary basis. And that would never do for her, she knew.

He answered her in that sarcastic tone she had come to dread. "Are you so sure they would be pleasures, infant? I think I have told you often that virgins are not really worth the effort."

Just as she expected, any mention of a real relationship between them caused him to retreat into that cynical mocking attitude which she despised. Refusing to acknowledge how his words pained her, she burrowed distractedly among the toiletries on her dressing table.

"I cannot find my makeup. I lent the jar to Molly and see she has forgotten to return it. I will just pop into her room and retrieve it. Won't be a moment," she explained and rushed out of the room before he could wound her further with his callous words. She was not much of an actress if she could not hide her dismay at his rejection, she decided ruefully, hurrying down the hall.

The corridor was strangely silent. Most of the company had not yet made an appearance to prepare for the evening's performance and in the somber hall her footsteps echoed eerily. She was a prey to odd emotions, engendered by Theron's harsh treatment, and an increasing feeling that she struggled helplessly in a morass of loneliness. She drew a deep breath, trying to still her pounding heart and hesitated a moment to regain her composure before knocking on Molly's door. She did not want the character actress to ply her with questions, and she hoped that Alison was not within as she felt unable to cope with that devious lady just now. Hearing no response she pushed open the door. Alison was there, certainly, but sprawled across the floor, her body at an unnatural angle, her face beneath her golden curls a horrible mottled colour, her eyes distended. Melissa choked down a scream, stupefied with terror. Backing away hurriedly from the dreadful scene, she turned and fled back to the safety of her own dressing room.

"Theron, Theron, come quickly, something has happened to Alison. She's . . . she's . . . I think she's dead," Melissa choked out the words as she threw herself at the Marquis who had risen to his feet and received her slight form as it sought the comfort of his embrace. Melissa shook with the effort at self-control as she tried to explain the gruesome sight she had

:umbled upon. She was near to fainting.

"Hush, poppet, it's all right," he murmured soothingly. Come, sit down here, and try to compose yourself. Damn it, hat you need is brandy. But this will have to do." He poured er a glass of water from a carafe on the table and held it to her 'an lips. She gulped it down, hardly aware of what she was oing.

"It's a nightmare. She looked so . . . so . . ." Melissa could ot bear the picture which seemed imprinted on her eyes. "Oh, o go see. It cannot be true."

"Rest here, that's a good girl, and I will investigate." Theron ut her gently on the chair, stroking back her disheveled hair, nd patting her shoulder, appalled at her condition.

"Who could have attacked her and left her so? Oh, Theron, ou must go and investigate. I will be fine," she said bravely, aking a valiant effort to subdue her trembling.

"That's my brave girl. I will be just a moment," he said, orried at her wan face and tear-filled eyes.

The corridor was still silent. No one appeared to question his resence as he entered the actresses' dressing room. He knelt y the girl, feeling for a pulse, although he had little doubt, eeing her purpled face and bulging eyes, that she was indeed ead. He noted the scarf wound tightly about her neck, not by er own hand. She had been strangled, murdered, probably urprised by her attacker as she was changing into her ostume, for she wore a peach silk negligee over her chemise.

He looked about the room carefully, grimacing with epugnance. Although he had seen dead bodies before, the ight of a young and lovely young woman in such a condition vas far from pleasant. Restraining his distaste he examined her ody more closely and noticed that one hand was concealed by er body. Moving the dead girl gingerly he saw that her fingers 'ere clutching a scrap of paper. Cooly he unclenched the tiffening fingers and removed the crumbled shred which roved to be the top of a Majestic playbill advertising "The 'aming of the Shrew." Much like the advertisement he had

seen once before, and in similar circumstances, he remembered, in the pocket of the agent murdered on the Devon coast.

He put the paper in his pocket, his face drawn into a thoughtful frown. This could not be a coincidence. Somehow this paltry little actress was involved in the conspiracy he was trying so hard to uncover. Well, there was nothing he could do for the poor girl now. She was beyond help. His chief concern must be to find her murderer for then the leader of the spy ring would be revealed. He had no doubt that the killer of Alison Andrews was the man he sought. But his first responsibility was to Melissa, and how he could protect her from the scandal and horror which would accompany this death. Why had he ever allowed her to enter upon this masquerade? She could have been the victim instead of this poor girl lying there.

Theron, usually cool and ruthless in the face of danger, felt suddenly powerless and confused. Murder could not be hidden. This meant the Bow Street runners would be called into the case, and Melissa's discovery of the body might bring her under suspicion. Well, by God, he would protect her. His first duty was to inform the authorities. Then Whitebread must be told, and tonight's performance cancelled. Most of all Melissa must be kept out of the affair. Somehow he would contrive to shield her.

Giving a last glance at Alison Andrews' grotesque body, he left the room, quietly closing the door behind him, locking it and pocketing the key.

Chapter Twenty-Two

Although Theron insisted to George Whitebread that the Bow Street runners be called in to investigate Alison Andrews' death, he intended to keep the reins of the investigation in his own hands. Whitebread himself, although he professed to be shocked, seemed more concerned over the effect of the murder on his box office receipts, a callous indifference which did not surprise Theron who cynically accepted that the impresario's first responsibility was to his theatre.

On Theron's insistence Whitebread called the company together in the Green Room and told them of the tragedy. They had been aware on their arrival at the Majestic to prepare for that evening's performance that something was afoot, but Theron believed he might discover a tell-tale reaction if the announcement was made to the cast in a formal manner. But only Molly behaved emotionally, her tender heart touched by Alison's fate. Robert Rathbone seemed almost as indifferent as Whitebread. The poor girl had obviously not endeared herself to her fellow thespians. As for the rest of the company, the members looked upon the murder with dismay, but it did not seem to affect them personally. Their chief interest lay in how the actress's death would alter their own careers. They did not appear frightened of being suspected. And Theron although realizing that acting was their profession, could not discern that any of them were hiding guilty knowledge.

Rathbone spitefully offered his own assessment of the situation, "I understand that Miss Langford found the body. I do hope this will not cause problems for you, Melissa," he said to the pale girl sitting quietly in one corner of the Green Room.

Theron's hackles rose immediately at the actor's innuendo, but he did not display his anger. "Miss Langford is not a suspect, Rathbone," he said calmly. "I was with her from the moment she entered the theatre this evening, and in any case it is unthinkable she could have perpetrated such a crime. Miss Andrews was strangled, undoubtedly by a man, for few women would have the strength to commit such a task. At any rate, I have vouched for her."

Melissa barely noticed the actor's reference to her, still in shock at what she had discovered. Whitebread seemed content to let the Marquis handle the questioning, worrying solely about the arrangements for the coming performances.

He turned to the Marquis, his heavy brows rising in interrogation. "The Majestic must remain dark for several days until this regrettable affair is cleared up, I suppose my lord."

"Yes, indeed. I have sent for a Bow Street Runner, but whether the man is competent to solve this crime is questionable. I believe we cannot rely entirely on Bow Street in this affair," Theron replied, unwilling to show his hand but determined to keep a careful eye on the investigation. He found it difficult to believe that any of the company were members of the spy ring and had been in danger of disclosure from the actress, but the evidence of the playbill was irrefutable, he thought. He did not intend to reveal that clue to Bow Street until he had taken further advice.

His musing was interrupted by a cry from Molly.

"I think you are all heartless rogues. Yes, even you, my lord. There is poor Alison lying dead on our dressing room floor, and most of you don't care. Can you not even mourn her decently?"

"Molly is quite right," Melissa intervened, not looking at 'heron for she was as disgusted with him as the character ctress. Granted that Alison's death might reinforce his uspicions of the Majestic as the headquarters of the French raitors, but had he no compassion for that poor girl?

"We are not indifferent to Alison's death, my dear," Guy ;ordon, the character actor, reproved. "We are all shocked by he tragedy, and you most of all, I understand, discovering her, frightful sight for a gently-bred girl, but we can do nothing for er now but discover the perpetrator of this crime. That is the est way to mourn her and avenge her. Don't you agree, my ord?" he asked quietly, turning to the Marquis, recognizing in hat gentleman the arbiter of the company's fate.

"Yes, Mr. Gordon, I do. And Melissa, I know you are upset, nd I will send you home, as soon as I have put a few matters in rain," he said firmly, crossing the room to her and raising her hin with a firm hand. "Now don't fret, there's a good girl. We vill get to the bottom of this matter, and you will not be vorried." He spoke with determination and distaste, reluctant o admit how much he disliked Melissa's involvement, and the uilty knowledge that she would not have been, except for his nsistence upon her role in their scheme.

"It's all very well for her," Nell Beatty, one of the ingenues nuttered to her companion, another young actress. "His ordship will see no harm comes to his mistress, but the rest of is are not so fortunate to have such a powerful, well-born rotector."

"Hush, Nell, do not rile his lordship. He is not the man to ake kindly to any criticism," her companion warned, and Nell ould only subside, unappeased, but accepting the truth of the tatement.

"For the moment, I must be about putting up a cancellation nnouncement. Do you think we can reopen in a few days time, ny lord? We can put on a Vanburgh play, which will not equire Miss Langford's presence, but I cannot afford to have he theatre dark for too long. Surely you understand that no

matter how shocked we are by Miss Andrews' death, the rest c
us have our livings to make," George Whitebread offere
tentatively, not eager to incur the Marquis' scorn, but dogge
in his responsibility to the Majestic which he had struggled t
bring into the audience's favour.

"Of course," Theron replied. "You must do what has to b
done. I will see the Bow Street runner and make arrangement
to have Miss Andrews removed to the mortuary. You will be i
your office for further consultation, I gather," he added in
tone that brooked no defiance.

"Of course, my lord. And I suppose the company mu
remain until the runner questions them."

"Yes, but we should not have to keep them long."

Just then there was a knock on the door, and old Joe, th
stage door keeper, called out, "That runner's here."

The company seemed to shrink back, as if accepting for th
first time the horrible reality of the events. Theron strode t
the door to let in a burly creature, of middle years, thick set an
florid-faced, with piercing cold blue eyes beneath a wid
brimmed hat, which he doffed respectfully as he entered th
room.

"Hal Borley, Bow Street runner, your gracious," he saic
acknowledging Theron as a blood of the first water an
obviously the man in charge. He cast an appraising eye on th
rest of the company.

"At last, Mr. Borley," Theron said wryly. "We have calle
upon you because a murder has been committed and we wil
need your assistance. I intend to take the matter higher but fo
the moment you may begin your investigations. I will sho
you the victim." Theron took one last look at Melissa befor
ushering the runner from the room, leaving behind a group o
very frightened people.

The Bow Street runner would have preferred to make hi
investigation without the disturbing presence of the Marquis
but that haughty gentleman made it quite clear he intended t
oversee the whole operation. The runner, unaccustomed t

meeting members of the aristocracy in his normal pursuits, could not gainsay him. Theron stood disdainfully watching through his quizzing glass, as Borley examined the dead girl and searched the dressing room cursorily. Nothing incriminating could be found in her belongings, not even the note Melissa had discovered. At this omission Theron frowned thoughtfully but kept his own counsel. He suspected that Alison had been strangled by someone who knew her, probably the author of that note. The murderer must have caught her unaware, drawn the scarf around her neck and throttled her, but how had he entered the theatre without being noticed?

In questioning the stage door keeper the runner learned that the Marquis and Melissa had been the first to arrive that evening. Joe, who liked his pint, had obviously not been at his post when Alison had come. She must have had an assignation with whomever killed her. That could be the only explanation for her appearance so much in advance of the rest of the cast. Of course, Whitebread had been in his office upstairs, but he rarely came through the stage door entrance. Joe, a garrulous gossip, offered the information that Miss Andrews had incurred the impresario's wrath the night before because she had forgotten her lines, causing some confusion which earned her a dressing down from Whitebread.

"His nibs was proper put out," Joe explained, remembering the drubbing Miss Andrews had suffered. "If she had come in at her regular time she wouldn't be lying there, a cold corpse," he finished with some relish, not at all dismayed by the sight of the poor victim stretched out upon the floor of the dressing room.

Although the Marquis said nothing he doubted that Joe was right. The actress had apparently stumbled upon some evidence which revealed the identity of the traitor and had been killed for her pains. That her murderer was upon intimate terms with her, and knew the environs of the theatre seemed certain. Perhaps she had tried to blackmail the villain and he had taken this method of silencing her, which brought up

several possibilities. Theron made no mention of his suspi
cions to the runner, who was inclined to favour a crime o
passion, a conclusion inspired by his experience among th
tawdry ragtag whose sordid lives were his normal concern
Theron said nothing to disabuse him of this theory. Borley
although a trained tracker of petty criminals, had littl
experience in dealing with a man of the Marquis' stamp. Hi
manner swerved between truculence, which stood him in goo
stead with his usual prey but would not serve with this hig
and mighty flash cove, and an obsequious air which se
Theron's teeth on edge.

In the end the runner decided to bully the cast, payin
special attention to Robert Rathbone, to that gentleman'
anger and dismay. Rathbone tried to brush through th
interview with a combination of disgust and condescensio
which did not serve him well and increased Borley'
suspicions. His own inclination was to think that Rathbon
and Alison had quarreled over the actor's attentions t
Melissa, since he had been apprised of her recent addition t
the company. But with the Marquis standing by, eyeing th
proceedings with that supercilious hauteur which he coul
assume so easily, Borley hesitated to put his beliefs to the test

Balked of subjecting Melissa to hard questioning, he at las
dismissed the cast but warned them all that they had not see
the last of him. The Marquis, unimpressed with Borley'
badgering, suggested that the runner postpone furthe
examination and busy himself with making arrangements t
remove the body of the poor girl.

Unwilling to leave Borley to his own devices, Theron at las
sent Melissa home with Molly, hoping the actress might be o
some comfort. He advised them not to sit up all nigh
discussing the tragedy. Melissa, in some part recovered fro
her ordeal, looked at him appealingly and pleaded that he
would not leave her long in anticipation of his own investigations. She had a great deal more faith in the Marquis
discovering the murderer than any results that the blustering

Mr. Borley might uncover.

"Do let us hear what transpires, Theron. Until Alison's killer is unmasked we are all under suspicion," she said, looking up at him, worry and fright shadowing her violet eyes.

Theron patted her shoulder. He would have preferred to take her in his arms and offer more personal reassurance, but with the company watching avidly his every move, he denied himself and Melissa that comfort.

"If Borley comes around to question you, which I doubt, say little," he warned, as he wrapped her in her pelisse. "There is a great deal more to this business than he can possibly understand. I will confer with his superiors. And be careful what you say to Molly. But you might try to discover what she knows about Alison's associates. She might know who Alison's current lover is, and then we would have some lead on who the traitor might be." He gazed at her, frowning with concern. She should never have been exposed to such a horrifying sight. He wanted to pick her up and carry her away from this nightmare and instead all he could do was ask for her assistance in the investigation. He was disgusted at his powerlessness to protect her from the inevitable scandal and disagreeable attention which lay ahead. "Try to get some rest, and put this out of your mind. I depend on your natural good sense to prevail. You look pale and unhappy, but a good night's sleep will banish some of this horror, I know."

He then surprised her by kissing her tenderly on the forehead, ignoring the company who were watching the two of them. "Don't worry, poppet. We will come about."

Molly, who had not overheard their soft conversation, looked curiously at the Marquis, taken aback a bit by his tenderness toward Melissa, a quality she had never before noticed in the reserved and enigmatic nobleman. Following in Melissa's wake as he escorted her to the door, she hurried to reassure them both with her kindly concern.

"I will have a care of her, my lord. She's too young and innocent to be mixed up in this sordid affair. Should be in the nursery, she's such a baby." She shook her head over the contemplation of the naive young woman whose proper sphere was far from here.

Melissa, wanting to deny such a description, felt too tired to argue when the Marquis replied, "Quite right, Molly. The theatre and the company of a hardened rake is not at all proper for our infant. I must see what I can do about restoring her to her proper milieu." He did not like being reminded that it was entirely due to his own actions that Melissa had endured such a frightening ordeal.

Handing them both into his barouche, he bade his coachman deliver them to Stanhope Gate without more ado. His last sight of Melissa, huddled wanly in the corner of the coach as it drove away, haunted him. This was all his fault and he could not forgive himself, an emotion so uncommon to his usual indifference to others. He surprised himself with the strength of his self reproach. Damn the girl. She was coming between him and his chief responsibility. He must be mad to think he wished devoutly to forget the whole miserable business and take her away to safety. Shrugging off his distaste he reentered the darkened theatre to come to terms with the hectoring Mr. Borley.

Chapter Twenty-Three

"Well, infant, you seem to have survived last night's ordeal in good shape. I suppose it's youth," Theron sighed tiredly as he greeted Melissa the next morning.

She did indeed appear recovered, her violet eyes sparkling and a warm glowing tint to her cheeks. She was wearing a lavender sprigged muslin morning gown accented at the puffed sleeves and rounded neckline with an edging of Alencon lace, fitting apparel for the sprightly September morning which beckoned beyond the door.

"I can't say the same for you, Theron. You look exhausted," Melissa responded.

"What a wifely remark, my dear," Theron mocked, his mouth drawn into a cynical line as he surveyed the fetching picture Melissa made. Although he was dressed impeccably as usual in a midnight blue coat of super fine cut by Weston, and cream kersey britches, his boots shining and his linen pristine, he did have a fine-drawn cast to his features.

"Not at all. Most likely your exhaustion stems from unimaginable dissipations," Melissa retorted, annoyed that he might think she was overly concerned as to his welfare.

"For once I do not deserve your scorn, although an orgy would be most enjoyable in contrast to the evening I have spent. And this morning I went around to Bow Street to see the magistrate and insure his cooperation. Samuel Rommilly promised that Borley would leave you alone, not chivy you with unnecessary questions. It was in your behalf, Melissa, I used my influence. You are an ungrateful chit."

Melissa ignored his reproof. "Have the magistrate or the runner come to any conclusions as to who was responsible for Alison's death?"

"They are inclined to think it was a rejected lover, Bow Street's experience in these affairs being confined to the more lurid motives," Theron said. "But I do not think the young woman was killed in a jealous rage by some besotted fool. Rather, I believe she somehow came across proof of our spy master and he did her in."

"Did you tell the magistrate of your suspicions?" Melissa asked, remembering with a shudder how Alison had looked on the floor of her dressing room. She had not found the actress sympathetic but she could have wished the young woman had not suffered such a wretched fate.

"I rather brushed over our belief that she might be involved in some kind of blackmail, which is what I do think. But what did Molly have to say? She must have known of Miss Andrews' latest paramour."

"She did say that Alison had a new lover. For some months she had been Robert Rathbone's light-o-love but that affair seems to have come to an end, by mutual consent. The new man in her life remained a mystery, and all Molly could suggest was that there was a new protector, but Alison was very secretive, not of a confiding nature. Molly was inclined to think he might be connected with the theatre as Alison did not often have lovers from among the dandies and bucks who frequent the Green Room. I wonder why not, for she was attractive, ambitious and, I think, avaricious." Melissa frowned perplexed.

"Puss, puss," Theron teased. "Did you consider the late Miss Andrews a rival? You astound me, infant. I had no idea you entertained such spiteful thoughts."

"Don't be nonsensical. And stop calling me infant. I am far from that, and the reputation you have given me certainly denies any childishness, I would think," Melissa replied angrily, weary of his constantly referring to her youthful innocence. Today she felt a hundred, veritably hag-ridden by the events of the past twenty-four hours, even if her appearance belied it.

Theron frowned. Her reaction was one he had feared, her humiliation at the position in which she found herself, and for which he alone was responsible, in pursuit of his own selfish aims. It was all very well to argue that the masquerade on which they were employed was inspired by patriotism, in protection of their country, but she would be the one hurt. His reputation, already beyond repair, would not suffer. Why this caused him such soul-searching he could not explain, but at least he had taken steps to correct the situation.

"You are quite right, of course. You are not a child, although your incredible innocence is a continuing reproach to me. But you will no longer be exposed to the embarrassment of parading your charms for the motley to gape at. I have told Whitebread that you are retiring from the Majestic. He will have to find another actress to rescue his theatre from obscurity."

Melissa stared at him. "Really, Theron. That is beyond all. I have quite enjoyed my career as the reigning star of the Majestic, and you have no right to interfere. Your arrogance and ruthless disregard of all wishes but your own is the outside of enough. Someday you will get your comeuppance and I hope I am around to see it!"

"I doubt it, my dear. By that time you will be happily wed to some bucolic squire, surrounded by a bevy of brats, your unhappy partnership with me entirely forgotten. And I will have gone to the devil by then, as you expected," he answered bitterly.

Melissa, seeing his reaction to her unconsidered words, regretted she had been so fierce. After all, he was doing his best to protect her.

"Perhaps you have been a bit arrogant, my lord, but I understand that the current situation is enough to try all our patiences," she said, hoping to conciliate him. Why his bitterness should affect her so she could not imagine, but that was where Theron always had the advantage over her. Her sensibilities, which he could rouse to righteous indignation, were easily touched by this strange emotion he could evoke even at his most outrageous. What had inspired his bitterness toward life and women in general? She wished she knew, and did not wonder why this should be so important to her.

"You do not owe me an apology, Melissa," he said, forcibly banishing the black mood that had dogged him earlier. "It is quite the other way round. But enough of these vain regrets. Come, I will take you around to the Ravenshams. A ride will cheer you up, and the company of such undemanding friends is just what you need. Lady Ravensham, Sarah's grandmother, is all agog to meet you and has been pleading with me for days to effect an introduction."

"Lady Ravensham wants to meet me?" Melissa cried, astonished. "How peculiar. I would never have expected she would receive one such as myself—your acknowledged mistress."

"Lady Ravensham knows me better than most. Whatever appearances, I think she is quite assured that you are not what you seem, and if she had any doubts, Sarah would have dispelled them. That young woman is quite awake on most suits. We did not deceive her, I vow." Theron smiled dryly. "You have this uncanny ability to inspire chivalrous, protective instincts in your champions, Melissa."

"Even in you?" she asked pertly.

"Even in me, poppet. Now come along. My horses have been standing long enough and it is a lovely day, a great tonic to dark thoughts."

Their reception at the Ravensham's impressive house in Park Lane was all that Theron had promised. Lucien and Sarah were both on hand to greet them warmly, and the colonel and Theron almost immediately went off to the library to discuss recent events while Sarah invited Melissa to partake of some chocolate with her grandmother in the morning room. Melissa's spirits rose immediately under the tactful and kindly manner of the dowager who seemed genuinely pleased to meet her.

"Theron tells me, my dear, that he rescued you from a frightful situation with your guardian, an enforced marriage he explained," Lady Ravensham probed, liking the fresh, open countenance of her young guest. Melissa was not at all what she had expected, having the usual prejudice of her class against actresses. That this young woman was of an uncommon type she sensed at once and wondered anew at Theron's involvement, and his protective air toward the girl. One look and she was convinced that the relationship between the two was far from what it seemed to the world. Melissa's pointed, piquant face, her elegant figure, and most of all those wide, drowning violet eyes reminded Lady Ravensham of someone, a face from the past to whom she could not put a name.

"Tell me, my dear, your real name. I understand that Langford is just a professional title," Lady Ravensham asked.

Somewhat surprised at the dowager's interest, Melissa hesitated and then, unable to resist the kind and welcoming smile of the older woman, acquiesced. "Mansfield, Lady Ravensham. My father spent most of his life in India, which is where he met my guardian, I understand."

"And your mother's maiden name?" Lady Ravensham insisted, feeling that here was a mystery to which she had the key if only she could find it.

"I don't know. I was only nine when my parents died, and they never spoke of her family. All I have is a locket, a portrait of Mama when she was a young girl," Melissa offered, a bit baffled by Lady Ravensham's insistence.

"I don't mean to pry, my dear, but you bear a striking resemblance to someone I once knew. I cannot put a name to her, it just eludes me, but I will remember," Lady Ravensham said with determination.

"Just as I thought, Grandma," Sarah intervened nodding her head with satisfaction, for she had felt all along that Melissa's heritage was exceptional. "There is some quality out of the ordinary about Melissa, and we will discover her mother's people. I am convinced there is a great deal here which needs investigation."

"My parents led me to believe, from what I dimly recall, that my mother's family abandoned her when she married Papa. He was a bit of an adventurer, I fear, and spirited her off to India before Mama's father could protest the match. They obviously disapproved of him, although I remember him as a gay, charming, and affectionate man. I still miss them both a great deal." Melissa sighed, unhappy at the old memories this discussion evoked.

"Well, we do not want to distress you with glum thoughts of the past. Come, let us talk of better times, but do let me see that locket one day. It might jog my memory," Lady Ravensham turned the conversation, aware that Melissa found this delving into the past disturbing. She began to question her about her life in the theatre and how she happened on such a career.

When the gentlemen joined them they were deep in a discussion of Shakespeare's heroines and arguing spiritedly about the merits of Portia over Katherine. Theron smiled to see Melissa so comfortable with Sarah and Lady Ravensham, and reproached himself, yet again, for placing her in the equivocal position in which she found herself.

"Well, Lucien, did you and Theron solve the problems of state which were causing you such disquiet?" Sarah asked, wondering at the sober faces of both men.

"Not completely, my dear. Theron has stirred up a veritable hornet's nest and whether we shall come about is very problematical," the colonel replied.

"The important thing is to keep Melissa well out of it now," Theron said. "Murder has been committed, and this proves how serious our conspirators are about protecting their identities."

"And how do you feel about the sudden end to your triumphs on the stage, Melissa?" Sarah asked, knowing she was stirring up controversy, but eager to see how Melissa handled the domineering lord.

"I am not going to accept it, Sarah, but leave me to deal with Theron. He's much too fond of having his own way," Melissa declared, to Sarah's amusement. That sprightly matron found the idea of the notorious rake acting the possessive chaperone of a young woman of unimpeachable virtue a treat. It was high time someone took Theron in hand or he would soon be beyond redemption.

All Melissa earned for her defiance was a frosty smile from his lordship and a glance which promised retribution at some later date. Lady Ravensham, noticing that the two were at odds over this matter of the theatre, tried to avoid further unpleasantness by mentioning Melissa's mysterious likeness to someone she had known.

"Mansfield is not a name which strikes a chord, but we must discover Melissa's mother's people. I feel sure they would welcome her after all this age. Often parents regret turning their children away for some misdeed which seems so dreadful at the time, but which can be misconstrued and lead to unhappy years of estrangement." Lady Ravensham sighed, remembering her own tragedy when Sarah's father had been unjustly accused of dishonourable activity.

Theron, knowing how much that old story, now fortunately dispelled, still disturbed his gentle friend, attempted to distract her. "I see you had no difficulty in confiding in Lady Ravensham, Melissa. You have been more effective than I was, madam. No doubt my satanic past is responsible. She tried to fob me off with some tale and name, but I soon made short work of that. Melissa has this strange notion that I am not to be trusted," he explained with some chagrin, acknowledging that Melissa had justice on her side. As it turned out, he had used her in a blameworthy fashion.

"I believed Theron only wanted my real name and directio so that he could return me to my guardian. He threatened t wash his hands of me, abandon me by the roadside. He is a nasty customer," Melissa explained more in truth than jest.

Theron sighed. "Well, we will see, poppet. That might stil be in the cards. Perhaps that mysterious gentleman can dea with you more soundly than I can. You are a great re sponsibility. Since we have met I find myself embroiled in al kinds of mischief I could well do without."

"Nonsense, Theron, protecting Melissa is a new role for yo and for once you must put your own selfish, libertine desires t one side and consider another's well being. About time, too,' chided Lady Ravensham in admonitory tones. Behind he words was the implication that Theron would do well to respec Melissa's virtue or she would enter the lists. "I hope Meliss brings you your just deserts."

They all laughed, but Theron had to admit that Lad Ravensham had analysed the situation acutely. Melissa coul very well cause him to regret the day he discovered her hidin in his coach. They might yet both regret it, he concede ruefully to himself.

Soon after, the two departed, Melissa promising to bring he mother's locket to Lady Ravensham, but without much hop that anything would come of it. She had long accepted the fac that her mother's family wanted naught to do with her. The could have discovered her whereabouts before now if they ha really wanted to know, she felt.

In the privacy of their carriage, on the way back to Stanhop Gate, Melissa broached the issue which she had not wanted t pursue in the Ravensham drawing room.

"Theron, I must protest your cavalier attitude in telling Mr Whitebread that I would no longer appear at the Majestic. No more than ever I should be on the scene for we could be withi an ace of unmasking the traitor if what you believe abou Alison's dreadful murder is true." She watched him closely t see how he accepted her reasoning. She knew he did not entertain interference with his plans, but she could not allow him to dominate her in this fashion.

"It is too dangerous," he replied curtly. "If our spy will go to the lengths of murder to avoid discovery who knows what could happen to you. I will not put you at risk any longer."

"I may owe you a great deal for rescuing me from my guardian and securing my place at the Majestic, but you do not control my every action. I intend to finish what we began. You refine too much on the danger. I am going back to the Majestic when it reopens and that's the end of it," she declared, peeking at him from under her bonnet to see the effect of her provocative words.

"You try my patience, you obstinate wench. For a chit of a girl you have a vast determination to go your own way."

"Just as well you see that, my lord. I may owe you gratitude but not blind obedience, and you would be wise not to challenge me. I cannot turn down a dare." Melissa felt quite triumphant in her belief she had scored off the maddening Marquis. They parted without the matter being resolved although Melissa had decided that she would insist on her way. After all a mistress, even a masquerading one, did not owe obedience. Only a wife could be so compelled. And there was certainly little likelihood that she would ever enjoy that condition!

Chapter Twenty-Four

The Majestic, without its star, remained dark for a week, and finally reopened with a turgid melodrama, one of the company's standard offerings. Audiences, upon discovering that Melissa was not in the cast, failed to patronize the theatre in significant numbers and often the company played to a half-filled house, much to Whitebread's disgust. Molly O'Hara reported to Melissa on the tepid reception the current play was receiving and hoped that the young actress who had brought the theatre such acclaim would soon return. She had hard words for Mr. Borley, the Bow Street runner, who continued to haunt the theatre trying to find some clue to Alison Andrews' murder with little success. Nervous and insecure, members of the company tried valiantly to brave out the notoriety and scandal. For her part, Melissa was bored. Her anger with Theron increased when he virtually ignored her, leaving her with too much time to brood over events and his strange new attitude. She was forced to conclude that he no longer had any use for her and had abandoned her to her fate, not a prospect she viewed with equanimity.

Determined to take charge of her own destiny, she decided to approach Whitebread herself and plead with him to restore her to the stage. She refused to be a pawn in Theron's game, waiting patiently until he could deal with her affairs, if he ever condescended to do so. After several days of enforced inactivity, enlivened only by a visit to the Ravenshams when she had delivered the promised locket, she prevailed upon the faithful Percy to drive her to the Majestic. She chose a time when the cast would be absent, not wanting the members of the company to witness her humiliation if Whitebread refused her. Bearding the impresario in his office she came immediately to the point.

"Mr. Whitebread, I know that the Marquis de Lisle has informed you that I would no longer appear on the Majestic's stage," she began, "I might say he did this without my permission and I have no intention of abiding by his edict. I realize that you would never have engaged me originally if he had not offered to subsidize my appearance, but my reception by audiences has surely proved that I can attract patrons with my own ability. I understand that the Majestic is playing to half-empty houses and I know that is not to your taste. I want to come back to the stage."

Whitebread looked at the young woman who had brought his company so much success, noting her fresh, eager appeal, wondering not for the first time what it was about Melissa which projected so effectively over the footlights.

She had dressed carefully for this interview, determined to look her best. Her ivory silk dress under a sky blue redincote faced with a matching collar and cuffs complemented her gold streaked hair and wide violet eyes beseeching under an ivory straw bonnet trimmed with blue flowers. He was tempted, but remembered the stern orders of the Marquis, a man whom he hesitated to cross even though he yearned to see his theatre again the cynosure of all eyes.

"Surely, the success of 'The Shrew' brought you the box office receipts you needed, and even without the Marquis' patronage you can afford to take a chance with me," Melissa urged, unable to tell from the impresario's impassive face what he was really thinking.

"I must admit we miss you, Melissa, but the Marquis was

quite adamant about your retirement. Would it be wise to go against his wishes?" Whitebread said, remembering that august gentleman's orders, and wondering not for the first time about the relationship of this disparate couple.

"The Marquis does not control my life, whatever he may say, and I wish to return to the stage. If the Majestic will not employ me, I am convinced Drury Lane or the Theatre Royal might be interested in giving me a place," Melissa threatened, knowing how Whitebread felt about his rivals.

"Now, now," he said quickly. "If you are sure you can talk the Marquis around, it might be possible. There is no doubt that we miss your star quality, and the audiences are clamouring to see you." He pushed impatiently at the play bills piled on his desk. Melissa wondered what he was doing with the advertisements. When she had entered the office after a perfunctory knock he had been busy with the playbills, writing something on each one carefully.

"I was hoping I could prevail upon you to let me play Juliet. I had quite a success with it in Bath," Melissa offered. "You can safely leave the Marquis to me. After all, if I am the success you claim, we will not need his financial support. As a draw, I can surely make up for the money he has expended on the Majestic," she continued bravely, not liking to push herself forward in this brazen manner, but seeing that Whitebread was wavering.

"You must realize, Miss Langford, that it would be unwise of me to antagonize the Marquis. He has a great deal of influence even if we deny the help his patronage brings. He could make things very awkward," Whitebread said, obviously torn between two difficult choices. He knew he needed Melissa but he was reluctant to allow her to return if it meant incurring the wrath of one of London's most noted bloods.

"Theron de Lisle believes he can order the world to suit his desires. It's time he learned differently. I cannot see how he can cause you trouble. Surely the fate of the Majestic is in your hands, Mr. Whitebread," Melissa replied, cleverly attacking the impresario's pride and vulnerability. She knew how much the theatre meant to him, and his plans for its future.

"Well, I think I will grant your request. You are a powerful advocate, Miss Langford. But I must rely on you to talk the Marquis around," he agreed with some reluctance, his dour expression lightening as he thought of his theatre once more enjoying full houses and popularity.

"Thank you, Mr. Whitebread. You will not regret it. I promise," Melissa smiled in gratitude, barely restraining a crow of delight. She would show the Marquis, Whitebread, and all of London she was a force to be reckoned with. "When can we begin rehearsals?" she asked quickly, before Whitebread could have second thoughts.

"Tomorrow. The sooner the better. If only this investigation of Alison's murder could be cleared away, we would be in a far better case," Whitebread said, frowning.

Melissa anxious to distract him from thoughts of the slain girl hurried on. "Well, I am sure the industrious Mr. Borley will accomplish that before too long. It is hardly fair for the company to suffer under all this suspicion until he does. We will come about with a new play, I am convinced," she said blithely with more confidence than she felt, remembering that dreadful evening. "Until tomorrow then, Mr. Whitebread," she said. "I will be ready to rehearse."

"Yes, yes. Well, I must busy myself with the arrangements. There is much to do." He dismissed her with a careless wave of his hand. Now that the die was cast, he put his doubts behind him.

Melissa smiled at him, and bade him goodbye, barely able to restrain her triumphant feelings. For once she had won over the intransigent Marquis and she must capitalize on her victory. She went to rejoin the patient Percy waiting in his phaeton outside the theatre.

Theron de Lisle would have to accept that he was not in control of her life, and although she was grateful for his protection, he must realize she would make her own decisions.

For some reason this resolve did not afford her the satisfaction she had expected. Well, she would worry about that when the inevitable confrontation arose. By his recent indifferent manner it could scarcely matter to him what she did, she decided. She must just relegate the Marquis to the past. No doubt at this very moment he was pursuing some light skirt, and had become bored with his former protégé. Only a niggling doubt about the wisdom of her actions remained. She disliked abandoning the investigation into the spy conspiracy for she felt she was ignoring the danger to her country, but if Theron had decided he no longer needed her to play that role, she must go along as best she might without his direction. Shrugging off her unease, she greeted Percy with a sunny smile completely captivating that young man, and they rode off together in good spirits.

Theron, deliberately distancing himself from Melissa, had spent his days conferring with the boffins at the Foreign Office, persuading himself that his first responsibility was intelligence affairs, not the welfare of a young woman who had engaged too much of his attention by far. Distrustful of women in general and cynical about the emotions Melissa had aroused in him, he had decided that he must sever his connection with her. He had already endangered her reputation and possibly her life. The least he could do was protect her since she had so cheerfully gone along with his schemes, and to no purpose. They were no closer to unmasking the traitors. He railed inwardly at the idea that the miscreants had balked him at every turn. He was annoyed, too, at the King's ministers, a craven lot who wanted to sue Napoleon for a truce, a disastrous turn of events, he thought. He spent many fruitless hours arguing for a more ruthless attack on the French, but his suggestions met with a cool reception. If he could tie up this spy business, round up the traitors, his opinions would carry more weight with the powerful men who directed the country's destiny. That must be his first priority, and Melissa had distracted him long enough. Ruthlessly he pushed her to the back of his mind and pursued those pleasures—drinking, wenching, gambling—which had been his wont in the past. But his attempts to find oblivion in the tawdry round of dissipation brought little relief.

Lucien Valentine, meeting him at White's one evening, noticed his friend's preoccupation but hesitated to interrupt his brooding, for Theron was deep into his cups and frowned ferociously at the few bold souls who tried to engage him in conversation. Lucien sighed, remembering his own follies, and felt he must make some effort to bring Theron around. Sarah and Lady Ravensham were worried about the hot-headed rake and were both convinced that only in Melissa would he find his salvation. Lucien, more worldly and experienced, was not so sure, but Melissa's welfare was very much in his mind when he approached Theron, determined not to be put off by the Marquis' sullen mood.

"Well, here's a case, Theron. I see you are blue devilled. The French affair not progressing, I gather." Lucien offered this gambit, though he was convinced it was not the frustration of the spy ring which had brought Theron to such a pass.

"Damn the traitors. I can make no progress and Castlereagh now thinks I am a fool to continue," Theron replied, rousing himself to face his friend's interrogation. Valentine was a good fellow, a brave soldier, and not a member of the curious dissolute crowd which frequented the club. Here the country was going down the drain and the ton ignored the danger, preferring to gamble and drink away the hours. And Theron thought himself little better. Self-disgust darkened his face as he thought of the last few days and his reckless attempts to banish the cloud of anger and mistrust which had pushed him into his recent fruitless round of dissipation.

"I am sure you will come about and this is only a temporary setback. Surely the murder of that actress lends weight to your suspicions about the Majestic as headquarters of the ring," Lucien said, choosing his words carefully. "Has the runner made any progress? I take it you have not confided in him."

"Oh, Borley believes the girl had some disgruntled lover who did her in, but I think differently, as you know. Someone in that theatre is directing events. But who? And there are other factors. The French must have a conduit to the Foreign Office, some villain there who is selling his country to the enemy. Our every decision is delivered to them on a plate," Theron railed, going over and over again the miserable state of affairs.

"I am sure you are right about the Majestic. Has Melissa any ideas on who among the company might be involved?" Lucien asked, determined to introduce Melissa's name but wary of his reception.

"I have removed her from the theatre," Theron replied arrogantly, implying that was the end of it and he would brook no further questions. "It is not a proper place for her and I was a fool to introduce her there in the first place. She is not suited to such a role."

"Yes, well, I believe you have a responsibility for the young woman," Lucien suggested tentatively. He eyed the peer warily. How far could he go?

A heavy frown darkened the Marquis' face, and his eyes looked cold and inscrutable. "What are you suggesting, Lucien? That I marry the chit? I think you know my feelings on that matter. And I would hardly prove an acceptable husband to such an innocent if I were so inclined. I am surprised you should entertain such a shocking thought," he jeered.

"I don't entertain it, but Sarah and Lady Ravensham, of a much more romantic disposition, thought you might have been caught at last. Surely you want an heir to all those acres in Devon," Lucien suggested, trying to maintain an indifferent tone.

"Sarah must just be content with her own matrimonial venture. A stubborn lady, your wife, but I am not available for her maneuvering." Theron dismissed the conversation coldly, making clear that he would offer no confidences on this matter.

Eyeing the Marquis speculatively, Lucien decided he could venture no further. Theron was an ugly customer when crossed and he had little hope that any more information would be forthcoming, although he suspected the Marquis cared more for the young woman he had rescued than he would admit. He turned the talk to the latest political situation and the possibilities of a truce with the French, a subject on which Theron held violent views. Lucien, a skilled campaigner, knew when to retreat, and in the matter of Melissa he felt he must make a strategic withdrawal, in order to fight another day.

Chapter Twenty-Five

In the depths of Devon, Horace Hawksley and his nephew Algernon were also preparing a battle plan. Algernon had posted down to his uncle's gloomy manor house soon after the encounter with Melissa in the Majestic's Green Room. Despite her rebuff he was far from convinced that she was not the wench whose fortune he intended to claim. He lost no time in appraising his uncle of events, and was gratified to learn that Horace Hawksley was inclined to agree with him.

"That damn girl has been nothing but a trial since the day she arrived at my doorstep. Why couldn't she behave in a seemly fashion, obey my orders and carry out my wishes as any right-thinking chit would? Far too independent. I knew she would embroil herself in some outrageous ploy. The only bright aspect to this affair is that she has irretrievably ruined her reputation by appearing on stage. This high born protector she has attracted will not marry her, and no other respectable young man will take her on after this jackanape." Horace rubbed his fat hands together in satisfaction.

"No, I suppose not, but that damn Marquis keeps a pretty close eye upon her, has set her up in a fancy house in Stanhope Gate, and his affection does not appear to be cooling," Algy reported, wondering what his uncle could do to alter events.

"In my experience these top-of-the-tree bloods lose interest in their ladybirds after a short time in keeping. And then what will milady do? I doubt her acting abilities are such that she has earned herself a permanent niche on stage. She must then look about for another protector. Not beyond her powers, but certain to sink her beyond redemption. Unfortunately, with your proclivities for spending my blunt, we cannot wait for her to fall to the depths she deserves. We will have to remove her from London. Much as I dislike the prospect I will have to drive up to London and see to the matter myself. You seem to have come a cropper over the affair, plus putting up her hackles. But once you are shackled you can surely keep her in order." Horace glowered at his nephew. A paltry fellow with little to attract a girl, t'was true, but if Horace wanted to keep Melissa's fortune in his hands he had to use the material available and that could only mean Algy.

The two settled down to their nefarious plans. Nothing less than an abduction would serve, and they had to learn much more about Melissa's current situation before they could effect that drastic action.

The Hawksleys were not the only couple intent on bending Melissa to their will.

"And how do you plan to carry out your revenge on the girl, Major?" Aimee de Frontons asked, late one evening in her house.

Major Gratton had been careful to call when dark had drawn in, and he had left his curricle some distance away. It would not do for any observers to think that he and the Comtesse were conspiring together.

"Since the wench has rebuffed my most ardent lures, I must just take her under duress. Rather adds to the spice of the adventure, wouldn't you say?" he grinned lasciviously, contemplating the delights of seducing Melissa.

"If that is your taste. The Marquis will not take kindly to your seduction of his mistress, you know. Had you taken him into account?" Aimee thought that the Major was either a fool or more vainglorious than she had suspected if he contemplated coming to odds with the Marquis. Oh, la, la, what a coil. She chuckled to herself, looking the Major over. He would soon be at point non plus with Theron, despite his belief in his powers. And all over that wretched brat, too. Men were surely unaccountable.

"From what I have learned of that top-lofty lord, he wouldn't give a tinker's damn. I believe his interest is already cooling, small wonder. She is hardly up to his touch, a silly ignorant light skirt," he scoffed. "He will return to you, madame, at any rate. How could he resist your obvious charms over that of an untutored bit o' muslin."

Aimee, as vain and shallow as the Major, smiled smugly. She agreed, and certainly she had her own score to settle with both the Marquis and Melissa.

"Now this is what I have in mind. I want you to write her a note asking for an interview, saying you have important news concerning the Marquis you feel she should know. That will fetch her," he said slyly.

"But I don't want her here," Aimee protested, unwilling to risk any kind of exposure. If the Marquis discovered she had conspired to harm Melissa, his wrath would be formidable, and she could not chance losing his support, even if he had tired of her practiced lovemaking.

"She will never arrive here. If we choose our time properly. Just as evening draws in or early in the morning. I will be able to spirit her away before she reaches your doorstep. She will have to order a hackney, and that is where my plan is foolproof," Gratton explained, congratulating himself on his cleverness.

"And then where will you take her? And do you think she will submit tamely?" Aimee asked, a bit aghast at Gratton's brutality.

"There is that safe house, not far from Hampstead Heath. It should serve, I think. I am looking forward to having her at my mercy. She will change her tune soon enough then, I vow." He grinned evilly.

"As you will, *mon ami*, but you must keep me out of it. I need the Marquis' funds, if not his less obvious assets. I am in deep water and cannot prevail on the Jews any longer. My expenses are many and I am finding myself at my wit's end," Aimee confided.

"But surely our French paymasters are generous," Gratton replied in some surprise.

"Not unless we produce results. True, matters have been going at a fine pace, but I fear we are nearing discovery, and I must take care." Aimee frowned, worry marring the usual serenity of her smooth complexion.

"Well, I have quite a budget of news from my War Office contact, and I think we can satisfy the greedy beggars," Gratton answered coarsely. "But write that note. Tomorrow is the date. I will not wait longer," he threatened. "And Comtesse, remember we are in this together too deep now to fall out, so no second thoughts, eh?" he sneered.

For a moment Aimee wavered. What had she done, collaborating with this shoddy fellow? He might fancy himself as a demon lover for a certain type of female, and he had a certain raffish attraction, but in no way could he offer any competition to a girl under Theron de Lisle's protection. For a moment she felt a real sympathy for Gratton's intended victim. Still, she owed Melissa a bad turn. That young woman had challenged her on the one front on which she claimed supremacy and had lured Theron from her bed. Her conscience would trouble her little if the girl came to a bad end. She had a score to settle with Theron, too, and this would be one way of paying it. He would not like to think his mistress had been despoiled by this graceless officer.

An encounter with the Marquis that evening only strengthened her determination to lure Melissa into the hands of her eager seducer. They met at the Seftons rout, which Theron had only attended in order to find Henry Addington and quiz him about the progress of the French truce talks. That stolid gentleman had proved strangely illusive when Theron had called upon him. Meeting Aimee at the supper table, Theron greeted her cooly, obviously not prepared to linger. But she placed a restraining hand on his arm, and politeness insisted that he listen to her.

"Well, *mon cher,* it has been some time since I have seen you." She smiled, hiding her chagrin at his indifferent air. "Too taken up with your little actress, I suppose. You must not entirely desert your old friends, you know."

"Not at all, Aimee. And I do not believe I owe you any explanations. I find Melissa a charming relief from the practiced attentions of more experienced females. It's always enjoyable to be first in the field," he answered sarcastically, but annoyed that he had been betrayed into speaking so crudely about Melissa.

"First in the field? Oh, Theron, I can't believe you have been so gulled by that wench. She is a clever girl," Aimee unwisely responded, her own temper rising to his sneering manner.

"So spiteful, Aimee," he jeered, one eyebrow lifting wryly. "Not the way to insinuate yourself back into my good graces, I promise. But I see Lord Alvaney making his way here, obviously in pursuit of you. Take my advice and accept what the gods offer. I am finished with you," he said brutally, his dark eyes flaring briefly before the lids lowered and he resumed his usual languid air. Then giving her a mocking and perfunctory bow, he left without more ado. It was all Aimee could do to turn a ravishing smile on Alvaney, one of the leaders of the ton, and not a gentleman who would suffer a snub gracefully. Well, Theron would discover she made a bad enemy.

"Damn all women," Theron cursed silently to himself as he made his way through the throng to the entrance hall. Aimee with her jealous insinuations, Sarah with her meddling, and Melissa most of all. He had been in a raging temper all day since viewing the posters plastered over the Majestic advertising Melissa's return to the stage in a new vehicle, "Romeo and Juliet." How dare she defy him! And was she so heedless of the danger she was incurring by returning to the theatre?

A combination of guilt and frustration had driven him to denying not only the Majestic but himself of Melissa's presence. He could not remember being so preoccupied by a female since his salad days, but she had managed to intrude on his every waking moment. He had kept away from her these past few days only by the utmost exertion of will, and yet he had not been able to banish from his mind her face, with its elfin features, those liquid violet eyes, her slight yet entrancing figure, and the audacious way she had of taking him to task, haunting him.

He kept reminding himself that he had a grave responsibility for her safety, that he had lured her into this dangerous masquerade, and owed her protection. But he knew this was not the whole of it. He wanted her, wanted to feel that slight form naked in his bed, responding to his love making, surrendering her body and her will, mindless with passion. He had never denied himself a woman he desired before so why was he proving so faint hearted now, so reluctant to take what he knew he could win from her, her innocence, her virtue. And that, too, surprised him. He had told Aimee de Frontons the truth. To be first in the field with Melissa had become a devouring thirst although it had never been important in previous amours. Why was he not living up to his reputation as a lecher, a libertine, a rake, a callous pursuer of women, and equally indifferent to their avowals of love?

Surely he could not be suffering from a conscience at this late date. He could not seriously be considering offering her marriage. Every prudent counsel was against it. Her innocence might attract for a spell, but in the long run her very naivete would bore him, and her independent nature meant she would never be a conformable wife, content to live quietly in the country, breeding, while he continued his rake's progress in town. Long ago he had decided no woman would catch him in her toils, and certainly this fledgling had not the ability when dozens of others had failed. She would do far better with the callow Percy or even Sir Harry, who admired her exceedingly.

He supposed that someday he must marry to secure that heir which Lucien believed so vital. But no need to rush matters. And did he want some East India Company cit's offspring to become his Marchioness? Like most of his class Theron saw nothing out of the way in seducing any woman who caught his fancy, but when the time came to marry would insist on a bride of impeccable virtue and lineage. He had a callous disregard for the women who graced his bed, waving them away without a thought when the liaison bored him, as it did within a short time. With the impures and bits of muslin he had in keeping he paid them off generously, finding their greed less tiresome than the protestations of love from members of his own set used merely as an excuse to satisfy their lust.

He had never met a young woman like Melissa, having carefully insulated himself from marriageable ladies, and finding most debutantes simpering and mindless. He could never say that of her. But he was tired of playing the bloodless elder brother or indulgent uncle, and marriage was out of the question. But he wanted her, and Theron de Lisle always got what he wanted. Why should he suddenly develop qualms of morality in Melissa's case?

True, she trusted him, and she deserved better of him than a careless seduction as a reward for helping his investigations. Could he marry her? And would she accept him? Probably not, he scoffed to himself. He had not forgotten the disagreeable guardian, hovering about waiting to force her into an unsavoury marriage. The image of some bumbling, coarse oaf taking Melissa to bed raised his temper to a frightening degree. He would not have it. She would be far better off with him, even without the legal sanction.

Uncomfortable scruples had never prevented Theron from satisfying his appetites in the past, but now he was hesitating ike some beardless schoolboy full of vague yearnings. Satiation would restore his senses, but he might have to deny himself that surcease. He must throw off this strange infatuation which had taken such a grip upon him, but he seemed helpless to prevent his mind from returning again and again to a picture of Melissa surrendering to his lovemaking. Labouring under the double burden of self-disgust and frustration Theron repaired to White's to seek some relief from the torturous thoughts and desires which were now his daily companions.

Chapter Twenty-Six

Aimee de Frontons' note arrived with Melissa's breakfast tray the following morning. As soon as Bessie had left the bedroom Melissa opened the missive, her eyes widening in perplexity as she read Aimee's words.

Dear Melissa,

I know in the past that you have had reason to suspect my motives in regard to you, but believe me I had only your best interests at heart. I think you should know the rather startling information I have learned concerning Theron. It shocked me and will, I am certain, cause you equal unease. If you will call upon me this morning at your convenience I will impart this disturbing news to you. It will affect not only your relationship with Theron but your own future. Please do not fail me, I will expect you any time before noon.

Yours,
Aimee de Frontons

At her first perusal Melissa had decided that Aimee was about to announce her marriage to the Marquis, but this would not be shocking even if Aimee expected it to cause her unease However, a more careful study of the letter gave Melissa econd thoughts. Her first inclination was to refuse the ıeeting, but her curiosity was aroused. She did not trust .imee but she doubted the Comtesse would request an nterview unless she had good reason, devious or honest. ıimee was undoubtedly up to some rig and Melissa had a ompelling desire to know what the lady had in mind. If 'heron was involved in some dangerous situation she owed ıim loyalty and help no matter how hurt and angry she was at ıis defection. She would certainly attend the Comtesse and ıear her story.

Asking Bessie to have one of the maids secure her a hackney, he hurried into her gown, and perched a fetching straw onnet on her curls. Bessie protested, wanting to know her lestination, but Melissa hesitated to confide in her.

"You have a rehearsal at two o'clock, dearie, and should not e dashing off on some mysterious errand now," Bessie omplained as she buttoned up Melissa's heavy silk cherry norning dress.

"Don't fuss, Bessie. I will be back in good time to make the ehearsal," Melissa assured her.

"I don't know what you are up to, but I don't like it. You hould be resting or studying your lines. I have a feeling you ıre up to no good," grumbled the dresser, always protective of ıer charge. "And it's a nasty morning, all grey and foggy. You von't want to catch a cold traipsing around the city so early."

"Oh, a little damp won't bother me. Now be a dear Bessie ınd stop complaining. I am not some tender flower unable to rave the weather, you know. I will be back before you know t," Melissa soothed, eager to be on her way.

When she paused on the step of the house, taking a Norwich hawl from the dresser, she had to agree that it was indeed an nclement morning, but she was all impatient to proceed. Aimee had piqued her curiosity and she would not be easy until he had satisfied it. No matter that she and Theron were at odds vith one another, she must discover what Aimee had learnt hat threatened him. However angry she might be at his cavalier manner toward her, she felt a deep sense of obligation toward him. She would not admit that some strong, unnamed emotion impelled her to try to protect him from any enemy who might wish to destroy him, and she persuaded herself it was gratitude not any warmer feeling which was moving her toward this uncomfortable confrontation with Aimee. Distracted and uneasy she hardly noticed the hackney waiting for her arrival and hurried down the steps, entering it without another pause. She had hardly settled herself in the carriage when she became aware of another passenger, settled in one corner. To her surprise and disgust she recognized Henry Gratton.

"Major Gratton, what are you doing in this hackney? There must be some mistake. I am on my way to an important appointment," she spoke with irritation, annoyed at his presence and feeling unequal to dealing with this bounder now.

"The mistake was yours, Miss Langford. You are coming with me, under duress if necessary, but I advise you to come quietly, and you will not be hurt," Gratton sneered, edging closer to her and putting a hand on her arm.

Trying to shrug out of his grasp Melissa felt the first suspicion and fear. Had she been lured into a trap?

"Unhand me, sir, and leave this carriage. I do not want your company," she spoke haughtily, unwilling to let him see she was frightened.

"I have had enough of your stiff-necked ways, my pretty. You will do what I say or it will be the worse for you. And don't think you can escape from this carriage. You would only injure yourself and I will have you anyway. Your high born protector isn't around now to challenge me. I was determined to have you from the first and now I have you just where I want you," he said brutally, drawing her struggling form closer. "Behave prettily and we will deal very well together."

Furious, Melissa fought back, striking him a few ineffectual blows before finally landing a hard smack on his face, as he tried to kiss her.

Infuriated by her reaction, Gratton lost his temper and narled, "If that's the way you want it, you miserable little oxy, you shall have it," and he slapped her back. Before she ould scream at this painful outrage, he took a vial from his ocket, easily restraining her with one arm, and forced the oxious potion down her throat. Gasping and sputtering, lelissa shook with fury at such handling, and continued to ight him, although her efforts became steadily weaker. Before oo long she fell back, insensible, drugged into a stupor.

Gratton threw her roughly into one corner of the carriage hich was now careening wildly on the road, the coachman hipping his horse to a frantic speed. Few pedestrians had entured out on the misty morning and those that were on the treets, hurrying about their business, paid no attention to the acing hackney, accustomed to vehicles driven with reckless bandon on London's streets. Melissa, unconscious, lay in a athetic heap. Her attacker viewed her with some enjoyment, or he had her at last at his mercy. Gratton had rarely been so oundly rebuffed by a female that he fancied, for his uniform, asy pockets and careless address had usually brought him any voman he pursued. That most of these women were not of lelissa's quality he did not consider important. He rather elished ravishing a woman who put up a fight and he grinned villy contemplating the outcome of this morning's work.

They continued northward, emerging finally from the city's venues into lanes with a more rural aspect, entering Iampstead Heath, the nighttime haunt of highwaymen, hickly covered with shrubs and trees. On this foggy morning he Heath lay silent and brooding, untenanted and shrouded vith gloom. After a few miles they left the wider road, putting he sparsely settled environs behind them, and jolted down a ough lane which led eventually to a cottage, lying hidden eneath a bower of dark greenery. The carriage stopped and Gratton emerged, carrying Melissa's inert body. The coachman, unmoved by the sight of his passenger and his limp ompanion, did not wait, but drove the equipage away at a fast

pace. The doings of the quality did not interest him. He ha
been well paid for his trouble and the fate of the young woma
was no concern of his.

Gratton kicked open the door and headed directly up th
narrow stairs into the cottage bedroom where he threw Meliss
carelessly on the bed. Then he stooped over her, his face draw
into leering anticipation, but to his disgust she did not stir, no
respond to his shaking or hard slap.

"Damn it, I have given the wench too much drug. But sh
will be coming around before too long. I can wait. No one wil
disturb us here," he muttered and repaired downstairs to th
sitting room, locking the door behind him. In that dust
apartment, equipped with the bare minimum of furnishing, h
threw off his hat and gloves, took a bottle from the cupboard
and poured himself a generous tot of brandy.

So far all had gone according to plan. When she did awake
with no help at hand, she would no doubt accept the situatio
for what it was and surrender to his possession without to
much demure. It was not as if she was a timid virgin, fo
Gratton had recognized in the Marquis a man of appetites t
match his own, and the peer would have tutored her well
These light skirts liked a masterful man, and she should hav
little complaint. He owed her a rough handling for he
contemptuous rejection of him in the past. Now she would pa
for her scornful spurning of his offers. He grinned lasciviousl
and dipped again into the bottle. No little bit of muslin woul
treat him with disdain without paying for it. She would b
begging for his lovemaking before he was through with her. H
grinned in contemplation of the scene ahead.

Upstairs in the bedroom where he had deposited her s
summarily, Melissa came groggily awake, at first befuddled
with a pounding headache. What nightmare was this, an
where was she? Then she remembered her struggle with th
vicious Gratton, and his forcing the drug down her throat. Sh
staggered to her feet, tottering to the door, which she tugged a
to no avail. Locked. She looked about the apartment in disgust

How could she obtain her release? She refused to think of the fate which Gratton obviously intended for her. But she would not submit tamely to Gratton's kidnapping and despoiling, of that she was certain.

Gradually, as her senses cleared, she considered her invidious position. The room was dark, no light piercing the dingy recesses of the room from the grimy small windows. Aside from the bed covered with a dingy counterpane, she saw a wardrobe, a rickety table, and two chairs. All were bare of any useful utensils with which she might defend herself. She tried the windows, which were secured, warped by weather and unbudging. On the table were a cracked pitcher and basin. These were the only possible weapons and they would have to serve. Shaking her head to clear the last fumes of drugs from her consciousness she considered the windows again. The frames seemed rotten. Perhaps there was a chance here, but before she could investigate further she heard Gratton's step on the stair.

Hurrying to the door, the pitcher in her hand, she listened, her fright now fading to a furious anger. She would not submit to this dreadful man. She would come about no matter what. But suddenly the steps stopped, and then retreated. Pressing her ear against the door, she heard him curse, and growl.

"What are you doing here? I want no interruptions, now."

Straining to catch a reply, Melissa could hear little but an indignant query in a deep voice which seemed somehow familiar, but try as she might she could not place it. The two men retreated to the lower room and all she could hear then was the mutter of harsh words, an altercation was in progress. Good, this gave her the respite she needed.

She crossed to the windows again and cracked the pitcher softly on the sill, leaving a rough edge which served as a knife. With this, she worked frantically at the framing, hoping the noise would not alarm her protagonists below. At last she succeeded in prying the glass from the frame, and the dank air blew into the room. Leaning outside she saw the branches of a large yew brushing the side of the cottage. Fright added courage to her determination and she considered the tree thoughtfully. Yes, she might do it.

She scrambled out of the window, almost too narrow to allow her slight frame purchase, but she accomplished it somehow, and edged herself onto a stout branch. Looking down she shuddered, but she had climbed trees before, this one should not defeat her. Carefully she clambered down, her hands scratched and bleeding from the effort, her ears pealed for any sound from the two in the cottage. Halfway down she thought she heard footsteps which only hastened her descent.

At last she reached the ground, and then looked warily about. What to do now? Put as much distance from this horrid hovel as possible, but in what direction? She darted quickly down a rutted path but had no idea where she was heading. On every side was dark shrubbery, impeding any view of an escape route. Looking behind her she saw no sign of pursuit, and hurried on. She did not see the dark figure looming up before her, until she rushed pell-mell into his arms.

"Rather strenuous exercise for such a cold morning, my dear. Where are you off to in such haste," came Theron's taunting tones. He held her strongly, black anger belying the mocking voice.

"Oh, Theron, thank goodness. I have been abducted by that nasty Major Gratton. He took me to this dreadful place and would have had his way with me, if he had not been interrupted. How did you find me?" she gasped, collapsing with relief in his sheltering hold.

"Never mind that now. I must get you away from here before that rotter appears. Not that I would not bring him to account with relish. Lucien has the carriage down the road. Let us be off. I can deal with Gratton later." Theron's manner boded no good for that gentleman.

But before he could hurry her away, the door of the cottage opened and Gratton appeared in the entrance. At one glance he took in the situation—his victim was escaping, and into the arms of the very man he feared would seek a dire retribution upon him. Recklessly, in a passion of anger and frustration, he drew a pistol.

"Release that chit. She's mine," he demanded of Theron.

"I think not, you damned scoundrel," Theron responded, and to Melissa's horror, he too drew a gun. Gratton, unsteady from the brandy he had imbibed and the furious disruption to his morning's sport, fired recklessly at the couple. His shot went wide, but Theron's did not. It caught the Major in the shoulder and he fell gasping to the ground. Ignoring the wounded man Theron picked up Melissa cooly and walked away, down the path to his waiting carriage, sublimely indifferent to the fate of his opponent, writhing and cursing on the ground.

Chapter Twenty-Seven

Once in the safety of the carriage, Melissa tried valiantly to restrain her tears and shaking. The ordeal had taxed her spirits to the utmost. She wanted comfort and cosseting, but she would receive neither from Theron, who once he had greeted Lucien relapsed into a dark silence. Lucien, driving the curricle, tried to discover what had happened but Theron turned aside his questions with a brief remark, promising to explain all later. When Melissa stammered a few words of thanks for her rescue, he ignored her, glaring balefully at her as they rushed down the road toward the city.

"But Theron, old fellow, you cannot just leave the man, bleeding on the path, you know," Lucien protested.

"Why not? He deserves no less. But I will send someone to see to him when we get back to town. And I will see to you, too, madam," he glowered, thoroughly aroused as he thought of what might have happened to Melissa.

Timidly, recognizing his mood, Melissa asked, "But how did you know where to find me, Theron? That mean cottage was so isolated. I am truly grateful for my rescue, but how did you discover my whereabouts?"

Theron, however, did not see fit to confide in his companions, and only replied, "I will deal with you later, madam. You have been a confounded nuisance, and you have a lot of explaining to do, yourself."

"Really, Theron, don't chivy the poor girl," Lucien said. "Can't you see that she is a sad case. Look at her hands, all scratched and bleeding, aside from the shock to her sensibilities, of being abducted."

"No more than she deserved. I have warned her, and now she has come within an ace of getting herself raped or killed. The stubborn little fool, thinking she could manage affairs on her own."

"I'll have you know that I did manage fairly well, Theron, and I can't see how this was my fault," Melissa responded with more spirit. Now that they had reached safety, her normal sensibilities were restored and a healthy anger was brewing at Theron's attitude.

But Theron refused to be mollified, and one look at his closed, hostile face persuaded Melissa she would do well to hold her tongue. At any rate with Lucien as a spectator she was not inclined to wrangle with Theron, especially tooling along at a hectic pace in the curricle.

Lucien, too, decided in view of Theron's intransient attitude, to take refuge in his own thoughts. His friend's violent reaction to Melissa's abduction reinforced his belief that the rakehell Marquis cared more about the girl than he would let on. Both Sarah and Lady Ravensham were convinced that Theron loved the girl, but Lucien had remained dubious, knowing far more about the Marquis' libertine proclivities than his womenfolk. Sarah, whose heart often ruled her head, was too apt to be swayed by her romantic sympathies, but in this case Lucien was inclined to agree with her. He smiled to himself. If that was indeed the case they were in for some turbulent times before the affair resolved itself in the manner his impressionable wife desired. With his two companions glowering at one another, Lucien contented himself with imagining the fireworks ahead and concentrated on his driving.

In this manner, the trio finally reached Stanhope Gate where Lucien deposited his passengers bidding them a pleasant farewell and rode off chuckling to himself.

Once inside the doors of the house Melissa was greeted with lamentations by Bessie, who looked appalled at her disheveled mistress.

"Take her away and clean her up, Bessie. I will wait in the drawing room until she is fit to be seen," Theron ordered. "And send me a bottle of Madeira." He stalked off toward the drawing room, leaving Melissa to Bessie's tender ministrations.

Bessie swept Melissa upstairs, muttering all the time, and Melissa was hard put to keep from screaming. They acted as if the abduction and subsequent terrors were her fault. Her resentment and anger fueled by Theron's callous manner, increased with every minute. Not even a soothing bath and a restoring bowl of soup dampened her ire. She instructed Bessie to call a carriage as she must be off to the theatre for rehearsal. Bessie, shocked, refused, saying she would send a message that Melissa had taken ill, as she was in no case to join the company. Too weary to protest further, Melissa settled before the fire in her dressing gown and relived the ordeal again. She had to think that Aimee de Frontons had lured her to the frightful fate Gratton had planned, and she determined to seek her revenge on that conniving lady. She was in no mood to be dragged over the coals by Theron, and she wished she could postpone an interview with the Marquis for she felt unequal to the confrontation.

Theron, his temper not improved by dipping into the Madeira, strode into her bedroom, dismissing Bessie with a negligent wave of his hand, much to that woman's distress, for she had every intention of quizzing Melissa on events.

"Not now, Bessie. You can have your innings later, but I have a few words to say to Miss Langford." He bundled her out the door without more ado, throwing the bolt behind her.

"Really, Theron. You take too much on yourself," Melissa protested, girding herself for a battle royal. He would not cow her with his highhanded ways.

"You are the outside of enough, madam. If I had not taken the precaution of setting a man to watch you, the Lord knows what would have happened to you. Do you realize that much vaunted virtue you cling to so stubbornly would be gone by now. And I doubt you would have appreciated the manner of losing it," he snarled, standing before the fireplace and glaring down at Melissa, seated in a slipper chair warming her toes. The sight of her pale face and lacerated hands only seemed to fuel his wrath.

"I did not provoke Major Gratton to act in such an odious way!" Melissa cried. "The fault for that lies at your door. Your precious Comtesse had much to do with what happened to me."

"Excuses will avail you nothing," he replied curtly, "And I have dealt with Aimee, don't worry. But this experience teaches you that you are not impervious to attack. You cannot rush headlong into danger, thinking you can handle matters which are far beyond your talents. You delight in defying me, and I will not have it."

"Theron, I know I owe you gratitude for a great deal, but I will not be chivied and ordered around in this fashion. You do not control my every action," Melissa hurled back at him. She knew she should try to cajole him since he did not respond to defiance, but she was in no mood to play the pitiful waif. He must learn she was not one of his simpering women, content with whatever he offered, but a person of independence and in charge of her own destiny. If she surrendered to him now, she would be lost.

"You try the patience of a saint, my girl."

Before Melissa could protest, he dragged her from the chair and into his arms.

"For weeks you have challenged me with your innocence and I have respected your limits, but no longer. Before this day is past you will know what it is like to be loved—whatever your virtuous fears." He lowered his head and kissed her sensuously, forcing her mouth open to his invading tongue, his hands roaming slowly over her back and drugging her with languorous strokes. She lost all desire to struggle. These kisses were not a bit like the gentle caresses he usually bestowed, nor were they the practiced embraces of the skilled controlled lover. His passion threatened to break all bounds as his hands slid down the length of her body evoking a fiery response.

"I've burned with desire for you," he murmured, his voice harsh.

"Please, Theron, don't do this. We will both regret it," Melissa whispered, as aroused as he by the sensations his lips and his hands evoked.

His mouth took hers again, moving from her lips to her neck, and finally to the cleft between her delicate breasts. She gasped, shuddering, unable to fight against his strength and her own desire. What was happening to her that she allowed him such liberties? He groaned as she melted against him, hardly aware that he was removing her robe and freeing her from the restricting nightgown. Her body flamed with passion as he lifted her, naked now, and placed her on the bed. She stared up at him, mesmerized, as he quickly shed his own clothes, and then he was beside her, his hands lulling her with seductive strokes, his dark eyes glowing with need. She made an ineffectual attempt to evade his hands and mouth, clawing at his back, and struggling to escape the hands which were determined to subdue her. He caught her back as she struggled to the edge of the bed and kissed her ruthlessly, arousing her with the force of his passion. Weak with the unfamiliar emotions which were coursing through her limbs, still she fought, but he easily countered her feeble struggles. With every touch of his hands and mouth she felt her resistance fading. Now his lips were gentling, as he moved her under him and parted her legs. An intolerable tension which had been building within her shattered under a sudden pain which slowly dissipated to a throbbing pleasure. Her flailing hands stilled and she found herself responding to the rhythm of his violent movement within her. With a shuddering gasp he released himself. For a moment she lay in stunned disbelief, his possession of her throbbing body beyond her wildest imagination.

"Now, at last you know what it is to be a woman. I should regret it, but I cannot. You tempted me beyond all control," he murmured, smoothing her hair with a gentle hand and watching her reaction.

His hands were gentle, but his words angered Melissa. He had not taken her from love, but from lust, of that she was convinced, and now she had become just another of his legion of women. He was no better than Gratton. She pulled away from him in disgust.

Theron rose leisurely and stood beside the bed, watching her cynically as she strove to pull the coverlet around her nakedness.

"It had to happen eventually. I only regret that I forced you when you were vulnerable. But you aroused the devil in me. Next time it will be different, *ma mie,*" he said softly, his eyes hooded as he saw the blush of mortification which flooded her cheeks.

"There will be no next time. I am not some doxy, eager for your attentions. I will not forgive you for this, my lord. Now leave me," Melissa answered coldly, her innermost fears justified by his calm assumption that she had now become his until he wearied of her.

"We will see. For the moment I will leave you to repine in private. But we are not finished, my dear," he said firmly, and turned away to don his clothes. He dressed quickly, and then turned to the shrinking figure in the bed, his gaze roaming over her possessively. He bent and kissed her resisting lips. "You will come to enjoy it, believe me. You are a passionate young thing and need a lover to content you. I will see you later today," he promised and left her, a prey to a welter of confused thoughts. Tears rose to her eyes, and flowed down her cheeks. He had used her vilely but the ruthless possession of her body only reinforced her deepest fears. She had fought the knowledge long enough, but now admitted, lying bruised and unhappy on her bed, that she loved Theron, and she feared it was a love destined to bring her only unhappiness.

Chapter Twenty-Eight

With conflicting emotions, Theron stalked away from Stanhope Gate in search of a hackney. He had not wanted to take her in anger, but the morning's events had provoked his darkest humour—fear for her safety, dismay at her reckless behaviour, and rage at her defiance, compounded by a tempestuous interview with Aimee de Frontons.

When he had decided to remain aloof from Melissa he had not been unmindful of her well-being, and had deputized a man to watch over her. It was this agent who had seen her enter the hackney that drove away at such frightening speed. The man had hurried to Theron's Grosvernor Square house to tell him of the strange journey. Theron, recovering from a massive overindulgence in wine, was toying with a beefsteak and cursing his folly at dipping so deep the evening before when the man was ushered into the dining room. Immediately he had feared that either the French spy master had learned of Melissa's involvement in the attempt to unmask him and had taken dire measures to restrain her or Horace Hawksley had spirited her away. Either possibility placed her in jeopardy.

As he made ready to leave in pursuit of her captor, Lucien Valentine arrived, and Theron prevailed upon him, after a few terse words of explanation, to accompany him. Lucien, too, was worried, as much by Theron's devilish mood as by the contemplation of Melissa's unenviable fate.

The two men drove off without more ado to Stanhope Gate. There they faced a distraught Bessie, who was already worried by Melissa's strange departure and secretive manner. Bessie could tell them little except that Melissa had decided within moments of receiving the morning's post to dress and leave on her mysterious errand. Theron, determined to learn the cause of such behaviour, stormed into Melissa's bedroom, searching for the discarded missive which had inspired her journey. He found Aimee's note crumpled on the dressing table and read the request for an interview concerning him which only increased his rage. Explaining curtly to Lucien that the Comtesse had lured Melissa to a bogus interview he rushed from the house, followed by the worried colonel.

When the two reached Aimee's house after a silent ride, Theron did not stand on ceremony. Confronting Aimee, who was still in her boudoir, looking charmingly disengagé in a ruffled dressing gown, he brandished the note before her.

"And what is the meaning of this, madam? You will tell me what inspired you to write such a farrago of nonsense to Melissa. What did you hope to gain?" he snarled, in a veritable passion.

Aimee, undecided at what tone to take, hesitated, searching for a soothing nostrum, but frightened by Theron's furious stance, could only pretend innocence. She could not maintain the facade for long, for he took her by the shoulders and shook her soundly.

"I have warned you, Aimee, I will not brook your interference in my life, and if this is some misguided attempt to cause Melissa pain, you will pay dearly for your impudence," he threatened.

"Perhaps I was wrong, Theron, but I was only inspired by my devotion to you. I cannot bear that you have abandoned me for that chit of a girl," Aimee whimpered. "I was jealous, and thought if Melissa was removed you would turn again to me, for you and that little doxy are not well-suited," she tried to appease him, but he was beyond her cajolery.

"Where is she? And who has kidnapped her? I want answers now, and no evasions or it will be the worse for you," he warned, his tone and his posture redolent of barely controlled violence, his grasp on her arms tightening. He was within an ace of throttling her, and Lucien who stood by, a silent spectator to the scene, wondered if he must intervene before Theron murdered the woman.

"Stop it, Theron. You are hurting me. I did not believe you could care what happened to her. You seemed to have tired of your unaccountable interest, and I only wanted you back. Believe me, it was because I love you so much that I was persuaded into this desperate design," she pleaded, shrinking from the implacable face of her tormentor.

"Don't gammon me, my lady. You cared about my bankroll, and had hopes of beguiling me into an alliance. My biggest mistake was to rescue you from Brittany. I should have left you to Madame Guillotine. You would have been well served. And this is how you repay me," he replied callously, completely unmoved by her protestations.

Aimee, seeing that she had chanced her luck and failed, gave not a thought to her co-conspirator, and told Theron about her intrigue with Major Gratton. She hoped to distract the Marquis by insisting that the Major's passion for Melissa had been the sole reason for the abduction, trying to protect her more dangerous secret, her connivance with the French spy ring. But Theron, despite his rage, now simmering into a controlled disgust, soon had the whole sorry tale out of her.

"You have exhausted my limited patience, Comtesse. Not only have you betrayed the country which sheltered you, and acted vilely toward an innocent girl, but you have earned my lasting enmity. It would serve you well if I turned you over to the magistrates and left you to moulder away in Newgate or the Tower. But I have no time for you now. It will go easier if you tell me everything about this nefarious plot. Come, hurry, for my patience is at an end," he finished, eyeing her with an ugly look which brooked no resistance.

Aimee was forced to comply after turning to Lucien and seeing no sympathy in his equally cold, disgusted disapproval. After a pitiful attempt to deny that she knew Gratton's destination she confessed the whole, hoping to salvage something from the disaster by an appeal to Theron's charity. She mistook her man. Before leaving he warned, "You would be well advised to cut your losses, Comtesse, and flee the country. I am sure, with your many talents, you can survive, even under Napoleon. Go back to your estates and salvage what you can. If anything has happened to Melissa, I will have my revenge," he said with chilling finality. Sweeping Lucien before him, he departed as abruptly as he had arrived, leaving behind a much frightened lady, who realized she had gambled and lost.

Spurred by Theron to greater efforts, Lucien drove at a careening pace to Hampstead Heath, where they made a few abortive forays before finding the lane leading to the cottage which Aimee had described. Theron's relief at finding Melissa unharmed had turned to a smouldering anger at her willful action, the result of which had been his own ruthless seduction of her for which he now reviled himself.

He had not meant to practically rape her, had not meant seduction at all. No, that was not true, he conceded ruefully as he sat brooding in his library. From the first moment he had seen her in his carriage at Exeter he had meant to make her his. He had never denied himself a woman he wanted, and he had seen no reason to make an exception with Melissa, although her uncommon qualities—her independence, her courage—had evoked his admiration and delight. But he had meant to woo her softly into bed, and charm her into mindless surrender with his skilled lovemaking. Instead he had ravished her in the most violent way and left her with a well-deserved hatred toward him. And the seduction had not left him satisfied. Despite her inexperience and her reluctance, he had found her passionate and provocative, leaving him strangely dissatisfied by the coupling. She had not deserved to be used in such a cruel way.

How could he retrieve his mistake, rooted in his selfish anger which had rebounded on her so disastrously? He was bound in honour to offer her marriage. But when had he ever worried about honour. His whole life was a journey of dishonour, a reckless disregard of propriety, of decency. Would any young girl want to join her future to such as himself, even if he promised fidelity, a vow he saw little chance of maintaining, knowing his past record. He would make a vile husband. Melissa should be the cherished prize of some respectable man who would protect her and give her the life she needed. Wife to a rake was not in the cards for her, and he could not sacrifice a lifetime of independence even for her. He must let her go. Even with her virtue gone, many a more likely man would want her. He frowned, as if in pain. He could not let some more worthy man have her. She was his. She had been since his first encounter with her. Good Lord, what was he to do? What was best for her? For the first time in his misspent life Theron was considering the welfare of another before his own. Since his mother's betrayal and rejection, compiled by that disillusioning love affair in his callow youth, he had decided never to trust another woman, but now he was truly caught, enslaved by a chit hardly out of the nursery, his whole happiness dependent on a girl who had every reason to despise him.

Determined to cast aside the grimness of his dilemma, Theron at last bestirred himself from his dark reverie, and went about clearing up the results of his set-to with Gratton in Hampstead Heath.

Runners were sent to the cottage to apprehend the wounded officer, but he was not to be found. No doubt Gratton had managed to find sanctuary in some other refuge of the French spy ring, but he had shot his bolt. He could not return to his regiment and his usefulness to the French was at an end. The Comtesse, too, would find her French paymasters unwilling to subsidize her any longer. But these two were unimportant. They no longer needed to be considered. Aimee had no more information to give. Theron suspected that few of the agents had ever met the ringleader. In that he was clever, hiding his identity and arranging some manner of collecting his reports without revealing himself to his minions. But he would be caught, Theron determined, and before much more damage could be done. The Foreign Office and War Department would heed his words now.

One encouraging result of this day's disaster was the information he had wrested from Aimee. He now knew he was much closer to finding the spy leader who had challenged him for so long. Although Aimee had not known the man's identity, she had admitted such a master mind existed. He had embroiled both Gratton and Aimee in his conspiracy, promising her the return of her husband's estates, and Gratton's cooperation had been secured by massive payments of gold. However, they were but weak pawns in a long chain. Theron suspected that Gratton had used whatever information he could pry from the War Office comrades to secure his French master's payments, and Aimee's entree in the ton had enabled her to discover snippets of information which might have had some value.

Somehow this whole affair culminated at the theatre, definitely the headquarters of the group, which left Melissa more vulnerable than ever. Eager for action, to postpone the agony of his thoughts, Theron called for a change of clothes, dashed off a few notes at his desk, and decided to pay a call on both Valentine and Castlereagh now that his deepest suspicions had been confirmed. As for Melissa, he must leave her to recover from her recent ordeals as best she might, for he felt unequal to facing her before he had resolved the finale to their tempestuous relationship.

Chapter Twenty-Nine

"So you see, Lucien, what we have here is a whole network of the traitors, centering on the theatre where their budget of information is collected by the ringleader, then turned over to the French. God knows, there are enough emigrés of dubious loyalties, gathered in London, determined on regaining their estates and not caring who they betray to do it. I've always thought it was the height of foolishness to welcome all the ragtag of Versailles leavings into society, influenced by their pitiable conditions as the result of the Revolution," Theron explained to his friend. "Castlereagh agrees that we have not been as careful as we might, and that the emigrés have entrée everywhere. Aimee is a good case in point, and her acceptance can be largely laid at my door. What a fool I was to be taken in by her posturings."

"Well, you can hardly be damned for rescuing a relative in distressed circumstances," Lucien responded. "You could not have known she would be so disloyal. A nasty woman that. London is a hotbed of traitors—our own, as well as the emigrés, French gold will tempt even our own people. Look at what we discovered not a year past. And Sarah almost losing her life in the discovery." Lucien frowned, remembering the danger his own wife had experienced in uncovering just such a master spy, a respected General in the War Office.

"Yes, we are gullible fools. But I can at last see an end to this particular set. I am pondering our next move. Much as I hate to see Melissa return to the theatre, it is our best hope of unmasking the ring leader. She will be on her guard now, and I will not let her out of my sight," Theron vowed, forgetting his recent decision to banish her from his life.

"I take it Melissa is agreeable," Lucien proffered wryly.

"We came to an understanding," Theron replied cooly. Not even to Lucien could he confide his dilemma over Melissa, and he would never allow Valentine to suspect what had really transpired between them. Lucien, although he had experienced his share of light amours before his marriage, was a man of strong principles, and now the most faithful of benedicts since wedding Sarah. Theron valued Lucien's friendship and Sarah's regard. If they knew how he had punished Melissa for her foolhardy independence they would turn from him in disgust. Theron had a great deal of practice in turning an aloof facade to the curious and his enigmatic manner stood him in good stead now. If he could do little else, at least he could protect Melissa, although he cynically admitted he was the last man to adopt such a role.

"I am sure you will see that she comes to no harm, but I believe you have your work cut out for you. She's an independent willful little miss and does not take direction easily, I warrant." Lucien eyed his companion with some question. Prudence and politeness precluded him from delving further into the relationship between the two, but he wondered just how affairs stood after the recent disaster. Rarely had he seen the Marquis in such a taking, for that gentleman usually met life with cool composure. This spy business was a nagging irritant, but Lucien believed Melissa posed more of a problem than Napoleon's most skilled agents.

"What we do know now is that someone in the theatre is using it as a focal point for collecting information," Theron said. "I think agents from all over London gather their budget of news and are instructed where to deposit it in the Majestic, where the unknown leader forwards it to France. That method protects him, because the agents never have to meet him face to face, and if they are caught they cannot reveal the identity of the leader. He must be a member of the company with access to the theatre at all times. There are a half a dozen men in the troupe who could play the role, dammit, and we are no further along in unmasking the traitor. All we have proved is that the Majestic is a center for the conspiracy. But I suspected that before. There are some who think the simplest way of dealing with this outrage is just to close the theatre down, but I think that would be a mistake. Our villain would just move his activities elsewhere, and we would be no better off."

Lucien looked troubled. "I know you have warned Melissa to go carefully. I keep thinking of that actress, throttled on the floor of her dressing room. Her murderer has not been found, either."

"When we find the traitor we will find the murderer," Theron said harshly, remembering Alison Andrew's pitiable fate. "At least the investigation keeps the Bow Street runner on the premises, and serves as a warning to the fellow that he will not get away with another such deed. Borley's chief use is as a deterrent to any more such incidents, and as such is a watchdog for Melissa."

Lucien, seeing that further discussion was only adding to Theron's burdens, turned the conversation. He reminded Theron that Lady Ravensham believed that she could discover Melissa's grandparents, and now was in possession of the locket to spur her memory. "If she could find Melissa's family, it would be a great relief. Once restored to them and under their protection, her reputation will be redeemed, and she need not rely on that guardian, who seems to have been derelict in his duties. Her grandparents will be able to arrange a suitable match for her, and that is as it should be," Lucien said firmly, determined to let Theron know that Melissa had friends and supporters who cared about her well-being and would insure her future. He respected Theron's ideas of honour among men, but he feared from his past record, that he entertained no such concept in his dealings with women.

"Oh, she has plenty of admirers, and serious suitors," Theron snapped bitterly. "That cub Percy Ashburton would marry her tomorrow if she allowed it. And Sir Harry Acton thinks she is some kind of goddess. Do not worry, Lucien, our little star can provide for herself very well. Have no fears on that score."

"I think Lady Ravensham has discovered some clue to her mother's identity. But she will want to tell you herself. Shall we join the ladies?" Lucien asked, treading gingerly. Theron's mood was touchy and he had some qualms about the Marquis' reaction to the latest revelations.

Sarah and her grandmother had many questions to ask about Melissa's latest adventure, which Lucien had vaguely discussed. Both men knew the ladies could be trusted to keep their own counsel about the French conspiracy and Sarah, in particular, had some experience in these matters. Theron greeted them and was able to reassure them that Melissa had brushed through the encounter with Major Gratton safely.

"As soon as Melissa gave me the locket and I examined it, I recalled whom she resembled," Lady Ravensham said. "When Ronald first went on the town he was quite taken with Elizabeth Carstairs. She and her twin sister, Maria, were both belles of the season, lovely girls, with many suitors. Maria was a very biddable girl, demure and quiet. She married the Earl of Cranston's heir, but died in childbirth. Her sister, Elizabeth, a much more lively girl, refused countless offers and ran away with a young man to India. I believe Elizabeth was Melissa's mother. I have written to Sir Claude and Lady Carstairs about her, and expect an answer soon. Sir Claude will undoubtedly want to come to London to see Melissa. I cannot believe the Carstairs, a charming couple, are still angry over the precipitate match. They will want to know their granddaughter, since they have no other heirs. I think it best not to mention the possibility to Melissa until my suspicions are confirmed."

Theron's brow darkened. He did not like the idea of Melissa's having relatives who would remove her from his protection. If she was indeed the granddaughter of this pair, his treatment of her could not go unchallenged.

"Are you sure, ma'am, that Melissa is this girl? You could be mistaken. Many years have past since you knew the mother," he offered tentatively.

"She is the very picture of Elizabeth Carstairs. I cannot believe my memory is at fault. Ronald was quite disappointed when she refused his offer, so I remember the girl well," Lady Ravensham insisted. "I wanted the match. But he married Margaret instead." She sighed, for her youngest son's wife had never been her choice and the marriage had not been a successful one. Lord Ravensham found little happiness in the domestic circle and spent most of his time at the Foreign Office where he was deeply involved with state business.

"I agree it would be best not to mention this to Melissa until the Carstairs confirm your suspicions. Even if she is their granddaughter, they might not want to receive her considering her reputation and current profession," Theron said. If she was indeed the daughter of this well-born lady, he had no choice but to offer her marriage. Somehow the prospect of having his hand forced in such a fashion did not seem disagreeable. He had to marry eventually, and he could do much worse. His own reputation did not bear scrutiny, and many parents would not accept him as an eligible parti. He refused to admit he hoped Melissa would indeed turn out to be a Carstairs and prove to be a proper bride for him. But he was not yet willing to confide in the Ravenshams. He had to settle affairs with Melissa first. He smiled grimly. She would take it in bad odour if he proposed to her after he discovered her background. Well, he would not accept any refusal. She would obey him.

Sarah, bolder than her grandmother and her husband, watching the effect of Lady Ravensham's words on the Marquis, intervened, "Are you going to offer for Melissa, Theron?"

"I see that marriage has not quelled your audacity, Sarah. You will just have to restrain your curiosity. I have not decided what to do about Melissa, but you have my assurance she will come to no harm through me," he answered austerely. Not even to such close friends as the Ravenshams could he reveal his indecision and his self-contempt. He had taken advantage of Melissa's vulnerability and, not for the first time, he realized how empty his life would be if he had to surrender her to another.

Lady Ravensham, more astute than the Marquis credited, smiled to herself. Affairs were turning out as she had expected. Theron cared more for the girl than he wanted to admit. His indiscretions would now be abandoned and she believed he would settle down and become a faithful and loving husband. Lady Ravensham, despite her own unhappy past, had never lost her taste for romance. She tended always to believe in the felicitous outcome of relationships, even one as turbulent as Theron's and Melissa's. They would make a match of it, she was convinced.

Theron did nothing to disabuse her of her notions, but he was a past master at dissembling and hid his uneasiness at the prospect of Melissa's grandparents wresting her from his influence. He promised the Ravenshams to keep in touch, and hoped they would let him know the outcome of Lady Ravensham's approach to the Carstairs before bidding them farewell.

Evening was drawing in as he left their Park Street house. He could not decide what to do. By now Melissa should have recovered in some part from her recent ordeal. He had promised to visit her, but he was reluctant to approach her. She might have taken him in such disgust that any attempt on his part to bring her around would only cause another argument. He did not want her to feel she must accept him because he had taken her virtue, but if he waited too long the Carstairs might make their claim and she would be forever lost to him. That was an eventuality he refused to entertain. The girl had completely ensnared him.

From the very beginning her rare quality had attracted him, her innocence allied to that spirited courage which led her into situations she was ill-suited to handle but which she faced indomitably. He acknowledged her rare quality, her fragile beauty allied to an unsuspected passion. Her response to his lovemaking had surprised them both and now that he had tasted the delights she offered he would never surrender her to another. Probably she could find a gentler husband but not one who would appreciate her as she deserved. They had already shared so much, and the end of their partnership was not in sight. Theron realized that Melissa would insist on fidelity and honesty in their dealings. But he was lost, and he welcomed the bonds which would tie him firmly to her side. Although he was willing to admit he must marry her, he was not yet ready to confess his love. That was an emotion he viewed charily, one which he had never entertained with any composure. He would marry her but she must not expect romantic vows. Never would he submit to that thralldom. She must accept him as he was, he decided. Arrogant still, Theron de Lisle would not surrender his freedom to any woman, no matter what her attractions. But he had walked alone for too long. Passion and compatability were reason enough to marry. A tender and selfless love did not enter into the arrangement he would make with Melissa.

Chapter Thirty

Melissa, both relieved and disappointed by Theron's absence that evening, tried to come to terms with what had happened between them. She could not deny her own love, but she was convinced he did not think of her in that way, and the prospect of their next meeting had her in a taking. How would she receive him? Should she ignore their tempestuous encounter, pretend his lovemaking had meant little to her. Pride came to her rescue. She would not join the legions of women who panted for his embraces, yearned for his kisses. He had used her in anger to satisfy his lust, and she must not expect any deeper emotion. She had little confidence that she had won what so many more attractive women had failed to secure.

In her heart she knew that no other man could ever win her. Theron had put his mark upon her and she must live with the knowledge that what was for her a never to be forgotten, heart-rending experience, was to him just another conquest in a long line of amourous sieges. Well, he would discover that this first explosion of passion between them was the last. She could not endure such soulless coupling, to be used in lustful pleasure with no softer emotion. She would deny the clamourings of her body for fulfillment, but she knew that her struggles to refuse him would cost her dearly.

The next morning, unrefreshed by a troubled, lonely night,

she and Bessie repaired to the theatre. Life must go on, and the rehearsal of "Romeo and Juliet" was her first responsibility. The company, still edgy from all the turmoil surrounding the investigation of Alison's murder, tried in the most professional manner to concentrate on the task at hand, but the rehearsal did not go smoothly. Robert Rathbone seemed especially distrait, and in any event, did not make a convincing Romeo. Melissa felt she read her lines, which she had mastered, with little conviction, and all in all Mr. Whitebread had every reason to complain. He could only insist it would all come together when they opened the play two nights hence. Melissa hoped he was right, for it was on her suggestion the company was attempting the tragedy.

Feeling drained by the hours spent on stage, she went to her dressing room to collect Bessie and leave for Stanhope Gate. The dresser was seated behind a welter of costumes, stitching away and shaking her head.

"I know we must practice economy but remaking these costumes of Alison's for Nell is a spooky task. Fair gives me the shivers," she said when Melissa questioned her.

"Yes, I can imagine. But can you not leave them for now, I am yearning for a cup of tea and a rest. Let us return to Stanhope Gate," Melissa urged, weariness apparent in every line of her fragile body.

"All right dearie. I will just finish this skirt. What's this, a nasty bulge." She ran her hand down the muslin gown and extracted a large handkerchief. "What's this doing here, I wonder?" she mused as she looked over the large piece of linen.

It was obviously a man's handkerchief, of fine white linen, and embroidered with an initial. Melissa, with a sense of repugnance, took the material from Bessie and looked at the initial, a scrawling scripted "W." What did that stand for?

And what was a man's handkerchief doing in Alison's costume? Quickly running over the possibilities in her mind, she conceded that the only man connected with the company who might own the handkerchief must be Samuel Whitebread himself. Running the linen back and forth through her hands, the idea came to her with stunning force. If this was in Alison's costume it meant that the late actress must have had more of a relationship with the impresario than any of them had suspected. Could he have been her paramour? And if that was so, it meant that he might have been her murderer, a chilling thought which Melissa could barely entertain. But it made sense, she thought, remembering the note she had discovered during her search of Alison's effects. She might be wrong, but it could not be a coincidence. This was a clue pointing to the unknown man with whom the actress had been involved. She must let Theron know immediately. Shocked and stunned by the discovery, Melissa folded the tell-tale handkerchief and placed it in her reticule.

"I will take care of this, Bessie. It might be well if you did not mention this matter to anyone. I am not sure what it means, but for the moment we must keep silent about it," she told the dresser, her expression troubled.

Bessie, who was equally puzzled, had enough shrewdness to realize that Melissa believed she had made an important find, a pointer to the late actress' dreadful death. Her chief concern was to protect the girl who had come to mean so much to her, and she agreed, eyeing Melissa in dismay. "Of course, I will say nothing, Miss Melissa. But don't you go poking around this affair. It means trouble. I can smell it," Bessie warned, a shiver of apprehension passing over her sturdy frame.

"You may be right, but until we have more information we must keep this a secret. I will consult the Marquis. He will have some ideas." Melissa realized that her reliance on Theron's protection meant she must face him and confess her concern. She sighed ruefully. She had always relied on her own instincts and ability to manage her own affairs, but his careless possession of her somehow had changed that independence. What a ninny she was, grabbing at any excuse to restore their relationship. But if this handkerchief proved Whitebread's involvement with the actress, she could not act alone. She needed his support and help.

On arriving back at Stanhope Gate Melissa found a huge bouquet of roses and a note from the Marquis saying he would join her for supper that evening. She told Bessie to order a light collation and repaired to her bedroom to make ready for the meeting with a mixture of feelings—embarrassment, confusion and excitement—warring with each other. She dressed very carefully in a demure gown of white lace over a blue silk underskirt, and after a moment's hesitation clasped the diamond and amythest necklace around her throat. Pinching her cheeks to bring some colour into her wan complexion, she sighed. She looked frightened and unsure of herself, not the picture she wanted to present to him. She must adopt a casual air for she would not want him to think that their last meeting and what had passed between them had completely overset her. She was convinced he would not be moved by what had transpired.

He arrived, as promised, at seven o'clock. In his austere evening dress, he appeared completely master of the situation. Accustomed to greeting his mistresses with aplomb, Melissa thought bitterly. Before he could launch into any explanations or even apologies, which she hardly expected, she produced the handkerchief and hurried into speech.

"Bessie found this in one of Alison's costumes she was remaking today. As you can see the initial embroidered in this corner is a "W." The only man with that initial connected with the theatre is Mr. Whitebread himself. It must mean something, that he had some intimate relationship with Alison, perhaps."

"Yes, it would seem so," Theron responded, his brow furrowed in thought. "This might be just the evidence we were searching for. I hope you did not tell anyone about this discovery, and that Bessie will keep her mouth shut."

"Do you think Mr. Whitebread is our spy and Alison's murderer? Why would he behave so? I never suspected him,"

Melissa said, shocked at the thought of what the impresario might have done.

"He is in the perfect position to run the ring, having control of the Majestic, and if Alison had taxed him with any suspicion he would be ruthless in silencing her. He has a great deal at stake. If he thought you suspected him, your life would not be worth a farthing," Theron replied harshly, anxiety over Melissa's safety overriding any satisfaction he might have felt at this incriminating evidence of Whitebread's treachery.

"He cannot know we have found this. If he is indeed the traitor, he has played his role with great finesse and skill," Melissa said, remembering the director's dismay at the time of Alison's death. "What an unnatural man, a veritable monster, to murder a woman whom he professed to care for in order to protect his secret."

"I doubt that he felt anything for her beyond a convenient liaison to satisfy his physical desires. He would not have confided in her." Theron eyed Melissa carefully, remembering their own last violent encounter. He winced at her reddening cheeks. "But enough of this. I must cast a more careful look at Whitebread. Now that we think he is the villain, there must be other indications. You are not to try to delve into the matter any further. Do you understand me?"

"Well, I will be most circumspect and careful, but I can make no promises. After all, that is why I am at the Majestic, to unmask the spy leader," Melissa argued. She would not sit tamely by and let Theron do all the investigating.

Theron took her chin between his long fingers and forced her to look up at him. "You are never circumspect and careful, and I have no intention of allowing my future wife to put her life at risk, no matter how willful she might be," he said softly.

Melissa gasped in surprise, loathe to believe she had heard him correctly. "What do you mean, Theron?"

"I mean that you are going to marry me, and before too long. Then I will be in the best position to protect you, and this masquerade will be finished. Do not argue with me, Melissa.

My mind is made up. I will marry you," he said.

Aroused by his cavalier manner, his assumption that she would hail his proposal with flattering gratitude, Melissa's hackles rose. He need not think that because he had seduced her she would fall at his feet in eagerness to make their relationship binding. No mention of love or affection could be glimpsed on his dark dominating face.

"You cannot be serious, my lord. Just because of what recently happened between us . . . I mean you do not have to make an honest woman of me," Melissa stammered, embarrassed and disappointed at his brusque, casual assumption.

Theron, realizing that he had handled the proposal badly, and equally irritated, did nothing to retrieve his mistake. "I have to marry someday, and you will suit quite well. At least I will know that my heirs will be mine. And I owe you some reparation for taking your virginity so brutally, Melissa. I regret that, but there is little I can do to repair the damage. Marriage is the answer," he said decisively, reluctant to admit to any warmer emotion than expediency. Curse the girl. She was so stubborn. She would marry him, if he had to drag her by the hair to the altar.

"What kind of a marriage will it be under these circumstances? You do not care for me in that way. You feel obligated, and that is not sufficient excuse," Melissa argued tiredly. If only he would take her in his arms and confess to some remnant of affection for her, how gladly would she embrace her fate.

Theron's dark mood vanished and he smiled gently at the perturbed girl standing before him in defiance and dismay. She was irresistible. Why could he not tell her his real motive, that he could not contemplate surrendering her to another. The idea of any other man claiming what he had possessed was anathema to him. But he could not tell her of the force of his feelings. He would not submit his life to any woman, even one as captivating and endearing as this one.

"Come, poppet. It will not be so terrible, better than the

odious Algy, you know. You will be my Marchioness, with a house in town, the place in the country which you might prefer, and I will make an unexceptional husband, not demanding and possessive, I promise," he coaxed, using all the persuasion at his command, and at last taking her in his arms and caressing her, his lips wandering slowly over her blushing face, eyes, and hair. Bemused by his careful lovemaking, so different from the hard sensuous demands he had made before, Melissa's defences weakened. Oh, he was a devil, and how could she continue to fight against her heart and this warm coursing emotion he evoked. "And I have discovered why your guardian is so eager for that disastrous match. He controls the fortune your father left to you, and when you marry he must account to your husband. If you wed Algy he need not surrender the blunt." His voice was persuasive as he continued his disturbing kisses.

Melissa, astounded, jerked herself from his arms. "What do you mean, my fortune? I know nothing of any fortune."

"Well, I had my suspicions money was at the root of his treatment of you," Theron said, allowing her some distance, and seating himself in a nearby chair.

"But he never told me, . . . I had no idea," Melissa stammered, appalled at the revelation of her guardian's duplicity.

"Well, he saw no need. If you married Algy you need never have known. The law may be an ass, as Shakespeare claimed, but it has its uses. My solicitor soon tracked down Hawksley's chicanery. He has been using your money all these years to support his manor, and, no doubt, the excesses of that nasty nephew of his who seems up the river tick. But when you marry, all this will be the business of your husband. Yet another reason to wed me, my dear," he explained, watching her through his hooded eyes, to see how she took the news of her changed fortune.

"What could my father have been thinking to deliver me into the hands of such a villain," Melissa responded, indignation her chief reaction. The shock of her changed status combined with his proposal completely confused her.

"Your parents probably did not intend to leave you bereft at such an early age. But living in India, so far from home and any family, your father provided as best he might. He could not have known that Hawksley would use you so. Incidentally, Melissa, what was your mother's first name? I have never heard you refer to it," he asked cooly, as though it was of little moment, but beneath his indolent air he tensed, awaiting her answer.

"Elizabeth. But I never knew her maiden name. I cared little for that sort of thing. I was so young," she said, wistfully remembering her gay, affectionate parents.

"You are still too young, but old enough to become a wife. And the sooner I wrest you from this unaccountable desire to cavort upon the stage, the better it will be," Theron said.

"I must continue with Juliet now that it has been announced. And I rather like being the toast of London," Melissa answered spiritedly, unwilling to surrender without a struggle. "And then there is this business of Mr. Whitebread. We must contrive to bring Alison's murder home to him, and unmask his traitorous activities." Her chin set and her eyes clouded recalling that dreadful scene.

Theron sighed. He had forced her to submit to him once and had almost immediately regretted it. Whatever reparation he made now would be a paltry recompense for his selfish mastery of her. But he would not let her escape. She had no recourse but to marry him.

Evidently she had not considered the result of his seduction. She could even now be carrying his child. Somehow this thought filled him with an overweening pleasure, but he could not use that weapon to force her. She would be overcome, and he doubted the possibility had crossed her mind. What a child she was despite her independence and belief she could rule her own destiny. A wave of possessiveness flooded through him. She needed him, and Lord knows, he wanted her badly enough to use almost any excuse to claim her.

"You will fulfill this one engagement, and then you will abandon this play acting. And I am going to see to it that you are protected. Borley is still hanging about the Majestic, but it might be wise to hire a few more runners to keep an eye on you while you are there. Whitebread knows if he tries any tricks in regard to you, he will have me to deal with, and I think that might give him pause. But your situation is far from easy. No more of this dashing off on investigations of your own. I have dealt with Gratton and Aimee, but they are not the only agents in French pay. There is a veritable hornet's nest of spies, all under Whitebread's leadership. I should have suspected him. Certainly he is more likely than Rathbone or Gordon, for example," Theron mused. He eyed Melissa. "The hour is late, and you look tired, poppet. No wonder, with all that you have experienced in the last twenty-four hours." He watched her carefully. She had drawn away from him, as if afraid he would claim further intimacies now that he had signaled his intention to wed her.

"Don't look so much like a scared rabbit. I have no intention of dragging you off to bed. That can wait until you are legally mine. Something for you to look forward to. For now you may return unmolested to your chaste couch," he assured her in that sardonic tone which always raised her hackles. Far better for her to be angry with him, than fear a renewal of his lovemaking. What an effect she had upon him. He was unaccustomed to putting another's welfare before his own, and surprised himself as much as Melissa by his forbearance. He could not imagine that she took his denial as a signal that he found her too innocent and unexperienced to be appealing.

"Good night, my lord," she rose and spoke cooly, unwilling to let him see her dismay. She was ashamed at how much she desired those passionate kisses which he bestowed so casually. For him she was just another in a long line of conquests, while for her he represented everything she yearned for in a husband. Whatever his reasons for marrying her they were not rooted in any sincere love, only in expediency and regret. He must never discover how she felt. His amusement and indifference would destroy her. Pride forced Melissa to bid him good-bye with the most superficial of smiles. He was not deceived by her offhand air. He knew he had given her several shocks and she needed time to absorb her changed circumstances.

"*Au revoir, ma mie.* I will be around tomorrow to drive you to the theatre. Try to get some rest. You are looking a bit hagged," he advised, leaning over and kissing her gently on the forehead.

"I wonder, my lord, that you should wish to marry someone whose looks are so disappointing. Perhaps you wish to retract your offer," she said pertly.

"Not at all. You will make an exceptional Marchioness. Now no pouting. Be off with you," he answered calmly, rather like an aged uncle soothing a recalcitrant child. And he was gone, leaving behind a much troubled girl. For all his negligent air, Melissa knew he would have his way. But he might still be in for a few surprises. She knew she should refuse to wed him, but she could not resist becoming his wife, even if an unloved one. Her own feelings were too overwhelming to be denied. She could only hope that in the intimacy of marriage she could inspire his affection if not the devotion and passion she would bring to their union.

Chapter Thirty-One

Backstage at the Majestic on the evening of Melissa's debut as Juliet the atmosphere in the dressing rooms and corridors throbbed with anticipation. Even the presence of Borley and his minions could not dampen the excitement of the company, convinced that the evening would be a triumph. The Marquis had not confided in the runner but had told him that the affair was marching toward a solution and he must not relax his vigilance. The front of the house was crowded with a glittering audience. The king's youngest son, the Duke of Cambridge, had reserved the royal box, and the stalls thronged with well-dressed aristocrats, their ladies displaying a dazzling array of jewels.

In the pit the less favoured members of the audience passed their time chattering and speculating, the level of noise rising to a crescendo as the hour approached for the curtain to open. From the glittering chandeliers hundreds of tapers cast their light on the scene which seethed with activity. Every seat in the theatre was filled, the normally blasé fans honouring the company by their early arrival, expecting to witness an unusual event in the history of the drama. Raucous bucks and gallants toasted the new star, impatiently awaiting a new vehicle for her abilities, and hoping she would not disappoint them.

Rarely had Juliet been so suitably cast, with a young glowing star whose youth and innocence could make the story of the star-crossed lovers so believable. Theron, surveying the house through his quizzing glass admitted the scene stirred the senses. No wonder Melissa was reluctant to give up the plaudits which would come to her this night. In his box, immediately to the right of the stage, and two removed from the royal box were the Valentines and Lady Ravensham, who had been joined at the last minute by a thin distinguished gentleman whose calm demeanour belied his inner qualms. For this guest was Sir Claude Carstairs who had arrived in London that afternoon in response to Lady Ravensham's letter.

In her dressing room Melissa was listening to the last minute instructions of George Whitebread. In his sober evening dress his mind fully occupied with the upcoming performance Melissa found it hard to believe that he was their culprit, the clever and ruthless master of a spy ring which was working toward the defeat of their country. Hoping that he would think her nervousness on meeting him was due to the imminence of the first night, she needed all her acting skills to hide her dislike and suspicion. She must trust in the fact that he expected the usual first night tremours from his star, and could sse nothing out of the way in her jittery reaction to his presence. Obviously his mind was entirely taken up with "Romeo and Juliet" at this hour and he had no idea that she viewed him as aught but the impresario concerned with the success of the drama.

"I have no fears that you will not acquit yourself creditably this evening," he said in what he believed was a comforting tone. "You know the play well, and have acted Juliet at Bath to an enthusiastic audience. I know that London will hail you with equal excitement. It is Rathbone who worries me. He does not project the image of the young, beset Romeo in quite the manner I find convincing. The burden of the evening rests with you, my dear."

"Robert will rise to the occasion I am sure, Mr. Whitebread.

I am not so sure about Nell. If only Alison could have played Lady Capulet," she suggested warily, watching him closely for a reaction. But to her disappointment his impassive face revealed no emotion.

He dismissed her comment with a brief, "Yes, she is sorely missed."

"There is no sign of the murderer, I understand. Mr. Borley seems to make little progress with the investigation," Melissa pressed him, unable to resist looking for some indication of his guilt.

"Unfortunately, no," he replied calmly. "But you must not allow that dreadful tragedy to overset you tonight. I rather think the perpetrator must have been some rejected lover. That is the theory the runner believes at any rate."

If he was indeed Alison's murderer how callous and indifferent he seemed to that poor girl's fate. His careless reference hardened Melissa's resolve. If he had killed the girl, he was indeed the ruthless monster she suspected, and deserved no compassion or consideration. His very insensibility convinced Melissa where a display of regret and horror might have given her pause. But she was careful to let none of her revulsion show.

Schooling her expression to one of timid apprehension she said, "Oh, I do hope the runners find the knave soon. It is dreadful to think a murderer may be lurking in the theatre."

He looked at her a bit sharply, then.

"You are in no danger, my dear. Now enough of this brooding. I will leave you to prepare yourself for your entrance and offer no advice but every assurance that you will bring the Majestic yet another success." He offered his usual nostrums smoothly, and, bowing, left her to her thoughts, which were not happy ones.

Melissa's portrayal of Juliet more than fulfilled Whitebread's expectations. The curtain rang down on a tumultuous ovation, the audience shouting its approval. The sophisticated theatre goers, moved by Melissa's youth and

fragility, had no difficulty in believing in the force of her il
starred love which drove her to her death. Many in the hous
were in tears as the final scene ended in the death of the tw
lovers. When Guy Gordon's last speech, "As rich shall Rome
by his lady's lie. Poor sacrifices of our enmity," rang throug
the still house, all conceded that the evening had provoke
powerful emotions. Melissa, with the rest of the company, too
many curtain calls, but the audience would not disperse unt
their reigning star at last received their tribute alone. Sh
bowed one last time on the empty stage and with a sigh of relie
watched the curtain descend for the final time.

In Theron's box, Sir Claude Carstairs could barely restrai
the tears which rose in his tired blue eyes. Lady Ravensha
leaned across Sarah and grasped him by the arm.

"Do you not see Melissa's uncanny resemblance t
Elizabeth, Sir Claude? I am right in suspecting she is you
granddaughter, am I not?" she asked in some anxiety, notin
the effect on the gentleman.

"I must agree, Lady Ravensham. She is the very picture c
our poor lost Elizabeth. I must see her at once. Do you thin
she will receive me?" he asked, remembering sadly th
estrangement from his adored daughter. "She gave a mos
touching portrayal, but I do not like to think of ou
granddaughter upon the stage. She must have been in di
straits to have been persuaded to such a course. Still I hav
no right to criticise since we have failed her so badly." H
sighed, guilt and sorrow obviously warring with his pride i
Melissa's talent.

"The Marquis has bespoken a small supper to celebrate he
triumph, Sir Claude," Lady Ravensham said gently. "You wi
meet her soon. We have told her nothing about you in case yo
did not want to claim the association."

For a moment it seemed that Sir Claude would make a shar
rejoinder. He was not unaware of the position of the Marquis i
Melissa's life. Unworldly he might be, but he had no illusion
about the Marquis' reputation and he felt he should take d

Lisle to task for compromising his granddaughter. She might appear on stage as an innocent but if de Lisle had her in keeping, how could he introduce her to his wife, a sheltered upright lady of the old school who would be shocked by her granddaughter's situation? Still, Melissa would not have been forced into her present way of life if he and his wife had assumed their responsibilities and not clung to the old resentment.

"Of course, we want to claim her. She must assume her rightful position, and give up this playacting. It is no role for a gently bred girl," he answered Lady Ravensham fiercely, gazing at the Marquis antagonistically. De Lisle, who had a good idea of what was passing through Sir Claude's mind, smiled ironically. Now was not the time to tell the older man what he had in mind for Melissa but he would brook no interference in his plans, even from Melissa's grandparents.

The meeting between Sir Claude and his granddaughter, which Lady Ravensham had engineered, would not be an easy one. Theron decided that she must be prepared for it, and reminded himself that no matter how Sir Claude received her it mattered little, since as his wife she would be accepted by society, and her reputation redeemed. The ton had a short memory, and would never shun his Marchioness. He had enough consequence to make sure of that.

The Marquis' guests went on to his Grosvernor Square house where he had ordered a light collation, and he arranged to meet them there after he had collected Melissa. He arrived in her dressing room determined to assert his claim as her affianced husband, which would enable him to protect her from any criticism of her past life from her grandfather.

"Well, poppet, another triumph," he hailed her as he ambled casually into the room, his appearance of negligent possession immediately apparent. Ignoring Bessie's hovering presence he bent over her where she sat at her dressing table removing her makeup and kissed her hard on her mouth.

Disregarding his air of ownership, Melissa tried to behave in an equally offhand manner. "Thank you, Theron, I think it went well. The audience seemed quite receptive." For some reason she felt shy and insecure under his lazy glance. She rose and darted behind the screen to don her gown. Bessie, glowering at the Marquis, muttered under her breath, not unmindful of the changed relationship between the two. Her darkest suspicions were being confirmed.

The Marquis settled himself in a chair and continued to chat about the performance, but within a few moments Melissa emerged, dressed enticingly in an amber silk and seed pearls.

"You may go, Bessie," he dismissed the dresser, turning Melissa around, and expertly beginning to fasten the buttons at the back of her gown.

Blushing in response to his attitude, Melissa tried to pretend indifference, difficult, as she felt his hard fingers on her back, sending a shudder of excitement through her. "Yes, Bessie. I will be going on to supper with the Marquis. You have had a long day. Be sure to take a hackney back to Stanhope Gate and do not wait up for me. I will probably be late." She smiled in friendly affection at the dresser.

"If you insist, Miss Melissa. But I will not go to bed until you return. I would not be easy," Bessie responded, eyeing the Marquis darkly.

"Now, Bessie, you may trust me with your ewe lamb. She will come to no harm, believe me," Theron quipped, amused at Bessie's attitude.

Much as she would have liked to challenge the noble lord, Bessie knew she could not sustain any objection and, giving Melissa an admonitory look and sniffing her disapproval, she finally took leave.

"There you are, my dear, and I must say you look not a day older than Juliet—fourteen wasn't she? Much too young for a grand passion, as you are," he patted Melissa gently on her backside and resumed his seat, watching her through narrowed eyes as she settled to finish her preparations.

"Really, Theron. You act as if I were still in the nursery, and you have seen to it that I have become a woman," Melissa reproved him sharply. What a maddening man he was, hiding his innermost feelings and yet expecting her to reveal hers.

"I fear you will be a far from obedient wife, Melissa," he mocked.

"I am not sure I want to be a wife at all," she snapped, her anger rising as he continued to treat her with amusement.

"That is not a subject for negotiation. Before we leave for supper, I have something to tell you which might disturb you, but it will in no way alter my decision about your future," he said, suddenly grim. Then he grasped the nettle. "Lady Ravensham has discovered who your grandparents are and your grandfather, who obviously regrets his treatment of your mother, has decided to make up for his past dereliction. Sir Claude Carstairs joined us this evening for the performance and is convinced you are his long-lost granddaughter. He is eager to make your acquaintance, and no doubt, prevail upon your forgiving nature, to accept him."

"Oh, Theron, how wonderful!" Melissa gasped. "I do want to be reconciled to my grandparents. I have so often dreamt of such a reunion." She glowed in happy anticipation.

"Do you feel no animosity at their attitude? Are you so willing to forgive them?" he answered harshly, thinking of the Carstairs' past transgressions.

"I am sure they have suffered badly and regretted their indictment," she said thoughtfully. "Of course, I want to meet them, and learn about mother's girlhood. And I will make them understand that she and my father were happy together, and their disapproval of the match was the only blight on my parents' felicity." Her face softened as she thought of her past life in India.

"Whether the Carstairs accept you or not is of no importance. As my wife you will find all the acceptance you need. And to signal our coming marriage, I have brought you this," he said, not liking the idea that the Carstairs sudden emergence might lessen Melissa's dependence on him.

He took a small box from his pocket and drew from it a sparkling huge sapphire ring which he slipped onto her finger "Before you meet Sir Claude I think you must wear this ring signifying that no matter what his attitude, your future is secure. You are my promised wife."

Confusion and disappointment warred with pleasure a Melissa looked at the lovely badge of ownership. Was he marrying her because he had discovered her respectable background and from a sense of responsibility and shame tha he had taken her virtue in a fit of anger and passion? Before sh could demur and question his motives, he had taken her in hi arms and began to kiss her with a thoroughness and hunge which swamped her senses and banished all her objections.

"Whatever the Carstairs' plans they do not matter," he murmured. "This is what is of paramount importance. I wan you and intend to allow no one to interfere, neither you grandparents, society's silly strictures, nor a whole regiment o French traitors. And don't you forget it my girl. Now let us b off to this confrontation, and remember, I will be on hand t protect you from any embarrassment or coercion. You ar mine."

His words effectively dismissed her immediate fears if no assuring her of his sincerity. If only he would admit that h loved her, she felt her happiness would know no bounds, bu that emotion was one the arrogant lord did not entertain.

Whatever he said, however adamant his decision, ought sh to refuse, now that she had some promise of her grandparent' protection? Removing reluctantly from his embrace, sh conceded that the possibility of winning his love once the were truly married, overrode any other thought. Eventuall she might break through to the passionate man who hid hi emotions beneath a facade of cynicism and reserve. How sh loved him, and how much she yearned for him to return tha love. But was it possible?

Hiding her doubts and questions, Melissa slipped into he pelisse which he was holding for her, and looked up at him with a challenging smile. "Well, let us be off to this meeting. It should prove interesting if nothing else. I wonder if Sir Claude will approve of a playacting granddaughter."

"The only approval which concerns you now, is mine, and that you have unstintingly, my dear," he replied as he escorted her from the theatre.

Chapter Thirty-Two

At de Lisle's sumptuous Grosvernor Square home, the guests rose as the Marquis and Melissa entered the drawing room, chorusing their delight in her performance. Melissa peeked shyly at the stranger in their midst while acknowledging with pretty humility their congratulations. Sarah, giving her an enthusiastic kiss, noticed at once the glowing sapphire on her hand and waited eagerly for some announcement of its significance, but Lady Ravensham interrupted the profuse compliments after a brief time, to take Melissa by the hand and lead her to the strange gentleman waiting impatiently by the fireplace.

She introduced the two in triumph, pleased at having solved the mystery of the young girl's background. "Melissa, I believe Sir Claude Carstairs has much to say to you. He is convinced, and so am I, that you are indeed his long-lost granddaughter."

Looking up into the faded blue eyes of the tall elderly gentleman who was returning her gaze with some fear of rejection, Melissa smiled and spoke softly. "If you are, indeed, my grandfather, Sir Claude, I am overjoyed to meet you at last." She waited for his words of either welcome or repudiation calmly. She was convinced that this distinguished old man, whatever his relationship to her, would treat her kindly.

"My dear child, this is more than I could have hoped for after all these empty years. You have such a look of your mother, and the locket Lady Ravensham showed me is all the evidence I need. We gave it to your mother on her sixteenth birthday. I hope you will come to forgive our estrangement, brought about by misunderstanding and stupid insistence that we knew best. My wife, your grandmother, will be overcome that we have met at last, and, I hope, will make an effort to repair past mistakes. Your forgiveness is our deepest wish, but we will have to accept whatever you offer." He spoke quietly, but was obviously under the stress of deep emotion. Melissa saw a tall, thin man, with tired eyes, thinning white hair, and a disciplined mouth, a man braced to face rejection, and her natural kindness rose to the surface.

"Thank you, Grandfather. I do not hold grudges, and we have all suffered enough from the past," she reassured him. "I cannot wait to meet Grandmother. I feel we have much to discuss." She reached up and kissed him on the cheek.

He sighed, as if he had been holding his breath waiting for his reception. He was not comforted by the possessive figure who stood by her side, only waiting to see if Sir Claude's acceptance was couched in the proper humility before defending his protégé. Sir Claude, although far from worldly, could not mistake the Marquis' stance, and he knew, from the little Lady Ravensham had told him of Melissa's adventures, that the Marquis was a dominant figure in her life. He would have preferred another protector for his granddaughter but was in no position to protest.

He smiled at her. "Thank you, my dear, for your forbearance and forgiveness. We must have a long talk about your future. So many explanations to be made and questions to be answered. Your grandmother will be arriving in London and our reunion can only bring great happiness to us both. We realize, of course, that you have been forced to make your own way without the guidance of your family, and we know a bit about Horace Hawksley, but all that can wait."

Theron, watching the two carefully, felt that the moment was in danger of becoming too oversetting for the company and intervened. He would stake his claim and make the position clear. "Before we go into supper, I must inform you all, so concerned with Melissa's welfare, that she has honoured me by promising to be my wife. So this will be a triple celebration—of our betrothal, her success as Juliet, and her reunion with her grandparents," he announced, leaving no doubt in his hearers' minds which occasion was the more important. He had no intention of asking Sir Claude's permission for the match, nor brook defiance from either Melissa or her grandfather. His smooth composure hid any evidence that Sir Claude's objection might weigh with his willful fiancée.

For a moment it looked as if Melissa would defy him, but she realized this was not the time to voice her arguments. However, Theron's ruthless refusal to entertain any but his own wishes would not go unchallenged. Sarah, delighted with the turn of events, came eagerly forward to offer her felicitations, and Lady Ravensham smiled benignly, all having marched as she wished. Before Melissa's doubts could surface or her grandfather could protest, Peverel, the Ravensham's stately butler threw open the drawing room doors and announced in his usual sepulchral tones that supper was served. Lucien cocked a wry eyebrow at Theron, and offered Lady Ravensham his arm, as if to say, "Let us have no arguments now, my good fellow."

The evening passed off smoothly, but underneath the jollity several of the company were far from easy. Sir Claude's delight in discovering his granddaughter was tempered by his reluctance to cede the prior rights which the disreputable Marquis so suavely asserted. He did not like that gentleman's proprietorial attitude and he wondered just how far the relationship between Melissa and the libertine had progressed. Lucien, too, had questions. Only Sarah and Lady Ravensham seemed genuinely pleased and accepted the fait accompli with delight. Theron, braced for a confrontation with both Melissa and Sir Claude, behaved with smooth address, a facade behind which he entertained grave questions as to the future. After the final toasts he suggested that he would escort Melissa back to Stanhope Gate as it had been a long and exciting evening.

"Children need their rest, you know," he explained in the maddening casual manner which annoyed Melissa so.

She refused to rise to his bait, and instead thanked Lady Ravensham prettily, promised Sarah to meet soon, and kissed her grandfather farewell before being whisked away by her dominating suitor.

In the carriage, riding to Stanhope Gate, she attempted to take issue with Theron on his high-handed efforts to settle her life.

"Perhaps my grandparents would prefer to be consulted as to my husband, Theron. You were a trifle ruthless in the way you faced Sir Claude with your demands," she challenged him.

"Your grandparents may wish to manage the ceremony, my pet, but they are hardly in a position to make objections as to your choice," he replied smoothly, eyeing her sardonically. "They would certainly not be pleased to learn we had anticipated the wedding night. They would insist on the nuptials once they knew the whole story of our relationship."

"I am not unprotected now, Theron. You cannot continue to run my affairs in such a cavalier manner. Perhaps I don't want to marry you. I don't remember that I was asked, only commanded," she answered, thoroughly aroused by his lordly indifference to her objections.

"If you expect me to play the besotted bridegroom, waiting on tenterhooks for a blushing virgin, you have chosen the wrong man, my dear. I have decided to claim you and that is the end of it," he answered brusquely, in no mood to pander to shrinking fancies.

"You are impossible, completely insufferable. I wish I had never met you!" Melissa stormed, now thoroughly angered.

"Now, now. Let's have no more of these theatrics. Save

them for the Majestic's stage and your adoring fans," he said, not one whit discomposed by her threats. "What you require right now is your lonely bed. I would seal our arrangement by showing you just how much you want to be my wife, but I feel this is not the evening for such an impassioned performance. I am quite willing to wait until you are legally mine. I want to clear up this Whitebread business before the knot is tied."

Melissa, in the stress of emotion, had almost forgotten the traitorous impresario. How much was Theron's determination to wed her based on their partnership in unmasking that monster? Once they had brought him to his deserts would Theron lose interest in her, relegating her to the background of his life, available for an occasional spate of lovemaking, before returning to his rakehell pursuits? Glumly she conceded that was what marriage to the notorious peer would probably entail. Could she stand meaning so little when he was so vital to her happiness? She might be better off to sever their connection and retire to the country with her grandparents—if they would have her once they knew the truth. But could she bear to banish him from her life? She desperately hoped that marriage might give her the chance to make him love her as she loved him, but he was not a man to be cozened. Which would bring her the most grief, to be an unloved wife, or never to lay in his arms again? She remained silent, and when they reached Stanhope Gate allowed him to escort her to the door without any further demur.

Theron smiled grimly at her downcast face. "It is rather lowering to my self-esteem that the prospect of marriage with me is so abhorrent to you, poppet. Never fear, we will come about. You are weary beyond belief. Forget your doubts and your troubles now. You may rake me over the coals tomorrow. I will come around to take you driving in the afternoon. You need a little pleasuring." He pushed her through the door with a careless caress and returned to his waiting carriage.

Exhausted from the tempest of emotions stirred by the reunion with her grandfather, the excitement of her debut as

Juliet, the problem of George Whitebread, and her hopeless love for the Marquis, Melissa fell asleep quickly. Tomorrow would be soon enough to face her myriad problems. However, in reviewing the events of the evening before dropping off, she gave no thought to Horace Hawksley. She could not know that her erstwhile guardian had been in the audience that night watching her avidly as she portrayed the doomed Juliet.

Later in Algy's rather squalid lodgings, after a sketchy supper, Horace and his nephew reviewed their plans to take Melissa and her fortune into their permanent custody.

"We have our work cut out for us, with that nasty nob guarding her every moment," Algy muttered in disgust, drinking deep from his glass of brandy.

"Yes, and I thought you said he was going off her. I was around to the stage door and saw her emerge under his escort and rush off after the performance," Horace reproved testily. As a co-conspirator Algy was proving more of a hindrance than a help, he thought, his small, narrow eyes darkening in frustration. "This abduction is going to take some clever planning."

"Why an abduction? You have a perfect right to carry her off to Devon. You are her legal guardian, after all," Algy protested. He was loathe to exert himself in any intricate doings. Only greed, and his pressing creditors impelled him to cooperate with his uncle. Melissa, as a wife, held few charms for him. He preferred a more lush and experienced consort, though she might have learned a few tricks from that Marquis. After all, she could expect little being soiled goods, so to speak.

"I am not too anxious to press my claim. Some nosey parker of a solicitor has been rooting around, I understand from my man of business. No, t'will be best to have you firmly shackled before any investigation can be mounted by that hoity-toity nob. He's probably in queer street himself, for these quality types are always at the duns. He probably fancies her blunt as much as we do. When she marries, her money goes to her husband, don't forget. We must do the job now, if we have to drag her to the altar." Horace nodded sagely, convinced he had the matter in hand. "We will have to force her, and be quick about it, too. I have a suspicion that affairs are coming to a head."

Several methods were broached, but the two, now well in their cups, could not come to an agreement. Finally, they decided that the best plan was a bold one. Horace would take her by surprise. She would not be expecting him, and certainly could be cowed into submission when he turned up demanding his rights. If they could just catch her when the damned aristocrat was absent their task should not prove beyond their powers, and delay would not serve. The sooner the better. The two argued back and forth, with Horace finally giving Algy the instruction to secure a minister to stand by for the hurried ceremony. Then they could all repair to Devon and once Melissa was beyond the reach of her protector and shackled, the Marquis would have no recourse but to accept her loss.

"It will have to be a special license and that costs, more's the pity. But it's her money and well spent in a good cause, eh, nephy?" Horace chuckled, thinking of the funds soon to be at his disposal."

"And I can use my share," Algy reminded him. He did not completely trust his uncle to divvy up when the time came, but he intended to see to it that he was lavishly compensated for taking the chit to wife.

"You will have to settle up here and isolate yourself for some time in Devon. We want no awkward questions asked, and if you are not available so much the better. After a time, if you want to return to London I will keep an eye on your wife. She should be breeding by then, if you are half the man you claim to be," he leered coarsely.

"Oh, I'll quite enjoy that, never fear," Algy responded, smacking his loose lips in anticipation.

The two, at last in some agreement, continued to drink away the hours, secure in the knowledge that they had plotted Melissa's future to their satisfaction.

Chapter Thirty-Three

Melissa had not known quite what to expect from Lady Carstairs. Somehow she had thought her grandmother would embody her dreams of a gentle, kindly woman, mourning the loss of her daughter, and as willing to admit to her transgressions as her husband. She was mistaken. Lady Carstairs, who arrived in London two days after Melissa's reunion with her grandfather at the Ravenshams, offered her granddaughter a rather chilly welcome. The two met in the rooms Sir Claude had taken in the Fenton Hotel on St. James Street. Lady Carstairs, an imposing, tall woman, her severe dark brown hair lightly touched with gray, wore a magenta silk taffeta gown of rigid fashion, heavily accented with jet. Her frosty dark eyes held little compassion. It was soon apparent to Melissa that whatever joy the discovery of their abandoned granddaughter had brought Sir Claude, his wife had reacted in a more temperate fashion to the discovery. It was evident that she was the dominant member of the two, and most probably had persuaded her husband into the intransigent attitude he had previously adopted toward the Mansfield marriage. Time may have eased her disappointment and dislike of Melissa's father, but she was far from overwhelming in her reception to the child of that union. Sir Claude, his own enthusiasm somewhat dampened by his wife's obduracy, tried to soften matters.

"Melissa has kindly forgiven us for not trying to discover her whereabouts after Elizabeth's tragic death. We should have made more of a push to locate her, and we must try to atone for our negligence now," Sir Claude urged, worried as to how Melissa would respond to his wife's cool reception.

"My husband has assured me that you are indeed Elizabeth's daughter, the proof being your locket," Lady Carstairs said, unimpressed by her husband's championship. "It is no secret that we disapproved of Elizabeth's foolish elopement with a man of whom we had some reason to be chary. He tells me that your parents were happy together, and their life in India very successful."

"We were indeed a happy family, Lady Carstairs, and I miss both my parents still. Their early death was a terrible tragedy for me," Melissa responded firmly. She would not apologize to this rather formidable lady, and could not bring herself to call her grandmother. Any disparaging remarks about her father would be dealt with summarily. Disappointed and ill at ease under Lady Carstairs' scrutiny, she could only sympathize with her mother's predicament, and understand more fully why she had run away from home.

"I also understand that because of your father's unfortunate choice of a guardian for you that you spent an uncomfortable childhood, and were, in the end, forced to escape his protection into a life which seems to me to be far from respectable," Lady Carstairs continued, her tone full of condemnation.

Melissa, now thoroughly irritated by this catechism, hesitated over a response. What right had this rather austere lady to judge her actions? If she had behaved with a little tolerance and affection, Melissa's situation would be far different today. Before she could rush into hasty speech, Sir Claude intervened.

"We must not criticise Melissa for her youthful imprudence, my dear. Naturally, she felt unwilling to wed a man abhorrent to her. Her guardian seems a paltry fellow to me, attempting to coerce her in such a fashion." He smiled coaxingly. Long experience had taught him how to mollify his stern wife.

"Perhaps, but she has merely escaped from one coil into another. We have never had a . . . an *actress* . . . in the family and I cannot approve of such a position for my granddaughter," Lady Carstairs sniffed.

"Since I was unaware of your existence, I could not seek your approval, Lady Carstairs," Melissa said sharply. "In all fairness you must agree I had to grasp whatever opportunity was offered. Life in the theatre may not suit your notions of propriety, but I have found it quite to my taste. And I believe I have the right to choose my own husband, since I have been without the protection of a family who might have guided me down a different path."

Lady Carstairs gazed coldly at her granddaughter. "The Marquis de Lisle has a frightful reputation as a womanizer and a debauched libertine. Hardly an acceptable party for a gently bred girl."

"But, as we have both agreed, I am not a gently bred girl, but a disreputable adventuress, and quite fortunate to have lured the Marquis into marriage, don't you think?" Melissa was by now as angry as she could ever remember being.

Lady Carstairs lifted her eyebrows in haughty surprise at such a rebellion. "Don't be impudent, Melissa. Your welfare must now be our concern, and I am not convinced that we can countenance this union."

No wonder her mother fled with her father. Trying to win a concession, even minimal understanding, from this stubborn and rigid old lady was impossible, and Melissa no longer even wished to make the effort. How different had been Lady Ravensham's reaction to the Marquis' proposal. She, too, had suffered from a child's estrangement, but had done all in her power to atone for it. Lady Carstairs was determined to accept

Melissa into her family only on her terms, and those terms were unacceptable to Melissa.

"Well, Lady Carstairs, I can see we must agree to differ about Theron, and a great deal besides, for I have quite made up my mind to become his Marchioness. The only permission I seek is my own. You will excuse me for speaking frankly, but you appear to approve of forthright discussion and I can only agree it is best." Melissa met her grandmother's gaze with a hard stare. She would not be intimidated, nor humiliated, by references to her past or her present way of life. Lady Carstairs could accept her or not as she pleased. Much as Melissa yearned for people of her own, who truly cared for her, she would not be bullied or coerced. Horace Hawksley had tried that and he had not succeeded. She would not submit to such dominance again.

Sir Claude hastened to soothe both irate females. "Come, come, let us not wrangle. De Lisle and Melissa will have their own way in this matter of the marriage, and at least, you will concede, Mathilda, he will remove Melissa from the theatre. A great loss, I feel, for your Juliet was very appealing, my dear." This reunion had not gone quite the way he had envisioned, and his disappointment was obvious to Melissa, who pitied the old gentleman caught between two stubborn protagonists.

Nodding her head regally, Lady Carstairs, aware that she had handled the interview badly, saw she must make a few concessions. "The Marquis may do for a husband. There are few mothers who would allow him to court their daughters, but your situation is a bit different. It might serve," she allowed graciously. Most of the time she could manage her gentle husband, but once he dug his toes in about a matter, he could prove surprisingly stubborn. And he was quite determined to acknowledge Melissa and make amends for past mistakes.

Melissa, admitting that she could never envisage earning her grandmother's love, and after this critical interview, not particularly eager for it, allowed Lady Carstairs to turn the conversation to unexceptional matters. How shocked that virtuous lady would be if she knew how far affaires had progressed between the rakehell Marquis and herself. Then she would press eagerly for the marriage, no doubt, fearing for her granddaughter's future. She had expected her grandparents to be, if not tolerant, at least penitent and understanding of the dilemma which had forced her to her present pass, not unaware of their own abandoned responsibilities. Sir Claude obviously entertained such feelings, but Lady Carstairs had a different view. Beneath that aloof facade might lurk the kindly doting grandmother of legend, but Melissa was aware she had not played the part Lady Carstairs expected in order to win her acceptance. Fallen beyond redemption, Melissa thought wryly.

Describing the interview later to Theron, she explained that they could not count on Lady Carstairs' sponsorship in respectable society.

Theron reacted with commendable anger. "Damn the hypocrites. She should have hailed your spirit and independence in coping so well, instead of ringing a peal over you."

"Actually you and my grandmother have a great deal in common. You should become devoted allies, both determined to subdue my more outrageous tendencies toward adventure," Melissa quipped, her distasteful interview now becoming an object of raillery rather than sorrow.

Theron, secretly impressed by her resilience in rebounding from what must have been an uncomfortable and disappointing reunion, failed to rise to her baiting. "Don't try to deceive me, my girl. Your grandmother's attitude is unfortunate, but hardly surprising. If she had been a compassionate kindly woman your mother would not have been forced to elope. She will be the loser once again, in not trying to atone for past misjudgments, and seeking your forgiveness. But enough of this, you may not have had a loving family to cosset you in the past, but soon you will have a husband upon whom to practice your wiles and well on the way to establishing a family of your own to command your affections."

"You are certainly eager to enjoy the delights of domesticity, Theron. Quite a shock. I cannot see you as a model family man," she taunted, unwilling to let him see how the vision of carrying his child thrilled and excited her.

"I might surprise you yet, wench. Reformed rakes make very complaisant husbands, I understand. I am in danger already of coming under your thumb," he admitted with more truth than she could envisage.

"I am not such a pea goose as to believe that," she scoffed with a gurgle of laughter. "But now that we have solved the identity of my parentage and background, we must return to our chief concern, George Whitebread's treachery, and how to bring him to brook."

"Yes, well, you are not to concern yourself with that any longer," Theron said firmly. "Now that we suspect him he will be under constant surveillance. So far he has not put a foot wrong, and acted in no exceptional way. I want to catch him in the act of conspiracy, and round up his agents. We still have little proof on which to take him into custody, and until he is safely under lock and key with his adherents, you are still in danger," he warned. "Henry Gratton has never surfaced despite our best efforts. Of course, he could not return to his barracks, and I can only think that he has escaped to the Continent." Theron was reluctant to tell her that he believed Gratton had suffered the same fate as Alison Andrews for that would do nothing to calm her uneasiness.

"Well, he is certainly no loss. I feel quite relieved that he will not be hovering about, ready to pounce on me. I did not enjoy our last meeting."

"Forget about him. And I suppose it is naive of me to believe you will also forget about Whitebread. My solicitor has approached Sir Claude about this guardianship business, and your grandfather is willing to give his permission for our marriage so I do not think we need contact the odious Mr. Hawksley. If he intends to make mischief, I believe I can cope with him," Theron reassured her, anxious to get the matter settled to his satisfaction. With Melissa he could not be certain until they were firmly shackled, for who knew what rig she would be up to. Lately he had begun to fear she had accepted him as the least obnoxious of her options, and that was not what he wanted. Damn the girl. She had truly managed to enmesh him in her toils although he acquitted her of deliberately seeking that end. He had reason to regret that seduction, taking her in anger. And he wanted her now. Only by the most stringent self-discipline had he refrained from beguiling her again into his bed. He sensed that would finish his chances for all time.

"Well, poppet, I am willing to let you continue at the Majestic for a while, even if your grandparents prefer you to lead a more respectable life. But this playacting cannot continue indefinitely. I hope you have accepted that your days as a star are shortly to come to an end," he said hiding his concern at the danger she faced.

"Do you imagine that I will be a complacent wife, Theron?" Melissa taunted, as eager as he to hide her feelings.

"Not for a moment. I would never be so foolish. But I must admit to some pleasure at the thought of taming your volatile spirits," he mocked in return. And so they left matters, neither willing nor able to express what was in their hearts.

Although she granted the necessity, Melissa now found the protection upon which Theron insisted, a real obstacle to her freedom. He installed two burley footmen in Stanhope Gate for she refused to move either to the Fenton Hotel under her grandparent's chaperonage or to accept Lady Ravensham's invitation to stay in Park Street. She felt she could not expose either the Carstairs or Lady Ravensham to the danger she faced. At the theatre she was guarded by the Bow Street runners. Theron felt he had taken every possible precaution, although he was not completely easy in his mind. Negotiations between France and England were progressing at a snail's pace toward the inevitable truce, but until the pact was signed the

French agents remained an active threat. Even after the truce became a reality, the French would not cease their conniving. Castlereagh was all for pulling in the impresario, and Theron agreed that eventually they might have to arrest the man even if the evidence of his treachery was not forthcoming. With Whitebread in custody Melissa's safety would be assured, but she herself scorned this cowardly expedient. Not given to indecision, Theron chafed under this lack of action, but he was persuaded to give the affair a few more weeks, although he felt time was running against them.

In the matter of their marriage, Theron acted in his usual high-handed way, placing the announcement of the coming nuptials in the *Gazette*, where the publication caused many a raised eyebrow and a great deal of murmuring among the ton. Few were foolhardy enough to question the inscrutable Marquis, and even his intimates were reluctant to probe, for it was generally conceded that Theron would not take such curiosity kindly. De Lisle was an experienced hand at parrying awkward remarks and not a man to challenge. As the Marquis seldom answered invitations tendered by hopeful London hostesses, he avoided much of the tittle-tattle of the gossip mongers, and in any event would have ignored it in his usual lofty manner. The Carstairs had agreed to stay on for the wedding, lending some respectability to the affair. Even Lady Carstairs had to accept the marriage or forever alienate her granddaughter, which her husband would never allow. Melissa managed to subdue her irritation at her grandmother's attitude for Sir Claude's sake. She felt a real affection for him, which was eagerly returned. Lady Carstairs and Melissa achieved a reluctant truce, but their relationship would never be a warm one.

Soon after the announcement appeared in the journal, Whitebread suggested to Melissa that they ought to discuss her plans and how her new status would affect the company. She did not contemplate the interview with equanimity, in light of her new knowledge, but consented to his request, suggesting they meet before that evening's performance. Mindful of Theron's warnings she dutifully sent off a note to his Grosvernor Square house, telling him that she would be leaving early that evening to confer with the impresario. She did not wait for a reply. He was certain to offer some objections and she was weary of his meticulous surveillance. Her love had in no way tempered her independence of action.

Escorted by the Marquis' two watchdogs, in his crested barouche, she left Stanhope Gate with Bessie, as dusk was falling, the foggy dank October evening a fitting backdrop to her dark musings. As the carriage passed through Piccadilly en route to Shaftesbury Avenue, the vehicle suddenly rumbled to a stop. Aroused from her deep study by Bessie's cries of alarm, Melissa looked from the windows of the coach to see the reason for the abrupt halt. All she could glimpse in the gloom were three or four cursing men, the tall hat of one of her footmen, who was arguing with the crowd. Then the door of the barouche opened and her coachman stuck his head into the carriage to explain the disturbance.

"Some stupid cove has a spavined old horse and cart blocking the turning, Miss Langford. We will be held up for a bit, but shouldn't take long to move them. Sorry for the delay," John, the coachman explained.

"That's quite all right, John. Should we get out of the carriage?" Melissa asked, always willing to be helpful, an attitude those who served her found as considerate as it was rare in the quality.

"No, ma'am. Won't be a trice. Stay cosy here," the coachman suggested, aghast at the thought of her leaving the protection of the coach.

Melissa, deep in her uncomfortable thoughts, could only be grateful for the postponement of the inevitable meeting with Whitebread. She looked casually out of the window of the coach, watching the scene absentmindedly. A flaring torch suddenly illuminated the dimness and she noticed a play bill advertising "Romeo and Juliet" on a nearby post. The sight jolted her memory.

Playbills. They were tacked on sidings and buildings all over London. And Whitebread had held a sheaf of the advertisements in his hand the last time she had seen him. She remembered suddenly the day she had confronted him in his office about the projected drama. When she entered he had been writing on a similar sheaf of playbills. He seemed to take an inordinant interest in the announcements. Surely once they were printed with the required information, he need not bother about them.

They were distributed throughout the city, for Whitebread believed in plastering the notices so that they would catch the eye of any possible customer, not just affluent ones, who, at any rate, booked boxes and stalls. But the Majestic depended on the motley as well to fill the pits and gallery. Playbills. In a blinding revelation, Melissa believed she had solved the method by which the impresario notified his agents. What could be easier. On those playbills he must signify some cache which would be safe from prying eyes, a secret rendezvous where his contacts could deliver their treacherous messages without meeting Whitebread face to face. How simple and foolproof. Why hadn't she realized it earlier. She choked back a startled exclamation as the barouche suddenly rumbled forward. That must be it. The playbills notified the agents as to the time and location of the drop. She must let Theron know immediately about her suspicions. Perhaps once she reached the theatre she could discover more, without letting Whitebread know that she had uncovered his scheme. That must be it. How else could he gather the information and protect his identity?

She shuddered at the thought of confronting him while hiding her discovery. He was a dangerous, ruthless man, who had already killed to protect his secret. It would take all her acting prowess to circumvent him. Should she postpone this meeting, return to Stanhope Gate until she could contact Theron? No, that was fainthearted. Surely she could dissemble, lull the impresario into a damaging disclosure. After all, she had entered into this masquerade with just that in mind. Surrounded by the protection Theron had instituted he could not attack her, and if she could beguile him into some inadvertent clue, how pleased Theron would be that their designs had at last borne fruit.

As the barouche rolled to a stop near the stage door, Melissa set her chin with determination, and stilled the small tremours of fear which shook her. She would do it.

Chapter Thirty-Four

In her dressing room, awaiting the coming interview, Melissa looked distractedly about her. She had sent word to the impresario by Joe, the stage door man, that she would receive him here for their discussion. She felt she needed the advantage of familiar ground, not the isolated aerie in which he conducted his affairs. Outside the door, just yards away a Bow Street runner lingered, on duty as usual as the cast would be arriving within the hour to ready itself for the evening's performance.

Bessie puttered about, watching Melissa grimly. She disapproved of her charge continuing on the stage now that her marriage was an accepted fact. Bessie was not convinced that Melissa had chosen well, but she thought a bit better of the Marquis, who had come up to scratch, done his duty by her darling. Whether he could make Melissa happy was another question, but at least she would now be respectable, an end Bessie had devoutly wished but which had seemed very doubtful at the beginning of this strange association. She resented not being completely in Melissa's confidence, and she still held the Marquis accountable for that unfortunate circumstance, but she tempered her suspicions. He was offering Melissa a secure future, and even if he did not remain faithful, the girl would still have the comfort of his wealth and title, although Bessie realized that might not be enough for the mercurial, vulnerable girl. Still, buried in the country, under Hawksley's domination, she might never have achieved so much. Bessie had learned in a hard school that women were often victims, and rarely able to choose their fate. She was not unaware of Lady Carstairs' grudging acceptance of her granddaughter, and viewed that austere lady with dislike. Miss Melissa was certainly not well served by those who owed her protection and affection.

Bessie's muttering and Melissa's dark thoughts were interrupted by a sharp knock on the door. Whitebread entered, looking to Melissa as inscrutable and as calm as usual. Suspecting what she did about the impresario, Melissa could hardly believe this self-contained man, so engrossed with his theatre's success, could be a traitor and a murderer. Had she made a mistake? Well, she must steel herself to finding the proof of his infamy.

Dismissing Bessie, Melissa welcomed Whitebread with apparent calm.

"Good evening, my dear. Readying yourself for another triumphant evening?" Whitebread greeted her. She waved him to a chair and turned to face him not sure how to proceed.

"Not very many more, I fear, Mr. Whitebread. Naturally the Marquis does not wish me to continue my career after we are wed," she said with a tentative smile.

"Well, I can quite understand he would not wish his Marchioness to tread the boards," he said agreeably. "I cannot deny it is a deep disappointment, but it does not come as a complete surprise to me. Will you want to retire after this run of 'Juliet?'"

"I think that will be best. We will be wed shortly and then repair to Devon for a short honeymoon. The Marquis is much occupied with government business and must not be absent from London for long," she explained, watching him closely to gauge his reaction. Did he guess that Theron's business was tracking down French agents?"

"His abilities are much prized, I am sure," he answered smoothly, but his dark opaque eyes had become harder.

"It is rather unfortunate that you have advertised the program so widely," she said daringly. "Everywhere I look in London I see playbills hawking the play. Surely that is not necessary with the box office turning away customers?" She was gratified to see his hands clench.

"I believe it prudent," he replied. "We don't want to lose momentum, especially since we are losing you, my dear. I intend the Majestic to continue its present popularity. We have become quite the rage, and must capitalize on the current interest."

"Surely all these playbills—the printing and distributing—are very expensive," Melissa remarked artlessly, although she could feel her hands becoming cold and only by the most rigid discipline did she restrain her fear.

"Yes, very costly. But don't trouble your little head about the playbills. Believe me, they are vital," Whitebread insisted warily. What was the girl implying?

"I wonder, Mr. Whitebread, if they do not serve another purpose," she said recklessly, weary of this fencing.

The impresario flushed, and looked at her carefully, "What do you mean?" he queried sharply.

"Just that there are an excessive amount of them, in very odd places, and I am puzzled about the reason. But since you assure me they are important to the success of the Majestic I must accept your word," she said firmly, now more than certain he understood she knew their real purpose. For a moment she thought he might lose his control and threaten her. His mien was most forbidding. But with some effort he kept his temper, although his regard never wavered.

"Well, soon this will be of no concern to you. You will be acting on another stage. Perhaps one that will not receive you so enthusiastically," he sneered.

"Oh, I am assured by the Marquis that London society will welcome me kindly," she said blithely. "And we will be spending more time in the country once all this turmoil with the French is settled."

"If you have no further questions I will return to my office," he said sullenly. "Let us be in agreement then that Juliet will come off at the end of the week, in five days time, then. Is that agreeable to you?"

"Of course, and I must take this opportunity to thank you for giving me this chance. You have been most cooperative." Melissa smiled sweetly in gratitude, but Whitebread, distracted, only nodded and rose hurriedly to his feet, anxious to depart. Without another word he left her.

She wondered if she had shaken him at all. In her own mind she was now sure that the playbills hid the secret of his conspiracy. Somehow through them he announced to his agents where and how to deliver their traitorous information. But now that he knew of her suspicions, was she in danger of suffering Alison's fate? She had not liked the way he had looked at her at his departure, a considering, brooding stare which left her full of apprehension.

Suddenly she longed for the comforting presence of Theron. The performance ahead seemed more than she could manage, and she needed his bracing and protective support. How he dominated her and not just as her partner in this attempt to root out the French spies, but in every aspect of her life. Suddenly exhausted by the recent confrontation with Whitebread and the turmoil which contemplation of her relationship with the Marquis inspired, she felt desperately weary. How could she appear on stage? Shaking off her troubled thoughts, she reproved herself. Was she becoming such a milk-and-water miss that she had lost her courage and conviction? She must stop this wretched wavering and get on with her responsibilities. Comforted by the thought that Theron would join her after the performance, and persuading herself into her natural ebullient belief that affairs would march in the required direction, she turned to her dressing table and the makeup pots.

Whitebread returned to his office a much disturbed man. Lulled by his long record of success, he had relaxed his vigilance, secure in the knowledge that he was omnipotent, able to gull the Bow Street runners, and even the haughty Marquis, for by now he was convinced he knew the reason for the peer's interest in his theatre. De Lisle was in pursuit of the French conspirators. But he could handle that nosey gentleman, and his paramour. Melissa had obviously found some hint of his methods, perhaps from that bungling ass Gratton. Still he had dealt with that paltry opportunist and he would deal with her, too.

He had become enmeshed in this treasonable game because he needed the money to insure the continuance of his theatre, for the Majestic was the overriding passion of his life. He had every reason to take pride in his talent to deceive and conquer. So far, he had not put a foot wrong, dealing with any threats to his position. And Melissa represented a dangerous threat, hinting that she knew of his activities, probably a preface to some blackmailing demand. Alison had tried that ploy, and what had it cost her? Success had made him arrogant and somewhat careless. Alison had damned near upset the whole scheme with her prying insistence. But he had settled with her, and with Gratton. Cornered, he was ruthless. His intricate method of collecting and distributing the information his network of spies compiled through the device of the playbills had proved productive and would continue to do so. None of the couriers knew him. They learned through the playbills the time and position of their deliveries. He wrote on the notices the date and seat in the theatre for which they must secure a ticket, not always the same one, but reserved by him. The clerks at the box office assumed they were saved for his friends and important customers who were interested in the theatre.

Soon he could abandon the whole intrigue, although Melissa's departure might reduce his profits. One more delivery and he could cancel the whole affair. His French masters need not think they could rule him. They were in for a disappointment and so was that intriguing little madam if she attempted to threaten him. He was cleverer than all of them, and they would see that George Whitebread knew how to deal with his enemies. Opening his desk he took a small vial from the drawer. This would settle Miss Langford once and for all.

Although the audience that evening saw nothing untoward in the performance of their reigning star, Melissa was only too aware that she was only walking through her part. Robert Rathbone looked at her quizzically after the second act, puzzled by her distraction, but reluctant to question her. He knew he would receive short shrift, for she did not entertain any advances from him at all. Molly, too, noticed Melissa's distrait air with concern. But she put down the star's manner to troubles over her affair with the Marquis. She hoped nothing had come amiss between them.

Finally, Melissa escaped to her dressing room after the many curtain calls which were the usual reception of her performance. Bessie greeted her and noticing her expression for once did not ply her with questions. On the table stood a cooler of champagne, which Bessie indicated had just been delivered.

"The Marquis must have sent it. There was no note, but who else would be so thoughtful?" Bessie explained.

"Yes, yes, but I do not want any now. I wonder what has delayed Theron. He promised to attend tonight, at least part of the performance," Melissa fretted.

"He will be here, dearie," Bessie soothed, putting Melissa's gown over her chemise, as the actress removed the heavy makeup leaving her creamy cheeks unusually pale.

Before Melissa could reply, the door to the room swung open with a crash and Horace Hawksley swaggered into the room.

"So there you are, missy. At last. You thought you could escape me forever, I vow. But I have caught you now," he blustered, standing over her in a threatening manner.

After her first surprise, Melissa controlled herself admirably. "Hello, Uncle Horace. I suppose Algy ran to you with the knowledge of my direction. Well, you have no power to coerce me now. I have other protectors." She supposed she should have expected his appearance once the announcement of her coming marriage had appeared in the *Gazette*. She just wished he had not chosen this moment, when she was beset with fatigue and worry, to confront her. But she had lost her fear of him. There was little he could do to her with Theron protecting her. Why didn't he arrive?

Hawksley, prepared to bully and bluster, looked a bit taken aback by her resolute stand. A bulky man, with bettling brows, tending to fat, and light brown eyes rather like boiled sweets, he had little about him to inspire affection. Melissa, looking him over in a considering fashion, wondered not for the first time what her father had found to attract him in such a man, and why he had entrusted his daughter to this far from prepossessing specimen. He was sputtering now, uneasy at having the initiative taken from him.

"You cannot marry without my permission, missy, and I am not inclined to give it. I have other plans for you," he growled, not exactly sure how to continue in the face of Melissa's calm reception.

Before she could answer a knock came on the door, and then it opened. One of the runners stood there, solid and menacing, looking at Hawksley with a sceptical eye. "Is this fellow bothering you, Miss Langford? He got by me before I knew what he was up to."

"It's quite all right. He will be leaving soon. Thank you for your concern. Perhaps you had better stand by to see that no one else interrupts us. Except the Marquis, of course. I am expecting him," Melissa reassured him, thankful that her protectors had not been caught napping. Hawksley could hardly drag her from the theatre with the runners standing by.

"That's all right, then. But I will be right outside the door in case of trouble, miss." The runner cast a jaundiced eye over Horace Hawksley, thinking him a nasty customer and ready to take issue with him if he seemed likely to cause trouble. But having made his presence known there was little more he could do. Giving a short nod he left the room. At Melissa's request, Bessie also left, not without a baleful look at Hawksley, who had not recognized her.

On their departure, Hawksley determined to return to the battle, although he felt increasingly unsure of his ground. Heavily guarded as Melissa was, he could not now put his intention into effect and take her from the dressing room. His temper was sorely tried by events, as he had been waiting for days for the opportunity to abduct her, but that damned Marquis had seen to it that he had no chance. Gathering his wits about him and glowering at the girl who had frustrated all his plans, he decided that cajolery might be the ticket.

"Now, Melissa, we must not come to daggers drawn. I want what is best for you, and I am concerned about your future," he whined, seeing her fortune eluding his greedy grasp.

"I have told you, Uncle Horace, you need no longer be concerned with me. I have been reunited with my grandparents who are far better fitted to be my guardians, and, in fact, are taking steps to have your custody revoked. In any case, it hardly matters as my husband will have charge of my affairs very shortly," she said firmly, intent on letting him know his stewardship would be called into account.

Before Hawksley could protest, the door opened again, to admit Theron, looking, as usual, the pattern card of the Corinthian, in his superb black evening clothes. He raised his eyebrows on seeing Hawksley but crossed to Melissa and raising her to her feet, gave her a warm kiss.

"Please accept my apologies for my tardiness. I was delayed at White's. Will you be ready to leave shortly?" he asked, searching her face for signs of anger or fear. Raising his quizzing glass, he stared quellingly at Hawksley. "And who is this fellow, my dear. Is he annoying you?"

"This is Horace Hawksley, Theron. My fiancé, the Marquis Theron de Lisle, Uncle Horace. I am sure he can answer any questions about my future which seem to disturb you," she said archly, knowing Theron would make short work of her guardian.

"Ah, yes, the odious guardian. At last we meet. I quite see why you felt you must escape from his care, my dear. What a propitious reunion. Saves me the bother of looking him up. What do you want with Melissa, my man?" he asked suavely, his supercilious air at variance with the steely look in his hooded eyes.

Hawksley, distinctly uncomfortable under Theron's gaze, and aware that he had met his match, attempted to be conciliatory. Like most bullies, he cringed before superior force, and the Marquis looked a formidable foe.

"Now, let us not quarrel, your lordship. Naturally, as Melissa's legal guardian, I have been distraught at her disappearance and am only relieved to see she has landed on her feet," he replied ingratiatingly. "Why don't we sit down and have some of this champagne and discuss matters amicably. I have no quarrel with you, my lord." He took up the bottle of champagne standing in the cooler, and tried to act with assurance. Nervously eyeing the two who remained silent, he opened the bottle and poured the golden liquid into the waiting glasses. "Let us have a toast to Melissa's future?" he suggested, downing the wine in a gulp, and turning to them in expectation.

Before they could answer he clutched his throat, and gasped. Within minutes he had fallen wretching to the floor, writhing in pain.

"What the devil!" Theron exclaimed and bent over the tortured man. Hawksley attempted to gasp out a plea for help, but only a groan issued from his grimacing lips. His contorted body arched in agony and suddenly was still. Theron bent over him, feeling for some signs of life but found none. Horace Hawksley was dead.

Chapter Thirty-Five

"By God. He's been poisoned!" Theron exclaimed looking at the distorted figure, lying on the floor. "That wine must have been meant for you, Melissa." He turned to the girl, who watched shuddering with horror at the still, agonized man whose death shocked her beyond all imagining.

Theron bit back a curse, and went to her, drawing her into the comfort of his embrace. "Don't look, Melissa. Don't even think of it. I must get you out of here. Where's Bessie?" he looked about, for the moment distracted, his one instinct to remove Melissa from the harrowing scene.

"I don't know. I sent her out when Uncle Horace appeared," she burrowed closer into his protecting arms, appalled at the turn of events, not understanding, but feeling that she had barely avoided terrible danger.

Theron reluctantly unloosed her arms, and put her gently into a chair, then opened the door and called for assistance. The runner stationed on guard came into the room, took one look at Hawksley on the floor, and bent to examine the man.

"He's dead, my lord. What happened?" the runner rose and seemed unsure what to do, unable to challenge the darkly frowning figure who faced him.

"He drank some poisoned wine intended for Miss Langford. I must get her out of this horror. Call her dresser. She should be nearby."

The runner, accustomed to obeying the quality, hurried to do his bidding.

Within moments, Bessie entered the room. Casting one look at the scene, she immediately took charge of Melissa. She shepherded the confused and shaking girl from the room, leaving Theron to make arrangements.

Repressing his anguish at what might have been Melissa's fate, Theron capped the champagne and wrapped the bottle and glass which had fallen from Hawksley's rigid fingers in a napkin. "This must be examined. But there is no doubt it contains poison, and was meant for Miss Langford. There does not seem to be any indication who sent it," he mused to the runner, who stood by awaiting his instructions. "Call Borley in here, my man," he ordered. "This is a serious affair, and must be investigated immediately."

"Yes, my lord," the runner hurried to obey, out of his depth with this latest murder and eager to let the Marquis take charge.

While Theron, Borley, and the other two runners, discussed Hawksley's death and examined the evidence, Melissa, hardly comprehending how nearly she had met an agonizing end, struggled to regain her wits under Bessie's ministrations. The dresser had taken her into Molly O'Hara's dressing room, turning aside the character actress's frantic questions. Waving a vial of smelling salts under Melissa's nose, she tried to restore the shaken girl. Soon Melissa's natural resilience came to the fore, and she pushed aside the salts, straightening her shoulders and reassuring the dresser that she was recovered.

"Mr. Hawksley drank some of that champagne in my dressing room and fell immediately into a spasm. Theron says he's dead, and that the poison was meant for me. Who could have planned such a deed? Who sent the wine, Bessie?" she asked immediately grasping the essential fact.

"I don't know, dearie. I thought it was the Marquis. No note accompanied it. Joe, the stage door keeper brought it in, said it had been left with him for you," Bessie explained, as puzzled as Melissa by the strange gift.

"Why are you in danger? Why would someone want to kill you?" Molly asked, aghast at the revelations, and baldly asking the question they all feared to face.

"I believe I have some idea. I must see Theron. Please get him for me, Bessie. I will be quite all right here with Molly," Melissa said stoutly, repressing the horror of what had so nearly happened.

"Yes, you run along, Bessie. I will watch over Melissa," Molly directed the dresser.

"Please hurry, Bessie. I have something of great import to tell the Marquis," Melissa said.

Suddenly George Whitebread came through the open door of the dressing room, apparently in great perturbation.

"My dear, Melissa. How dreadful for you. Such a shock. Who was this man who has died in your dressing room? I can get no sense from that Borley," he said, watching her narrowly.

"My guardian, Horace Hawksley, drank some poisoned wine meant for me, I believe. Do you know how the wine came to be delivered, Mr. Whitebread?" Melissa asked, taking her courage in her hands. She confronted the impresario bravely, forgetting her fear in her eagerness to bring the perpertrator to justice.

Before he could contrive a soothing answer, Theron joined them.

"Yes, Whitebread. What is your knowledge of this latest outrage? I am sure you have some explaining to do," Theron asked, holding Whitebread's shifting gaze, watching as the impresario struggled to find the words to answer him. Caught off guard by the Marquis' accusing stare he suddenly seemed to collapse.

"Why would I know anything about this miserable mischance, my lord? Are you accusing me of some involvement?" he stuttered, for once not in command of himself, a betraying flush rising to his cheeks.

"I believe you do, Mr. Whitebread," Melissa intervened. "When I challenged you earlier about the playbills, my suspicions were confirmed. I think you are the leader of a ring of spies, which you have directed from the security of this theatre. I must tell you, Theron, I think I have discovered how he has managed the whole intrigue. He notified his agents by means of playbills posted all over London as to where and how they could deliver the information they collected. He is our spy," she said secure in the safety of Theron's protection, and convinced at last that the solution to the treachery which had baffled them for so long, was at hand.

"How dare you accuse me, you little chit. I'll have your head for this," Whitebread, completely overcome by passion, lunged at Melissa, his hands raised, determined to silence her. But Theron quickly stepped between them.

Without a word, without even seeming to move, he hit Whitebread with a hard right to the jaw, leveling the impresario to the floor, where he lay stunned. The Marquis, regarding his bruised knuckles thoughtfully and adjusting his coat sleeves, stood over the fallen figure as if waiting for some further reaction, but the impresario did not stir. Turning to Melissa, who had watched the whole encounter in shocked surprise, he reproved gently, "You know I quite sympathize with the man, trying to throttle you. I am inclined often to do so myself, and only by the utmost exercise of self-control have I been prevented from squeezing the life out of you. You would be well served if I treated you thus," he concluded, gazing at her with a warm admiration which belied his words. "But I have to commend your detective work if not your behaviour. How in the world did you expose this business about the playbills?"

"Really, Theron, you are the outside of enough. Within the space of an hour I am almost poisoned and strangled, and in addition have unmasked a spy ring which baffled the great minds of the Foreign Office for months, and all you can do is reprove me," she complained, dimly realizing he was treating the disasters of the evening in a light manner in order to defuse the emotion. But really, what she needed now was comfort and praise, not criticism as to the wisdom of her actions.

"You are quite right, poppet, and I am in awe of your skills. You deserve a huge reward, but then, I am forgetting, you are getting me," he mocked, taking her in his arms, and raising her chin with one hand, the light in his eyes refuting his jeering words. Before she could challenge his provocative remark, he had kissed her hungrily, for beneath his careless words lay anguish and relief at her safety, so often at risk in the invidious role she had played so bravely.

Molly wisely chose that moment to slip away.

"No more questions, now. This is all that is important," Theron murmured, moving his lips in drugging languor over her hair, her cheeks, her throat, her lips, his desperation belying his casual words. Responding to his caresses, Melissa felt the burdens of the past weeks slip from her, the recent horrifying events becoming a distant dream, for surely this was reality. Theron could not kiss her in such a way if he did not have some deep affection for her. Whitebread, who lay senseless at their very feet, Hawksley, the runners, the outcry and speculation from the corridor beyond their sight, all faded from her consciousness. She cared nothing for all the questions and explanations which must be answered and offered, as long as she stood here in the warm shelter of Theron's arms, believing he might, against all hope, have come to love her. How long those desperate caresses might have continued, Melissa could not imagine, but they were interrupted by a cough and a shuffling of feet from the entrance way.

"Excuse me, my lord, I am sure, but just what is going on here? That cove at your feet, who you seem to have given a wicked facer, is he our villain?" Hal Borley, stood looking in some bewilderment at Whitebread's prone body and the embracing couple, who reluctantly parted at his words. The events of the past half hour had sorely tried Borley's attempt to manage them, and although he was loathe to admit it, he realized that the Marquis and Melissa probably had the answers to the problems that vexed him. Reluctant as he was to coerce the quality, he had his duty and was determined to do it.

"Ah, yes, the ubiquitous Borley. Of course, my man, you want some explanations. And I suppose we cannot wait until this varlet here is dragged before the magistrate. Some of his machinations are still a mystery, but there is little doubt he is the murderer of Alison Andrews and the author of the attempt on Miss Langford," the Marquis explained, repressing a shudder at the remembrance of how barely Melissa had escaped the fate Whitebread intended for her. He nudged the prone figure disgustedly with his foot.

"You had better secure him well, Borley, and haul him off to Bow Street. I will be along shortly to explain the whole business to your magistrate, but I must see that Miss Langford gets home safely. She has been through a dreadful ordeal."

"Well, my lord, if you say so, but there are a few things I want to know first," Borley began, but quieted in the face of the Marquis' quelling glance. Melissa, still bemused from Theron's kisses, stood uncertainly.

"May I return to my dressing room, Mr. Borley?" she asked. I must finish dressing. Is my guardian . . . is Mr. Hawksley . . . ?" she hesitated over the words, but she could not reenter that room if his poor body was still on the floor.

"The corpse has been removed, miss. You may have the use of your room, but there are several questions I would like answered," Borley insisted, clinging to his official manner, and jealously insisting on his rights. The lady might be under the protection of the Marquis but she still had to obey the law represented in all its majesty by Borley himself.

"That will do, Borley. Miss Langford has endured enough for one evening. I will answer all your questions, once I have escorted her home," Theron said decisively, and Borley had the good sense to accept his directive. Beneath Theron's

egligent casual manner lay a possessiveness, refined by
nerations of autocrats, accustomed to having their words
eeded, their orders obeyed. Borley recognized in the Marquis
ı intelligence far superior to his own, and much as he might
uster and bully, knew that the Marquis' influence was far
ore powerful than any inducement of Bow Street. He had no
course except to follow the Marquis' instructions.

Bessie bundled Melissa into her gown, while the weary girl
ood meekly allowing herself to be dressed, avoiding any
tempt to think of the night's events which had climaxed in
ıch a horrible way. Her immediate concern was to seek her
d, for all explanations must await upon the morrow.
omehow the whole farrago of spies, conspiracies, even the
urder of Alison, seemed of little importance now that a
solution had been made in the frightening intrigue which
ad engaged them for so many weeks. Even her relationship
ith Theron lacked substance. Numbly Melissa knew that they
ad much to discover and discuss, but for this evening she felt
ie could not endure another emotional moment.

Theron, well aware of the traumatic nature of her
cperiences, took her from Bessie's kindly hands, and whisked
oth women into his carriage. The dresser's presence
evented any significant conversation and the ride was made
ith only a few desultory remarks. Theron bid Melissa
odnight on the steps of the Stanhope Gate house, realizing
ie was in no condition to suffer either questions nor his
arely subdued passion. Tomorrow would be soon enough for
oth, he promised himself.

Chapter Thirty-Six

"But he shouldn't go free. He is a dangerous snake, wh betrayed his country," Melissa wailed in dismay, upon hearin Theron's plans for the disposition of Whitebread the followin afternoon.

"Such a fiery little termagant with passionate conviction on the right and wrong of every situation. You will be ver difficult to live up to, my dear, quite straining my usua equanimity," Theron taunted, watching with pleasure as sh rose to his bait, her cheeks flushing with mortification. No she looked more like herself, rather than the wan, pale littl creature he had deposited on the doorstep last evening. He ha not wanted to leave her. He had wanted to accompany her t her bedroom and reassure her in the only way which woul satisfy them both, but events had not allowed that outcom However, her usual resilience and a night's sleep had prove restoring. Melissa looked quite enchanting in a lilac sil redingote, cut away to show an embroidered cream underskir the whole picture a foil for her huge violet eyes and gami features beneath the careless gold-streaked curls.

"You are so maddening, Theron. What I want to know why Whitebread is not ending on the gallows, where h belongs?" Melissa insisted, not allowing him to distract he

He sighed wearily. He had had a long night of interviews, ar even longer morning of persuasion and arrangements. But certainly, Melissa was entitled to know the whole of it. He looked at her with appreciation and beneath his languid manner a desire he could barely restrain, rose in him, a longing which must be appeased.

"Well, in return for his life, Whitebread, a craven coward now that he has been unmasked, has agreed to reveal the whole network. A clerk in the Foreign Office, several Army officers, and smaller fry, but the biggest catch is the emigré, one Count Henri Francois de Grimond, who was the direct conduit to Napoleon, a supercilious knave, who had gulled us all with his pretence of the persecuted aristo. No doubt he was Aimee's contact, too. He collected the material from Whitebread and forwarded it directly to Napoleon's minions. Whitebread, through those iniquitous playbills you so cleverly discovered, arranged for the agents to place their information under a seat at a designated performance at the Majestic. Somehow Alison, who had been Whitebread's mistress, found out some damaging indication of what her paramour was doing and tried to blackmail him. No doubt she wanted you turned from the theatre and coveted your star roles. It was her death knell," he explained. "We have rolled them all up, a stunning coup, for which the Foreign Office has congratulated me fulsomely," he added in some disgust. "But it hasn't aborted that dratted truce, which Pitt warns them will yet cause us deep regret."

"But what is going to happen to Mr. Whitebread?" Melissa persisted, her gorge rising at the thought that her attempted murderer would get off his punishment.

"He will be deported to the West Indies, which he will find not at all to his taste. The climate there is most insalubrious, I understand. And de Grimond is being shipped back to France. The others will get long terms of imprisonment. The important aspect is that we have destroyed a damaging network, which was privy to all the plans of the War Office and the Foreign Office. I suppose Napoleon is far from defeated. He will busy himself putting another group of traitors in motion, and we will have the whole mess beginning again. But for the moment we have triumphantly routed the curs," Theron said with some satisfaction.

"And now we can concentrate on our own affairs, far more interesting to me at this moment," he eyed her suggestively, wanting to put the recent disagreeable events behind them. "With Hawksley so tidily, if dreadfully, dispatched, no more than he deserved, I warrant, we need not worry about his objections to our marriage which will take place two days hence in St. Margaret's. I want no more delay or demur on your part. I have waited long enough. The Majestic, perforce, must close down, and your career there is ended. The Foreign Office has had enough of me. All my talents must now be directed into transforming you into an obedient and adoring wife," he taunted, unwilling to rake over the business any longer, but anticipating in some amusement Melissa's reaction to this outrageous statement.

"About this marriage, Theron. Now that we have solved the conspiracy and found my grandparents, even settled the problem of Horace Hawksley, and poor Algy, who must be aghast at the outcome of events, there is no necessity . . ." she trailed off uncertainly, as Theron releasing the hard hold he had kept on himself drew her into his arms and muffled her faint objections with the force of his kiss.

She responded to his hungry caresses, despising herself at the ease with which he answered all her objections, but unable to resist his compelling passion.

"I will not listen to any more doubts, and I will wait no longer. Don't you know, you little fool, that I want to marry you quite desperately, to possess you always, to keep you from any more crazy escapades, to fill you with my children. You will never get away from me now, however you try, and someday you will learn to love me as much as I love you. Do you really think I am coercing you into wedlock just because I took your virginity? You cannot fail to see that I am obsessed by you, and it is not an obsession which will wear off with possession," he said hoarsely, for the first time impressing her with the strength of his emotion.

Melissa, gazing up at him in awe, could only gasp, "Do you really love me, Theron? You have always said that no woman would bring you to such a pass."

"Well, you have turned the trick. I am besotted with you, just as much in your toils as that callow Percy or any of the other miserable puppies who follow you about, grateful for any trifling sign of your attention. Who would have believed it? The most notorious rakehell in London falling under the spell of a wench barely out of leading strings," he said bitterly, prepared for her scorn, but not letting her escape from his arms, watching for her reaction with a desperate intensity. For a moment she saw an unbearable pain in his eyes, and she wanted only to reassure him.

"Are you certain, Theron? You won't tire of me, as you have of all the others, and find yourself trapped in a suffocating marriage, yearning to return to your usual round of pleasure? I will not be relegated to the background, used only to produce heirs, ignored and pitied," Melissa insisted, unwilling to believe in this unexpected happiness, unable to comprehend that this libertine lord, who had scorned all deep feelings could indeed be professing his love for her.

"I will be the most devoted of husbands. You have spoiled me for any other woman, and I can only conclude you have woven some witch's spell over me which will last a lifetime. But what of you, little one, are you willing to join your future to one as notorious as I, with a reputation that frightens respectable society? You are not very respectable yourself, if it comes to that," he asked, trying to lighten the tense moment, but waiting for her reply with a certain apprehension.

"Oh, Theron, I have known I loved you for ages past, and not just because you are so skilled at . . . well, you know. I quite intended to lure you into marriage from that first kiss in the inn, but was not sure I could contrive it. I am only afraid you will become bored with my love, and I could not bear that," Melissa admitted, casting all her doubts to the wind, astounded at the depth of sincerity her normally enigmatic lover was displaying.

"Thank God. I have you and I will never let you go," he exclaimed, gathering her more securely to his breast. If she had any lingering objections she abandoned them and taking the initiative kissed him soundly in return, shuddering with the tempest he could arouse in her.

"And I do not intend to wait until the vows are spoken, or you might change your mind. It has been so long since the night I claimed you," he asserted masterfully, gathering her up in his arms and marching toward the stairs.

"Am I allowed any choice?" she countered saucily but contradicted her words by nestling securely into his grasp as he strode steadily toward the bedroom, shouldering open the door to be greeted by Bessie's shocked eyes. Standing Melissa on her feet and turning her around he began cooly to unbutton her gown.

"Your mistress will not need you again today, Bessie. Begone with you, that's a good woman," he murmured paying no heed to the dresser's shocked disapproval.

Melissa, afire with impatience, hardly noticed Bessie's hasty departure. She was as frantic as Theron to consummate their love, and boldly began to untie his stock. Her dress fell unnoticed to the floor, as he placed her upon the bed and followed her down, covering her bared body with passionate kisses. "I am glad to see you have decided to be an obliging wife, eager to obey her husband in all things," he teased, his hands roaming enticingly all over her.

For the moment, Melissa made no protest, swept away by the ardour of his lovemaking, but she was not so lost to sanity that she did not heed his words. The rakehell Marquis would learn differently but now was not the time to challenge him, and she sighed with delicious anticipation of the delights ahead.